SONG
OF
FIRE

SONG OF FIRE

JOSEPH BENTZ

THOMAS NELSON PUBLISHERS
Nashville • Atlanta • London • Vancouver

Copyright © 1995 by Joseph Bentz

Published in Nashville, Tennessee, by Jan Dennis Books, an imprint of Thomas Nelson, Inc., Publishers, and distributed in Canada by Word Communications, Ltd., Richmond, British Columbia.

Scripture quotations are from the Holy Bible: NEW INTERNATIONAL VER-SION. Copyright © 1978 by the New York International Bible Society. Used by permission of Zondervan Bible Publishers.

Library of Congress Cataloging-in-Publication Data

Bentz, Joseph, 1961-
    Song of fire / by Joseph Bentz.
      p. cm.
    "A Jan Dennis book."
    ISBN 0-7852-7882-6
    I. Title.
  PS3552.E6S65 1995
  813'.54—dc20
                                                    95-14040
                                                       CIP

Printed in the United States of America
1 2 3 4 5 6 — 00 99 98 97 96 95

FOR PEGGY

His word is in my heart like a fire, a fire
shut up in my bones. I am weary of holding it in;
indeed, I cannot.

—Jeremiah 20:9

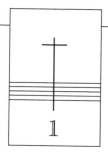

1

Anne skated away from me and headed toward the light at the edge of the frozen lake. I was left alone in the darkness to regret everything I had said to her.

I glided off in the opposite direction from her, toward the darkest, most secluded corner of the lake. This area was supposed to be off-limits because the park could not guarantee that the ice was safe. But I knew that the park rangers were always too cautious. The entire lake had been frozen solid for days. Besides, the solidness of the ice was not my biggest concern at the moment. I needed to be alone to think.

I had brought Anne, my almost-fiancée, to the lake because it had always been our favorite place to come for serious talks. We could glide around in the vast silence without any distractions. We often wandered off into what we considered our own private alcove, one of those "unsafe" areas where we had never been caught.

On most trips here we had been able to talk things through until they were resolved, but this night had been different. I told Anne that earlier that day, against her fervent wishes, I had quit my job at the bank.

I could not explain to her why I quit, or at least I couldn't put together any coherent explanation that sounded like anything more than a weak excuse, even to myself. To Anne my job at the bank was a respectable, reasonably well paying position that, in addition to her own income, would allow us to afford getting married and starting a home. I had been at the bank since graduating from college—nearly a year—and my bosses encouraged me with promises of a bright future in the organization.

I could not explain to Anne what the job was doing to me. I could not describe the mind-crushing boredom of it, the way time seemed stretched out of all proportion there, my legs vibrating restlessly under the desk as I glanced at the clock repeatedly and thought, *Still seven more hours to go, still six hours and fifty-seven minutes to go . . .*

I hardly seemed to breathe while I was at the bank; I just kept quiet and tried to endure the endless passage of time, tried not to let anyone see my frustration, tried to smile and laugh and answer at the appropriate times, tried to keep my pen moving on the page, tried not to run desperately out the door and into the sunshine. There had to be something besides this. Some of the people around me seemed to thrive on the work, but it was killing me. This I could not explain to Anne. She, and just about everybody else, would simply say, "Oh, everybody gets bored with their job sometimes. It will pick up."

Angry though Anne was that I had suddenly quit my job, she was even more upset about what I had decided to do while I looked for another job.

In college, before I met Anne, I had been a member of a band that played in the college bars on the weekends. I had quit after graduation, but my best friend Will had kept the band going, and a few weeks before I quit the bank, he had asked me to come back to the group. I told him maybe. It was only part-time, and it wouldn't pay enough that I could afford not to work somewhere else, but I felt a strange need to do it, a powerful hunger for the music.

Anne immediately jumped on the band and the sinister influence of Will as the real reasons I was quitting my job.

"You're going back to your old life," she said.

"No," I said. "I'm just going to play with the band. Weekends mostly. Just playing with the band."

"No, it's not just the band. It's all that goes with it. You're going back to your old life, and it's a place you know I'll never fit."

———○———

Anne and Will were the two people closest to me, but they distrusted each other completely. I kept them separate from each other, like two warring sides of my own personality.

To Anne, Will was a dangerous force drawing me back to my self-destructive past. To Will, Anne was responsible for what he saw as my weird embrace of her Christian beliefs. He viewed my Christianity as an unfortunate side effect of my relationship with Anne, and he thought my faith would fade as soon as my passion for her cooled. He never said that in so many words, but I knew him too well not to figure it out. I could not explain my Christianity to Will because he did not even want to discuss the subject. I could not explain to Will the intensity of the Spirit that burned inside me. I could not explain the months of raging in my soul, the questions and doubts, the struggle with the Spirit that led to my becoming a Christian. He could believe in the spiritual power of our music, which we had talked about many times, but he scorned the idea that the power in the music was only a shadow of the power of the Spirit. He patiently waited for my "Christian phase" to end.

Anne could not understand why my friendship with Will stayed so strong and why I felt such a need to get back to the music. To her Will was cynical and aimless. She did not see the side of him that I saw. She did not see the friend who was full of life, totally accepting, expecting nothing more from me than to be there in the band and have a good time. He wanted only to feel the music, to sense the pleasure of the crowd.

———○———

I hardly knew where I was skating. The moon was gone. It was very dark. Nothing looked familiar. I wished Anne were still beside me. I needed to reach her, to make her understand.

Going back to the "old life," if that is what I was doing,

certainly did not mean leaving Anne behind. I loved her more than I had ever loved anyone, and the changes she had brought about in my life could never be undone.

I had met Anne during our final semester in college. From the night we were introduced at a friend's house, I couldn't stop thinking about her. The first time we went out alone we went to the state park, the same one where I now skated alone in the dark. But that day was warm and sunny, and we walked to the waterfall on the river that cuts through the park. We stood arm in arm in the stream looking at the waterfall crashing down from twenty feet above us. Anne's face was wrapped in the spray of it, her black hair gradually getting wet, her brown eyes sparkling. I knew I loved her in that moment, if I hadn't known it already. We found a place along the edge of the fall where we could climb up.

She climbed ahead of me, the water drenching her, sometimes pushing her hard against me. For some reason the water made her laugh so hard that I was afraid she would fall. I tried to steady her with my arms. "Don't laugh," I said, but she couldn't help it. When we finally got to the top, she ran along the smooth rock, splashing water into the air with her feet. Before long she was ready to climb back down.

When we got to the bottom she pulled me right into the center of the spray, so powerful it nearly washed the blouse off her shoulders. She screamed and laughed. I held onto her as tight as I could until the force of the water knocked us into the cool pool below.

—◯—

I decided to try to skate back to Anne, but I had wandered so far out that I wasn't quite sure of the direction. So dark. I glided off toward where I thought she must be. This area just didn't look right. The ice didn't feel right.

During our argument Anne had said that quitting my job was just one more way of drifting back toward self-destructive patterns and that before it was over I would drift away from my faith and away from her too. What I could not get her to see—what I could barely believe myself—was that quitting the bank was an act of faith, a desperate plea to the Lord to show me where He wanted me to go. I did not seem capable of finding Him in a simpler way like other people did, through quiet reflection or prayer.

I skated out of an alcove and onto a broader part of the lake. I was pretty sure I was skating in the right direction finally, and I was relieved when I saw a figure—and then two figures—up ahead, and distant lights on the bank. I would skate toward the light. No problem.

I hoped that one of the figures was Anne, but soon I could tell that they were both men. None of this looked right. I heard nothing but a squeaking noise under my feet. The light on the bank must have been where Anne was, I thought, but it looked different. What part of the lake was I on?

I might have been headed toward the wrong bank, but at least it was a bank, and, I reasoned, the ice must be better over there than here. I didn't get much farther before the front tip of my right blade caught on something and I feel on one knee. "Dear Lord, protect me." My knee smashed through the ice. I felt the frigid water surround it. I lost my balance for a moment, but then I jerked myself up and plunged forward again. The two men saw me. They waved their arms.

Everything around me seemed to be cracking. The entire lake seemed to be falling into a huge abyss, sinking, ice upon ice. I fell again, my legs in the wetness turning to stone. As water covered me, I turned to cold, hopeless stone. Anne's face flashed in my brain. My father's face. I felt myself thrashing, heard my voice try to scream for Anne, but she was nowhere. I was a stone. Sinking. I could not breathe. *Dear Jesus. Anne.*

Not knowing whether I was dead or alive, I did not stop falling until I crashed through what I can only describe as a blackness, a door. When I woke up, if waking up is what I should call it, nothing would ever be the same.

2

I came down in a swirl of music so bright that I couldn't see anything else around me.

The light and sound were not separate things but were part of one another. Each sound had its own appearance, each bit of light its own sound. In my hands I held my guitar. I played it and sang, but the sound was intertwined with the sound of violins, trombones, pianos, trumpets, drums, and other sounds I had never heard before. I stepped into the melody and let it carry me. I found my body could move as fast as my thoughts. At what must have been millions of miles per hour, I pierced through a melody that was faster and more complicated and glorious than any sound my ears had ever been able to hear. As I sliced through the music, it pierced through me like bolts of energy. Every cell in my body tingled with power, with the very Spirit of God. I never wanted to leave the music. I wrapped myself in it, flung myself thousands of miles through it, sang in it, and danced in it.

I could change the melody any way I wanted to, slow it down, make it quieter or louder, add variations, just by thinking about them. The other instruments followed whatever I did and sometimes surprised me with little variations of their own, as if we were speaking to one another in some elaborate language.

I was surrounded by such a blaze of energy and sound and

spirit that it took a long time before I realized I was in a place with other people. After half an hour or maybe an hour or two—the music distorted all sense of time—I saw an old man penetrate the light. His body was skinny and wrinkled, but the power in the light had given him the strength of a young man. He danced and revelled in the music. The light began to break apart and fly off as bright projectiles. The old man reached out to grab one, but when he touched it, it shattered into a mist of millions of tiny sparkles and floated outward and upward. The ring of light that had kept everyone away from me began to disintegrate, and as it turned to mist I could see that I was in the middle of a crowd of people clothed in the same brightness that enveloped the old man. As the light dissipated, so did the music, each instrument falling away one at a time. The change in the sound was slow, but by whatever force it is that controls the everyday world, this bright and spirit-filled sound turned into ordinary earth music.

As the sound and light evaporated, an unbearable heaviness swept down on me, as if the force of gravity had suddenly multiplied. It pressed me to the ground, where I lay helpless as the mob cut through the light and got closer to me. I began to hear their voices over the music. Their pleasure in the music gave way to panic, and they yelled at me and pointed down the street as if someone were after us. They pushed at me and gestured at me to stand up and go with them, but the force was so heavy on me that it was impossible even to lift my head. The crowd surged in closer, and I thought any minute I would be crushed. I saw my guitar being tossed from person to person. A man knelt down behind me, grabbed my shoulders, and lifted me up. Another man grabbed my ankles, and together they carried me several yards and tossed me into the back of a horse-drawn wagon filled with straw. One of them grabbed my guitar and tossed it in with me, and then the wagon started to move.

One of my captors stayed beside me in the wagon while the other one drove. Part of the crowd followed us, but many of them, scared by whatever threat they had been pointing toward, ran inside the ramshackle buildings that lined the street. We drove away from the remaining mist of light, and for the first time I realized it was night. The only light I saw came from the windows of the tenement buildings, where people huddled close and stared down at us to see what all the commotion was about. I could smell the food from their kitchens and the refuse from their sewers as we passed through the narrow streets. What few people I could see were dressed in rags, and everywhere I could hear the cries of children.

We drove through block after block of slums, the crowd getting thinner all the time. The tumbledown buildings were made of a white plaster that looked like dried foam. They were three or four stories high, and some of the top stories leaned out precariously toward the street, making the place seem even more crowded. When we finally got out of the city, we came to dusty flatlands covered with only scrawny bushes and an occasional shack. The road was bumpy and, even with the straw under me, I took quite a beating. I was powerless to shift my weight to absorb the shocks. I felt as if some huge wrestler were lying on top of me and trying to squeeze the life out of me. The man beside me kept chattering, but after an hour or so he got exasperated and shut up. We drove through this desolate country for several hours. I grew tired but could not sleep. We finally stopped in front of one of the white foam buildings out in the wasteland. Realizing that I would be unable to stand, the two men picked me up and carried me inside. An enormous woman wearing a red scarf and what looked like several layers of unmatching blouses and skirts met us at the door, and the men held onto me in her front room while they poured out their story. When they finished, she looked at me and spoke in a soothing tone words I could not understand. The woman smelled like greasy hamburgers, and her smile revealed that most of her teeth were gone. She seemed to carry great authority in this house, for all the men's comments were directed at her, and they waited for her to tell them what to do next. She pointed the men toward a narrow staircase, and they carried me upstairs to a dark room where they laid me on a pallet.

Before long the woman, whom I heard them call Moll, came in with a tray filled with meat, steaming vegetables, pie with some sort of fruit in it, and two large rolls. Even though I was hungry, the force pressing down on me had exhausted me to the point that it was too tiring even to lift my head off the pallet. Moll coaxed me with her soft voice, but I couldn't move. She tried to feed me some of the vegetables with a wooden spoon, but it was so messy and difficult that finally I just shook my head, closed my eyes, and she took the food away. Miserable and confused, I fell asleep.

—⊖—

I woke to the sound of a baby crying. In those first few seconds of half-sleep, I was not completely aware of where I was or what had happened to me. I lifted my head and felt the force slam it back down. Then I heard these words in a language not my own: "Moll! He's movin'!" The language was not one that I could remember ever having learned, but I understood it perfectly. When I opened my eyes, I was staring into the face of a teenage girl I had not seen the night before. Her gaze bore down on me as if she expected that at any moment I might spring up and try to escape, or that I might magically fly off in a puff of smoke. But I was going nowhere. The force that pressed me down seemed slightly less heavy than the night before, but it still took every bit of strength I had just to lift my head a few inches. I wanted to lean my head against the wall so that I could see the room better. I finally managed this, but as I struggled to do so the girl wailed "Moll!" over and over, as if I were committing some act of violence on her. Moll came running, as did eight or nine others, including a woman holding the screaming baby.

When they burst into the room they all started talking at once, and the commotion was so startling that it knocked the understanding of the language right out of me. Their words were nothing more than gibberish again. As I relaxed, though, and concentrated, I found that the phrases began to make sense. Where had this knowledge come from? Though I could not remember exactly what had happened to me between the time I fell through the ice and the time I arrived in this strange world in the swirl of music, I did have the vague impression that I had been *somewhere*. The place was extremely fuzzy in my memory, but I must have learned this language there. I did remember one other thing: I had the clear impression that, for my own safety, I had been told—by whom I did not know—that I was not to tell anyone about my home and that I was allowed to say only that I was from the "Bright World."

I managed to get my head propped against the wall, and once everything calmed down, Moll hovered over me and said, "At least he's lifting his head. I wonder if he wants something to eat now."

I was monstrously hungry. I stammered, "I understand—some—words. Very hungry."

Moll squealed and reached out to hold my head in her hands. The whole room erupted in a similar way, and for a few minutes their blizzard of words was incomprehensible again. Moll made them shut up and then she asked me something, but I couldn't follow it. She repeated the word, "Hungry. Hungry. Hungry," and I nodded. She said, "I'll go down and get you some food."

I said, "Yes. Food."

"Beautiful," she said. "You speak beautiful."

I also desperately needed to go to the bathroom, but I had no idea how to say this. Moll kept her patient gaze on me as I came up with what I thought was the word *toilet*, but I later realized it was a similar sounding word that meant *waterfall*. After I tried the word a few more times, the girl who had screamed at my awakening whispered something into Moll's ear and the woman's face lit up with understanding. "Can you walk?" she said.

I shook my head no.

Moll called down the stairs, and two men came up and carried me to the outhouse in Moll's backyard. Moll's rooms downstairs were crowded with people who stared at me as I was carried out. The force had let up enough that I at least was able to sit on the toilet without help. I still could not walk, so after I finished they carried me upstairs, where my meal was waiting. It was fabulous. Juicy slabs of meat covered with gravy, steaming vegetables, a loaf of bread, a gooey, sweet dessert. Moll sliced the meat for me and gave me only a large wooden spoon to eat with. Thankfully, I was strong enough to maneuver the spoon on my own. While ten or twelve people stood and watched me eat, Moll, seemingly the only one allowed to speak to me, tried to ask me questions.

"Can you tell us your name?"

"Jeremy."

"Jeremy. We never heard that name before. Where are you from?"

"The Bright World," I said, hoping they would not press me for details about what that meant, since I did not know.

"Oh my," said Moll, and several of those behind her began to whisper among themselves. "Is there somebody we should take you to?" she asked.

"No."

"What have you come to do?"

"I don't know," I said, though I had to repeat this a couple times before they understood my pronunciation.

The young man behind Moll said, "Are you a follower of Emajus?"

"No." This brought some more murmuring from my spectators. I had no idea who Emajus was. Were they glad I was not his follower, or did this bother them? I couldn't tell.

He said, "Did you know that making the music the way you did is a crime punishable by death?"

"Shut up, Manu," said Moll.

Manu said, "Did you know we could all be killed if we're caught hiding you here?"

"SHUT UP, MANU!"

"Well, it's ridiculous!" he shouted. "We've got a house full of people who all know we've got him here. The soldiers are going to find out. Shutting me up is not going to change the fact that if they catch us they'll slaughter us. We've got to get him out of here."

Moll stood, grabbed Manu by the arm, and practically dragged him down the stairs. Everyone else followed, breaking into a flurry of speech too fast for me to understand.

I ate my meal alone. There was still an air of unreality to this whole experience, as if someone would come back at any moment and grab me out of it.

Moll came back up as I finished the dessert. She cleared away the dishes and sat down beside me. She smiled at me and patted my hand before she began to speak. Her manner made me feel about ten years old, but I didn't mind. There was something reassuring about her. She could be big and tough enough to drag Manu down the stairs, but she could be cuddly and motherly too.

"Don't you worry about a thing," she said. "Manu is a wimp. Scared of everything. Ain't nobody going to get around Moll and do you any harm. But we are going to take you somewhere. We're going to take you to see Tarius Arc. Do you know who he is?"

"No."

"Well, he's a great man. A godly man. He knows all about the music and Emajus, and chances are he'll know what you're doing here. They're going to be after you, that's for sure, but Tarius will know what to do. Are you feeling any stronger?"

"Yes. Feeling stronger. Good food."

"God bless your heart. You don't worry about a thing. You see Tarius, and he'll have it all straightened out in no time."

—⊖—

Late that night I was awakened by someone shaking my shoulder and shining a light in my face. It was Manu. We had the room to ourselves because Moll had ordered everyone to leave me alone for the night. I had told her I didn't like people staring at me all the time.

"My curiosity wouldn't let me sleep," he said.

I propped my head up against the wall.

Manu said, "Do you really not know why you're here, or have you been ordered not to tell us?"

"I really don't know."

He said nothing for a moment. "Do you really not know who Tarius Arc is?"

"No."

"There is not a single person in the world who does not know who Tarius Arc is."

"I have never heard of him before today."

"Then why are you going to see him?"

"They told me he would straighten everything out. They said he's a great man."

"You think he is a great man? They didn't tell you every-thing."

"Tell me."

"They didn't tell you that his greatest accomplishment was inventing the bombs that destroyed most of Persus Am, including the Temple of God, during the War. They never talk about that. They never tell about the people he killed."

"Why are they taking me to him?"

"They think you're Emajian, and he's the spiritual leader of the Emajians."

"I am not Emajian. I don't know anything about Emajus."

"That's what I don't understand. That's why I'm not sure you're telling the truth. Only Emajians make music. If you get caught, you're a dead man. The only safe place for you now is the Rock of Calad. Do you know about the Rock?"

"No."

"It's where the Emajians live. If you wanted to come from some other world and play the kind of music you played—with the lights and everything, for heaven's sake—then you should have gone to the Rock of Calad. They love that sort of thing. They would have eaten it up. But you land right smack in the middle of the Utturies, which is swarming with soldiers from Persus Am. It's a miracle you got out of there. Just a miracle."

"What do you think Tarius Arc will do with me?"

"He won't do anything for you if you say you're not an Emajian. I'd tell him you are one if I were you. The Emajians are your only hope now. If the soldiers catch you they'll kill you."

As he finished we heard Moll coming up the stairs; Manu hid behind a cabinet while she checked on me, and after she left he sneaked silently down the stairs without another word.

—◯—

They told me I was in a country called Persus Am. It was a valley surrounded by mountains, and Tarius Arc lived over the mountains east of Moll's house at a place called the Rock of Calad. They originally planned to take me to his home, but by the time we left the next morning, the plans had changed because they heard that the way to the Rock of Calad was blocked by soldiers who suspected I would try to go there. Instead I was to meet him in a village called Breone in Persus Am. They said he was risking his life by coming to see me.

I was strong enough to walk out of Moll's house on my own, though I still felt as if an invisible force were trying to smash me to the ground. She hugged me and kissed me and wished me well, and several of the others gave me gifts of candy, which was their custom. We traveled for two days in a covered cargo wagon pulled by the animals that looked like some strange, squatty breed of horse. We arrived mid-morning at a house built into the side of a hill. It looked deserted from the outside, with weeds growing up everywhere and most of the windows boarded up. There were no other wagons or any other signs that other people had traveled there. The wagon did not pull up very close to the house, and it took nearly five minutes for me to walk to the front door. The force that weighed me down was still so great that I felt like I was walking shoulder deep in thick mud. By the time I got into the house I was so exhausted that I collapsed into the first chair offered me. The house was not deserted. There were eight or nine people in the front room, all helping themselves to delicious-smelling food at a rickety wooden table. They all gathered around me and chattered away with introductions and words of welcome and questions, but I was too exhausted to pay much attention. They got me something to drink, and in a few minutes I had pulled myself together enough to say a few words to them.

Tarius Arc was not in this room, so I had to fight my way through the heaviness to the next room to meet him. I walked into a smaller, dimly lit room where Tarius sat surrounded by about twelve men and women. He played a stringed instrument on his lap. As soon as I entered he stopped playing and stood up to welcome me. Everyone around him started talking all at once, most of it directed toward me. The room was suddenly flooded with so many voices, and I was so distracted by the painful numbness in my legs that I lost the power of the language again and did not know what Tarius Arc said to me as he clasped my arm. It seemed that whenever I got tripped up on a word or two, the whole language would collapse into an incoherent jumble.

Tarius sensed my confusion and made everyone stop talking. He motioned for me to sit in a chair, and when everyone sat down he began to play the instrument again and sing.

It was a marvelous song. He had the most Spirit-filled voice I had ever heard. Everyone kept their eyes on me, but Tarius seemed to watch me most intently of all. It was unnerving. He had sky blue eyes so penetrating they seemed ready either to love me or hate me. They were eyes like your conscience has. They were eyes of spirit.

He had a neatly trimmed white beard cut close to his face, and his shoulder-length hair was totally white. His rugged face made him look younger than the white hair indicated he was. The intensity with which he played his instrument and sang, and the intensity with which he watched me, made him seem completely self-assured, but not arrogant. He paid no attention to those who gathered close to him to fawn on him. He kept complete concentration on what he was doing.

The music sounded incredibly good to me. The others in the room soon joined in the singing, flooding the room with sound. The music in this place seemed different from the music at home, in ways difficult to describe. It seemed to remain longer in the air and to penetrate it more. The sound seemed to be not just in front of me but all around me. I was drenched in its warmth and brightness. Tarius sensed how much I enjoyed it, and he continued to play even after many of the others had stopped singing and seemed antsy to get back to business. Trays of food and drink were brought in, and I ate while Tarius sang. As I sat there enjoying the music and the food and the return of strength to my body, I felt for the first time a relief from the fear and homesickness that had preoccupied me. I was able, for the moment at least, to just enjoy being there. Before long my mind became clear enough to understand most of the language again. Tarius's song was about God's promise to restore His voice to the world and to sing again in His mighty temple.

When Tarius stopped singing, he said to me, "Brother Jeremy, I hope you feel better now."

"Yes, I do. Your music is incredible."

"Well, music is better than words when you want to make someone feel at home, isn't it? I've heard a lot about your own music and how full it was of the voice of God. I've heard how brave you were to sing your songs right there in the middle of the Utturies, where you could have been killed. I've heard how the whole sky lit up with the light from your songs. We set out from the Rock of Calad to meet you the moment we got the news. All we believers are ready to hear why you have come and what you plan to do."

"I'm not sure I can answer that," I said.

Tarius kept his gaze on me. He was waiting for me to say more. When I failed to break the uncomfortable silence of those next few moments, he said, "Maybe we could talk alone for a while instead of making you face this crowd." A few of them got up reluctantly to leave. Tarius said, "Why don't you all go get something to drink in the other room and let Brother Jeremy catch his breath for a few minutes. You'll have plenty of time to hear from him."

Only two men, apparently Tarius's assistants, stayed with us in the room. After everyone else was gone, Tarius said, "We've come a long way, brother, and we've put ourselves at great risk by being here. Now tell us why you're here."

"I'm not trying to hide anything from you," I said. "I just don't know why I'm here. I came from the Bright World. When I got here, the music was swirling all around me and I was playing it. Then it disappeared, and the air was so heavy I couldn't move. They scooped me up and took me to Moll's house. I couldn't understand the language at first, but then I could. And now they've brought me here. That's all I know."

"I see," he said. "Are you an Emajian?"

"No. Everyone asks me that. I don't know anything about Emajus."

"But your music. They tell me it was Emajian music."

"It was just music."

He looked at the other two men, but they gave him no clue about how to proceed. He said, "So why have you come to see me?"

"Moll said you would straighten everything out and tell me what to do."

"What do you know about me?"

"Not much. They told me you are a great man, a spiritual and godly man, a leader of the Emajians. A musician." Tarius stayed silent, so I added the only other detail I had heard about him. "They also told me you invented bombs that destroyed a country during the War."

As soon as I said this I wished I hadn't. The wide-eyed glances Tarius's men gave each other made it clear I had hit on a sensitive subject. But how was I to know? He seemed to want every bit of information I had. His personality seemed to draw it from me.

"So that's the fact in my background you came to torment me with," he said.

"Believe me, I don't want to torment you at all. I'm just telling you what I've heard."

"So someone told you their story. But did they tell you mine? Did they tell you how my daughter was stolen from me and raped and driven insane? And did they tell you how I have had to live alone all these years without my wife?"

"Honestly, I don't know about any of this. I'm sorry to offend you. I'm completely lost here."

"I'm not after your apology, brother. I just want you to understand."

"Then tell me. Explain things to me. That's what they told me you would do."

He turned to the men behind him and said, "Leave us, brothers. Be sure they bring us food and drink from time to time, but otherwise don't let us be disturbed. Brother Jeremy and I have a few stories to tell."

We were left alone then for several hours. Tarius played his instrument much of the time he talked, particularly when he spoke of the distant past, for it seemed to make his memory more vivid. When I think back to his extraordinary story, I remember it as a song sung to that instrument. I have tried to piece it together just the way he sang it.

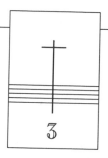

3

Song of Tarius Arc

I

Everybody wants to talk about the bombs! You'd think they were all I ever invented. Do you see this globe here that lights up this room? Who do you think invented it? I did. Before the War we invented all kinds of things. We thought nothing of it. But do they tell you about the globes of light? No. Nearly every home in the world is lit by them, but bombs are what they remember. Most people who talk about the War don't know anything about it. Most of them weren't even born yet. I'm the only person in this house right now who actually lived through the War. I remember it. I remember many things that other people have forgotten.

I remember that before the War the voice of God filled the city of Persus Am. I remember His Temple, with the lights sparkling through the Dome, the whole place vibrating with the music that was His voice. I remember the swords of red light and blue light flashing through the Temple to the rhythm of the music. I remember standing there under the Dome and dancing in the light and music.

Do you think I was the one who destroyed all that? I was not.

When I was young there was no such thing as war. We didn't even have a word for it. When I was young all of Persus Am was incredibly beautiful, full of forests and gardens and rivers. It was not a dusty desert as it is now. Seven hundred years before I was born, the Lord brought my ancestors to the land and told them it was all theirs to enjoy. He gave them more land than they could ever use. The whole valley of Persus Am was bordered by mountains. The Lord gave them the entire vast valley, but He told them not to stray beyond the mountains. Back then the mountains seemed impossibly high anyway, and besides, the people were already in paradise.

For seven hundred years they obeyed Him. When I was young, however, the mountains loomed as a giant temptation to some. What was beyond those mountains, they wondered, that the Lord was afraid for us to see? By the time the people began to consider the possibility of going over the mountains, I was a young man living in the country with my wife and our young daughter. We had a marvelous life there, in a beautiful house by the river. Those years were a time of great discovery. It was then that we invented the globe lights—right in the workshop behind my house. We invented refrigeration, cloth that would not wrinkle, new machines of all kinds, and new sources of energy from minerals in the ground that would power the machines. I did not invent all these things, of course, but all of us did, all of us young men and women living just outside the city of Persus Am. Within less than fifty years we made discoveries that have changed the world. We had giant celebrations of thanks to God after each new invention. It was the most exciting time of my life, probably the most exciting in history. The power of God filled the air.

There was very little government in those days. But we did choose one man or woman each year to oversee the building of roads and the funding of schools and that sort of thing. That person was called the Administrator and served for just a year at a time. Most people considered the job a nuisance because it took them away from whatever else they were doing, but everyone served their turn. One year in the midst of the great discoveries I was elected Administrator. At the time I was heavily involved in my experiments with light and energy—experiments that later led to the bombs and other inventions. I asked if someone else could be chosen that year and I would serve another year.

The council in charge of nominating candidates chose one of my best friends, Umbriel, who had worked with me on a number of experiments. Umbriel was considered one of the brightest men in Persus Am. He was a great musician. When he sang you knew the Lord Himself was singing to us through Umbriel's voice. I was surprised that Umbriel agreed to be Administrator that year because he was involved with some important experiments with music. But when he took the job, he did things the government had never considered doing before. He poured money into loans for businesses that were trying to produce all the inventions we were coming up with, like the globe light, motorized carts, and new musical instruments. He sponsored huge festivals of music and food and theater unlike anything the world had ever seen. He had new streets built, new bridges over the river. He came up with a way for us to pay taxes gradually throughout the year rather than all at once. He was a great Administrator, and everyone loved him.

When his year ended, people began to ask, When have we ever had an Administrator as good as Umbriel? Why should we follow a law that says each Administrator may rule for only one year when we have the best man in the job right now, and he's willing to go on serving? He *was* willing too. At the time I was amazed by this. No one had ever really *wanted* to be Administrator. But he relished it.

The only problem with keeping him on was that it was against the law. We had always had a new Administrator each year, since the beginning. Very few laws went all the way back, but that was one of them. We had never changed any of the original laws. Some of Umbriel's supporters called for a special election to throw out the law so he could continue to serve. Many people were against this change, especially older people, who thought the old laws were sacred and should not be tampered with. But the younger generation and many others considered the law outdated and unnecessary. It was a rule made by men, not by God, they said. Within weeks Umbriel and his followers brushed the old folks aside and changed the law, and he served as our Administrator for the second year in a row. What did we care about tossing out an ancient law? We were too busy to worry about it. We were having too much fun. It was the most exciting time in history to be alive, and we knew it. We thought there was nothing we could not do.

II

It was during this time of our greatest confidence and our greatest triumph that some of Umbriel's advisers began to make serious plans to explore beyond the mountains. They said, Why should we not explore the whole world? God has given all of it to us. The old-timers spoke strongly against the idea, because God clearly had said we must not go beyond the mountains. But was that command for all time? Umbriel's people asked. Didn't the Lord make that law to protect our ancestors, who were few and could not afford to be separated from one another in any way? Our ancestors were unequipped for exploration or for protecting themselves against the beasts that were said to live beyond the mountains. But look how God has equipped us now, they said. We have weapons that could kill any beast. We have tools and equipment that can get us over the mountain. Our people have prospered. They have covered the land. It is time to move beyond. Why would God make a way for us to go and then forbid us from going? Why would He create a land beyond the mountains if no one ever would be allowed to go there? He has made us clever and mighty, and He will glory in our discoveries.

These were clever arguments, so cleverly presented that those against the exploration sounded like people of little faith, when in fact those good people were simply trying to obey the written law of God.

Umbriel cleverly stayed out of the debate until a consensus was established that there was nothing wrong with the exploration. All along he simply said he was studying the issue and praying about it. And we were so naive back then about duplicity and treachery that we believed him. When his praying finally ended after many months, he concluded that it was safe to push ahead with exploration. The people had rationalized breaking the law of God and had convinced themselves that it was an act of faith. Never could we have imagined the horrible consequences of that decision. It seemed such a brave and admirable thing to do. The Lord's prohibition seemed quaint and outdated, as if we had progressed beyond His overly cautious way of thinking.

Umbriel put together a large team of explorers, more than a hundred. His lust for power had risen higher than any mountain in Persus Am, but he was clever enough to keep it hidden behind a veil of humility, pretending that the whole idea had been pressed on him by others. He publicly kept saying that we must move cautiously and in accordance with God's will, but in his heart he yearned to be ruler over not only Persus Am, which was beginning to seem small to him, but the entire world, however vast it might be.

The explorers headed off with great fanfare—there were feasts and bands and gift-giving. They cut through the section of mountain that is now called the Damonchok Pass. It's easy to get through there now, but back then it was quite a feat. When they got to Damonchok they found a gorgeous, untamed land. They found all kinds of trees and plants that bore exotic fruits the Lord had never provided us in Persus Am. They found the fabled beasts and slaughtered them and ate their meat. They found lush forests and vast lakes and birds and other animals unlike anything we had ever seen. They sent back some of the fruits and animals, and the messengers who brought them told of what a marvelous place it was. There was great excitement about this discovery in all of Persus Am. Everyone came to see the animals, and the stories spread. The consensus was that we had made the right decision in going to Damonchok. The Lord had given us a brand new world.

The explorers continued their work, and we did not hear from them for many months. They studied the southern part of Damonchok, clear to the eastern edge, where another mountain range stopped them. Damonchok had been so amazing that they decided to find a way to get across that eastern mountain range and go into the territory they named Wilmoroth. They did find a way, and what they found there changed our lives forever. They did not find anyone living in Damonchok, even though there are people living in the north. But in Wilmoroth they found a number of tribes, most of them at war with one another, as is still the case today. These people seemed very strange, with their dark skin and styles of dress that were totally unfamiliar to us. Our people were frightened and confused too by the fact that the tribesmen could not understand our language and spoke in strange sounds of their own. We knew only one language. It had never occurred to us that people somewhere else might use different words. This is how naive we were.

Our people had never heard of any human being killing another human being. It had never happened in our entire history. When they came across the first tribe, that tribe thought it was some sort of trick of their enemies, and they slaughtered twenty-seven of our explorers, more than a quarter of the total number. Our people were too stunned to defend themselves. Such bloodshed was beyond their wildest imagination, and they were totally unprepared.

Once the tribe had killed so many of our people and saw that we stood there helpless and stunned, they took pity on them and tried to befriend them. The group was so overwhelmed with grief and confusion they had no idea what to do next. Some of them wanted to come home, and some of them insisted they should stay and finish their mission. In the end about half of them decided to return with the bodies of their slain comrades. This became such a gruesome and difficult task that they abandoned most of the bodies along the way. When they finally returned home, though, they had a few of the corpses still with them, and Umbriel ordered them displayed in the courtyard of the Temple, exactly where the animals and fruits and other treasures from Damonchok had been displayed before. The news of the massacre of our people was devastating. We did not think such a tragedy was possible. We had conceived of the idea of great beasts killing people, though the ones in Persus Am had never done so. But the thought of human beings murdering other human beings filled us with horror.

We were also filled with an irrational fear of the tribe who had attacked our people. Somehow the rumor got started that maybe the savages (that's what we always called them) would come to Persus Am and attack us. There was no real reason to believe this rumor at all. The Wilmorothian tribes had rarely even wandered into Damonchok, so they certainly would not be inclined to go to all the trouble of trying to get across the mountains into Persus Am. We found out later, in fact, that their religion forbade them even going near those mountains. But Umbriel allowed this talk of their possible invasion to go on, until many people were in a frenzy over it. People talked about what they would do if one of those savages ever tried to kill anyone in their family, how they were peaceful folks but they could kill if they had to protect their children.

Umbriel pretended to try to calm their fears. He said the thing to do was not to get all worried but just to be prepared for whatever might happen. He set up a Band of Protectors (there was no such word as *army* back then—there had never been anyone to fight!), and these Protectors were given weapons and were trained to repulse any attack of invaders. It was the silliest thing you ever saw, such a weird overreaction to a nonexistent threat that I thought Umbriel had lost his mind.

He hadn't. He knew exactly what he was doing. A crisis atmosphere was just what he needed to rally the people to him and continue his reign. The Protectors became an elite group, and all the young men wanted to be part of it. They had to pass through rigorous training to qualify, and once they made it they played war games and wore special uniforms, which they loved to strut around in to show they were part of the exclusive group. Just about everybody praised Umbriel for responding so quickly to the danger we faced, and supposedly we all felt safe and cozy with his band of teenagers marching around and protecting us against nothing.

Umbriel also sent back over the mountains a new group of explorers, several hundred this time. Part of them were to go "rescue" our kinsmen in Wilmoroth, who needed no rescuing. The others were to go claim and settle the land of southern Damonchok in the name of God and Persus Am. This they did.

III

While Umbriel tried to build his empire, I played with the light, making discoveries with my friends day after day about what we could do with its energy. My wife had another baby, a boy, and we named him Rickeon. The four of us lived in perfect contentment. We celebrated at the Temple. We had wonderful parties and feasts at our house, where my wife and her collaborators would play the new instruments they were creating. My daughter was growing up to be a beautiful young lady. These were happy days, and we put Umbriel and his maneuverings out of our minds most of the time. In our exploration of light and energy, my friends and I had invented explosives that used the energy from light in combination with certain chemical reactions. We thought, of course, that such an invention would have all sorts of productive uses—from blasting mines and tunnels to reshaping the landscape as we needed. Umbriel heard about our experiments and came out to see us one day. He took me aside and said, "You realize the value such weapons as these might have for the protection of Persus Am someday."

"I have not created a weapon," I told him. "I am a scientist."

"When the land the Lord has given us is threatened, we're all soldiers and weapons makers," he said.

"You know as well as I do those savages mean us no harm," I told him. "And even if we were in danger, I wouldn't trust Persus Am to your bunch of kids marching around in their costumes and stabbing at posts in the ground."

My words made him angry. We were not used to speaking so harshly to one another then. I knew he was fuming, but he held back and just said, "I came here to encourage you in your work. Persus Am needs you."

I said, "Thank you, brother. But I wouldn't get too excited yet. Right now our explosions aren't powerful enough to scare a baby."

"But I've heard they have great potential," he said. "Everyone believes you're onto something big. Just keep working on it, Tarius. You're the miracle man. Everybody says so."

From then on he always referred to me as his miracle man, in public or private. I tried not to be taken in by it. I didn't want to be known as one of his inner circle. But my colleagues and I did keep experimenting, and in time we were able to come up with some pretty good blasts—powerful enough to blow away a tree or a small house. We felt we were on the verge of something bigger—a really big explosion, that would rock the earth. It was amazing what we had learned about light and energy and the way matter is put together, but I won't tell you about that because I don't talk about bombs anymore, not about how they work or how we created them. I am forever silent on that subject, and when you hear what happened, you'll know why.

Now while we were making our discoveries, Umbriel was trying to take over Damonchok and Wilmoroth, the very thing he and his son have been trying to do ever since. Back then southern Damonchok was pretty open, and within a couple years he had a few communities settled there in what is now called the Disputed Territory. Our people in Wilmoroth stayed with the tribe that had massacred those first twenty-seven; they learned their language and lived in their villages. A few of our people intermarried with theirs. People at home, particularly Umbriel, were repulsed that any of our people would marry those savages. Umbriel wanted them to have nothing to do with those people, but having the Wilmorothians as allies was the only way they could survive.

We had disobeyed the Lord in going beyond our mountains, and the fabulous life He had given us in Persus Am was just about to be ripped away from us. Some of the Wilmorothians decided they wanted to see that land beyond the forbidden mountains. They could rationalize just as well as we could, and they decided that since the Amians had come to Wilmoroth and told them what a paradise God had created in Persus Am, God must want them to see it, in spite of His earlier command. So they planned an expedition of about a hundred of their people, as many as we had first sent them. Our people acted as guides.

When word reached Persus Am that the savages who had killed our people were coming, there was panic. Umbriel allowed this, probably even caused it. He let the news leak out, with no explanation that the barbarians were coming in peace and friendship escorted by our own people. The war games intensified, and the leaders of the army declared they were ready to meet any challenge. Some more responsible people finally brought it to

Umbriel's attention in a public forum that the barbarians were coming not as attackers but basically as tourists. He did not deny this, but said he would have the army ready to meet any unexpected threat.

IV

While the army got ready to repulse the invasion of the barbaric hordes, my friends and I reached a crucial point in our research. We had been experimenting with ways to make the explosions bigger. We were trying different combinations of forces, and finally, by accident really, we hit on the source of what could make the explosions very powerful. Once we had observed it in the laboratory, we had to set up an experiment to see how it would work on a big scale. To tell you the truth, we had no idea what to expect. Our theories told us the blast might shake the earth, but experience told us it might be just an embarrassing fizzle. We set it up far away from any houses or buildings, out in a flat open area, and we built a metal building with thick walls and heavy windows covered with screens. We told very few people what we were doing because if it fizzled we didn't want to look ridiculous.

It didn't fizzle. The explosion was so incredible we were nearly killed by it. Rocks, dust, and trees piled up on our building, the windows were sucked out, we were smashed against the walls. It was amazing. Debris flew farther than we had projected even in our most extreme scenarios. Houses that we thought were far too far away to be touched at all by the blast were covered with debris and their windows were smashed. No one was killed, miraculously, but some people were hurt. It scared us to death, but it was also exhilarating. All that power! And we knew we could make it bigger. The blast was heard for miles around, and everyone came running. I was hurt and had to be carried away on a stretcher, but I was praising God for the power He had let us unleash.

I thought we would be in big trouble for all the damage we had caused, but Umbriel himself came to see me in the hospital that night to congratulate me for what we had accomplished. He said he had heard the blast all the way in the city. When I got out of the hospital, he had me take him all around the blast site. He was enthralled with every detail. Seeing the crater at the blast site thrilled him. He wanted to see the trees that had been uprooted and the houses that had been damaged. He wanted to know every detail of what the blast had looked like and sounded like. He wanted to know precisely how it worked.

I was very vague with him. I was the leader of the team, and I had sworn them all to silence about how the explosive worked. I knew Umbriel was just looking for ways his military forces could use the bomb, and I was determined not to let him do it. He never mentioned the military, though. He treated the bomb only as a scientific discovery, just as he would have done in the old days. He talked about how amazing it was that the Lord was opening up so many secrets of the world to us in such a short amount of time. The way he talked almost made me ashamed of being so suspicious of him. There was so much that was admirable about him—I don't know if you can see that. But there was something about him that was so strong and enthusiastic and self-assured that you just wanted to believe that he was right, you wanted to be on his side and share his vision. He inspired loyalty like no other man I've known.

I told him we still had a long way to go before we perfected our discovery (the word *bomb* was not in our vocabulary yet). He told me by all means to keep working on it, and he would keep checking our progress.

After that day his attention was turned to other things, for the time of the savages' visit had arrived. Umbriel had his military waiting for them at the base of the Damonchokian Mountains and promised the people the soldiers would accompany them every step of their visit. Umbriel said we would try to meet them in peace, but we would allow nothing that would put Persus Am in danger.

What happened next is one of the most shameful episodes in the history of our nation. The true story may never be known, for there are many versions of it. But what apparently happened was something like this. The savages came across the mountain at a different place from where Umbriel's army expected them to.

When the soldiers finally saw them, the savages and the Amian explorers who were escorting them were already down the mountain and were headed toward the city. This is where the story gets a little fuzzy. The story Umbriel's army gave was that the savages, as soon as they saw the army, ran toward it as if to attack, waving their weapons in the air and screaming. The army had to defend themselves, so they attacked and killed nearly the entire party, with only a dozen or so escaping and a number of others taken prisoner. Thirty or so soldiers were also killed. But survivors on the other side of the battle say the savages had no intention of attacking at all and gave no indication they were going to. They were just running to greet the Amians and held no weapons. They were massacred, some say, as retaliation for what had happened to our own explorers.

Whatever the case may be, Umbriel now had a bona fide enemy to fight, because when word of the massacre reached the tribes in Wilmoroth, several of the tribes joined together to proclaim war on Persus Am. Many of them were already angry that Umbriel had sent so many people to settle southern Damonchok. They were afraid that eventually he might try to take their land as well, which in fact was probably true. They gathered their armies and attacked the Amian settlements, which were totally unprepared for battle. Our explorers thought Damonchok was safe, and until then it had been, so they had built villages rather than fortresses. They had never fought a battle in their lives, and the Wilmorothians marched in with no warning. Our people were sliced down. It was another massacre, but instead of losing twenty-seven as we had before, this time we lost more than two hundred.

News of this loss threw Persus Am into a panic, and we began to prepare for all-out war, something we knew nothing about. Umbriel came to me again, and this time he told me the importance of making our explosives available for the protection of Persus Am. He said, "That is one weapon the savages have never even dreamed of. We can stop them in their tracks with it. We can slaughter them before they ever get off the mountain."

I told him God did not open His secrets to us so we could use them to murder other human beings.

"They're not human beings," Umbriel says. "They're savages who attacked peaceful settlements and killed over two hundred people, and they will wipe us all out if they get the chance. If you won't let us use those bombs, you're saying you think we should just surrender our nation to those animals. Let them slaughter your wife and children as they've done to so many others."

"Is your mind that corrupt?" I said. "We've got to put a stop to this killing once and for all. You disobeyed God when you first crossed that mountain, and now you're paying the penalty. Instead of finding ways to kill those people, you ought to be looking for ways to stop the killing. We're becoming as barbaric as they are."

"You're very naive, Tarius," he said. "Dangerously naive. Do you think we can just go to them and say, 'All right, we've had enough, let's just call the whole thing off'? We're not dealing with rational people. They want to overthrow our whole nation, and they won't stop until they win or we crush them."

"I don't believe that," I said. "They never would have bothered us if we hadn't massacred them when they came over the mountain."

"But they attacked us!" he said. "Whose side are you on?"

I said, "I just believe we could work this out peacefully, and my conscience will not allow me to use my discovery to kill people."

After our talk I went immediately to all six other members of the team and made them promise they wouldn't release any part of our discovery to Umbriel. I figured he would go around me to get to them, and he did. They promised to keep the secret, and I trusted them to do so.

V

Umbriel directed all the nation's energies into preparing for war, but when war came, we still were not ready for it. The Wilmorothians had been warriors for hundreds of years. For us war had only been a game. The Wilmorothians gloried in war. They were vicious and relentless. Killing was easy and commonplace for them. Our soldiers were young men who had been born into a nation that had never known killing. Until the massacre, none of them had ever killed a man. Strangely enough, we had some good weapons. We had "fire pellets" which could kill instantly and from a considerable distance, and the barbarians mostly had swords and bows and arrows. But we did not have the viciousness of the Wilmorothians, or their eagerness to kill.

As the Wilmorothians marched out of their own country, across Damonchok toward Persus Am, Umbriel worked the public and his soldiers into a frenzy of fear and paranoia. He got them ready to fight and kill. Umbriel's plan was to stop the barbarians before they even got over the mountain, but they so outnumbered us, and they were so much better than we were in battle, that they poured over the mountain in wave after wave, and while I suppose you could say our soldiers fought valiantly, the barbarians trampled right over them. Not that we didn't kill hundreds of them, but they just kept coming and coming, and as they headed toward the city they destroyed everything in sight. They burned down houses and killed children. I remember having to move three dead children out of the road on my way into the city the next day. Each one of their little heads had been crushed and was crusted over with blood. That is what our nation had come to.

Our army was more successful protecting the city. We held the invaders off for a couple of days, but whenever some of them finally got through, they headed straight for the Temple and established it as their base. They had found out from our explorers that the Temple was the most sacred place in the nation, and they believed it would not be attacked. And they were right at first. This may be hard for you to imagine in this day when nothing is sacred, but for those soldiers the thought of attacking the Temple and committing murder in it would have been too horrible to consider.

Umbriel knew the situation was desperate. In a matter of hours, or at most another day, the Wilmorothians would control our nation. He did the only thing left for him to do. I was just outside the city when I heard the blasts. They happened almost simultaneously, and I knew as soon as I heard the sound and saw the incredible clouds of smoke and felt the earth shake underneath me that he had used my bombs. I had been betrayed. I turned around immediately so that I could get to my wife and daughter to protect them from what was to come. I felt certain the destruction had only begun, and sure enough, even before I got back to my house, there was another horrible blast, closer this time, and the sun was blocked out by the cloud of dust and debris in the air.

My wife and children and I hid in one of my laboratories underground. We stayed there for three days. I was in despair. I remember my wife's face when I first got home after those bombs went off. She knew they were the bombs I had invented. She hugged me, and then I looked into her eyes and she began to cry. "It is my fault," I said.

"No, no, no," she said, and she held me for a long time right there at the doorway. She said, "You invented something good, and they used it to kill. Never say it was your fault. This is bad enough already."

"But I made the discovery. I led the team."

She said, "The discovery isn't what did this. Umbriel did it. The Lord will deal with him. Now we just have to trust in the Lord."

When we came up after three days, everything was quiet. The war was apparently over, but we had no idea who had won or how bad things were. I decided to go into the city to find out what I could, while my wife stayed home with our children.

The destruction I saw as I rode toward the city was unbelievable. It was very dark, first of all, because the dust from the explosions had filled the sky and blocked out the sun. I saw burned corpses, I saw bodies dangling from the remains of buildings. I saw a man whose body looked perfectly intact, but a wall had caved in and had crushed his head. People walked, dazed, along the streets; others screamed for relatives they couldn't find or who had been killed. I rode to the Temple, which was nothing more than a chaos of bricks and glass and corpses. People prayed amidst the rubble, rummaging through it, crying and wailing. It was a devastating sight. This building had been the most fabulous structure on earth, where the Lord sang and His light swirled around the domes and we felt more alive than we ever thought it was possible to feel. Now it was a trash heap. I could smell nothing but dead bodies and could hear nothing but the high-pitched wails that seemed to fill the world in those days. I stood there knowing that my own discovery had caused this destruction. In those first moments standing in the ashes of that Temple, I wished that I had been lucky enough for the walls to fall on me. But my punishment was to come later.

I talked to people and found out Umbriel had won his war. Much of the Wilmorothian army had been killed by the bombs, and the rest had retreated in fear. But Umbriel had not realized how powerful the bombs would be, and he killed at least as many Amian civilians as he did barbarians.

The two members of my team who had given the bombs to Umbriel were killed in the war, and three other innocent team members were killed; that left only two men alive who knew the secrets of the bombs. Umbriel called me to his headquarters in the city to try to talk me into joining him to prepare more bombs in case the Wilmorothians decided to make another attack. He offered me a place in his inner council. He offered me a home in the new palace he was planning, which he said would be the greatest and most luxurious building ever built. He talked about a glittering dome and swimming pools and banquet halls, but all I could think about were the burned carcasses and wailing women I had just seen on the streets. He repulsed me. He said he regretted what had happened with the bomb, but now we should all join together to build up the city to be even better than it was. He said we needed to put aside our differences and remember that we fought against a common enemy.

I was so angry that the whole room became a blur around me. "You are the enemy!" I shouted. I felt like I could kill him. I had to get out of there. I turned away from him and walked out of the room, but before I got out of the building they arrested me and put me in prison.

Having failed to persuade me to join him, Umbriel did the next best thing. He used me as a scapegoat, blamed me for what had happened with the bombs. He wrote in an informational—

that was what they called the publications that came out every day to give the news—that I had lied to him about how powerful the bombs were. He said I had assured him that the bombs would kill their targets and nothing more. He mourned the loss of our own people and said he had imprisoned me for what I had done. He took credit for the strategy that defeated the Wilmorothians, but he put the blame for the bombs' devastation at my feet. I was unable to defend myself, of course, and by then everyone knew I had in fact invented the bombs, so they had no reason not to believe Umbriel. Those who could have defended me were given no access to tell my side to the informationals.

Umbriel, had taken not only the informationals but all other powers unto himself. He pared down his inner council to only a dozen or so of his closest supporters. He imprisoned anyone who publicly spoke against him or whom he considered his enemy. The military could make no move without his permission, nor could any other arm of government.

To revive the people's spirits and keep them from turning against him, he came out with elaborate plans for a new Temple to be built in place of the old one. He commissioned a gigantic painting of it to be displayed at the site of the old Temple. The building was actually going to be his palace, but at that time he referred to it as the Temple. All those who had lost their homes were to work on this project, some of them supervising Wilmorothian slaves, who were given the hardest jobs.

The biggest problems were beyond Umbriel's control. Some peculiar things had happened as a result of the War. It was as if God, seeing that we had chosen sin, removed His Spirit from our world. The most frightening and debilitating thing for us was what happened to the music. From the moment of the destruction of the Temple, the music had a flatness, a deadness to it, as if it were nothing more than sound. Before, it had been alive with the voice of God. It had been saturated with His energy, just as we heard in your music when you arrived. For the first time in the history of the world the music was dead, and we had been so dependent on it that it left us in despair. Nothing could replace it.

Besides being deprived of the nourishing music, we were also deprived of light because the bombs had sent an enormous cloud of dust into the air that blocked the sun for many days. After that, deadly gray ashes covered everything. Crops were destroyed all over the country. What food remained wasn't distributed very well, so for the first time ever people were starving in the streets. Animals were dying. The whole countryside was a wasteland. Even when the sky gradually cleared, the land did not recover. It was as if the ground was cursed. Every year the land produced less and less, and now it's practically a desert. There is no scientific explanation for this that I know of. It's as if God simply withdrew His blessing from the land.

People were homeless, sick from the ashes, despondent because of the lack of light, spiritually wounded from the loss of the music. Umbriel tried to get the people to concentrate on the rebuilding and the glorious city that would come of it, but he wasn't very successful. People were not inspired with hope by watching bands of prisoners being forced to build a "Temple" that seemed to take forever to construct.

I remained in prison during this time, separated from my wife and children, who were in another prison. I was incredibly lonely and discouraged. Sitting there day after day in that smelly cubicle, having nothing to do, and not being able to see my wife or children at all nearly drove me crazy. For all I knew my imprisonment would last months or years, perhaps even the rest of my life. I didn't know if I would ever see Amandan or our children Ona and Rickeon again, and the images of their faces burned in my brain.

VI

There were some very revered people among us, whom we simply called the Old Ones, because some of them were nearly three hundred years old. There were nine of them at that time, and they all lived very close to the Lord and were marvelous musicians. They were among the few voices that all along had warned against Umbriel's schemes. They predicted all the destruction that eventually took place. Their prophecies had seemed far-fetched, and Umbriel managed to brush them aside as senile and outdated. But once their prophecies came true, the Old Ones gained new influence because everybody was looking for the way out of the agony we found ourselves in. Umbriel imprisoned most of them, but he did not kill them, and their words seeped through the prison walls. Some of them heard from the Lord through dreams, and the dreams as they were reported were remarkably similar, even though none of the Old Ones spoke to any of the others. I was able to talk to one of the Old Ones, Turi Marek, in prison, and he told me personally of the very vivid and frightening dreams he had almost every night. The specifics of the dreams were different, but the message was always this: Persus Am had plunged itself into sin and had cut itself off from the Spirit of God. His Spirit had departed from the music and from the land. But because God still loved His people, He would send someone, His very own Son in the form of a man, to save us. We would know this Man by the Spirit of God in His singing. All those who wanted to turn away from wickedness would trust in Him, and He would lead them to a new land, called Caladria, which means "land of hope." They would stay there while the Savior accomplished their salvation, and then they would return to Persus Am.

This message was repeated so many times in so many of the Old Ones' dreams that we all believed it must be from God. We knew only His intervention could save us from the mess we found ourselves in. Umbriel gathered the Old Ones together and executed them in secret, but not before their prophecies were already widely known and believed. They had fulfilled their mission. After that it was a matter of our wondering how long it would take for this savior to come. Would He come immediately, or would He even come in our lifetime? We had no idea. We just clung to the hope that He would come and that it could happen any day.

It seemed as though He would never come, but in fact it was just over a year from the first prophecies when He emerged from among us. At first all He did was play the music, but what music! It wasn't the dead post-War music. It was the Spirit-filled song we had always known. He was the only person in the world who could play it, and as the word spread people flocked to hear Him. They were starved for the Spirit that had been so much a part of their lives, and at times the crowds nearly crushed Him in their eagerness. Umbriel hated Him, but he had trouble getting at Him because the man's followers were so good at helping Him elude the soldiers. We believed, of course, that He was surrounded by God's protection. Umbriel made a few attempts to capture Him, but he only ended up looking ridiculous. Then he laid off for a while, not willing to risk his popularity further by inflicting bloodshed on his own people just to capture one man. Some said Umbriel believed the people's interest in this criminal would wear off soon.

The man's name was Emajus. He not only played the music, but He began to heal people who had been injured in the War and who were sick from the diseases that the bombs had caused. It was amazing. He also began to proclaim a message that was similar to what the Old Ones had said, that the world needed repentance and salvation from God. This is when Umbriel realized what a threat Emajus was. He believed Emajus wanted to overthrow him and rule in his place. Umbriel sent soldiers to kill Him, but Emajus always seemed able to evade him. Emajus began to speak of Caladria, just as the Old Ones had, and He invited anyone who believed in His message to follow Him there. On this point Umbriel tried to challenge Emajus's credibility. Emajus said Caladria was at a certain place beyond Wilmoroth, and even the Wilmorothians testified that no such place existed, that the place Emajus identified was in the Gray Desert, where nothing lived but horrible black creatures about the size of your fist that could kill you with their bite. But because the Spirit so pervaded Him, people believed Emajus anyway and were ready to follow Him.

Before He could get His group together though Umbriel finally got to Him in a late-night raid conducted by his best soldiers. He didn't kill Emajus, but he captured Him and threw Him in prison. This was the only time I saw Him. They brought Him to the prison where I was. He was under heavy guard, but for reasons I have never known they did not stop Him from talking to people as they led Him down the hallway toward His cell. As He walked past me, He saw me watching Him and stopped. He reached out and clasped my arm. Someone must have told Him my name, because He said, "Don't be discouraged, Tarius. In

Umbriel's kingdom, a good man belongs in prison." I have treasured that moment all these years.

Emajus seemed completely unconcerned that Umbriel had Him locked up in prison. He was so cheerful you would have thought He had come voluntarily. To those of us who believed in His teaching, seeing Him in prison was a great tragedy. We knew the only reason Umbriel hadn't killed Him yet was that he was planning some sort of public execution. We knew Umbriel wouldn't wait long to get rid of Him. And then what would become of us?

It took only a few days for us to find out why Emajus was so unworried. It happened on the morning He was to be executed. We felt the ground sort of tremble. It stopped after just a few seconds, and we put it out of our minds. Then about an hour later it happened again, and in a few more minutes it happened a third time. No one had ever felt anything like it before, and everyone seemed to have a different idea of what caused the trembling. Some blamed it on the machines they were using to build the new Temple—the prison was pretty close to it. Others thought there must be a bomb exploding far off.

After those strange rumbles something else happened that was even harder to understand. We began to hear a sound—very far off—hard to identify. It was high and distant, but to me it wasn't unpleasant. As the day continued, the sound gradually got louder, and I thought, even though lots of other people denied this, that it sounded more and more like music. I was almost certain I could hear distinct notes in it and a melody. The sound began to bother some people. Our guards in particular were very annoyed by it. They covered their ears with their hands at first, and then most of them put plugs in their ears. At the same time, the rumbling became more frequent and more violent. The floors cracked. The doors of our cells rattled so hard we thought they would fall off. Bits of the ceiling began to break away. By mid-afternoon our building was crumbling so badly that we heard the guards talking about getting themselves and the prisoners out of there. The sound was also hurting them very badly, even though their ears were plugged. The next thing we knew, the guards fled their posts, and we thought we had been abandoned to die in the crumbling building. Before long, though, the hallways outside our cells were filled with people from the streets, shouting and cheering and unlocking the prison doors. I can't tell you how thrilling it was. The earth was shaking, this sound was everywhere, and we were being liberated. It was utter chaos. No one seemed to be in charge of anything. When they opened my cell, I asked a man, "What about Emajus? Did they kill Him?"

"No," he said. "He escaped. Umbriel's soldiers are running from the sound, his new buildings have crumbled, and all the prisoners are being set free."

That very night word began to spread that Emajus would leave for Caladria the next morning and that anyone who wanted to go with Him was to meet at a certain place at the edge of the city. I planned to go, but the first thing I was determined to do was to find my wife and children. I looked everywhere and asked everyone I saw, and finally late that night I found Amandan. She had our little boy, but she didn't know where our daughter was. I have never been so happy to see anyone in my life as I was to see my wife and baby that night. My only worry was finding our daughter. We couldn't bear to leave Persus Am knowing she was still there. Emajus was to leave at dawn, so we had only a few hours. We went to the edge of the city where most of those who were planning to go were staying, and I talked to one of Emajus's closest followers, who was helping to organize the journey. "We can't leave without her," I said. "You have to give us time to find her."

He said, "The Lord has told us that no one who wants to go will be prevented by anything. We will leave at dawn."

"Well my daughter is not here. Obviously she's being prevented," I said.

He said, "The Lord has said everyone has been set free. If your daughter is not here, it is because she has chosen not to come."

"You don't know what you're talking about. If she's free, she just hasn't found us. We have to find her."

"I hope you find her," he said. "But be sure you are here at dawn, because we're leaving then, and once we go, you can never catch up with us."

We heard his warning, but we were determined to find Ona before dawn. Since we had checked everywhere in the city we could think of, we decided to go to our house and see if she might be waiting there. She wasn't. Our house had been ransacked and was in ruins. We didn't have time to worry about the house, though. Our daughter wasn't there, and none of the few neighbors who were left had seen her. We had to get back to Emajus, because there was no time left. My wife said that the Lord promised that no one who wanted to go would be prevented, so maybe Ona had found her way there by now. We clung to this hope on our way back.

We got to the camp less than an hour before dawn. As soon as we were in sight of it, one of our friends, who had been in prison with me for months, came with news of our daughter. His words were horrible. I can still picture him standing there, and I remember just how I felt, with my wife and son there, all of us dirty and tired and anxious beyond description. And then he told me Umbriel had invited my daughter to live in the palace with him and she had accepted. He said he had received this word from someone who worked for Umbriel, and he was certain it was true.

If anyone else had told me this, I wouldn't have believed it, but this man had been our friend for years. We had been through all kinds of adversity together. He had reliable sources in Umbriel's inner circle. Still, even though deep down I knew it must be true, right then I denied it. I had to. It made me crazy. "He has her in prison," I said.

Yorion said, "No one is in prison, Tarius. The Lord set them all free."

"She wouldn't choose to be with him," I said. "It's ridiculous. We have to rescue her."

Yorion knew my pain, and he didn't want to argue with me. He said, "I'll speak to you very frankly since we don't have much time. They told me your daughter was in prison, but it was very hard on her, harder than on most. She nearly lost her mind. When Umbriel offered to let her out for a while and gave her gifts and good food and comfort, she could not resist him. One thing led to another, and they decided to get married."

"Married!"

"I'm told they got married, and Umbriel is planning a public ceremony as soon as he has things under control again."

"It can't be true!" I said. "They just can't be telling you the truth!" But Amandan just stood there and cried because she knew it was true. I was out of my mind with rage and hurt. I said, "I'm going to go find her for myself."

"You can't," Yorion said. "I know what you must be feeling, but there just isn't time. In less than an hour we'll be leaving, and even if you found her right away, you'd never make it back. You've just got to put her in God's hands now. There's nothing you can do."

Amandan tried to stop me too, but I was out of control. I regret my decision now more than anything I've ever done in my life, and I wish someone had forcibly stopped me, but I told Amandan to wait for me while I made one last attempt to find Ona. She begged me not to go. I promised her I would be back in time. I said, "If I don't find her before it's time to go, I'll come right back."

VII

It was a wasted mission from the beginning. The soldiers guarding Umbriel's quarters wouldn't let me anywhere near my daughter or allow me to speak to anyone who would know if she was there. I stormed and raged and nearly got arrested, but I got no closer to my daughter. As you must have guessed by now, by the time I got back to the camp, Emajus and his followers were gone, my wife and son included. Even though I was at the brink of total physical exhaustion, I chased them for nearly a day before I collapsed unconscious on the road.

The next couple weeks are a blur in my memory. The family who found me on the road took care of me for a few days, but I was so distraught I don't remember much about them. Then I went back to Persus Am with this impossible idea of rescuing my daughter. While I was outside Umbriel's quarters one afternoon,

I was amazed to see a group of Emajians coming toward me. I knew several of them and thought they had all gone with Emajus. They took me to a home where it was safer to talk and said the Lord had left a group of them behind to set up a place to keep His message alive in the world and to await His return. My wife was not among this group. The Lord had told them to go to a mountain in Damonchok, and they asked me to go with them. I told them how much I wanted to find my daughter, but they gently helped me realize what a hopeless cause it was, and I was so distraught and so tired and so relieved to see someone I knew that I agreed to go with them.

The place we named the Rock of Calad was south of Damonchok near what is now called the Disputed Territory. The Rock of Calad was a large plateau that was uninhabited. There was only one way to get to the top, and that made it easier to defend. We got to work right away making a fortress of it because we knew that as soon as Umbriel got control of the crisis in Persus Am, he would come after us. There were just over a hundred of us that first year, but our numbers would increase dramatically over the years as Emajians from all over the world joined us. We farmed the land near the Rock and even some places on the Rock, where the land was rich enough. We built storehouses for food, cisterns for water, houses to live in, and all the rest of it. My friends also hounded me into making another bomb just in case we needed it. I didn't have all the tools and necessary materials to make one of the big bombs, and I had vowed never to do it again anyway; but I made some smaller ones that would certainly be adequate for anything we needed. We made other kinds of weapons too and bought some from the Wilmorothians and even from Damonchokians, who were selling them illegally.

We had one year of peace. It was a horrible year for me, separated from my wife and children and knowing I had given up my chance to go to Caladria. We had no idea when the Lord would return, and we still don't know. Before long I found out for certain that Umbriel had married my daughter. I have never been allowed to speak to her.

During that year, while we were building our homes and

preparing our defense, Umbriel was rebuilding his army and reenslaving his people. He was ruthless, but he built his palace and amassed all power unto himself. He did everything he could to keep the Spirit of the Lord from ever returning to Persus Am. The music had gone bad, but that wasn't enough for him. He declared in speeches and in his informational that the Lord had laid on his heart a new way that the Almighty must be worshiped in this new era. The music was dead because it was music of the old order. The old instruments of music would no longer work and must be changed. He ordered them all to be collected so he could have his own musicians "transform" them. All instruments were carefully numbered and inventoried, and each person was given a date by which his instrument would be returned. Then, after the soldiers had searched nearly every building in Persus Am to make sure all instruments had been collected, Umbriel quietly and systematically destroyed every one in his collection. It was thereafter declared illegal to possess or manufacture a musical instrument of any kind in Persus Am. Umbriel said the Lord had told him that this is the way it must be.

All these things happened during our year of peace. But once Umbriel had taken care of the problems in his own country, he turned on us. He apparently thought that since his army outnumbered us three to one, stamping us out would be no problem. He must have been misinformed about the strength of our fortress because he fought the battle as stupidly as it was possible to fight it. We were well armed, and we were on top of a plateau whose sides—except for one—were sheer cliffs. The side you could climb was difficult in the best of conditions, let alone when someone's firing on you. But still they attacked, and we dutifully killed them. When we had killed probably half their army, they decided to lay in a siege while they waited for more troops to arrive. We had plenty of food and water in storage, but Umbriel's army began to run out of supplies in just a few weeks. Incredibly, they attacked again, this time in the middle of the night, apparently hoping to catch us by surprise. They were surprised about halfway up the Rock when they detonated two bombs we had hidden there. The blast killed dozens of them and tore away a good chunk of the mountain too. That was the end of that battle. They retreated, and Umbriel turned his attention toward other matters for a while. But later he sent troops to harass us and to try to make it difficult for us to get supplies to the Rock. And they built catapults that sent swirling balls of fire onto the Rock to set our buildings on fire. They've made life rough for us over the years, but they've never really been much of a threat to our existence.

After a few years my daughter gave birth to Umbriel's child, and he was called Umbriel II. When he grew to be a man, his father died—some say he was murdered—and this man, my grandson, though I do not claim him, became the ruler of Persus Am. He still rules it today. Part of my punishment all these decades has been to see my own offspring outdo his father in evil. He is a nuisance to the world and has brought it again to the brink of war even as we speak. I think of how my wife's heart will break when she comes back to find that her grandson is a monster and that her daughter is lost to her forever. Every day I spend on the Rock is a lost day that I should have spent with the woman I love. Every day I feel the emptiness of not being with her, and I wonder if she still could love me as much as I love her. I imagine all kinds of horrible things. Every day that is the punishment I receive.

But the Lord said He will send a messenger to tell us all things are ready. The messenger will take us to Caladria, and we will escort our people back home. Then the salvation the Lord went away to prepare will be proclaimed to everyone. The Lord's Temple will be rebuilt in Persus Am, and His own voice will sing in the music of that place. These are the things we wait for, so when we heard of your music in the Utturies, we prayed, "Lord, let him be the messenger."

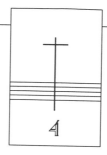

4

When Tarius Arc finished his story, he asked that the evening meal be brought in. I had questions to ask him, but he seemed so tired and lost in thought that I stayed quiet while we ate.

It was a meal we would never finish.

We heard a horrible crash in the outer room, followed by screams and shouts. Tarius told me to follow him through a side door, but before we even got to the door a group of soldiers burst into the room, and three of them knocked me hard to the ground. My chin smashed against the floor and sent spasms of pain through my body. They tied my hands behind my back, picked me up, thrashed me against the wall, and shouted questions I could not understand because the language had been knocked out of me again. They pinned Tarius against the wall too, but they weren't abusing him quite so much as they were me. The soldiers were strong, muscular men, neat and clean shaven, dressed in impressive red jackets and black pants. Around their waists were sashes of various colors covered with colored horizontal bars according to their accomplishments and positions. Their hair was short and slicked back. They were utterly professional, almost mechanical, in every move they made.

As they dragged us through the outer room, I saw the other

soldiers smashing the musical instruments against the floor. Sometimes as the instruments hit the ground they breathed one last musical note, and this seemed to infuriate the soldiers, who thrashed them all the harder. One of them picked up my guitar to demolish it, but the commander yelled at him to stop. It was too late. The guitar splintered into several pieces against the stone floor. The commander screamed at the soldier and ran over to pick up the pieces of the guitar, but before I could see what he would do I was dragged outside.

At first Tarius and I were thrown together into the back of an enclosed wagon, but a few minutes later one of the soldiers came and pulled Tarius out. I was left alone for the rest of the trip.

The journey took more than two days, during which the only light I saw was what came through the slits of wood of the wagon walls. They didn't give me much food, and the wagon smelled bad. But this discomfort was nothing compared to what I was headed toward. Nobody said anything to me. I had no idea where I was going or what would happen to me when I got there. I spent much of my time praying that God would take me out of there. I did not belong there, I told God. None of this had anything to do with me.

During this trip my dreams about Anne started. My visions of her grew more vivid even while I was rapidly losing most of my other memories about home. I could remember, for example, working at the bank, but by the time I had been in the new world three days I could no longer remember what route I took to get to the bank, no matter how hard I struggled to bring it to mind. I could remember my car, but I was not sure what color it was. Each day more details faded.

The one memory that became sharper was the memory of Anne. In my dream on that first night in the wagon Anne was far away, lost in fuzziness that I was trying to cut through to get to her. I heard her voice just as clearly as if she were in the wagon with me. Despite her distance, she did not yell. She repeated my name in a loving, undisturbed way, but I don't know if she saw me. When I woke up, I had the strangest sensation that her hand had just brushed through my hair and over my forehead. I literally felt the warmth of her hand. The wagon was totally dark. I heard my voice say "Anne," and for a minute I was certain someone was in the wagon with me. I ran my hands over the whole area, but I was alone. The image of her face, the sound of her voice, and the touch of her hand burned in my brain, and I did not get back to sleep for a long time that night.

To see anything outside the wagon I had to press my face against the walls and peer between the boards. I saw that the animals that pulled the wagons were not horses, as I had thought, but creatures called camucks, shorter and stouter than horses, with longer necks and smaller heads. I also saw three-wheeled motorized vehicles about the size of golf carts. They were quiet and quick. I don't know why the soldiers didn't have one to take me away in, except that some of the roads we traveled were awfully bad, and those little cars didn't look as if they could take much abuse. The land was pretty barren the whole way, as Tarius had told me. We went through several small towns, with their clusters of houses and shops, a few made of stone or wood, but most made of the white material that looked like dry foam. The poorer people, like Moll and her family and many of the people I saw along the streets, wore shirts and pants of rugged-looking heavy cloth or a leathery material. The wealthier or more refined people like Tarius Arc wore looser-fitting garments with bright sashes and puffy sleeves and pant legs. My own clothing—I had only the outfit I had arrived in—looked rather peasant-like. My pants were black and felt like denim, and my shirt felt like flannel. I wore boots and heavy socks.

Traffic got heavier the closer we got to Persus Am. Whole families traveled together on wagons loaded down with tents and pots and pans and bundles of every kind. I had no idea why they would all be going to the city. Eventually the traffic got so bad that we stopped. I heard the soldiers screaming at people to get out of the way, and pretty soon we pulled past them as they sat in the hot sun and waited. Many of them tried to press against the wagon to look inside, but the soldiers knocked them away. Soon on one side of us I could see a brick wall, about twenty-five feet high. This was the wall of the city of Persus Am, though I did not know that

until later. We followed along the wall until we got to the point
that the crowds were headed for—the Great Gate with its magnificent archway bearing Umbriel's seal. In the opening of the gate
were three small brick guardhouses for the soldiers who stopped
each group that entered. The lines in front of the guardhouses were
long and the people noisy and eager, the children trying to peek
past the crowds to see what was on the other side of the gate, the
adults rearranging their supplies on their animals and taking
drinks from brown leather sacks that they passed around for
everyone. The soldiers pushed us through while people banged on
the wagon and, if they were a safe enough distance away, shouted
obscenities at the soldiers.

As we drove through the gate, I saw why the travelers were
making such a commotion to get inside, for here was beauty unlike
anything I had seen in this land. Wide green lawns stretched as far
as I could see on both sides of the road, which was made of the
same rectangular bricks that formed the wall. Various sections of
the lawns were being watered by unseen sprinklers spraying up
from the ground, sending a fine, silent mist over the landscape. In
the midst of the lawns were carefully trimmed shrubs, flower beds,
and trees. Servants were everywhere clipping bushes, removing
dead trees, pulling dead flowers, and planting bright new plants.

While the landscape was gorgeous in itself, all of it—the lane
we traveled on, the slope of the hill, the carefully manicured lines
of trees—pointed toward what lay ahead, Umbriel's magnificent
palace at the top of the hill. There, blazing as if it were its own
source of light, was the Dome of Persus, the onion-shaped dome
that formed the top of the palace. It was no illusion that the Dome
seemed to blaze with its own light; its golden light, with occasional
flashes of red when the sun hit it a certain way, was not simply a
reflection of the sun. Rather, the jewels with which it was covered
collected the energy from the sun and with this energy projected
their own light, so that it shined the same way day and night. The
bluish white palace itself would have been impressive enough,
with its graceful arches pointing toward heaven, imposing in size
but delicate in its beauty, but I could not stop looking at the Dome.
The way it pulsed forth its light gave it a sense of being not a part

of the building but a separate, living force all its own. It looked like a bright helium balloon that might carry the whole palace toward heaven, the graceful points of the arches pointing the way. I knew all the horrible things Tarius had said about Umbriel, and I knew I was going to this place as a prisoner and not a guest, but in those moments heading toward the Dome of Persus I was glad to be there. I thought it must certainly be a magnificent nation that would build such a palace. Maybe Tarius Arc was wrong.

As we got closer we came upon fountains placed so that the lane split into two half-circles around them. The palace had its own wall, its gates guarded with elaborately dressed soldiers. In front of the palace, just inside the main gate, was a long reflecting pool in which the brilliance of the Dome shimmered. I hoped the soldiers would take me through the intricately carved archway of the main entrance of the palace, but instead we went around to the side to a smaller gate. Once inside they stopped the wagon and made me walk. We left the wide lawns and fountains and sunshine and went inside the palace, down the stairs to a windowless prison.

The prison was the most foul-smelling place I have ever been in. Before I was in my cell five minutes I began to vomit into a can in the corner of the room. I have no idea what the can was there for—the toilet was outside the cell—but my tiny room contained only a mat to sleep on and this can, which remained in the corner for two days filled with vomit, until one of the men sent to observe me insisted that it be removed.

The smell of that place was like nothing I have ever known— a rank mixture of urine and burnt flesh and rotting vegetables. The stench was so overpowering that I could concentrate on nothing else. I could not eat. I did not even try to eat until the end of the second day, and then I vomited immediately.

For those first few horrible hours I was alone. The guards came to the cells only when they had to. They stayed one floor above us, in less unpleasant rooms. I could not see the other prisoners, but I could hear them moving around in their cells. For the first few hours I simply lay on the mat and tried to keep from vomiting. I prayed furiously, "Lord Jesus, get me out of here." I prayed, "Jesus. Jesus. Jesus," over and over again. But I sensed no Spirit of Jesus or anyone else in that place. I was desperately alone.

The next indignity I had to endure was the observers who came with their pencils and drawing pads and their endless tedious questions. There were nine or ten of them at first, but the smell was so unbearable that only five of them stayed. Before anyone spoke to me, two of the artists began to draw pictures of me, and a third began taking notes of some kind, apparently describing my behavior, for every time I moved or spoke it sent him into a flurry of scribbling. The other two—apparently in charge of the scribblers—talked about me as if I were a mannequin in a window.

"Do you think he looks Damonchokian?" the woman said.

"No. Not dark enough," said the man. "His hair sort of looks it, though. His clothes definitely look it."

"But they gave him the clothes. Those weren't the clothes he was wearing when he played the music."

"This smell is *awful*," the man said. "How does he *stand* it?"

As if I had any choice.

"Maybe he enjoys it," she said. "Maybe where he comes from they like this smell."

"He must be Damonchokian then," said the man, and all five of them laughed.

As I stood up and walked closer to the bars of the door, the observers backed away as if I were some monster. The scribblers worked furiously.

"Let me out of here," I said. "What do you want with me?"

"That accent," the man said, "is it Damonchokian?"

But the woman spoke to me. "We have questions. You have broken our laws in a very heinous way. Who are you?"

I told her my name and said I was from the Bright World. She asked the other questions I had already heard, and I gave her the same answers as always. No, I was not an Emajian. No, I had no malicious intentions toward Umbriel or the nation of Persus Am. No, I had not chosen the Utturies in particular as the place to play my criminal songs. No, I could not tell them why I had come, because I did not know.

The woman believed me, I thought, but the man did not. He

said, "He's hiding things. I don't believe he's from the Bright World or any other world. I think he's an Emajian redneck troublemaker from Damonchok."

The woman kept her eyes on me. She did not answer him for a moment. Then she said, "You may be right."

"It isn't the first time they've pulled this Bright World routine."

"That's true."

"I don't believe him at all."

"Well, let's leave him for Councilor Dakin. He dealt with the others. He'll be able to tell. When's he coming?"

"He's been sent for. I don't know."

"Let's get out of here. I feel sick."

I said, "I feel sick too. I've answered your questions. Now let me out of here."

"Only Father-King Umbriel himself can let you out now," the woman said. "Or maybe Councilor Dakin."

"Get them," I said.

The man said, "They'll get here soon enough. You should have thought of this before you decided to play your music in the Utturies."

The questioners left, but the scribblers stayed, making endless drawings and notes of me doing basically nothing. They even followed me into the toilet when it was time, until I screamed at them to get away.

As if those pests weren't bad enough, another group of observers soon arrived, pointing cameras the size of microwave ovens at me, and roasting me with bright lights set up all over my cell. The head photographer, in sugary tones that seemed intended for a child, asked me to remain completely still on my mat while he recorded my image. I later saw these "photos," which were called shadow pictures because they were nothing more than dim silhouettes that artists would paint over to make a picture.

I became quite an attraction, and by my second day of captivity, crowds of thirty or more huddled outside my cell to catch a glimpse of me. They stayed for as long as they could stand the smell, and then they moved on to make room for others. Hungry and feverish and miserable, I turned my back on them and tried to concentrate on other things. Once I started to sing, but a guard came in and stabbed me with his pointer until I stopped.

Some time in the afternoon the guards ordered the crowd to make way for Councilor Dakin. They made space for him immediately, nodding or slightly bowing to him as he walked by and murmuring among themselves. He walked through the gap and it closed behind him. He seemed not to notice them. His attention was on me. He had gray hair so thin it poked out in all directions on top, but it hung below his shoulders in back. He had thick black and gray eyebrows that seemed to slant downward and inward toward his nose, as if he were squinting. The frazzled hair and squinty eyes gave him a bewildered look, though in every other way—his walk, his manner of dress, the way he spoke—he was full of dignity.

He held onto the bars and stared right at me. "My God," he said, "why have they brought him down here? I want these people out of here. Get them away." With a wave of his hand he ended their gawking and scribbling. The guards ushered everyone out while Dakin put a handkerchief to his mouth because the smell made him sick.

Only Dakin's young aide remained with him. The young man said, "Councilor Vanus is on his way down here. Should I try to stop him?"

"No," said Dakin. "Let him come and see the man, and then we'll do business."

Councilor Vanus—fat, red-faced, nearly bald—came in a few minutes later. Dakin seemed annoyed by him and merely nodded. Vanus said, "Cheer up, Dakin. We got this one and we got Tarius Arc. Not bad for one day, is it?"

"You have no idea what we got. You have no idea who this one is."

"Who is he?"

"I have no idea."

Vanus laughed in a wheezing, fat way, his face turning instantly red.

Dakin said, "We can't keep him down here. It's awful. They tell me he's not eating."

Vanus said, "He's an Emajian. He deserves to be here."

"I want to take him up to my residence where I can talk to him."

"Don't do it, Dakin. Umbriel would never go for it. He's a prisoner. We don't want to give anyone the impression he's anything else. He's probably just another hoax from Damonchok. Like the others."

Dakin's voice was tight with anger: "We don't know about most of the others, though, do we? We killed them too fast."

"We followed the orders of Father-King Umbriel. Are you saying he made a mistake?"

"No. I would like to question this prisoner if you don't mind."

"Fine, Councilor. But you just leave him here." Vanus turned to walk away. "It is pretty sickening, though, isn't it?"

"Don't you want to stay for the questioning?" asked Dakin.

"No need. I read the transcript of his answers. Same old stuff. He's an Emajian fraud. Every time it's the same old thing."

After Vanus left, Dakin turned to me and asked, "You are a Visitor from the Bright World?"

"Yes."

"You just heard how skeptical Councilor Vanus is about who you are. We all are skeptical. Over the years we have arrested seven people who have claimed to be Visitors from another world. Our investigations showed that at least two of the seven were hoaxes. Believe me, if you are a hoax, we will find it out, and you will face torture more savage and painful than anything your mind has ever conceived. You are a friend of Tarius Arc?"

"I met him on the day we were captured."

"Let me be blunt with you. You are in a very dangerous position. We are investigating you now very thoroughly, and if you are a fake, we will soon find it out. We have the best information in the world available to us. You will not get away with this. But we realize Tarius Arc is a dangerous and ruthless man. He has led many people astray, perhaps including you. If you confess now that he put you up to this trick, I can arrange to have your life spared. Many people have been his victims. But if you wait until we expose you as a fake, you will certainly be killed."

"I am not a fake. Everything I've told you is true. Tarius Arc should not be held responsible for anything I have done."

"Do you know anything about the other Visitors who were sent across the years?"

"No."

"All of them brought something as a sign that they were from another place. As far as we know you brought only a musical instrument."

"Which your soldiers smashed."

"Yes, unfortunately. But your possession of it is a crime. Did you bring nothing else?"

"No."

"That does not help your chances for survival. Your only possession is a criminal instrument."

"What's wrong with it? It can't hurt anyone."

"Is that what you think? You have a lot to learn. Not much time to learn it, either." He turned to his aide, who carried a large case. "Take out the books," he said.

As the young man took out the objects, Dakin said, "All the other Visitors brought what they said were holy books, though you'll see that two of these don't look like books at all." One "book" was a metal disc and the other was a spongy, sphere-shaped object. "I want you to look at them and see if any of them are familiar to you." The aide took each book out of its plastic pouch and placed it in my hands. I had no idea how the piece of metal or the sponge would even be read, and the first regular book I was given was written in an alphabet completely foreign to me. The next book, however, had a leather cover on the front of which was stitched a cross. The cover had a snap on it, and when I unsnapped it and opened to the first page, I read, "The Holy Bible," and underneath that, "New International Version." I found the copyright date, 1978, and saw that the book was published in Grand Rapids, Michigan. In English I said aloud,

"Grand Rapids, Michigan. Thank God. Somebody from home has been here."

"You know this book?" asked Dakin, pressing close to the bars.

"Yes."

"What was that you said?"

"I said, 'Grand Rapids, Michigan.'"

"What is this?"

"It is a city, in the country where I live. It is where they printed this book."

"Is it a holy place?"

"No."

"Is it a holy book?"

"Yes."

"And you can read it?"

"Yes."

The aide smiled for the first time and looked relieved. Dakin said, "Good. You may have just saved your life. Do you know the language of that book and our own language well enough to translate that book into our language?"

"I think so, if someone could write it down for me. I don't know how to write your language very well. Who brought you this book?"

"Her name was Elaine. Do you know her?"

"What was her last name?"

"Her name was Elaine, first and last."

"Where I come from there are thousands of people named Elaine. Where did she come from? What else do you know about her?"

"Her name was Elaine. She was from the Bright World. That's all I know. We killed her before we found out much else."

"Why would you kill her?"

"Killing her—just like killing all the other Visitors—was not my idea. She came just like you, playing music and stirring up trouble with the Emajians. They thought she was their prophet, and she was very uncooperative, and we thought she was a hoax, so we killed her."

"Is that what you're going to do to me?"

"It's very possible, but I hope not. I think that after years of talking I have convinced Father-King Umbriel of the value of finding out what is in these books. If you can translate one of them, that may be enough reason to keep you alive."

"I'll do it, but get me out of here first. This place is killing me."

"If I get you out, you must promise no music."

"All right. They smashed my guitar anyway."

"No singing."

"If that's all it takes, fine."

"I'll see what I can do. In the meantime, this is my assistant, Filbus. Translate one page of this book for him, and I'll be back tomorrow."

Filbus didn't care which part I translated. I could tell he was in a hurry to get out of there, but it took me a while to decide what to translate. It felt so good to read English again and to have this one solid connection to home that I just wanted to read for a few minutes instead of thinking about how these words would be translated into Amian. I read the first part of John, which has always been my favorite book. Filbus stood there with his pen poised over his notebook and asked, "Have you found something?" I just wanted to hold the book and let the English words of the book of John fill my brain. I asked him if I could keep the book when we were finished, but he said no, that was not allowed. I knew the lights would be turned off anyway.

I finally decided on a psalm, since it would be a complete unit and short enough to translate easily. Or so I thought. It was not easy at all. I knew English. I knew Amian, mostly. But translating from one to another was terribly difficult. The phrases often sounded awkward, and some ideas just didn't have exact correlations in the other language. Filbus was impatient. I think he suspected I didn't know the language of the book after all. After leafing through the Old Testament, I chose Psalm 101 because it seemed easy to translate. It begins, "I will sing of your love and justice; to you, O LORD, I will sing praise." I forgot to consider that the psalm mentions singing, which to the Amians is an abominable act. After I translated the first phrase, Filbus said, "Is this stuff Emajian?" So I had to use *speak* instead of *sing* wherever it came up. I didn't know what to do with *psalm*, so I used the Amian word for *praise*. When we got through the psalm, Filbus took the Bible away from me and left. The guards turned off the light in my cell, and when I fell asleep, I had another of those startling visions of Anne. Her face was close to mine. Her hands caressed the side of my head. I was unable to speak, but I kept my eyes locked with hers until she went away.

—⊖—

When I woke up the next day the light was already on, and Councilor Dakin was standing outside my cell looking in, twisting one strand of his hair round and round his finger. He looked just as frazzled as he had the night before, but I soon learned that this look never left him. He was a nervous and fidgety man, though sometimes his slanting eyebrows and the uncontrollable wisps of hair on top of his head made him look more frazzled than he really was.

Dakin said, "I have good news for you. At least for the time being you will not be executed."

"Will you get me out of this cell?"

"Yes. If you agree to my conditions, I'm going to take you to my residence to stay."

"What are the conditions?"

"No music whatsoever."

"I agreed to that already."

"You must continue to translate your holy book."

"I'd be glad to."

"I have to warn you. You are the first Visitor ever to be let out of prison alive. My own reputation is at stake. If you betray me, the Council will not hesitate one second to put you to death. Have I made your situation clear to you?"

"Absolutely."

Dakin said he had to take care of some things before I could be released, so he left me sitting in the stinking prison the entire day. Time has never crept by as slowly as it did that day. With every creak of a door or scuffle of a rat outside my cell I jumped up to look, to see if Dakin was coming to set me free. I had absolutely nothing to do in the cell. I was still too sick to eat more than a few bites without vomiting. The smell seemed to get worse with each passing hour. My head ached. I prayed endlessly for God to send Dakin quickly, but prayer was not much comfort to me right then.

Dakin finally came. He was alone. He said, "Are you ready?"

"Yes," I said. "I have nothing to pack."

What a relief to rise up out of the rotten prison and walk up the wide stone staircases to the residential section of the palace. Dakin was one of four leaders who lived in Father-King Umbriel's palace. He was a senior member of the Council of Ministers, Umbriel's inner circle of twelve men and women who ran the nation. Only Umbriel himself, whose power was absolute, held more authority than the Council. Beneath the Council in authority was the Assembly, a group of 220 legislators and bureaucrats who had authority over the day-to-day workings of government.

Our way led us through a maze of corridors and up several staircases, to what was known as Councilor Dakin's Wing, nearly half of one floor of the immense palace. This wing contained not only Dakin's residence, but libraries, places of study for scholars and priests, editorial offices for the informationals, and the offices of Dakin's personal staff. As we walked through the wide corridors I thought how impressed Anne would be with a palace like this, how often she had talked of her dream of living in a place just like this, with the high, rounded ceilings, the plush rugs, the enormous pots of flowers on their gold stands all along the hallway. The doors of the libraries were open, and for the first time since I had come to the palace I saw light from the outside streaming through the high windows. It was evening sunlight that cast long shadows through the room. Dakin seemed a little impatient with how slowly I was walking, but everything to me looked new and exquisite, and I wanted to take in every detail.

Everyone we passed seemed to be well dressed like Dakin, the men in their short jackets and silky shirts, and the women in dresses and robes of various kinds. After three days in prison my clothes were filthy, my hair was greasy, my face was dirty and unshaven. The people we passed usually gave Dakin a slight bow or nod of respect, but they merely stared at me. Dakin seemed not to notice them at all. He headed straight for his residence.

When we got there, a guard costumed in a plumed hat and colorful sashes opened the high double doors for us, staring at me the whole time. Dakin asked me to wait in the entry hall while he gave the guard some instructions. Covering most of one of the walls of this room was an exquisite tapestry depicting a great outdoor feast. People dressed in brightly colored clothes passed bowls of food around a wooden table in a clearing in the woods. It was a joyous scene, with mothers chasing children who had strayed from the table, a fat-bellied old man laughing uproariously and nearly dropping a tray of meat, some kind of furry pet licking drops of milk that fell through crack in the table, and other such happy details. When Dakin came in, he looked at the tapestry with me and said proudly, "That is by Halliobard!"

When I made no reply, he said, "He was one of the greatest artists who ever lived. This one was almost lost, but I saved it just before they would have destroyed it."

"Why would they destroy it?"

"After the War many things had to be destroyed. Not that I'm questioning the wisdom of it. Halliobard painted many vulgar things—singing and dancing and the light from musical instruments and so forth—but I felt that was no reason to destroy *all* his work. Much of it is still good and inoffensive, like this one, and should be preserved."

Dakin's residence contained seven or eight sitting rooms whose walls were covered with paintings and tapestries he had saved from the post-War destruction. He had to take me through three of these elaborately furnished rooms on our way to the room I was to stay in, and on a sofa in one of them sat an enormous woman who at first did not hear us come in. She was sprawled out in a very unfeminine pose, with one foot propped up and the other one on the floor. She fanned herself with a turquoise-colored fan that matched the housecoat that draped her. Her hair was black with gray streaks and was swirled on top of her head in the fashion of the older women of the upper class.

"Ah, Miri!" said Dakin, and the woman let out a hoot of surprise.

"Oh, how embarrassing," she said. "I'm not even dressed. I had no idea you were bringing him up here now."

Dakin said, "Jeremy, this is my wife, Miriaban."

"I'm delighted you're going to stay with us," she said, sitting upright and pulling the housecoat over her legs. "I think it's absolutely barbaric of them to put you in that prison. We'll get you a big meal and a bath and whatever else you need."

Her words were friendly, but her hesitant expression made me realize for the first time that I carried the smell of the prison with me. I stepped as far away from her as I could.

Dakin said, "I'll introduce him to Pannip and get him ready for dinner."

"Fine," said Miriaban. "Don't you worry about a thing, Jeremy. We'll make you forget all about that prison."

—☉—

The bed in my room was king-sized and round. Like most furniture in Persus Am, the bed was lower to the ground than I was used to. I also had a low chair in a permanent reclining position, and I had two short, wide couches. In the corner of the room, looking out a window, was a tilted drawing board and stool where I was to work. My window looked out onto the great lawns, where servants were still tending to the trees, shrubs, and flowers, even though it was getting dark. Beyond the lawns and the palace walls was the skyline of Persus Am, great stone buildings outlined against the sky.

Dakin interrupted my survey of the outdoors by bringing in my servant, Pannip, a boy about fourteen years old. Pannip bowed low but said nothing when Dakin introduced him. Dakin opened a tall wooden wardrobe, revealing a closet full of clothes. He said, "The observers gave us your measurements, so we had some things brought up for you. Later we can have some other clothes custom made to your liking if—ah—all goes well. Let us know if anything doesn't fit right, and we'll have it tailored. Pannip will show you to your bath and help you with these things, and then I'll be back to get you for dinner."

The bathtub was round and big enough for me to stretch out completely in it. It was filled with hot, soapy water that swirled as fast or slow as I wanted it to. Dirty and smelly and miserable as I was, it was the best bath I have ever taken. Pannip brought me a cold fruity drink in a big glass, and I drank it slowly out of a straw as I let the water swirl all around me. He gave me soap and shampoo that made my matted, itchy hair feel tingly clean. After the bath I wrapped myself in a soft full-length robe and just lay on the recliner for a while feeling totally refreshed. It was up to me to choose the outfit I would wear to dinner. Pannip held out each shirt and jacket and pair of pants until I chose one I liked. I put on soft, white underclothes and then a silky maroon-colored shirt, black pants, and a short black jacket. Pannip fastened jewelled pins onto the front of the jacket, in the style of the aristocracy of Persus Am. As he did so, Dakin returned, and after I had picked out a new pair of shoes, we went to dinner.

The dining room was huge, with a table that looked big enough to seat fifty. The table sat very low, and rather than sitting on upright chairs we reclined on little couches that were placed parallel to the table. The couches sloped up at one end so that a person could lean against it or rest an arm on it. Dakin told me upright chairs were used only when there were many guests and space was a problem. Whenever chairs were brought in the table was raised. But Amians considered upright chairs quite uncomfortable. Reclining was considered the best position for eating.

Miriaban came in soon after we did. She wore an enormous blue gown, and her hair was held in place by jewelled pins. She looked completely unsuited to be Dakin's wife. Where he was thin and fidgety, she was large and completely at ease. Where Dakin was formal and strained, Miriaban was naturally open and friendly. She had the habit of slanting her head toward me in a very confidential way when she spoke, as if there were some secret understanding between us that did not include Dakin.

As they brought out the first part of the meal she said, "I know they've hardly given you anything to eat since you got here, but I want you to know it's not for any lack of complaining on my part. I kept telling Dari"—that was her nickname for Dakin—

"that whoever else you may be, you're a Visitor here until someone proves otherwise, and you shouldn't be made to sit in that stinking hellhole and eat that swill they try to pass off as food."

Dakin interrupted, "If I may say a word in my own defense, Jeremy, I am not the only person in the kingdom who has authority to say how strangers are treated in Persus Am, in spite of my wife's exalted view of my power."

"Ha!" sneered Miriaban. Then she turned confidentially to me. "Jeremy, let me tell you something. You will find that in the bureaucracy that governs this place, people like my husband will lead you to believe their power is infinite until such time as it becomes convenient for them to want you to believe they have almost no power at all." Her hand made a brushing off motion toward her husband, and then she reached out and squeezed my arm. I liked Miriaban very much.

The change of atmosphere had improved my appetite tremendously, and the food was excellent. We started out with pastries filled with fruit that tasted something like peaches. I ate four of them. Then we had chunks of meat smothered in green and red vegetables. Then we had ice cream that tasted better than any I had ever eaten. Each dish was brought out one at a time and removed before the next course was served. Every time my plate was empty, Miriaban ordered the servants to fill it up again. Miriaban ate as much as I did, but Dakin seemed distracted and hardly ate at all.

At one point Miriaban asked me, "Are you a friend of Tarius Arc?"

Dakin said, "Let's not get into that now."

"Dari and I used to be very good friends with Tarius and his wife, before the War, of course."

"Not now, Miri."

"His wife Amandan. Did Dari tell you that?"

"No, he didn't," I said.

"No. He wouldn't. It's not something he ever wants to get into right now."

I asked, "What is going to happen to Tarius Arc?"

Dakin answered, "Believe me, Jeremy, for your own good,

you'll be much better off if you forget about Tarius Arc entirely. It looks very bad for you that you were caught with him. It only increases people's belief that you're an Emajian."

"But I'm curious. What will happen to him?"

"It hasn't been decided. It's up to the Father-King. I assume he'll be executed, but maybe he'll be traded or something."

"And what's going to happen to me?" I asked.

"The first thing is you're going to translate that holy book, and we're going to try to show how valuable you are for research purposes. We're also going to try to show them you're not an Emajian and are no threat to them at all. But it's up to Umbriel. I cannot promise you anything."

"When will he decide about me?"

"No one knows. He is being very careful not to say anything at all at this point."

Miriaban said, "I think Umbriel's finally realizing how foolish it is to kill off all the Visitors just on suspicion they're Emajian."

"Not that Umbriel's actions were foolish," corrected Dakin. "But I believe you could be very valuable to us."

We had reached the end of the meal, and Miriaban asked her husband, "Shall we have the vapors now?"

"No," said Dakin. "I'm not sure we should expose Jeremy to that just yet." Miri huffed her disapproval, but Dakin held firm. The mysterious pleasures of the vapors—whatever they were—would have to wait until later.

———○———

Nothing, I thought, could keep me from having the best night of sleep in my life that night. I had finished a good meal; I was in a huge, comfortable bed, wrapped in silky sheets and soft blankets; I was finally cleaned up, finally away from the horrible smell, and most of all, I was totally exhausted. When Pannip turned off the lights and left my room, I was just moments from sleep.

Then I heard noises.

I heard scuffling sounds, similar to the sounds the rats in the prison had made at night. The sound had horrified me in prison because more than once the rats—or whatever they were—had stumbled across me as I slept, and I had knocked them across the room, causing them to screech in anger and even once to bite me.

The noises were coming from the wardrobe. I turned on the light next to my bed, got up and put on a robe, and called for Pannip. He ran in immediately from the room across the hall.

"Something's in the closet," I said. "A rat or something."

"There are no rats up here, sir," he said in a timid voice.

"Well, something's in there."

Pannip seemed not at all concerned about what might be in the wardrobe. He did not even look in that direction; he kept his eyes on me as if my hallucinations, and not the rats, were his real worry. But then I heard it again. A scuffling sound. The sound of the clothes being ruffled.

"What is it?" I asked.

"Something's in there!" said Pannip, as if that were the first time such a possibility had been suggested.

He walked to the door of the wardrobe and put his ear against it. A puzzled look came over his face. He stepped away from the door. "Who's in there?" he shouted.

The door burst open from the inside, and there sat a man, short, dark-haired, bearded, well-dressed, wearing one of the short-jacketed suits like the one I had worn.

"Jank! What are you doing in there?" asked Pannip.

"Who is he?" I asked.

The short man said something that sounded like, "Spreckle me not, Goat Pillows. I deem you to know harm."

I could not translate this. Apparently the confusion had startled the language out of me again.

The man crawled out of the closet and stood before me, less than five feet tall, muscular, his mustache slightly curled up at the ends.

"If you can confound my mealing, I sneer astride you as Jank, a nimble servant on his excellent see the Paramour Father Humboil."

I was still flustered, but Pannip, who until this time had been too timid to express any emotion whatsoever in my presence, could not keep from laughing.

The man from the closet said to him, "I up here to have mested up his line of tinkering."

Pannip said, "Quit fooling around, Jank. He doesn't like it."

"I'm sorry, sir," said Jank, thrusting out his hand to me. "My name is Jank. I heard that you sometimes had trouble putting together the meaning of our words, and I thought I would have a little fun."

I clasped his arm in the Amian way but said nothing.

Pannip asked, "What are you doing down here? How did you get in the closet?"

"What I am doing down here is waiting for Jeremy. Getting into the closet wasn't so easy, what with all these clothes they've lavished on the Visitor."

I said, "Maybe I should go get Dakin."

"No, no!" said Jank. "I don't think we want Dakin to be here just now. I come with a message from Tarius Arc."

"Who are you?" I said. "I thought there was to be no contact between me and Tarius Arc."

Jank answered, "That's right. At this very moment you must decide what kind of man you choose to be. I have a message for you from Tarius Arc. You may refuse it, you may turn your back on him and on your music and on truth and decency and everything you know is right, and you may do only what Dakin says you are allowed to do. On the other hand, you may accept the message and decide for yourself what your fate in this kingdom will be."

I asked Pannip, "Do you know this man?"

"He's Jank," said Pannip. "He's the servant of Umbriel's mother. I won't tell if you take the message. I promise."

Jank said, "Pannip is a smart boy. You are lucky, Jeremy, to have such a good young man as a servant."

"What is the message?"

"Tarius told me to tell you alone. Pannip, you'll have to leave the room."

"You can trust me!"

"Of course I can trust you, but Tarius said give it *only* to Jeremy. Just wait outside."

Pannip reluctantly left, and Jank took me as far away from the door as we could get before he said, "Pannip is a good boy, but he likes to know everything that's going on. I trust him, mostly, but there's no need to take chances. Tarius Arc knows that Dakin has brought you to his residence, and he advises you to be very careful, because he is afraid Dakin and Umbriel will try to use you for their own purposes."

"He's just having me translate a holy book from one of the previous Visitors."

"A holy book! From which Visitor?"

"Elaine."

"Elaine! I knew her. Did you know her?"

"No, but she brought a book from the land that I come from."

"She came among the Emajians many years ago, much like you did, and as soon as Umbriel caught her he killed her. You're lucky to still be alive."

"What are they going to do to Tarius Arc?"

"Well, any other time, I would have said they would kill him, but strange things are happening in Persus Am right now. Umbriel seems to be shifting his strategy. That's why Tarius wants you to be careful."

"I thought you worked for Umbriel. Are you an Emajian?"

"I am, yes. There are only two Emajians in Persus Am who can admit being one, and I am one of them. I work for Umbriel's mother, Ona, who is Tarius Arc's daughter. Umbriel is very protective of his mother, loves her more than probably anyone. She is an Emajian, and she insists on having Emajian music three times a day. I am her musician."

"You play music right here in the palace?"

"Yes. Shocking, isn't it? Officially it's all denied, of course. Officially I do not exist, and Umbriel's mother is an invalid who is not well enough to be seen in public or to take visitors. I'll have to bring you up to play music with us when I can arrange it."

"I don't think they would allow it, would they?"

"Well, what they allow and what goes on are often two different things. Remember, officially I do not exist. And not existing gives me certain privileges. As long as Ona is alive I am virtually untouchable. Umbriel protects her, and she protects me."

"But still, Dakin said I could play absolutely no music."

"Right. But with just a little courage on your part, I can get you up there without Dakin or anybody else ever knowing. But that comes later. Before that I'll want to take you down to visit Tarius. He has some things he wants to talk to you about. But we'll have to wait for the right time."

"Let's just don't do anything that will land me back in that prison."

"Courage, brother. These are hard times, and you are in a risky situation regardless of what you do. In a place like this, good men have to take chances. Tarius tells me you are not an Emajian in name, but you are sympathetic to our cause."

"I like music."

"And from everything I've heard your music was absolutely as Emajian as you can get, filled with the very voice of God."

"I feel like I'm being pulled in two directions and don't know which way to go. I don't even know what I'm doing here. Tarius tells me one thing, Dakin tells me another. I feel like I'm in the middle of something that has nothing to do with me. Actually I just want to get out of here."

"Jeremy, I'm just a servant. I'm a little guy—in more ways than one. So take your advice from the great men like Tarius Arc, and not from me. But let me tell you one thing. The other Visitors I met—and I've known four of them—all felt exactly the way you did, and the way they all got out of here was being executed. I'm hoping that won't happen to you, but what I'm saying is you're in this too deep now just to ride the fence. You're going to have to take a stand whether you want to or not. Tarius is asking you to stand for Emajus. You have His Spirit in you; you sang His song. Pray to God and see if that isn't the right thing for you to do."

"I have prayed, believe me. I just don't get any answers."

"Then just jump in and do what your guts tell you is right. You can't wait on definite answers. Nobody gets them. We just make it up as we go."

Pannip opened the door and looked in.

"Just a minute, Pannip," said Jank. Pannip reluctantly closed the door, and Jank whispered, "Don't tell Pannip anything I've said, and whatever you do, don't tell Dakin or anybody else that I've been here. I'll take care of Pannip so he won't tell, but we might as well not take any more risks than we have to. I have to go now. As soon as I can arrange something, I'll be back. You'll probably never see me during the day." He gave a devilish, playful laugh, and added, "But at night, the palace is mine! Good night, Jeremy."

———◯———

Each day brought more challenges to my survival. At times I became resigned to the fact that I would lose my life the same way Elaine and the other Visitors had. On the day after I found Jank in my closet, Dakin came to me as flustered as I had ever seen him. He twirled his hair furiously around one finger. His eyebrows furrowed downward and his lips were pressed into a tight frown. When he came into my room, I was translating the book of John with the help of Filbus.

"Bad news," said Dakin. "The Council met this morning to discuss what to do with you. I was hoping they would just let me have charge of you until you finished your translation. But some of them are opposed to this whole idea and think you should stay in prison or even be executed. So the compromise was that the matter would be put before the Assembly, and they'll decide your fate."

"What do you think will happen?"

"It's just impossible to tell. On the Council there are only twelve of us, so it's more predictable. But there are 220 members of the Assembly, so anything could happen. All this could be resolved if we could just get Umbriel to make a decision about you. But he won't even see you. His people have made it clear he's going to let this thing run its course."

"When does the Assembly vote?"

"Not for ten more days. That's when their next session is scheduled, and I'm told this vote will be first on the agenda. But at least ten days gives us some time. We'll have to do a lot of convincing between now and then."

"I appreciate what you've done to get me out of that prison and keep me alive, Dakin."

"Well, just be ready to work hard the next ten days. We're going to have to get these people to meet you. You're going to have to make a good impression. If we can get them to like you, they won't be as likely to vote to execute you."

———◯———

Miriaban was my only refuge in those next ten days. Dakin was so jittery and uptight that I never felt comfortable around him, but Miri was almost instantly my friend. Several times throughout the day as I translated with Filbus, she interrupted our work so that I could take a break.

The first time she came to get me she said, "I want to take you to what I think is the most beautiful place in Persus Am. Dari doesn't like me to take people there, but I know you'll just love it. It's my garden."

She took me down a hallway and stopped in front of a set of double doors. "You'll never guess what's beyond these doors," she said. "It's a whole other world."

Walking in there felt just like being outdoors. A brick pathway wound through the forest, but weeds broke through the cracks—the place was stuffed with life. Sunlight filtered through the leaves. Miriaban said this light was one of Tarius Arc's inventions, though Dari, she said, would have been irritated with her for telling me so. Birds screeched and flapped their wings in the trees all around us. The ones I saw perched on branches were orange and blue and green and looked something like parrots. In the distance a furry creature, something like a rabbit, scurried across the path and into the bushes. We crossed a bridge over the little stream that flowed through the woods. Miri took me to a clearing in the center of the garden, where there were reclining chairs and a table.

"This is fabulous!" I said. "Why would Dakin not want you to bring people here?

"He thinks it's too eccentric. He says I'm trying to live in the past, when all of Persus Am looked like this. I tell him if this is living in the past, then the past is where I want to be."

"I think it's beautiful. It even *feels* like you're outside. And you can sit and listen to the stream, and hear the birds. It must be very relaxing."

"Oh it is. But Dari just *hates* it. He says I've put too many trees in here and he feels like any minute they're going to reach out their arms and choke the life out of him! But for me it's just like where we lived before the War, where we had a garden of our own and the trees and plants weren't like they are now outside, all scrawny and dying all the time and servants always pulling the dead ones. They grew as high and healthy as you wanted them. If you cut them it wasn't because they were dead but because they were getting too big."

We reclined in the chairs in the center of the forest, and servants brought us pastries and cold drinks. Whenever I think of Miriaban I think of her on that day, sitting queen-like in the middle of her forest, sipping her drink and smiling as she listened to me. She was so enormous that her recliner had to be larger than the others, and the servants had to help her get up when we left.

For Dakin any talk of anything that happened before the War, when everyone, even Amians, enjoyed music, was taboo, but the forest evoked the past for Miri, and she spent much of her time telling me about the days when the world was unspoiled and when men like Tarius Arc were her and Dakin's friends instead of enemies.

"Did you know Tarius Arc very well?" I asked her.

"Oh yes. Dari and I were very good friends with Tarius and Amandan. We went to their house all the time. It was a country house—gorgeous!—and we used to spend the summer evenings with them. Umbriel—the first one, not his son, who is the Father-King now—was with us sometimes too, and we all ate together and sang and talked. Who would have guessed how everything has turned out!"

"Why did it happen?"

"It was—I don't know—it was the War. The War ruined everything. Before the War you didn't have Emajianism and all these other things to come between people. The War took something out of everybody. I don't care what they say about the

'Glorious Age of Umbriel II' that we're supposedly living in now. That's bunk, of course. Everybody knows in their hearts that the War took something away and it's impossible to ever get it back. Just look at Dari. You should have seen him before the War. Handsome, strong, popular. Now he's just a bundle of nerves. We are richer now than we've ever been, but Dakin is constantly uptight. I hate to say this, Jeremy, because I love him more than I love my own life, but in many ways he is a ruined man."

"Before the War, did you enjoy music the way the Emajians do now?"

"Oh Jeremy! What a question! Darling, let me give you some advice. It's fine to ask me that question. You can ask me anything. I have made myself your friend. But don't ever ask that of Dari or anyone else in Persus Am. Music is one thing we do not talk about, except to condemn. We do not reminisce about it. We do not acknowledge that it ever was a good thing."

"But where I come from it's a beautiful thing. Everybody enjoys it. I can't imagine why people here think it's bad."

"You'd change your mind if you ever saw an Amian have to listen to music. It is not a beautiful thing. It is a hideous thing. It makes people violently ill."

"But it doesn't make the Emajians ill."

"That's because they are corrupt and twisted people. They're as bad as the savages from Wilmoroth."

"But once you liked music."

"Yes, but music is just one more thing the War ruined. You can't recapture what is lost. Believe it or not, Tarius's wife Amandan and I used to play the thesola together when we went to the Temple. Yes, I enjoyed it. Everybody did. But it's gone now. The music is dead and it's harmful. Tarius believes in it because he's a desperate man. He lost his wife and he's trying to hang onto the past by believing in music and believing that Emajus is going to bring his wife back someday. His wife's not coming back. She's dead. Emajus is dead. The music is dead."

"Do you think they should kill Tarius Arc?"

"Heavens, no. I don't condone what he's done, but I know he's just trying to hang onto the past. It's just like this garden I've built. I've tried to make things like they were before the War. It's impossible, but I've spent lots of time and money trying. Tarius is just trying it a different way. He's a silly old man. I'm a silly old woman."

"No you're not. Your garden is magnificent, and you're the friendliest person I've met since I've been here."

She laughed and said, "You just say that because most of the others you've met have been trying to kill you! But you like Tarius Arc too, don't you?"

"Yes. Should I admit that? He seems so full of conviction."

"I used to like him too. But I think it's going to turn out badly for him. Just like it did for his wife. Just like for all of us, really. Sometimes I just sit in my garden and wonder how we ever made such a mess of things."

—◯—

Dakin introduced me personally to as many members of the Assembly as he could. He wanted them to see that I was a regular human being and not some Emajian monster. To that end, Dakin and Miriaban hosted a series of elaborate dinner parties five nights in a row.

The pattern was the same each night. I stood with Miriaban in the entryway of her residence and greeted each of the fifty or more guests. I was dressed in a new set of clothes each night, the lapels of my jacket studded with jewels in the manner of the rich Amians. Dakin wanted me to meet the guests, but he didn't want me to talk to them very long because he was afraid of what I would say. He told me to deny any connection with Emajianism, which was easy to do since I was unconnected to it, and he told me to say nothing about the music I played on the night of my arrival. If they asked about that night, he said, I should tell them how confused I was and how I collapsed and had to be dragged away.

Most guests, however, just briefly greeted me and then were escorted to the dining room, where waiters walked in and out carrying huge trays of meat, vegetable casseroles, warm bread, cakes, cookies, and hot and cold drinks. The guests were seated at round tables of ten. At each table Dakin placed at least two of his allies from the Assembly or the Council, who spoke to the guests during dinner about the advantages of keeping me alive to translate Elaine's holy book.

When I came into the dining room, I was seated at a table with Miriaban and some of Dakin's allies, who talked to me only about the most trivial topics, such as how I liked the food, how I liked living in the palace, how I was adjusting to the new language. After giving me barely enough time to eat, Miriaban escorted me from table to table, and I engaged in similar small talk with the remaining guests. If the conversation moved to "dangerous" topics like Emajianism or other political issues, Miri quickly but politely moved me to the next table.

After I had made the rounds to each table and all the guests had finished their main course, my favorite part of the evening arrived. The tables were cleared of food, and four servants brought in what at first glance look like brass pole lamps. Each pole was about seven feet high and supported a brass bowl at the top. At each pole a servant climbed a step ladder so that he hovered over the bowl. Then from a pouch he carried over his shoulder, he took out a fuzzy purple ball about the size of a coconut. He placed the ball into the bowl and climbed back down. A chain hung from the bottom of the bowl, and while everyone watched or whispered to one another in anticipation, he pulled the chain, causing the mechanism inside the bowl to squeeze the ball much the way a trash compactor squeezes garbage. As the ball was squeezed, a purple haze poured from the bowl and slowly permeated the room. These were the vapors, one of the favorite vices of the upper class in Persus Am.

More dessert was served as the vapors filled the air. I remember eating frothy dishes of whipped cream and ice cream and fruit as the smoke twisted all around my head. The vapors smelled like lilacs at first, and then they didn't smell at all. I remember the utter calm and friendliness that slowly filled the room. The entire course of the conversation changed. Miriaban no longer needed to guard me from the dangerous political topics because in that atmosphere no one thought to bring up such topics. Everything seemed to move in slow motion. We ate our desserts one deliberate bite after another, and we savored each mouthful. As I listened to the people around me speak, I lost the power of the language for several minutes at a time, but it made no difference. They needed no response. I spoke English for ten minutes or more, and everyone listened attentively. The people around my table felt a complete sense of togetherness. We were wrapped in well-being. If the vote on my fate had been taken then, it would have been impossible for any of them to vote for execution. But at that point in the evening the entire concept of votes and proposals and long, logical trains of thought were impossible. Our thoughts focused on individual details that required no connection to any thought before or after: the chill of the ice cream, the exquisiteness of the pile of hair on Miriaban's head, the impenetrability of the purple haze.

I do not know how long the parties lasted, but I know that Pannip escorted me to my room each night about an hour after the vapors were released, while most of the guests still lingered. Every morning Miriaban congratulated me on how well I had done and showed me the thank-you cards that had come in the morning mail. She gave me confidence that the vote in the Assembly would go my way, but Dakin shattered my optimism. He said thank-you cards after a party meant nothing; everyone sent them, and the vote was still too close to call. He was unhappy with my daily translations because they sounded too Emajian. I told him I had no idea what he meant by that. He pulled out a verse from John and read, "I am the true vine, and my Father is the gardener. He cuts off every branch in me that bears no fruit, while every branch that does bear fruit he prunes so that it will be even more fruitful."

"That's how it translates," I said. "Emajus has nothing to do with it."

"Well, can't you translate something less—Emajian?"

"The whole book sounds like that."

"Well, if I show this kind of stuff to somebody in the Assembly, they'll say it's Emajian, so why should we keep somebody alive who's just going to translate more Emajian trash?"

5

The guest that Dakin most wanted to come to one of the receptions was Umbriel, because he knew that if the Father-King gave me his blessing, I would be saved. Umbriel as yet had not said one word about me publicly. He was letting the scenario play out a little longer on its own, as Dakin explained he often did before making a decision.

Still, Dakin invited him to every reception, sending a separate invitation to each one. On the afternoon before the fourth reception, a blue envelope bearing the royal seal arrived at Dakin's door by messenger. Miriaban rushed into my room as soon as the envelope arrived. She shook the envelope at me as she walked toward me. I saw the seal that she flashed before my face, but I had no idea what it was.

Filbus said, "It's the royal seal. Is he coming?"

Miriaban said, "I don't know. I'm too nervous to open it. Jeremy, if this note says Umbriel is coming to your reception, your troubles are over. We just need one handshake from that man. One picture in the informational of you and him standing side by side drinking a glass of cherion."

"Open it," I said.

She cracked the seal and pulled out a flimsy blue sheet of paper that had the texture of cloth. "He sends his regrets," she said at once. "But he says he'll send his daughter to the final reception tomorrow night."

"Which daughter?" asked Filbus.

"It doesn't say. Well for crying out loud. What does that mean? He'll send a daughter. Now what in the world are we supposed to conclude from that? Is it an endorsement or not?"

"It might be," said Filbus.

"Or it might not be," said Miri. "Why doesn't he at least say which daughter is coming? That might tell us something."

"How many daughters does he have?" I asked.

"Two," said Miri. "Shellan is the oldest daughter, and some people think she's his favorite and maybe even heir to his throne. Tracian is the youngest. If he is sending Shellan—"

"Hasn't there been some—problem—with Shellan," began Filbus, but Miri's glance cut him off. Sheepishly Filbus said, "Not to gossip about Father-King Umbriel's family, but it might explain why he doesn't say which daughter—"

"Well, it's useless to speculate on things we can't know," said Miri. "One of the daughters is coming, but Umbriel's not. I'll tell Dari. Maybe he can make some sense of it."

—○—

When I got back to my room after the reception that night, feeling woozy and at ease from the vapors, Pannip stood fidgeting with the door of my wardrobe, looking startled and guilty. Miri, who was also tipsy, hazily asked, "Is everything all right, Pannip?"

"Yes, ma'am," he said.

She looked at me, tossed back her head and laughed, and then stared at me again, losing all interest in Pannip, forgetting he was even there. "Well," she said, struggling to climb onto any train of thought that might roll by, "so then." Laughing again, she waved her hand in a final, flourishing gesture and strolled off down the hall.

I shut the door and said, "What are you doing, Pannip?"

"Nothing, sir."

"Why do you look so guilty?"

Just then the wardrobe doors burst open and Jank uncurled

himself and crawled out. "Ah!" he shouted. "His wies are ide!
Swigs of vapors shamble scrambly bits in his brain."

"You don't fool me, Jank. I'm not *that* vapored."

"Oh, vapored he is not that. Swims on the screaming floats
of the night, but not vapored."

"What are you doing here?"

"I have news, unless you have already heard."

"What?"

"A princess is coming to your party tomorrow."

"I have heard. But they didn't know which daughter. Do you
know?"

"Things are getting so strange that it could be either of them.
Maybe Umbriel has decided to marry off Shellan, and he has
picked you to be her husband. What do you think of that,
Jeremy?"

Pannip looked down and tried not to laugh.

"I know nothing about her," I said. "What is she like?"

"Let Pannip describe her," said Jank.

I looked at Pannip, but he blushed and kept his head down.
I said, "Pannip?" He answered, "I'd rather not say, sir."

Jank said, "Oh, come on, Pannip. What kind of wife do you
think she'd make for Jeremy? Tell him what he has to look forward
to."

Pannip squirmed.

"Go *on*, boy," yelled Jank.

"She's weird," said Pannip.

"Is that all?" asked Jank. "I ask you for a description, and
you say 'she's weird'? What do you mean weird? Is she weird
because of those bizarre-looking puffy skirts with the gigantic
flowers on them? Or is it because of her skinny neck or the way
she jerks her head back and forth like some exotic bird? Or is it
the way she spits out her words like she's an actress in a third-rate
play who has to shout a little bit so the people in the back rows
can hear her? Is that what makes her weird?"

I said, "Filbus said she's in some kind of trouble."

"Oh yes," said Jank. "She is supposed to be Umbriel's heir,
but the more she learns about what it takes to run his job—the

deception and squashing people and all that—the more she's starting to question everything, and one thing Umbriel can't stand is to have people disagree with him. All this is just rumors, of course."

"But if it's true, why would he send her to represent him at my reception?"

"He wants to find her a husband is all I can figure out. Congratulations, Jeremy."

Pannip thought this comment very funny, but I said, "What about the other daughter?"

"Tracian. He never uses her for these kinds of things. Too bad. She's pretty."

"Well, Jank, if Umbriel hasn't even decided whether or not he's going to let me live, I doubt if he wants me to marry one of his daughters."

"Maybe not. But marriage is used to solve a lot of political problems in Persus Am. That's the main reason some people have children, to negotiate them away when the time comes. Anyway, I also came to tell you that Tarius Arc sends greetings, and he asks you as a brother not to make any deals with our enemies just to spare your life. He said to remind you that Emajus has said that those who suffer for the sake of the truth in this life will be rewarded in the next."

—◯—

Umbriel's daughter was to make an appearance after dinner. Miriaban took the decision to skip dinner as a bad sign. Umbriel's letting his daughter eat only dessert with us was not considered a very strong endorsement of me. Furthermore, the princess did not plan to stay for vapors, another bad sign. Even worse, she did not arrive on time, causing Miri to have to fill the awkward gap between the end of dinner and the princess's arrival. It was during this lull in the action that I confronted my most hostile dinner guest.

I remembered him instantly as the fat, red-faced man from the prison who had urged Dakin not to let me out. When I greeted him at the door, he merely nodded and walked on by. But after dinner, while we waited for the princess, he walked up to me as I stood at the drink table with Miri and a few of the guests. Miri stiffened as he walked up, and I knew I should be prepared for trouble.

"Mr. Jeremy, in all this talk about you I've never really heard what your position is on grangicar rights in the Disputed Territory. What do you think about it?"

Miri said, "Honestly, Vanus, this is hardly the time to talk about grangicar rights."

"Oh? I guess somebody forgot to give me the list of topics that are off-limits at these receptions."

"Jeremy is a Visitor. Why should he have taken a position on grangicar rights in the Disputed Territory?"

"To tell you the truth," I said, "I don't even know what a grangicar is."

Everyone but Vanus laughed at this. He kept his emotionless attention focused on me. "You have said you're not Emajian?" he asked.

"That's right."

"Are you aware of the contention your presence has provoked among the Emajians in the Utturies?" he asked, referring to the slum area, not far from the city of Persus Am, where I first arrived in the cloud of music. "Just this week we've had to arrest almost fifty criminals in the Utturies because they were singing what they said was the song you sang on the night of your arrival. Some of them are calling you an Emajian prophet who has come to lead the Emajians to Caladria. What do you think about that?"

"He knows nothing about it," said Miri.

"Let him answer," Vanus snapped.

"She's right," I said. "I haven't heard about any of this. I also never heard of Emajus until I came here."

Miri said, "There now, Vanus. You have your answer. Now if you'll all excuse us, I think it's time for us to go greet the princess."

Vanus had captured the attention of many of the guests and was unwilling to let us go. He said, "What about the music, Visitor? You've committed one of the most heinous crimes there is. Why should we throw receptions for you and buy you new clothes and let you live in Umbriel's Palace? Why should you be able to commit crime and get away with it?"

Miri said, "Vanus, it has been explained over and over that just because the Emajians thought it was music doesn't mean it *was* music. Jeremy is a Visitor who came into our world from the heavens. Wouldn't you expect some sort of cosmic noise and commotion when that happens? Let's go, Jeremy."

"What about you, Visitor? Do you think it was music?" Vanus asked, but Miri and I were already to the dining room door. "DO YOU THINK IT WAS MUSIC?" Vanus shouted, but we kept right on walking.

The princess finally came, but only after Miri and I had waited alone for nearly half an hour in the entry hall, wondering every moment what kind of gossip Vanus was spreading in the other room. Miri considered having him removed by force, but that would only cause more commotion and would make us look defensive. This way, Miri hoped, much of the crowd would think Vanus was a rude boor.

The princess was surrounded by bodyguards dressed in green and blue, colors no other servants but Umbriel's could wear. I knew immediately that this princess was not Shellan, the "weird" one that Jank had talked about. This was Princess Tracian, dressed not in a wildly flowered skirt but in a long, narrow dress of stunning blue. She looked about twenty years old, with black hair that was long and wavy. She had an attractive way of tilting her head slightly downward and peering up at those around her, making her look shy but dignified, mysterious. The dress was perfect for her figure, which was petite and well-proportioned. Miriaban was of high enough status and was popular enough with the Father-King's youngest daughter that she was able to drop the expected formality and give the princess a slight hug. Tracian said, "Hi, Miri. I'm sorry I'm late. The servants are impossible."

"That's all right, dear. It was sweet of you to come. Princess Tracian, may I present the Visitor Jeremy."

She took my hand for a moment and said, "It's a pleasure to meet you. You've caused such a commotion."

"I never intended to. Thank you for coming."

"Well, I don't mind a commotion personally. This place can get rather dull, though I'm sure it's been anything but dull for you."

"That's for sure. When your life's on the line, it focuses your attention."

"Well, Jeremy, unfortunately, there are a lot of people around here who seem to just look for reasons to execute people. It's a charming nation we live in."

Miri said, "And one of the charming guests is here tonight."

"Vanus? What a pleasure. How kind of you, Miri, to invite us on the same night. You'll probably seat us at the same table, too, won't you?"

"I will if you'd like me to, dear."

"No, that's all right. Why don't you share him with somebody else? I've been outraged enough today."

"Fine. Then why don't you walk in with Jeremy, and you can sit at his table."

As Tracian and I walked toward the dining room, I said, "It sounds like you don't get along too well with Vanus either."

"He is an ass. But my father likes him."

"He hates my guts."

"My father?"

"No. Vanus. I don't know what your father thinks of me. That seems to be the big unanswered question."

"I know you're probably hoping I can answer it, but I can't. He hasn't told anybody. Keep that in mind. Anyone who says they know what my father thinks about you is lying."

When we walked into the dining room, everyone stood and applauded, and the princess and I sat at a table with Dakin, Miri, and a few of Dakin's friends. I asked her, "Why did your father send you?"

"He was unable to come, so he sometimes sends me or my sister in his place. This time I got chosen."

"I see."

"But if you're asking me what message was he trying to give by sending me, the answer is I just don't know. I'm sorry. I know it must be frustrating to be toyed with like this when your life is threatened. But I don't know anything else. They don't normally use me for the political stuff. I'm more for social functions," she said, with the barest trace of a smile.

Tracian stayed for just under half an hour, most of which was spent greeting guests and about five minutes of which was spent eating dessert with me. Just before she left, she said, "When my father asks me about tonight, I'll tell him what a fine person you seem to be. I'm sorry I can't do more."

—⊖—

Afterward Miri tried to persuade me that Tracian had sent signals of support, but to me her behavior seemed decidedly noncommittal. In any case, in the remaining days before the vote, Umbriel sent no signal at all. Dakin lobbied the Assembly members tirelessly in my behalf, as if his own life were on the line. He showed them my translations of the book of John (except those passages he thought were "too Emajian") and tried to convince them of the scientific benefits of keeping me alive. But when the morning of the vote came, I could tell he believed he had lost.

I met him and Miri in the entry hall that morning as they stood under the mural and talked about the day's events. Dakin was not as fidgety as usual, but he was grim. He said nothing as I walked up, but Miri, with her hair piled high and her gown studded with jewels as if she were ready for a reception, tried to be cheerful. "I've planned a little celebration for tonight after we get the good news about the vote. Just a few people and a good meal and some vapors. I'm sure you must be tired of the big receptions by now. This will just be fun. You won't have to try to impress anybody at all."

"Are we sure we'll be celebrating?" I asked.

Dakin said, "We're not sure of anything. All I can tell you is that if we lose the vote, I'll personally lobby the Father-King to stop the execution."

"How long is this vote going to take?"

"By lunchtime it will all be over."

"Can I come and listen to the debate?"

Dakin looked at Miri and then back at me. "No. I'm sorry. I had thought about that. I had even thought of having you come to speak. But my friends on the Council think it's too risky. Vanus or someone might try to put you on the spot or embarrass you. Just wait here with Miri. Or work on the translations."

Miri said, "No translations! Not today. I'm sure he couldn't concentrate on it anyway. We're going to eat breakfast in the garden and wait until you send us word."

—○—

Throughout the morning I was haunted with the dread of what it would be like to be thrown back into that nauseating prison. The vivid memory of the stench and darkness in that narrow cell kept me from finishing breakfast. As for the possibility of being executed, the idea was so abstract and extreme that I could not conjure up a picture to match my sense of panic. I did not even know what method of execution they would use. No one had told me, and I had not had the heart to ask.

Even if the Assembly voted not to execute me, my problems still would not be over. I had promised Dakin very casually that I would make no music in his house, but since then my longing for music had risen to an intensity I had never known. At times when I was in my room alone, I would stuff my face in a pillow and sing as loudly as I could, just to feel the music. I had sometimes craved music at home, but that desire was nothing like the *need* I felt for it in this place. Music was different here. It was, as Tarius had told me, part of the very being of God. I longed for the music to swirl around me as it had on the night of my arrival, for it to take hold of me like the arms of God. Ever since I had come to the palace I had felt cut off from that Spirit, but I knew if I could just wrap myself in the music, I would know Him again.

Anyone who knew I felt this way would have accused me of being Emajian, so I kept my feelings to myself. I stuck my head in a pillow and sang in the darkness.

Music was not the only obsession I kept to myself. My visions—or dreams or vivid thoughts or whatever I should call them—of Anne became more and more frequent during those days in Dakin's house. These encounters with Anne did not occur only when I slept, though my dreams of her were as vivid as everyday reality. The dreams were always short. I would be face to face with her, sometimes touching her hair, sometimes kissing her, and then she would be gone. In one dream she stood in my living room and I watched her from the hallway. She saw me and walked toward me, but when she was halfway down the hall, the dream ended. In one dream Will also appeared. The dream began while I was hugging Anne, and when I looked up, there was Will, dressed in his cowboy boots and heavy coat, smelling like the cold outdoors. He smiled and gave the exaggerated shrug that was so characteristic of him, and then the dream was over.

Even when I was awake, there were times when I became as aware of Anne as if I had been with her just moments before. I never sensed that her presence was right there with me, but every detail of her—the smell of her hair, the feel of her hand, the expression on her face—was as vivid as if we had just spent hours together and then she had left the room for only a few minutes. I had the impression that at any moment she would reappear. My vivid sense of her made her absence incredibly frustrating and painful.

I was deprived of Anne and of music and of the Spirit and of everything familiar that had given my life stability. I feared execution, but there was a strange sense of hope in it, too, as if maybe execution was the way out of this world and back into the one I had left.

—◯—

Miri and I had breakfast in the garden while 220 men and women in the Great Hall of Assembly voted whether or not my value as a scientific specimen from another world outweighed my crimes against the nation of Persus Am. A dish of tart ice cream was always the last course for breakfast, and while we ate it a servant came into the garden with a note for Miriaban.

She looked at the note and said, "Dari wants me to come. You stay here and I'll see what's happening."

"Could they have decided already?"

"It's very possible. They've had all week to think about it. Dari thought they would probably cut the debate short."

I waited alone for nearly an hour. When I heard the garden door open and looked through the trees to catch a glimpse of a familiar fat red face, I knew it was all over. Councilor Vanus and a group of soldiers wound their way through the garden to where I sat. At first I considered running, since Miriaban's forest offered many hiding places that would have made the soldiers' job more difficult. Instead, I just sat there as nonchalantly as I could and finished my ice cream, thinking there might be a certain dignity in not seeming perturbed. I could hear Miriaban yelling in the hallway, but I couldn't make out the words.

The soldiers pulled me out of my chair and handcuffed me without ever saying a word. Vanus smiled his stupid red smile and kept his arms folded over his fat stomach. Not a word was spoken throughout this entire event. It was as if each person's part had been choreographed and no other comment was necessary.

When we got outside the garden, however, Miriaban was doing plenty of commenting. Two of Vanus's cohorts held her arms and had not let her into the garden. When I came out she was yelling at them about having no right to barge into her house, promising that Dakin would take action against them, and so on. She had completely lost the hostess-like composure I had always seen her maintain. Her chin trembled with anger as she spoke. As soon as Vanus saw that the men were holding her arms, he barked at them to let go of her.

"You've gone too far, Vanus," she said.

"They didn't mean to hurt you," he said. "You didn't need to be in there while we were arresting him."

"You've gone too far. We'll see what the Council says about assaulting a Councilor's wife in her own home."

"Nobody's assaulting anybody," he said, and walked past her, toward the door. The soldiers and I followed him. Miri walked beside me until we got to the entry hall.

"This isn't over, Jeremy," she said. "Keep your spirits up."

"Did they vote to execute me?"

"Yes, but it isn't over. The Father-King hasn't endorsed this yet. You just keep your hope up."

When we got downstairs and I caught the first hint of the horrible stench of the prison, my legs nearly collapsed beneath me. I was overwhelmed with dread at walking in there again. They took me into the same cell I had occupied before. The stench made me gag. I dropped to my knees on the floor of the cell and tried to keep from vomiting. I prayed, *Lord, if they're going to kill me, let them do it quickly*. But the Lord was as far away as Anne and home and everything secure, and I believed He could not hear me.

———○———

The only person who visited me in prison over the next two days was Jank. His head was covered with a hood that hid his face completely. I knew who he was immediately, though, for no one else had his stocky, short frame.

"How did you get past the guards?" I asked.

"My job supplies me with a number of privileges," he said. "I have access to lots of things people want. Guards are the easiest people of all to get around. How are you?"

"Terrible. I can't eat. The smell makes me too sick. I can't sleep. I don't even know when I'm supposed to be executed."

"Day after tomorrow."

"Oh. Isn't anybody doing anything to stop it?"

"Only Umbriel can stop it, and he's never shown much interest in Visitors. I'm sorry, Jeremy."

"Why do they want to kill me?"

"They're afraid of you. The Emajians in the Utturies demonstrate for you almost every day. And they keep singing that song. The Emajians all over the world—on the Rock of Calad, in Damonchok, in the Disputed Territory, everywhere—have taken you on as their hero and prophet. That scares people like Umbriel and Vanus. They're trying to stamp out Emajianism."

"Ever since the first day I got here I've said I'm not Emajian, but I'm still going to end up dying for it."

"I talked to Tarius Arc today, and he said that no matter what you call yourself, the Lord let His voice speak through your music, and that makes you Emajian. You may have a different name for him, but you serve Emajus. Tarius told me to come talk to you today, so that's why I'm here. He has prayed for you and has sung to God for you, and he wants you not to be afraid to die. He says that in a kingdom like Umbriel's a good man belongs on the fringe, as I am, or in prison, as Tarius is, or even dead. He says the Lord will reward you for singing His song in the Utturies. That is the message Tarius Arc sends to you."

"Thank him for me. Will you visit me again before the end?"

"I'll try. But Vanus has his people all over the place, and even for me, it's getting risky to be down here too much. But I'll try. I will. And who knows, maybe Dakin will think of something—"

"But you don't really think so, do you?"

"Honestly, no. I'm sorry, Jeremy. God must have a plan in all this. I'm sorry. Just keep the faith."

"Right. Keep the faith. Good-bye, Jank."

—◯—

On the morning of my execution five red-jacketed soldiers came to my cell. One handcuffed me and led me out into the hallway. None of them spoke as we made our way out of the nauseating prison and up the stairs to where the guards' stations were. We did not stop there. We walked down another hallway to another staircase that led to Dakin's wing of the palace. We walked up to the third floor, most of which was Dakin's.

"Where are you taking me?" I asked.

The soldiers remained silent.

When we reached the double doors of Dakin's residence, I felt a sudden wave of relief, though I didn't know if my feeling was warranted.

Dakin's servant let us in, and the soldier uncuffed me. Then he nodded at me, and he and his four companions walked out and shut the door behind them. By that time Dakin's servant had left the entry hall to announce me, so I stood there alone not knowing why I was there or what I should do next. The panic that had built up in me made me too restless to simply wait there until somebody came, so I walked through the house toward Miriaban's garden. Before I got there she found me, just outside the dining room.

"Jeremy! I was just coming."

"What's going on, Miri?"

"I don't know. They came a while ago and said they were bringing you here. Dari isn't here. He doesn't even know. I've been trying to track him down."

"Does this mean I won't be executed?"

"I have no idea. When Dari left this morning he said nothing could stop the execution now, but then the messenger from Umbriel's household came and said they were bringing you here. It's a good sign that it was one of Umbriel's servants, but he was just a houseboy, not one of Umbriel's aides, so I don't know what to make of that. And he knew nothing beyond the specific message, and that's kind of strange too."

"What should we do?"

"Just wait for Dari. I've sent just about every servant in the house to him with messages. Since he hasn't responded by now, he must be looking for answers. Come and I'll get you something to eat. I'm sure they haven't fed you well down there."

Dakin came in less than an hour while we waited in the garden.

Even before he reached us Miri asked, "Have they pardoned him?"

"No." He held out a letter on royal blue stationery. "They've invited him to dinner."

Miri took the letter as Dakin gave me a rare smile and said, "It's not over yet, Jeremy. You came to Persus Am at a very strange time."

"What does this mean?" asked Miri, still looking at the invitation. "Is Umbriel inviting him? It doesn't actually *say* Umbriel, but—"

"But it's from his household. So it's either Umbriel or one of the daughters. But either way we can interpret it as Umbriel delaying the execution, since he would have to approve of something like this."

"When am I to go to dinner?" I asked.

"This afternoon. Whatever they're up to, they don't want to waste much time," said Dakin.

Miri said, "I'll have Pannip get your bath ready and find some suitable clothes."

I had several hours to get ready, part of which I spent relaxing in the hot, swirling water of the tub while Pannip brought one glass after another of fruit drinks to quench my thirst. After my bath was finished, he gave me a crisp, new white shirt and a pair of blue slacks, baggy in the legs and tight at the ankles, in aristocratic fashion. Then Pannip held up a bottle that contained what looked like metal shavings. "Would you like the fire in your hair tonight?" he asked.

"What is it?"

"Fire—it—makes your hair glow."

I had seen a few people with "fire" in their hair at a few of the receptions, but I did not know how the effect was created. When light hit their hair it sparkled or glowed as if they were standing in a bright spotlight. I liked the effect.

"Do you think it's appropriate for me to go to dinner at Umbriel's wearing that?" I asked.

"Oh yes, sir. Everybody would wear it if they could. It's very expensive."

"Why not, then. Let's try it."

The shavings that Pannip poured onto my head turned to foam as soon as he started to work them into my hair. Then the foam gradually disappeared, leaving my hair dry, soft, and thick. Pannip brushed my hair, and as I moved toward the mirror the light reflected off small glints of gold all over my head. I put on my blue jacket, and Pannip placed the red jewels at the shoulders. Just below the collar of my shirt Pannip placed a brooch that Miriaban had given me, which bore the seal of Dakin's family. In just a few hours I had been transformed once again from a death row inmate into an Amian socialite.

Miriaban was delighted with how I looked, and she ordered Dakin's guards to put on their fanciest dress uniforms to escort me. "If Umbriel talks to you," she said, "he'll see right away you're no Emajian troublemaker. You absolutely look like a prince. He'll probably invite you to become part of his household."

"Right now I'd settle for him sparing my head."

"Don't you worry about that anymore," she said. "If he intended to let you be killed, you'd be dead already. I don't know what he's up to, but all I know is Umbriel doesn't execute his dinner guests."

Dakin said, "I wish we could be sure of that."

———○———

The Father-King's residence covered the entire top floor of the palace. Everything there was on a grand scale. It took two servants to push open one of the high double doors at the entrance of the residence. The entry hall had a cathedral ceiling probably thirty feet high in the middle, and it was nearly a hundred feet long and fifty feet wide. Ornately carved gold chairs and tables were placed at intervals along the walls, and the walls themselves were covered with tapestries like those in Dakin's house.

Even though this hall was needlessly long, it served as a stunning showcase for Princess Tracian, who appeared at the other end of it a few minutes after I arrived. She walked slowly toward me, like a model posing for the cameras. She wore a long dress, blue and silky and cut low in front. Her hair hung loose about her shoulders, not pinned up as most Amian women wore it. Her head was tilted slightly downward and she had the same shy smile I had noticed at my reception, but those were the only signs of her shyness. This stroll down the ornate hallway seemed too perfect not to have been planned. This was her entrance. All eyes were on Tracian.

When she reached me she hooked her arm around mine and said in a confidential whisper, "I'm glad you came, Jeremy. Why don't you dismiss your servants and let's talk." She smelled good. I felt like a boy on my first date, nervous but also fascinated by this woman so attractive yet so unfamiliar.

She kept her arm around mine as we walked alone down the long hallway. She said, "I know you've been treated horribly, and I'm sorry. You must be very confused by all this. I'm sure that by the standards of the place you've come from you've probably not even done anything wrong."

"That's right. I haven't."

"And I know you're wondering why you were invited here, and why we waited until the morning of your execution."

"And whether or not I'm still going to be executed."

"I understand. We're not trying to torture you, but things are just happening so fast that it's hard for any of us to keep up.

Amazing things are happening, and we're going to sit down and have a nice dinner and talk it all over."

"Just the two of us?"

"Yes."

"Does your father know you're doing this?"

"I haven't told him. He hasn't endorsed it, if that's what you're asking. I don't necessarily expect you to believe that, since almost nothing happens around here that isn't part of some strategy of his. But the truth is I did this on my own. He'll find out, of course. He may already have. But if we're lucky we'll at least get through dinner first."

She led me through magnificent corridors that outdid even Dakin's residence in their splendor. She said, "We'll be eating in my dining room. Daddy's is too huge and not cozy enough for just two people."

Tracian's "cozy" dining room turned out to be big enough to have seated at least a couple hundred people if it had been filled with tables and chairs. Instead of tables and chairs, however, it was mostly filled with water, whose source was a fountain in the center of the room. The fountain sprayed into a pool that fed into streams that curled around the room. Where there was not water, there were islands of flowers and trees. On one of these islands sat the oval table where we were to eat. We reached the table by a bridge from the door of the room to the dining area near the middle. The ceiling was domed, and from the center of the dome hung a delicate chandelier. A number of mound-shaped lights were attached to the dome, keeping the plants alive and making the room comfortably warm. Throughout dinner we heard the soothing sound of water spraying from the fountain and flowing about the room.

As soon as we were seated, servants began to cross the bridge with enough platters of food to feed a dozen people. They brought fruits of all types, carved meats, some mixed in vegetables and gravy, sculptured decorations of candy and other desserts, bread and rolls, and five pitchers of drinks of various kinds. Tracian took small portions of food and mostly talked rather than ate. My hunger was enormous, and I enjoyed generous portions of everything during our long talk. With the fabulous meal and the new clothes and this incredible room and Tracian across from me talking to me with such intensity and confidentiality, I felt happier than I had been in a long time.

As the servants spread out the food in front of us, Tracian said, "I could get in big trouble with my father for stopping your execution, but such an incredible opportunity has arisen that if it works out he'll be thanking me for years to come. And you'll be thanking me too, because you'll be alive. Jeremy, how much do you know about the Disputed Territory, which we call the Territory of Ur?"

"I've heard of it, but I don't know much because Dakin never wanted me to get too involved with political issues."

"Well, you don't have that luxury anymore."

Control of the Territory of Ur, as the princess proceeded to tell me, was the central political challenge of Persus Am, and my fate was tied up with the fate of that land. To understand the conflict over the Disputed Territory, I had to understand the nations that surrounded it. As I had learned from looking at one of Dakin's maps, this world I had fallen into was essentially a continent in the middle of a vast ocean. As far as I know, no other land had ever been discovered. Most of the continent was sandy and barren, but in the center, at the higher elevations, lay what was called the Known World, which was divided into four major political powers. Though the description oversimplifies the geography somewhat, the four powers could be thought of as controlling one of the four regions of North, South, East, and West. Persus Am was the power of the West and was technologically and culturally dominant in the world. Damonchok, with more than twice as much land as Persus Am, was the power of the North. The Rock of Calad was the Southern power, the smallest of all. The power of the East was vast Wilmoroth, made up of loose confederations of tribes.

The Territory of Ur was a strip of land near the center of the Known World. It stretched from the southeastern mountains of Persus Am to the western mountains of Wilmoroth. Its southern "boundary" was the Rock of Calad, and its northern "boundary" was the Santo River of Damonchok. Because of its location, it was of strategic importance to every nation, and every nation wanted to control it. Umbriel wanted it for two reasons. First, since so much of the countryside in Persus Am had turned barren since the War, the Disputed Territory offered Umbriel's nation much-needed farmland. But the most important reason Umbriel wanted the Territory was it would offer him a secure land route between Persus Am and the mines of Wilmoroth, which provided his factories with the raw materials they needed to maintain Persus Am's industrial superiority in the world.

For the Rock of Calad, the Disputed Territory was a source of food and other economic necessities, and it provided a buffer zone to keep its enemies away. Persus Am, the Rock's great enemy, had managed to cut the tiny nation off economically from most of the world through trade boycotts. Not only did Persus Am not allow its own people to trade with the Rock, but it also cut off all ties with anyone who did trade with the Rock. Therefore, Damonchok and most of the tribes of Wilmoroth, who wanted the farm equipment and globe lights and all the other goods and trinkets from the Amian factories, cut off trade with the Rock of Calad, who had comparatively little to offer them. The Rock of Calad had to rely on the black market and their sympathizers in the Territory of Ur to provide them with the basic necessities for living.

Damonchok claimed the Territory for historical and geographical reasons. The Territory lay between the mountain ranges that formed Damonchok's borders, and the earliest settlers of the region had been Damonchokian, so Damonchok saw no reason why the land south of the Santo River should be any less Damonchokian than the land north of the river. While the Damonchokians had probably been the first people to settle in the Disputed Territory, most of those settlements had died out hundreds of years before and some of the land had been taken over by Wilmorothian tribes. The ancestry of most of the residents of the Territory was Wilmorothian, so the Wilmorothians, who also coveted its rich farmland, believed the Territory belonged to them. In a peaceful world there had been plenty of room for the settlements from the various nations to coexist, but now each nation wanted complete sovereignty over the Territory.

In fact no one at all controlled the Territory. Umbriel had tried once to cut a route for grangicars, or trains, across the Territory, but Wilmorothian terrorists had slaughtered the workers. Umbriel drew back, but only because he had not yet had time to strengthen his military machine to the point that he could conquer the Territory once and for all. The withdrawal occurred many years before I came, and by the time I got there Umbriel had built the most powerful army in the history of the world. The other nations feared that unless they joined their armies together, which their political differences had not yet allowed them to do, they might not be able to stop Umbriel from overtaking the Territory. If he ever got the Territory firmly in his grip, it would be just a matter of time before he could conquer the rest of the world. Umbriel was doing everything in his power to keep the other nations from uniting against him. He only needed one of them as his ally to ensure his victory against the others, but so far all of them, except for a few stray Wilmorothian tribes, had refused to deal with him. By the time I arrived in Persus Am, rumors were rampant that Umbriel was losing patience and would soon launch his assault on the Territory even if he had to take on the rest of the world single-handedly.

It was into this political turmoil that Tracian intended to thrust me. Her questions were maddeningly cryptic at first. She asked, "Do you know anyone on the Rock of Calad?"

"No."

"Do you know of any reason why anyone there would speak on your behalf?"

"No. I met Tarius Arc and some of his friends, but—"

"But is it possible that there is another Visitor who is living on the Rock of Calad?"

"Not that I know of, but it's possible. What do you know?"

"Nothing definite. But I'm wondering—"

"Do you know of another Visitor?"

"No. It's only a possibility."

"Please. Tell me what you know."

"Jeremy, you seem like a trustworthy and good person. But you are a criminal sentenced to die. I could get in big trouble for just bringing you here at all. I have to tell you things my own way."

"All right. Tell me what you have to say."

"Emissaries from the Rock of Calad have approached me. They represent the governing council on the Rock. They pleaded for your life to be spared, and they want you to be sent to them. They seem willing to do almost anything to get you."

"What do they want me for?"

"That's what I was hoping you would tell me."

"I have no idea."

"Jeremy, if you know something, you have to tell me. I'm trying to help you."

"I don't know anything about it. I suppose they think I'm Emajian. Everybody else seems to think so. That's why they decided to execute me."

"But you don't know anything more specific?"

"Like what?"

"There isn't any certain kind of information that you have, that they need?"

"No. Like what?"

"Like something about Caladria, the place where they believe Emajus took his followers?"

"No. Tarius Arc mentioned that place to me, but that's all I know about it. Dakin told me the place doesn't exist."

"It doesn't. It's just one of their legends. But *they* believe it exists, and they think you know how to get them there. If you don't, then we could be in trouble."

"Well, I don't."

Tracian sighed and slumped back in her chair.

She said, "I can't understand why they are so certain you can help them. They're willing to make big concessions to get you."

"Like what?"

"They said my father could build tracks for his grangicars across the southern part of the Territory of Ur, the part closest to the Rock of Calad, and they would guarantee the safety of it."

"Could they do that?"

"Yes. They can't secure the whole Territory, but they do control a buffer zone around the Rock."

"But they'll only do that if I give them the information they need about Caladria?"

"The only conditions they gave were that you and Tarius Arc be released to them. But I could tell it was you and not Tarius they were really after. They seemed convinced that you could help them. If they think you can't, they may change their minds."

"But do you think your father would even go along with this?"

"Of course! He wants that Territory more than anything. He'd give them every prisoner in the kingdom to get it. And half the Assembly too. He'll jump at it."

"Why didn't they go directly to your father with this idea?"

Tracian did not like this question. She looked away from me and stared tight-lipped at the fountain for a moment before she said, "Jeremy, you may think, as other people apparently do, that I am nothing but a pretty airhead that Daddy just trots out for parties now and then, but I'm every bit as smart as my sister Shellan, and I know more than she does about how to use power."

"I wasn't meaning to question your—"

"They came to me rather than to my father or anyone else for the same reason that my father sent me to your reception. All this is very risky, and if it doesn't work out, nobody wants to admit they had any part of it. The other countries wouldn't like it if they knew the Rock was trying to make a deal with us, and a lot of the ministers and Assembly members here wouldn't like it if they thought we were willing to release you for *any* reason. They think it's safe to deal with me because most people don't think I'm a player. They could easily deny the whole thing if I let the word out. But I don't mind that. I *am* a player. That's what counts. And I can save your life if you'll help me.

"I would gladly help you, but I can't give them information about Caladria that I don't have."

"They haven't asked for that. It's not part of the deal. They want you released to them. That's all they've demanded."

"But when they find out I can't help them—"

"Then what? Will you be worse off there than here? If you stay here, they'll kill you. The Emajians are not going to kill you, I guarantee it. They're not that kind of people. All I'm asking you to do is to promise you will not tell them in advance that you don't know how to take them to Caladria. Don't tell anyone."

"What would you want me to tell them, then?"

"Nothing. Just agree to go along with this arrangement. If they insist on talking to you beforehand, say you can tell them nothing until you're in the safety of the Rock of Calad."

"But when I get there and they find out I can't help them, won't they back out on their agreement with your father?"

"Don't you worry about that. By then we'll have troops on parts of the Rock and the Territory where we've never been allowed before. Once the Rock lets those places slip out of their hands, they'll never get them back again. If they try, it will be war, but without this agreement that's what we're headed for anyway."

"So all I have to do is go along and keep quiet."

"Yes. For now that's all. You have nothing to lose, Jeremy. It's your only chance. I need to know where you stand."

"I guess I'll do it. Why not?"

She reached across the table and took my hand in hers. "Thank you, Jeremy. It's going to work out fine. Just do me a favor and don't tell anyone what we've talked about."

Tracian had no time to waste. As soon as I got back to Dakin's, Miri told me Vanus and his buddies were outraged that I was still alive, and they were appealing to Umbriel, the Council, and Assembly members to demand that my execution be carried out immediately.

"Did you see Umbriel?" Miri asked.

"No."

"Who did you see?"

"Tracian."

"Oh! Was she the one who stopped the execution?"

"Well—I'm really not supposed to say anything."

"Oh, I see," she said, following this comment with a long pause that she hoped I would fill. "It must be something big."

"Yes."

"But does Umbriel approve of the execution being stopped?"

"Well—"

"I know. You're not supposed to say anything. But—is it—whatever it is—do you think the execution will be called off for good?"

"I hope so."

"So now is there something you have to wait for?"

"Yes. We just have to wait."

"Is it something that is supposed to happen, or—"

"Miri, I'm sorry, but I just can't get into it."

"I know. If she told you not to talk, then you do just what she said. I'm going to find Dari to see whether Vanus has managed to cause any more trouble. I could just kill that man. I really could."

Whenever I get excited I have to walk around, and when I was at home I used to turn the music up loud so I could half dance, half pace. As soon as Miri left me I paced furiously around the room. My mind was obsessed with only one idea from my conversation with Tracian—the possibility that another Visitor was on the Rock of Calad. From the moment Tracian had mentioned the possibility of another Visitor on the Rock of Calad, my mind had begun to spin a theory that by the time I reached my room had established itself in my mind as an absolute fact: Anne was on the Rock. It only made sense. Why would my mind be tormented with those maddeningly vivid visions of her unless someday soon I would be with her again? And why would my mind crave music so desperately if I were going to be permanently deprived of it? Tracian's plan of sending me to the Rock would give me the two things I yearned for: Anne and music. I wandered the room thanking God and imagining what it would be like in those first moments when I saw Anne. I stretched out my arms to her and she came close, hugged me, and I said, "It's all right now, honey. Now it all makes sense."

———○———

When Dakin and Miriaban appeared at my doorway several hours later, their expressions were so contradictory that at first I couldn't tell whether their news was good or bad. Miri, whose enormous body and elaborately coiffed hair filled most of the doorway, beamed with happiness. Dakin, who always looked rather shrunken beside her, wore an especially haggard expression, his brows furrowed, his lips pursed in concentration, his fingers twirling his hair.

Miri said, "Jeremy, I don't know what you did, or how you did it."

"What has happened?" I asked.

Dakin shut the door behind him and said, "Umbriel himself has invited you to meet with him tomorrow. He has announced it publicly. It will appear in the informational tomorrow."

Miri said, "It's the first time he has made any public statement about you at all."

Dakin added, "He also will say that he himself called off your execution."

"So you're safe now for good," said Miri. "He won't execute you now that he's embraced you, and no one will dare oppose him publicly."

Dakin said, "No one seems to know what made him change his mind. What can you tell me?"

"I can't tell you anything. I'm sorry, but they told me—"

"That's fine. Play it the way they tell you to. I'm sure it will all come out soon enough."

"Yes. I'm sure it will."

Miri said, "Every time they think they've beaten you, Jeremy, you keep coming back. I'd love to see the look on Vanus's face right now."

"Miri—" chided Dakin.

"I don't care," she said. "You just keep it up, honey. You just don't let them get to you. They can't stop you now."

———○———

Umbriel was the number one celebrity in the world. The public was interested in every glimpse of his life that the informational would give them. They wanted to know whom he invited for dinner, how he spent his days, what his home looked like, what kind of clothes he wore, how he got along with his wife, how he handled the rivalry between his two daughters. Umbriel controlled the informationals, so they mentioned no unpleasant details about his life.

Whatever gaps were left by the informationals, rumors filled in. Every detail in the informational was believed to carry some clue about Umbriel's true feelings. If a picture showed Umbriel at a reception, for instance, and he had his arm around Tracian, a rumor might begin that Tracian was Umbriel's new favorite and that Shellan was for the moment out of favor with him. If Umbriel were pictured at a meeting with the Council of Ministers, the political observers paid close attention to who sat next to him. If Vanus, for instance, sat beside him, the observers took that as a sign that Umbriel was signalling his support for conservative, hard-line policies. If Dakin sat next to him, Umbriel was assumed to be taking a more diplomatic, moderate stance toward the issue of the moment.

Every activity of Umbriel's day was considered significant. At least once a day he took a walk in his private garden just outside the palace. Being invited to join him on one of these walks was considered a political triumph. Any guest list for receptions or conferences or any other gathering sponsored by Umbriel or his household was carefully probed by politicians and power brokers at every level for clues as to who was "in" and who was "out." Umbriel tolerated, some say even encouraged, wide diversity among the Councilors, but if a Councilor's name was consistently left off key guest lists published in the informational for several weeks in a row, it was a sign of his political demise, and he usually resigned to avoid the embarrassment of being forcibly removed from office.

Umbriel was younger than any of the Councilors, many of whom had served his father. His youthful appearance was particularly striking in a world where people often lived decades longer than they did where I came from, and where old people often stayed on the job until death. He was slender and athletic, with a thick head of brown hair cut short in the fashion of the younger men. Also like the younger generation, he was clean-shaven, and he preferred waist-length suit jackets to the traditional knee-length ones. His jacket preference had revolutionized men's fashion in Persus Am. When Umbriel's father reigned, no one in government wore short jackets. Now no one but very old men dared wear longer ones.

No expense was spared to prepare me for my meeting with the Father-King. Miriaban ordered her tailors to make a new suit for my meeting. She studded the jacket with new jewels. She ordered the barbers to trim my hair. One man brought dozens of bottles of cologne to the residence, and Miriaban had me test them all until we found just the right one. She picked out new shoes for me, with green jewels on the buckles to match the ones on my jacket. On the morning of the meeting I took a luxurious bath, and Pannip rubbed the metal shavings in my hair to make it sparkle. All the fuss, plus Miriaban's constant admonitions not to be nervous, made me every bit as apprehensive as I had been on the morning scheduled for my execution.

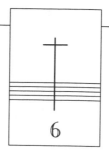

6

Six of Dakin's guards escorted me to Umbriel's residence, where I was met by a man named Hamlin. I had hoped that Tracian would meet me in her entry hall and introduce me to her father, but she was not there. Hamlin was a blonde-haired man in his early twenties. In a country where most important decisions were made by old men and a few old women, Hamlin was the youngest man I had seen with any significant amount of authority. A small crowd of well-dressed onlookers stood behind Hamlin, but he ignored them and did not introduce me to anyone.

Hamlin led me through the web of magnificently decorated chambers to Umbriel's Dome. As we left the entry hall he said, "I apologize for all the people straggling along to gawk at you. It was all I could do to thin out the crowd even this much. Everybody wants in on the action. You must be used to it by now."

"No I'm not, actually."

"No? Well, neither am I, and I've worked for Umbriel for two years. He's different from what you might think. He's very relaxed and friendly. You shouldn't be worried at all."

"The informationals make him seem so—"

"Godlike? Almighty? I know. I think he likes the image that's built up around him, but there's another side of him too, and he shows it when he's one-on-one with people."

"These rooms are incredible."

"Wait till you see the Dome."

"If it's like the pictures it must be pretty spectacular."

"It is. In fact, Umbriel won't be there when you first come in. He likes to give his guests a few minutes to look around and get adjusted to it. If he doesn't, he finds that people look around the room and can't concentrate on what they've come there to discuss."

The crowd that had followed us was not allowed into the Dome. The waiting rooms around it were guarded by soldiers carrying huge spears and wearing metal helmets with bushy red plumage. Four of them at the double doors of the Dome snapped to attention as we approached, and then they opened the doors to Umbriel's marvelous room.

A group of men waited for us at the opposite side of the room, but Hamlin stopped first to let me look around. What made the room especially stunning were the red jewels that covered the Dome and glowed as if emitting their own light. I did not know what made them glow that way, but they filled the room with the most pleasant rose color I had ever seen. The room was carpeted in white. In the center, on a raised platform, was Umbriel's black marble desk and a black marble conference table with twelve chairs. There were two sets of doors to the room. I had come through the main entrance, and the men who were waiting for me were at the smaller doors, which, I was told, led to the rooms in the palace where Umbriel actually lived. An enormous fireplace, which was blazing at that moment, covered another part of the wall. The Father-King loved art, so the rest of the wall was covered with murals and paintings he had commissioned for the room. He also had several sculptures throughout the room, most of them of great Amian statesman and warriors of the past. Near the group of men two of the large "shadow-cameras" were set up, though the lights that surrounded them were not yet glowing. Before I had time to inspect the art or to gaze any longer at the magical red dome, Umbriel's door opened and Tracian walked into the room.

The men who stood there seemed as surprised as I was to see her. All of them bowed, but she ignored them and headed straight for me. Hamlin bowed as she approached, and Tracian said, "Thank you, Hamlin. Give us a minute, won't you? I think Daddy's on his way."

When he stepped away, Tracian stepped close to me, clasped my hand and said, "I just wanted you to know that Daddy loved the proposal the Rock came up with. He hadn't been too thrilled about the idea of executing you to begin with, so now he's called off the execution for good. I just wanted to tell you myself. Everything's going to be just fine."

All I could think of was that all the men were staring at us. Tracian had made it a point to take hold of my hand in front of them. I felt uncomfortable. I said, "Thank you. Thanks for everything you did to help me."

"I have to go now," she said. "I wasn't invited to this, and Daddy doesn't like me just to pop in. But I just felt like I needed to talk to you myself."

"Good. I'm glad you did."

Without another word she turned and walked out of the room, saying nothing to any of Umbriel's men.

Hamlin came back and said, "Is everything all right? Did she say anything that—"

"Everything's fine," I said. "She just wanted to say hello."

"I see. Well. Let me make some introductions."

Some of the men were Umbriel's military leaders, others were heads of certain agencies of government, and others were advisers whose specific roles were not made clear to me. There were at least fifteen men waiting to be introduced to me, but before I had met even half of them, the private door opened and Umbriel himself walked in.

All eyes turned toward him. Hamlin dropped the introductions and watched the Father-King as he walked toward us. The lights for the shadow cameras now blazed, while the machines themselves recorded vague images that the artists would later enhance. Nearby two men stood poised to scribble every spoken word into their notebooks, and another sketched the scene. We were acting out a little drama for the informationals. By the next morning people all over the kingdom would sit at the breakfast table and try to interpret the words and images. Each phrase would be analyzed for multiple meanings. People would ask, *What signal is the Father-King trying to send about this strange Visitor, this almost-executed music criminal?*

Umbriel seemed the most relaxed person in the room. He smiled and nodded and looked vaguely surprised, as if he wondered what all the fuss was about. I was struck by how young he looked, his bushy hair and athletic stance so different from the worn-out look of most of the old men I had just met. It was hard to imagine that he was Tracian's father. When he reached us Hamlin said, "Father, may I present the Visitor Jeremy. Jeremy, may I present Father-King Umbriel, supreme ruler of Persus Am and the Territory of Ur."

"Yes," said Umbriel, "and you, Jeremy, are here to make sure that last phrase in my title is never taken away from me." Everyone laughed, and Umbriel clasped my arm in the traditional way. He said, "I know it's been a long, hard road for you here in Persus Am, but I would just ask you to forgive us. We have many enemies, and not everyone who has called himself our friend has proven to be one." After this and most other statements Umbriel made, his men either nodded their heads or punctuated his sentences with "Yes," or "That's right," or other words of encouragement. The Father-King never spoke to a silent audience. He continued, "But you have stood the test, Jeremy, and I'm happy to be able to stand here with you today surrounded by these men who have so loyally and steadfastly served me and this great nation and say that we welcome you among us as our friend." The men clapped and shouted words of agreement while I nodded and thanked them.

"Have you finished your introductions, Hamlin?" asked Umbriel.

"Not quite, sir. I had made it as far as Ambassador Bellohom."

"Well, let me help you," said Umbriel, and he introduced me to the rest of the group, adding words of personal appreciation about each man he presented. Once the introductions were done, Umbriel said, "Now, gentlemen, if you'll excuse us, Jeremy and I have a whole new world to create. May God help us!"

The camera lights were turned off, and the guests filed out.

The only one who did not leave was Hamlin, and he stood by the door while Umbriel led me over to one of the fireplaces, where we sat in ornate overstuffed chairs. In a moment servants brought a pitcher of a cold fruit drink and a plate of cake.

"So what do you think of my little room?" asked Umbriel.

"It's fabulous. It must give you a tremendous feeling of power just to sit and work in a room like this."

"Yes it does. In a room like this you feel you can accomplish anything. No vision seems too ambitious. That's why I wanted to make sure I talked to you here. I've talked to a lot of people about you, and I've read pages and pages of facts about you, but the one question no one has answered is, what is it you came here to accomplish?"

"I don't know."

He smiled at first, as if I were making a joke, and then he waited for me to finish my answer. When he realized I intended to say no more, he took a deep breath and said, "Jeremy, not a person who has walked into this office has come without an agenda. Now here you are. In just these few short weeks you've come out of nowhere and now you're sitting in the seat of power in the most powerful nation in the world. What's your agenda?"

"Sir, just yesterday morning my only agenda was to try to die with dignity when your men carried out your order to execute me."

He nodded and said, "Fair enough. But that must not have been your original plan. I want to know what you intended to do from that first day you appeared in the Utturies making Emajian music."

"If the music was Emajian, I certainly did not know it. No one was more surprised to find me here than I was myself. I did not know this place existed. I have absolutely no idea why I was put here, any more than you or anyone else has any idea why you were born in the exact time and place that you were born. Do you ask newborn babies what their agenda is? They don't have one. Neither do I."

He got up and poked the fire with an iron rod. He said, "It's strange, isn't it, that even though you fit into no identifiable category—you're not Emajian, you're not Amian, you're not Damonchokian—everybody still wants to claim you for their own."

"Yes. Or kill me."

"Right. But the point is, they wouldn't bother with you at all if they didn't have a sense that you are an important person, that you came here to do something big."

He paused to let me respond, but I did not.

"And my daughter told you that the Rock of Calad is willing to give me access to their part of the Territory of Ur in exchange for you and Tarius Arc. They've never been willing to give up *any* part of the Territory for *any* reason."

"So do you plan to take them up on their offer? What is *your* agenda?"

He smiled. "Well, Jeremy, as I said, in this room you begin to believe anything is possible."

"Meaning what?"

"What do you know about the Territory of Ur?"

"I know that it's a place that everyone wants to control."

"Do you know what life is like there? For the average citizen?"

"No."

"It is poverty stricken, it is violent, it is filled with constant fear. The people there haven't known a day's peace in generations. We control a sliver of it, and we've done the best we can, but a country torn in so many directions is bound to bleed. What it needs more than anything is stability. They need somebody to come in there and put a stop to the terrorism, to build some kind of solid economy for the people, to give them jobs and safe homes and schools that won't be bombed and stores that will have more than just empty shelves. Don't you think it's interesting that just at the very moment you came, we were considering a drastic measure—war—to bring about stability in the Territory of Ur? We knew it would be bloody and painful for everyone in the short run, but in the long run, we knew something had to be done. So we were prepared to do it. But then you came." He sat back and

smiled and took a drink from his glass. There was a certain
expression he had—a way of smiling and narrowing his eyes like
a mischievous little boy—that made him seem so conspiratorial
and young and hopeful that you couldn't help but want to go along
with him.

I said, "So you think stability will come when the Rock of
Calad gives you control of their part of the Territory?"

"No, I don't. The sliver of land they control is smaller than
mine. Of course, I would be glad to get it. It would certainly help
us, but for the average citizen of the Territory, it wouldn't mean
much at all."

"What do you want to do, then?"

"I want to do something bold and sensible. I don't want to
trade you in some tawdry little deal for land. I want to figure out
the reason you're here and then help you accomplish your mission.
Do you think the Lord sent you here just to be a bargaining chip?
Of course not. I want to know why the Emajians want you so
badly."

"They think I know how to take them to Caladria, the place
where Emajus is."

"But you don't know. Tracian told me you don't."

"That's right."

"Does anyone else know that you don't know about Caladria?"

"Just you and Tracian."

"You haven't told anyone else? Think."

"No. Nobody else has asked about it. I mean I've told
everybody I'm not Emajian—"

"Oh, sure, but nobody believes that. After all, the Assembly
voted to execute you because they didn't believe you. But as for
Caladria, you've discussed it only with me and Tracian."

"Right."

"Well, for your own good, you had better make sure that we
are the only ones who ever find out. Do you have any idea what
would happen to you if I went through with this deal and then the
Emajians found out you knew nothing about how to take them

to Caladria? You'd be dead before the day was through. They would have lost their best land only to find out you are a fraud."

"I am not a fraud. I've never pretended to be Emajian."

"Of course you haven't! But look at it from their perspective. They want one thing from you, and that is one thing you cannot deliver."

"So my choices are go there and be executed or stay here and be executed."

"No," he said. "There is a better way. After all, these people have been waiting for Caladria a long time. And do you want me to let you in on a little secret, Jeremy? Caladria doesn't exist. In the place where they think it is, there is only endless, cruel desert stretching farther than any person has lived long enough to go. So they're never going to Caladria, and even if they did, they would not find Emajus there ready to return with them, and do you know why? Because Emajus is dead. He died in that very desert, with His people following him. Caladria does not exist, and Emajus is dead. These are the two facts the Emajians have not had the courage to accept."

"And am I supposed to try to make them accept these facts?"

"No, no. Of course not. You're their hero. You've come here to help them, not to destroy their faith. You've got to ask yourself why they want Caladria so much in the first place, and why they want Emajus. They want Caladria because, like all of us, they want the world to be a better place. They want things the way they think they were before the War, with no poverty or violence. Caladria is that world, ready-made for them. And Emajus has told them it can be theirs for nothing, without any work or sweat, and without any imperfection along the way."

"I still don't see where I fit in."

"You, Jeremy, are the next best thing to Emajus. They were ready to claim you for their own the moment you arrived with your music and light show. You validate their fantasy. They believe you will deliver Caladria. But since you can't, you've got to redirect their fantasy, and that's where my interests and the interests of the Emajians coincide. Both of us want the world to be different, but they believe it will happen supernaturally, and I believe it will happen with lots of work and negotiation. I'm not asking you to deceive them. I'm only asking you to tell them the truth in such a way as to not destroy the foundation of what makes them strong. Don't tell them you don't know how to get to Caladria. Tell them that before anyone can go to Caladria to bring back Emajus, this world must first be prepared for him. Tell them you need to set things straight in the Territory of Ur, and then Caladria will come."

"You mean you want me to try to rule the Territory of Ur?"

"You're the only one who would be acceptable to everyone concerned."

"Acceptable to everyone concerned? Just yesterday my head was on the chopping block. Would I be acceptable to your people? And the Emajians only want me because they think I have information I don't."

He brushed his hand through the air as if to sweep away my objections. He said, "There are details to be worked out, there's no doubt about it, and I'm not saying this will be easy, but think with me for a minute. If you can deliver the Territory of Ur and at the same time help us avoid war, don't you think the objections my people have will vanish?"

"Do *you* think so?"

"Of course! Jeremy, I don't think you fully realize what kind of crisis we're involved in here. There is great pressure on me to win that Territory for Persus Am. Our whole economy depends on it. We're stymied without it. We've got to get it one way or another. I am a peaceful man, but many in my country are calling for us to take it by force if we can't get it any other way. But if we had an alliance with the Rock of Calad, which only you can bring us, then no one could stop us."

"And you think the Emajians would accept the fact that they have to wait longer to go to Caladria? I mean how long could we keep that up?"

"They can accept the fact that the world must be made ready for Emajus's return. I'm pretty sure there are even portions of their scripture that say something to that effect."

"I don't feel good about lying to them."

"You are absolutely not lying. What is Caladria, anyway? It's a place where people live in harmony with one another, where they are not hungry or oppressed, where they don't live in fear. That's the place you're going to create. You're taking them to Caladria. It doesn't exist out in a desert. It exists all around them. It is waiting to be created. You're fulfilling their prophecies. You are bringing them to Caladria."

"You seem to have thought of everything," I said.

"No, probably not. But before I can pursue this at all, I have to make sure you're with me."

"I don't know. It's an awful lot to think about. It seems sort of far-fetched."

"No. It's bold. But it makes perfect sense. The world is on the brink of war, and the Lord has sent a peacemaker. If we can get everyone to see that, then you will have saved thousands of lives, and you will begin the reconstruction of the world as a more prosperous and peaceful place. Don't you think that is worth the risk?"

"I think that none of this has to do with me, and I wish I could just go back where I came from."

"But now you're here, so you might as well try to do some good."

———◯———

I stayed with Dakin and Miri while I waited for Umbriel to "work out the details" of his plan. Part of me believed his idea was too far-fetched to ever work, but another part of me was wildly hopeful. Two visions kept racing through my mind. One pictured me on a high, rocky plateau, where I had been taken to meet the Visitor on the Rock of Calad. A house like the one where I first met Tarius Arc stood in the distance. As I got closer, I saw a woman dressed in white standing at the door of the house. Within a few minutes I began to see the details of her hair, her face. It was Anne. Then I was holding her, drowning in the warmth of her, saying, "I knew you were the Visitor. I knew it was you. I knew it."

The second vision showed Anne by my side as we stood on the balcony of our mansion in the Territory of Ur, where I ruled, and where I had brought peace for the first time in generations. The people had lavished Anne and me with gifts of gratitude, including this extraordinary white palace. Our home overlooked a forest, and beyond that was the faint outline of a village. Anne stood at the edge of the balcony and said, "Remember when we used to talk about what kind of house we'd like to live in someday? Who would ever have thought it could be this gorgeous? Who could have imagined all this would be given to us someday in a place we had never known?"

These were the lush fantasies that kept my hope alive while I waited on Umbriel to work his magic with those who wanted to kill me. Dakin urged me to keep translating the scriptures while I waited for Umbriel, but Miri, to whom translating looked like horrible drudgery, often found other activities to distract me. When I mentioned to her that painting had been a hobby of mine, she took me to a room that served as her private painting studio. "I used to paint all the time!" she said. "I have every type of paint in every color imaginable. I have enough canvases to cover every wall in the palace. You're welcome to it. Paint!"

"But Dakin wants me to translate," I said.

"I'll take care of Dakin. You just enjoy yourself." She flung open the doors of two closets that were stacked from floor to ceiling with brushes, canvases, and paints.

I painted several hours every day. I started with the landscapes from my fantasies of the Territory of Ur. I had trouble concentrating on the landscapes, though, for my mind was almost constantly bombarded with the sound—or rather *thoughts* of the sound—of music. My mind recreated every moment of sound from the night of my arrival in the Utturies. I remembered it as vividly as if it had happened just moments before. The sound was so gripping and distracting that I would often have to stand up and walk around the room, sometimes even talking out loud, to drown it out. What I really wanted to do was sing, but with great effort I managed to keep from it.

Finally I had to set aside my landscapes and paint the music. In Persus Am, unlike at home, every musical sound had a certain look to it. As Tarius Arc had told me, before the War it was common for music to produce the same swirls of color that had surrounded my music on the night of my arrival. After the War, when the music "died" because the Spirit of God no longer inhabited it, the colors disappeared from it and had reappeared at only a few miraculous times. Even though I had seen the music just once, on that first night, I knew the color of every sound.

I painted the music on the biggest canvases Miri had given me. I made two paintings on the first day, and they took nearly every color available to me, some of them carefully combined. It took me all day, probably ten hours or more, to finish the songs from the night of my arrival. Miri had some sort of engagement outside the palace that day, and Dakin was away in meetings, so I was left alone. I ordered Pannip to bring my meals to the studio, and I worked almost nonstop. Painting the music came close to satisfying my raging desire for it. I never got tired. I was flooded with energy. I felt completely good.

To anyone at home my work would have looked like a pleasing but meaningless series of colorful swirls. But for me it brought the sound instantly alive in my brain. I was finally interrupted when I was about an hour from finishing. I had expected Miri or Dakin to interrupt me, but instead I was surprised by a voice behind me who began to sing the song in my painting even before I knew he had come into the room. It was Jank. His strong tenor voice, so unexpected, sent chills through me as he sang the song that had been gripping my mind all day. I had been afraid to sing it out loud, but Jank sang without inhibition. I leaned back in my chair and listened until he finished the songs on both canvases. Then both of us were silent for a moment, the sound and Spirit of the music still echoing in our minds.

"Jeremy, those are beautiful! How do you know those songs?"

"This is the music that I arrived in the Utturies with."

"That is Emajian music."

"I didn't know that other people would be able to recognize what this was."

"I don't know of any Emajian who could have painted them

any better. They're fantastic. I wish Tarius Arc could see this. Does Dakin let you do this?"

"He hasn't seen it. I just thought of it today."

"The music is strong in you. You are filled with the Spirit of God."

I looked at my paintings and wondered how Dakin would react.

Jank said, "I can't stay long. I have a message from Tarius Arc. He knows that you met with Umbriel."

"Yes. Three days ago."

"Right. I saw it in the informationals. But it didn't say what happened at the meeting."

"No. It's a secret. I'm not allowed to discuss it with anyone."

"Well, today it's starting to come out, but I suspect that as usual Umbriel is keeping some of it to himself. I know this much at least: the Rock of Calad has offered Umbriel use of their part of the Territory of Ur in exchange for you and Tarius."

"That's right! Do many people know this yet?"

"No. Umbriel has told the Council of Ministers and a few others. But I've talked to Tarius Arc about it, and he isn't happy."

Before he could continue, Pannip rushed in and said, "The princess is coming."

"When?" asked Jank.

"Right now!"

"She's here in Dakin's quarters?"

"Yes! Get out of here, Jank."

"Are they bringing her back here now?"

"Yes."

"Then it's too late to run. I'll have to hide."

"The paint closet is the biggest," I said, pointing the way.

"That's fine. There are advantages to being short. I've probably hidden in close to half the closets in this palace."

"Hurry, Jank," said Pannip, and then ran out of the room.

Just before I shut the door Jank said, "Cover up those paintings."

I had just enough time to throw a sheet over the paintings and plop down in a chair before Tracian walked in, closely followed by three guards and an aide. She asked them to stand out in the hall and then closed the door behind her.

She was gorgeous. Her dress was simple, and she had shed most of the jewelry, letting her natural beauty speak for itself. To my eyes, which had been shut off so long from the sight of attractive young women, she was stunning.

I stood up and stepped toward her, but as she had done in her father's Dome, she took control of the greeting. She put her hands lightly on my shoulders and kissed my cheek, allowing me to do the same to her. Over her shoulder I could see that the closet door was cracked open a couple inches.

"I'm not supposed to be here," said Tracian, "but I figured as usual they had probably left you sitting alone wondering what was happening."

"That's true. I haven't seen Miri or Dakin all day. I haven't heard from your father's people at all since I saw him in the Dome."

Looking around, she said, "At least they've given you things to do. I didn't know you painted."

"A little."

"Well, let me see." She took hold of the sheet covering my paintings, but I caught her hand and said, "No, not these. They're not finished. Let me show you something else." I showed her one of the landscapes, which she said she liked very much.

"What is this place you've painted?" she asked.

"Oh, I just made it up. Would you like it?"

"Yes! Thank you."

"I'll have it framed."

"Yes, do. Well, I shouldn't stay, Jeremy. But I want you to know everything's going fine. Daddy started telling the Council and some of the Assembly Members about the offer from the Rock of Calad and some proposals of his own that he's considering, and he told me he's been getting a good reaction."

"Do you know when he'll talk to me again?"

"No. Just be patient. Don't worry about a thing. And don't tell Miri or Dakin I was here, all right? Things have a way of being misconstrued."

I glanced over to the partially opened closet door. "I won't tell. Thanks for coming, and for everything you've done."

"I'm happy to do it. Now don't you forget to send me that picture. Good-bye, Jeremy." She squeezed my hand and walked away.

After she left, Jank popped out of his closet and said, "Pretty friendly with you, isn't she?"

"She is a friendly lady," I said.

He smiled as if there were some secret between us.

I said, "So you were saying that Tarius doesn't like the deal the Rock of Calad has made."

"No, he doesn't. He sent me to warn you against making any deals with Umbriel whatsoever."

"But this wasn't even Umbriel's idea. Tarius Arc's own people proposed it. It will set him free and save my life."

"I know," said Jank. "But Tarius knows that Umbriel can't be trusted. Umbriel wants to destroy us, Jeremy. He wants to crush Emajianism and the music of our Lord."

I did not know whether or not Jank had heard about the Visitor on the Rock. Hesitantly I said, "The people on the Rock must have good reason to want to make this deal."

"Tarius Arc says they're weak."

"Tarius Arc is in prison. He doesn't know all the facts."

"And you are a Visitor. You don't know all the facts either. You don't know the people Umbriel has tortured. You've never seen the people he's had whipped until they bled to death, or the people he's hanged or burned to death."

"I'm not denying that, Jank. But Tarius's own people have made a peaceful offer, and it saved me from being executed. What good would it do for me to flat out reject it and let them go ahead and execute me?"

"Tarius says he would rather die in prison than do anything to help Umbriel destroy Emajianism."

"There has to be a better way."

"Well, I have delivered the message. Tarius wants no deal made with Umbriel on his behalf. I have to leave now before any more unexpected guests show up. I don't think you'll want Councilor Dakin to see those paintings. Why don't you let me take them?"

"Do you really think he would know what they were?"

"It would be just as obvious as if you started singing the songs at the top of your lungs."

"Take them, then. All that work for nothing."

———○———

The next day I sat alone in the center of the Dome, seated before Umbriel's great desk. Hamlin had brought me there and then had left to announce me to the Father-King. I leaned back in the chair and stared straight up at the magnificent glow of the red jewels that covered the Dome's surface. I hoped that Umbriel would not come for a while so I could just enjoy being in the room, but in a few minutes he came in alone. Hamlin soon followed, but he kept his customary place near the private door, close enough for Umbriel to call on him but not so close that I wouldn't consider our talk private.

Instead of sitting behind his desk, Umbriel motioned for me to come over to the chairs by the fireplace. He put his hand on my shoulder and smiled. "I'm sorry I've left you hanging for the last few days, but things are happening incredibly fast. It's unbelievable. Jeremy, you've changed the whole political balance. For the better too. I don't even think you've been *trying* to do it, either; that's the amazing thing. Sit down."

Umbriel lifted his hand and Hamlin opened the private door to a servant who brought us refreshments. Umbriel said, "I've hardly slept since I saw you last, but I'm not a bit tired. It's that rush of accomplishment, knowing that even though you're just sitting in these rooms exchanging words, you're changing the history of the whole planet. You're in the middle of that, Jeremy! It's going to be fun!"

As the servants fussed with the plates and cups, Umbriel continued, "Over the past few days I've talked to all twelve Councilors and the leaders of the Assembly and a few others about the deal the Rock of Calad has made. I've also talked to the ambassadors from the Rock to try to convince them that you represent the brightest hope we've had for solving the whole problem of the Territory of Ur. I've tried to convince them and our own people that the best solution is to stop this tug-of-war over the Territory once and for all before the whole world is plunged into war over it. The Caladans believe you are a man sent from God, and they're very receptive to the idea that you would rule the Territory. I told them of your desire to prepare the Territory before Emajus comes."

"You told them I said that?"

"I told them that was your belief. We agreed that this was the way to handle it. Right? They see it too. They understand preparing the world for Emajus's return. It's in their scriptures. We Amians want to bring peace to the Territory for our reasons, and the people on the Rock want to bring peace for their own reasons. Our goal is the same. You're not wavering on me, are you?"

In that vast room I had begun to feel closed in and smothered, exactly as I had felt at home when I sat in the office of the car salesman who wanted me to sign the papers right now, for hadn't he answered all my questions and objections? I could not find the words to make Umbriel understand why I could not be enthusiastic about his scheme. I could not explain the music in my brain or why I felt that there in his Dome I felt I was betraying the Spirit who lived in that music. I tried to lean on the idea that this political fight had nothing to do with me. I was fighting to save my life. This was a game. I had to play it out.

I asked, "What about your own people? What do they think?"

"They're delighted. Oh, a few of them are still suspicious of you, of course, but this is all very new and surprising for all of us. I expected some resistance. But for the most part they're thrilled. We'll have a friend ruling the Territory of Ur, we'll avoid war, and we'll be able to run our grangicars across the Territory to Wilmoroth. It solves a problem that has been vexing us a long time."

"So what do we do now?"

"Well, there are a couple of complications. First of all, the Caladans won't give their final agreement to the deal until they speak to you personally. I have spoken in your behalf until now so that you wouldn't get caught in any traps, but now they insist on speaking to your personally. That's no problem, really. You're going to have to speak to them eventually. But you're going to have to be very careful what you say because they are going to hang on every word. Don't promise things you can't deliver, but don't undermine yourself either. There's nothing wrong with being evasive. Prophets are supposed to be mysterious. The main two things to keep stressing are that you have come here to bring peace and that before Emajus returns, the Territory must be prepared for him. That's all they need to know. But we'll talk more about the particulars when the meeting is set up."

"And what are the other complications?"

"Just one. And I think you'll see it's very much in your favor. So far you've been perceived as being too much in the Emajian camp. Emajians are demonstrating for you in the Utturies, Emajians on the Rock are calling you a prophet, there's everything that happened on the night of your arrival—all that makes you look Emajian. In fact, we're going to make you an Emajian prophet. So it's going to look to many people like I'm surrendering to the Emajians in return for nothing but a sliver of land. I can't have that. I have to make my people see that you are one of us too. Words alone won't do it. It has to be something bold."

"Like what?"

"Jeremy, this may sound strange to you as an outsider, but I want to adopt you as my son."

"What! How could you—"

"I want to make you a prince of Persus Am. I know it's unexpected, but look how much sense it makes. You go to the Territory of Ur not only as a prophet of Emajus but also as Prince of the Amians. No one ever thought it would be possible. We will completely change old political definitions. We will break down old religious divisions. We will create a new political order. The problem in the Territory is too complicated to be solved by ordinary, old-fashioned solutions."

"I'm amazed. I mean, what about all those people who voted to execute me? What about Vanus? He hates my guts."

"He hates you because he thought you were an enemy of Persus Am, an Emajian troublemaker out to stir up the passions of the Emajians in the Utturies. He will not hate you as my son, as a man sent from God who will open up the Territory of Ur to us and help us avoid war. You shouldn't take these things so personally, Jeremy. This is politics."

"You really think people can change their minds about me?"

"Of course. They know so little about you, really. They were reacting to you out of habit and instinct. I'm not saying this will be easy, or that we won't run up against resistance, but I know that perceptions can be changed, and with the informationals and the other tools at my disposal, I have the power to change those perceptions. In the meantime, you must talk to absolutely no one about this."

"What would being a prince involve?"

"We'll have an elaborate coronation in the Stadium. We'll invite the Caladans, the Damonchokians, the Wilmorothians. Everybody—including your former enemies here in Persus Am—will see that you have a stake in Persus Am and will never betray it."

"By 'have a stake' do you mean—"

He held up his hand to stop me. He smiled. "The question of who will be heir to my throne will not be part of this. We need to keep that separate. We have enough issues to deal with without that. Besides, I plan to be around for a long, long time."

—◯—

Emajian prophet. Amian prince. I was becoming everything to everybody. I promised silence while Umbriel took on the arduous task of selling his plan to the Council of Ministers and Assembly members. Of course, as Father-King he had the power to adopt me without their approval, but he wanted their agreement and their commitment to this idea of a new political order.

In the meantime the informationals began to print one article after another proclaiming my virtues as a man of God and a visionary politician who had come to save the world from war. They published pictures of me standing side by side with Umbriel in the Dome, chatting with Councilors and Assembly members, and toiling over scripture translations at my desk. Photographers carrying their bulky shadow-cameras followed me much of the time. When the artists painted the dark photographs, they covered any flaw in my clothing or my hair and made me look just a little more muscular than I really was. I liked these pictures.

During the eleven days it took Umbriel to lobby for his plan, I saw him only once, briefly, when I met with the representatives from the Rock of Calad. Umbriel carefully staged the meeting himself so that I wouldn't get into any trouble. Shortly before the meeting, which took place in Umbriel's Dome, the Caladans were presented with a paper that detailed my position on Caladria, the return of Emajus, and my purpose in coming to the Known World. To be consistent with my earlier statements, the paper did not say I was an Emajian. It said I was sent from God to create a new political order "in the spirit of Emajus and all who yearn for peace." It said the "fathomless mysteries of Caladria and Emajus will never be revealed until the world is made ready for His coming. Caladria is not merely a spot on the map. It is an ideal toward which Emajus and others have challenged us to strive in this present world." By sending me, the Lord had given the world one last chance, the paper said, to avoid plunging the nations into chaos and destruction from which they might never emerge. It was time to lay aside our petty differences of politics and faith and be about the business that Emajus had left for His followers to do.

By issuing this statement in my name, Umbriel hoped to finesse some of the difficult questions the Emajians might have raised. The three officials insisted on seeing me alone. There were two men, named Eornus and Bashorn, and a woman named Doktol. Eornus, a smiling, friendly man whose teeth looked entirely too big in his gaunt face, was their spokesman. Umbriel introduced us and then left us sitting by the fireplace.

"We have studied your statement," said Eornus. "Let me ask you directly, sir. Do you know how to take us to Caladria?"

"As the statement says, that is a mystery that I cannot now open. We could never go to Caladria to reclaim the faithful until the world is ready for their return."

"Frankly, sir, that sounds like an answer that Umbriel would have asked you to give. We are prudent people, and the offer we have made to Umbriel is based on more than just the hysteria that has built up around your coming. We have reason to believe that you can lead us to Caladria, and we also have some indication that not everything has been revealed yet even to you."

"Just like you," I said, "I pray to God I'm doing the right thing. I suppose He hasn't revealed everything to any of us. He doesn't seem to work that way."

"We don't hold it against you that you don't yet have the answers we seek. What we need to know is, are you committed to acting upon the light that is revealed to you from the Lord, even if it means someday you may have to take action that Umbriel will find objectionable?"

"I will do what I think is right. Tell me, where do you get your information about me?"

"We can't tell you that."

"I've heard rumors there is another Visitor on the Rock of Calad. Who is it?"

"I can tell you nothing about any Visitor."

"Is it a woman?"

"Please, sir, I will tell you nothing whatsoever on that subject."

Eornus stood up then, as if eager to stop my questions, and at that moment Umbriel, who must have had some way of watching our meeting, opened the door and headed toward us.

Umbriel asked, "So then, is everything all right?"

"We are satisfied," said Eornus. "We will let the plan play out. We believe in Jeremy."

On the day after my meeting with the Caladans, I went to my desk after lunch to work on some translations, which Dakin had asked me to do. I kept my earlier translations in a folder Dakin had given me, and when I opened it I saw that about half of them were gone. I asked Filbus if he knew where they were, but he didn't. He suggested maybe Dakin had taken them, as he had done a number of times before. We went ahead with our work, and later in the afternoon I took some time off to swim and to rest in the garden with Miriaban. That night at dinner I casually asked Dakin whether he had taken my translations.

"I took some of your chapters from the book of John, but I returned them two days ago."

"You returned them?"

"Yes. Why?"

"I didn't see them in the folder today."

"Did you ask Filbus?"

"Yes. He was with me."

Dakin immediately stood up and said, "Let's go see."

Miri said, "Not during dinner!" But Dakin was already on his way.

I followed him, and when we got to my room, we found the chapters, not in the folder but underneath it, scattered among some other papers.

Dakin was flustered, his fingers furiously twirling a strand of hair at his shoulders. "Here they are," he said. "Please be more careful with these. They're still the most important thing you're doing."

I started to protest that I was certain the chapters had not been there earlier, but I decided against it. Dakin was paranoid enough, and I didn't want him to post a guard at my door. Besides, I had my own suspicions about who might have taken the translations. I asked Pannip later if he had seen anyone tampering with my papers, but he said no.

—◯—

I sent Tracian the painting she admired, but I received no response. On the third day after my meeting with the Caladans, I found out why. Jank showed up in my closet that night, his mustache curled, his jacket covered with jewels as if he were a member of the aristocracy.

"Have you joined the Assembly?" I asked him.

"Ona takes care of me," he said. "She doesn't think of me as a servant. She likes me to be well dressed. Umbriel and his goons get upset if they see me this way, though, so if I think there's a chance I'll run into them, I dress like a servant. No use pushing my luck."

"So you don't expect to see them tonight?"

"No. They're too busy running around talking to everybody about you."

"Oh? And what are they saying?"

"That's what I'd like you to tell me."

"Sorry, Jank. I can't discuss it at all."

"Come on, Jeremy. I'll find it out in the next couple days anyway. This will just save me some trouble. Nobody will know it came from you. Nobody knows I even know you."

"What do you know so far?"

"I know it has something to do with the offer the Caladans made for you."

"Right."

"And I know whatever it is, it has upset Princess Tracian something fierce."

Before I could think of a noncommittal response to that statement, my expression betrayed that it was news to me.

"Oh," said Jank, "so that was something you didn't know. I'll tell you more about it if you give me some information."

"Absolutely not. Jank, I can't. I told Umbriel I would be quiet about this and I'm going to. All I can tell you is it will all come out pretty soon."

"You disappoint me, Jeremy. We should be friends. You should trust me."

"Speaking of trust, I do have a question for you. Do you know anything about the disappearance of my scripture translations the other day?"

"You don't give me information; I don't give you information. I have some things to take care of now, Jeremy. Good night." He sneaked out without another word.

———○———

Two days after my talk with Umbriel, the Father-King had informed Dakin of his decision to make me a prince. Dakin was not as happy about it as I had expected him to be, though he wouldn't tell me why. He seemed even more preoccupied and fidgety than normal. Miriaban, when we were alone, told me she was worried about his health.

"All these maneuverings by the Father-King have upset him,

and I don't know why. It seems like things are finally starting to work out, but when Dari first came back with the news that Umbriel was going to adopt you, he was pale and quiet, even worse than when he found out they were going to execute you. He seems to take it as an ominous sign, but for the life of me I don't know why."

For the next several days I rarely saw Dakin. He was out of the house most of the day because of his work, and in the evenings he skipped meals or ate alone in his private study, a room that was separate from his regular office and a place where no one, even Miriaban or the maids, was allowed to go.

"I worry about him when he works there," said Miri. "It puts him in a bad mood."

"What does he do in there?" I asked her.

"He studies. It's in there that he keeps all the papers and pictures and everything from before the War. That's why nobody's allowed to go in there. He has things in there that are illegal to have anywhere else. But because of his position and because he studies those things, he's allowed to have them. He has Emajian scriptures even, and I think a couple of old musical instruments. But don't say anything about it. He doesn't like me even talking about that room."

The other Councilors found out soon after Dakin about Umbriel's plan, but it took seven or eight days for the news to trickle down to the servants. Pannip gave me the first hint that the servants knew what was happening when he broke his usual silence one evening to ask, "Sir, have you been happy with my work as your servant?"

"Yes, of course. Why do you ask?"

"If you were to ever—" he blushed before he continued—"if you were to ever move to a different part of the palace, I was wondering what your plans were about maybe taking me with you."

"Well, I don't have any idea, Pannip. I mean, you work for Councilor Dakin. I don't know what right I would have to take you—anywhere—with me."

"I understand, but if you were given your choice of servants, would you take me?"

"Yes, I certainly would. If that opportunity ever arises, I would be happy to take you with me."

"Thank you, sir."

Later that night Jank showed up, dressed all in black, like a thief. "I thought I'd be seeing you pretty soon," I said. "You found out about Umbriel's plan, didn't you?"

"Yes. How did you know?"

"Something Pannip said tonight made me think he knows what's going on, so I figured you must have found out by now."

"Pannip is a sharp one, isn't he? What did he say?"

"He said if I ever live anywhere else in the palace, he'd like me to take him with me as my servant."

"Oh. Looking out for his future. That would be quite an accomplishment for a kid his age, making it to Umbriel's household. You don't realize it, but even the fact that he's serving Dakin is considered quite a triumph. Of course, his parents helped him along, since they're servants of another of the Ministers, Councilor Drathe."

"So even among the servants there are political struggles going on."

"Oh yes. Sometimes it's fiercer at that level than what you're involved in. Serving a Minister is a sign of status in that class. When you serve in Umbriel's household, you've arrived. Speaking of which, you seem to be about to arrive yourself, Prince Jeremy."

"That's right. What do you think of that?"

"Well, I just came from the prison, where I've spent the last hour or so listening to Tarius Arc condemning the whole idea. He wants to see you."

"See me? How could he do that?"

"I can take you down there. Not tonight, because there are too many people out and about. But tomorrow night should be better."

"But I could never get down there without being seen."

"Sure you could. I have disguises. It'll be fun! You will be Dr. Manderlet, a specialist who has been called in to help Tarius Arc with his throat problems. I already have you down on the list of approved guests. What a feat! Smuggling in the future Prince of Persus Am right under their noses!"

"Jank, I can't take any chances with—"

"Nonsense! It's all set up. I do this kind of thing all the time."

"Couldn't Tarius just send a message?"

"Jeremy, he wants to see you face-to-face. He's down there in that prison suffering because of you—suffering because when you came he left the safety of the Rock of Calad to come out and see you. All he asks for is a visit. You owe him that much. You've got to see him."

"Things are just at a very delicate stage right now, and I don't want to do anything to mess it up."

"I understand. I'll come by late tomorrow night to get you. Be ready."

———○———

The next night, however, Umbriel called me to the Dome to say that he was ready to announce the adoption in the informationals the next day. Shadow photographers took dozens of pictures of Umbriel and me together all over the palace, particularly in the Dome and in the long entry hall, which looked great in pictures. We were also photographed with the Council of Ministers and with leaders of the Assembly. Certain Ministers and Assembly members also asked me to pose for individual pictures with them. Umbriel asked me to stay after the picture taking to talk with him alone. The pictures and congratulations took several hours, so it was late before Umbriel and I were finally alone.

"This is exhausting, isn't it?" Umbriel asked.

"Yes, it is. You must be used to it by now."

"I am, but I still get weary of it," he said, and in a rather unconvincing tone he added, "Sometimes I think I'd like to go off where nobody knew me and where I could just do a certain job during the day and then come home at night and forget about it. Just be with my family, play rogno, read."

"But that would get old too, wouldn't it? The same routine, over and over. You'd miss the exhilaration of power, of really making things happen. You've got the best job in the world."

"You're right! I shouldn't forget that. I think I'm just worn-out from all this arm twisting these last several days. But I think great things lie ahead. I won't keep you long, but I just need to clarify one thing. A few people are skeptical about my plan, but mostly people are supporting it, so I'm optimistic. The one thing the Ministers and the Assembly people are concerned about is this idea that if the Emajians see you as a prophet, they'll expect you to engage in music. The idea of a Prince of Persus Am practicing music is just too abhorrent for them to accept. So we're going to have to work it out so that you do not engage in music yourself."

"How would that be possible if they see me as a true Emajian?"

"It would be consistent with the rest of what we've told them. You have come to prepare the world for Emajus's return. How can you sing His songs before everything is ready? You will tell them that for yourself, you must wait until Emajus's return before you sing the songs again. For you, the highest way is abstinence."

"Do you honestly think they'll buy that?"

My tone of voice irked him. He replied, "They'll buy it if you do, and if you present it the way I just said."

"But Emajians have always sung songs, regardless of the fact that Emajus was not here. It's their main form of worship."

"I know that, Jeremy. And we're not so naive that we think we can stop them from engaging in music. You shouldn't even try. For the weaker Emajians, you will allow them to continue practicing music. But for you, there is a higher way."

We left it at this, but I had grave doubts about whether I could restrain myself from music when it was all around me. Already thoughts of those songs flooded my mind night and day. My longing for it was insatiable. But Umbriel was in no mood to debate anything that night, so I let it go.

—◯—

"Jank is waiting," Pannip told me as soon as I stepped into my room. I didn't need to ask where Jank was. I opened the closet and found him curled up asleep in the corner, resting his head against a bulky duffel bag.

"Jank!" I said, nudging him. "It's time for you to get up and go on home."

He crawled out of the closet, dragging the bag behind him. "I'm not going home. We're going to see Tarius. I've been waiting for hours."

"It's too late, Jank. They're announcing my adoption in the informationals tomorrow. It's going to be a busy day. I can't go running around the palace all night."

"It won't take all night. I can't keep you down there long. You have to go, Jeremy. Please. I promised Tarius I would bring you down there."

"I'm worn out, Jank."

"So am I." But as we spoke, he took out my costume piece by piece. He had a black wig, a mustache, makeup that darkened my skin, a black cloak and hood, and a medical bag. Jank said, "It won't take long at all to put this stuff on you. I've done it many times before."

Jank did a remarkably good job disguising me. He said the most dangerous part was getting out of Dakin's residence unde- tected. Pannip made sure our path was free of other servants and Dakin and Miriaban. Then Jank and I rushed from my bedroom to the kitchen, where I had never been before, and out a back door that I didn't even know existed. Jank had a fist-sized lantern to get us through the dark corridors, storage rooms, and stairwells that led to the prison. This was a part of the palace known only to servants, and at night it was mostly abandoned. We saw a few workers, but they paid no attention to us.

Jank knew the guard at the prison door, and he waved us in without a word. I thought I would vomit as soon as the awful stench of the dungeon hit my nostrils, but I recovered before we reached Tarius Arc's cell block. We heard him before we saw him. His voice was marvelous. To my music-starved soul his song was stunning, bursting with emotion. I wanted to walk slowly, afraid he would stop singing when he saw us. Jank grabbed my cloak and pulled me along.

Tarius Arc sat facing the back wall of his cell and was not aware of our presence until we stood at his door and Jank called his name. He stopped singing, turned around, expressionless, and looked straight into my eyes. His gaze seemed accusing and made me uncomfortable. He looked thinner and weaker than I remembered him, but the whiteness of his hair, the intensity of his gaze, and that marvelous voice gave him a sense of dignity that overcame his vile circumstances.

I said to him, "Your music is fantastic. I wish you hadn't stopped."

As soon as I said it, the old man walked over to the bars of his door, reached through the spaces, and grabbed my jacket. Before I could back away, he pulled me toward him with greater strength than I would have imagined he possessed and slammed my head hard against the bars. I closed my eyes in pain, but I could feel his awful breath against me as he said, "If my music is so fantastic, why are you doing everything in your power to destroy us?"

"Let go of me," I said. Tarius seemed almost out of his mind. I was frightened of what he might do. Jank stood back impassively, his arms folded.

Still clutching me, Tarius stormed, "I thought God would send us a prophet before I died, Jank, but all we get is a stupid little boy!"

"Let go of me!" I shouted, and pulled myself away.

"How dare you praise the music to my face and then try to wipe it out behind my back."

"I'm doing no such thing. You completely misunderstand what is happening."

"You're the one who misunderstands. You are agreeing to become the son and prince of Umbriel, a man whose sole preoccupation, no matter what other lies he couches it in, is to destroy the music of Emajus and the faith and Spirit that His music embodies."

"His preoccupation is to avoid war and bring stability to the Territory of Ur. I think that is an admirable goal."

Tarius threw up his hands and paced furiously around his cell. "What can we do with him, Jank? Why has the Lord done this to us? Jeremy, I do not want to fight with you. You and I, of all people, should not be enemies. But I need to ask you to listen to me a minute with your heart and mind open. I believe the very reason I am in prison might be to say these things to you."

"I am listening."

"Have you ever seen one of the Amians when they've listened to music?"

"No."

"I know you're not allowed to say much about where you come from, but is there no one there who is made sick by the music?"

"Music is different there. People play it or listen to it for enjoyment. Just about everybody likes it in some form or other. But it's not as—intense."

"Well, here it is the very voice of God. We don't just use it for enjoyment. And even now it isn't as 'intense,' if that's the word, as it was before the War. The War changed the music and made it only a whisper compared to what it was. Compared to the music before the War, the music now is like listening to someone sing behind a closed door in another part of the house. But even so, it has great power. It has the power to reach into the hearts of believers and make them remember the Lord. It can empower them and increase their faith. But for the Amians—or for anyone who tries to destroy the music—it is poison. It exposes their unforgiven corruption. To those who come to the music humbly, as believers, it can bring soothing love and forgiveness, but for those who oppose the Spirit that inhabits the songs, it can have a devastating effect. Not only does it force them to face their own corruption, but it has physical effects as well. It can make them vomit, scream, writhe in pain. Umbriel is terrified by the music. He fears Emajus. If Umbriel's people ever let the music purge their hearts, Umbriel's lies will be revealed to them and they will turn against him. When Emajus returns, having completed our salvation, the children of Emajus will sing once again in the new Temple of the Lord in the Lord's own city of Persus Am, and Umbriel will be finished. This is what terrifies him. This is why he'll do anything to stamp out Emajians and their music. He's using you as a tool to do it. You must not let him."

I said, "I know that you are concerned, Tarius. But your own people have asked me to do this."

"They're fools! Look, Jeremy, I don't know why they want you so badly. Maybe they know something I don't. But if they want you, fine, we can get you there. Jank can help you escape to them. But don't fall into Umbriel's trap. Jank can do it, right, Jank?"

"Absolutely. I can take you there any time you're ready, tonight if you want."

"No," I said. "I am sympathetic to you. I love your music. I sense the Spirit in it that you're talking about. I don't want to do anything to harm it. But I've agreed with Umbriel's plan, and I'm going to follow through with it."

"Jeremy! Look into your soul for once. Have you done that yet? Have you looked deep into your soul to see whether or not I'm right? Don't you see that you're not turning against me or my God, but that you're turning against your own?"

"I am not Emajian."

"You are! Look into your soul, son. Jank, give me those pages."

From his coat pocket Jank pulled out five or six sheets of paper and handed them to Tarius. Tarius looked over them for a moment and then read, "'I am the bread of life. He who comes to me will never go hungry, and he who believes in me will never be thirsty.' Let's see. 'Everyone who drinks this water will be thirsty again, but whoever drinks the water I give him will never thirst.'"

Looking at Jank, I interrupted, "Well, at least that explains why my translations were missing."

Jank put his hands in the air, smiled, and shrugged.

Tarius Arc continued, "'I tell you the truth, unless a kernel of wheat falls to the ground and dies, it remains only a single seed. But if it dies, it produces many seeds. The man who loves his life will lose it, while the man who hates his life in this world will keep it for eternal life.' Jeremy, is this the Lord you follow?"

"Yes, it is."

"These words are exactly the message Emajus brought us. Some of it is almost word for word."

"But there must have been lots of religious men who said things like this. Lots of religions have similarities. It doesn't prove they're the same. I can't risk everything on just a *possibility* that—"

"But the Spirit in the music! You recognize that, don't you, as the same Spirit of God that you know? Don't betray the Spirit. If you know that Spirit, you are Emajian. If you don't, you're not. Look into your soul and decide, Jeremy. That's all I'm asking."

My soul was the last place I wanted to look. I wanted only to get out of that putrid prison and get away from the old man's ranting.

I said, "I'm sorry, Tarius. I mean you no harm whatsoever, but I'm going to follow Umbriel's plan, and I think it's the right thing to do. Let's go, Jank." I turned and walked away, hoping Jank would follow. He did.

7

The next morning my adoption was announced and my coronation date was set for one month from that day. For most of that month Tracian refused to see me. She did not acknowledge my notes or in any other way explain why she had shut me out. Jank said the rumor he heard was that she was furious with me for having taken advantage of her help to usurp her place in the line of succession. Whenever I asked Umbriel about her, he just brushed my questions aside, saying Tracian was immature and impetuous and I should pay no attention to her moods.

Tracian was not the only member of her family who failed to welcome me with open arms. I met Umbriel's wife, Cashmel, only once, during a dinner for foreign dignitaries that Umbriel threw in my honor. She looked ten years older than Umbriel. Like Tracian, she had dark hair and a shy way of tilting her head slightly down while her eyes gazed up at you, but she rarely smiled and almost never spoke. She stayed for only the first part of the dinner and then was escorted away by an entourage of assistants long before dessert or vapors. Umbriel's oldest daughter, Shellan, allegedly out of favor with her father, never attended any of the dinners, and I never laid eyes on her until Coronation Day. Jank told me Shellan was hostile to my adoption, as she was to most of her father's ideas.

Despite his family's lack of enthusiasm for me, Umbriel spared no trouble or expense to keep me comfortable and to make my coronation the biggest event the world had seen since his own ascension to the throne. Entire industries shifted their resources overnight to prepare for my coronation. Some of the government officials involved in the planning were said to be complaining that a month was not long enough to plan the event, but Umbriel was determined to get me coronated as quickly as possible before any outside circumstances could interrupt his plan.

Hamlin, Umbriel's young assistant, was put in charge of planning the coronation. Early on he came to get my approval for his plans. "Every inch of your path from the palace to the Stadium will be decorated with flowers and banners. All along the path we'll have schoolchildren waving banners and signs in honor of you and the Father-King. They will have made the banners themselves in contests we're sponsoring in all the schools in Persus Am, the Territory of Ur, and the Rock of Calad. It will be a great honor for them to represent their towns along the pathway. We'll also have essay contests for the children, and the winning essays about you and the new hope that your coronation has brought to the world will be printed in the informationals.

"And we're building a fabulous new car," he said, "for you to ride in. I should have pictures of it in a few days. We're building you a throne for the Stadium, which we'll save for all time in memory of this event. And we're having commemorative coins made. I have one here somewhere," he said, searching through a bag he had brought. The gold coin had the diameter of a half-dollar, but it was about twice as thick, as were all Amian coins. It bore my likeness in profile on one side and the image of Umbriel's Dome on the other side.

From his bag Hamlin then pulled out a doll dressed in aristocratic clothes and royal blue colors. When he turned the doll toward me, I saw that it had my face! "Do you like this?" he said. "We're manufacturing these right now, and we know all the kids—and lots of adults too—will want one."

"I'm amazed!" I said. "I had no idea you were planning to do something like this."

"Oh yes. And we have commemorative books and key chains and lots of other things. And I haven't even told you about the ceremony itself. We'll have athletes performing gymnastic feats with streamers and all kinds of other things. And hot air balloons are being constructed bearing the seven emblems of Persus Am, and the balloons will take off from the Stadium right as you arrive. We have prizes for the crowd. And did I tell you tickets to the event will be awarded by lottery? We're opening it up to every nation. And did I tell you that a three-day holiday is being declared all over Persus Am? There will be parties and celebrations everywhere. The Father-King is going all out for you. His plan is going to work. No one can stop it now."

—◯—

Umbriel gave me twenty-five rooms on his floor of the palace that I was to remodel and use as my own until a palace was prepared for me in the Territory of Ur. Like the rest of Umbriel's palace, the rooms were already fabulously decorated, and I was bewildered by how I should order them to be remodeled. At one point I suggested to a group of Umbriel's aides that I would be satisfied if the rooms were left just as they were, but they thought I was only being polite and would not hear of cancelling the remodeling plans. They said the rooms should be redesigned to reflect my own needs and tastes. But my needs were few and were more than satisfied by my room at Dakin's. And my tastes were far too simple to ever be appropriate in Umbriel's fabulous palace.

It was during the remodeling that Tracian finally broke her silence. One week before my coronation I sat in one of the enormous rooms by myself poring over some plans the decorators had drawn for me. I heard the door open, and when I turned to look, there she stood, in a thin "afternoon dress," as they called them, smiling as casually as if she were showing up for a tennis date or for a walk in the garden. I started to take the papers off my lap so that I could stand, but before I could finish she plopped down beside me on the couch.

She looked at me with calm, steady eyes, waiting for me to speak first.

I said, "Well, you don't *look* like someone who'd tell the

servants to kill me in my sleep. That's what the rumors say you're thinking about doing."

"Oh, I hadn't heard that one. Last I heard I was planning to do the deed myself."

"I see. Well, that makes a much nicer story."

"Don't worry. You're safe. I'm not here to do you any harm. I was pretty mad at you, though." She said this without rancor, as if she were talking about someone else's anger.

"Why were you mad at me?"

She shifted in the couch so that she faced me. One of her hands rested on the cushion by my head. She smelled fresh and alluring.

She said, "I was mad at you because I thought you had taken my idea and used it against me."

"No! I had nothing to do with it. It was your father's idea. I even resisted it, but he said it was the only way. Even now I don't see why this has to work against you. Your father said my adoption has nothing to do with succession to his throne. This takes nothing away from you at all."

"I understand that now. But you've got to understand how things are around here. Everybody—especially people like my sister—is always playing power games, and because I'm the youngest, I haven't succeeded too well in all the struggles. I have to be suspicious of everything just to survive."

"I understand."

"But I've come to apologize for being mad at you and to ask you whether we can be friends again."

"Of course!" Something in her manner made me feel free to take her hand in mine, so I did, just for a moment. "You're the last person I wanted to compete with here."

"Good," she said, and she jumped up and spun around toward the open door that led toward all the other rooms. "So how are you coming with your remodeling?"

"Horrible. I'm beginning to wish your father had given me only two or three rooms instead of twenty-five. Nobody needs so many rooms."

"You certainly seem to have them all lit up nicely."

"Oh the servants do that. Every night in all the rooms. The decorators told them to keep the rooms lit until we were finished with the remodeling. I wish they wouldn't. There's something lonely about all those big rooms lit up and nobody in them."

"This whole place must seem lonely to you. You must miss your friends and family where you came from."

"I do miss them."

"It's strange, isn't it, that there are thousands of people out there who would give anything just to have a short conversation with you, now that you're such a celebrity, and yet you're stuck in here wandering around all these empty rooms by yourself. If there's anybody who shouldn't be lonely, it's you and me."

"You feel that way too?"

"Most of the time. I get tired of being locked up in the palace. I've thought about disguising myself and escaping into the city—just for a day or two—just to walk around and talk to people."

"Have you ever done it?"

"No. If Daddy caught me doing that, he'd throw a fit. I've had enough trouble without that." As she spoke she walked from room to room, while I followed. She said, "We've got to get these rooms remodeled."

"I know. But my heart's just not in it. It seems so unnecessary."

"But you've got to do it to show Daddy you can take charge of a project and see it through to completion. How can you run a kingdom if you can't redecorate a few rooms?"

From that evening on, Tracian spent most of every day with me, helping me order the plans for redecorating my mansion. We picked out desks, couches, drapes, tables, wallpaper, and countless other things. Some of these we chose from pictures in books, but other samples were brought to us by an endless stream of fawning decorators and furniture makers hoping to gain the prestige of having their work purchased for the royal palace.

Because we were together so much, rumors immediately began to spread that Tracian and I were romantically involved. At first these stories were not true, but I did nothing to stop them (not that I could have stopped them anyway) because frankly I was happy to hear myself linked with her. The rumors also said that Tracian's supposed boyfriend, a young man named Bortius, son of Councilor Eddle, was furious with Tracian and with me. When I asked her about this, she said their relationship was insignificant and it was presumptuous of him to think they were serious enough for him to be angry over her spending time with me.

Jank thought Tracian was only using me, and he told me so every time I saw him, which was every night that week. He preferred to hide in a different room each night. Then, when I turned a corner or opened a door, there he stood, his short, stocky frame as erect as a soldier, his mustache curled, his clothes courtly and impeccable. Without so much as a word of greeting he began his speech for that night. His opinion about Tracian was this: because she finally had realized there was nothing she could do to stop my coronation, she had decided to make the best of it and befriend me. That way her fortunes could rise with mine.

I knew there was some truth in what Jank said, that Tracian had plenty of political reasons for wanting to be with me. But for that matter, so did Jank, and Tarius Arc, and Dakin, and everyone else who had anything to do with me.

I spent my time with Tracian because I wanted to be with her. Besides the fact that she was gorgeous, or maybe partly *because* she was gorgeous, she was the only person who for long periods of time could make me set aside the aching isolation I felt in that place. Only Tracian could help me put aside for at least a little while my obsessive thoughts of Anne, whose presence seemed to hover all around me. I simply could not stop the dreams of her, when the smell of her hair, the touch of her hand, the sight of her face would seem so real that I could have sworn she was just inches away from me. Tracian distracted me, at least, and we had fun together, playing rogno (a sport something like racquetball), enjoying long, quiet dinners, and remodeling the mansion as if we were newlyweds planning our own home. Unlike almost everyone else in Persus Am, Tracian neither fawned on me, treated me like an alien, nor maneuvered me like a mere pawn in a political game. So I ignored what Jank had to say about her.

Jank did not visit me mainly to talk about Tracian, however. He came to persuade me to sneak away to visit Tarius Arc again. I refused. I told him I was never going down there again. My excuses to Jank were that it was too risky and that too many people were working on my behalf, toward the plan I had agreed to, for me to do anything to jeopardize my position. The truth was that Tarius Arc was like a throbbing conscience in my brain, calling into question everything I did. I was not convinced he was right that Emajus was Jesus and that by standing with Umbriel I was turning against everything I believed in. But the music and the Spirit that inhabited it gripped my mind day and night; sometimes I felt it so intensely that I had to sing into a pillow, but when I did, my conscience was so tortured that I had to stop.

I told Jank that Tarius would be set free on my coronation day as had been agreed, and then Tarius could come up to my mansion and visit me. Jank said that if being set free meant agreeing to one of Umbriel's deals, Tarius would refuse to leave the prison. Jank brought me "messages" from Tarius Arc each night. They usually went something like this: "Tarius Arc asked me whether Umbriel is doing everything in his power to make you rich and lazy and fat in order to dull your mind from how you are betraying the Lord."

"And what was your answer, Jank?"

"My answer was yes."

———○———

Coronation day. Finally I could crawl out of the near-isolation of my palatial prison and see the people I had been chosen to lead. Umbriel's actions had made it clear that he intended me to be nothing more than a public showpiece. He kept me away from all the important political discussions and decisions. Once he had decided what was to be done, he let me know and trained me with a response I should give to anyone who might ask me about it.

But to the people, I was presented as a great leader, second only to Umbriel himself. I was a mysteriously powerful Visitor who had come from the Bright World to avert the impending war, to permanently restructure the world order, and to bring normalcy to the Territory of Ur. In the tradition of Umbriel's father, I had to wear a long, flowing coat instead of the usual short jacket. The coat was studded with jewels of various kinds and was uncomfortably heavy to wear. Just before we left the palace that morning, Umbriel proudly told me the coat had belonged to his father. "I wore it at my own coronation," he said. "Besides my father and me, you are the only one who has put it on."

I was to ride in my own specially built car with only Tracian and Hamlin accompanying me. Umbriel was to ride just ahead of me in his own car, accompanied by his wife Cashmel, his daughter Shellan, and a couple of aides. Behind us would be the twelve Councilors and their families, and behind them the Assembly members and other government officials.

I truly felt like a prince as Tracian and I walked arm in arm through the fabulously decorated palace and down to the courtyard, where my car waited. A crowd, held back by soldiers, stood near my car. They clapped and cheered as we walked out the door of the palace. I waved to them, feeling like a true politician for the first time. Tracian had lost all reserve with me. She squeezed my arm and even kissed me on the cheek once while the crowd looked on. The car they had built for me looked like a giant aquarium on wheels. Every wall was made of glass, though inside there were curtains we could close if we wanted to. Tassels hung all around the top fringe of the caboose-sized vehicle, and flags sprouted from each corner. Two of the flags represented Umbriel's family, and the other two represented the nation of Persus Am. Though the Amians had the technology to motorize the car, tradition called for it to be pulled by six camucks, which were decorated almost as elaborately as the car itself.

A few minutes after we were seated in our car, Umbriel and his entourage emerged from the palace and were greeted with cheers. Cashmel clung to her husband and stared at the crowd with dazed eyes, though she attempted a smile. Shellan, wearing a flowered dress and a preposterously puffy hat—trademarks that had made her famous—strutted across the courtyard like an exotic bird, her neck long and stiff, her eyes darting nervously about.

Tracian laughed with delight at the sight of her sister.

"Doesn't she know how ridiculous she looks? It's no wonder nobody takes her seriously."

"Do you know that I still haven't met her?"

"Daddy's probably trying to keep you away from her. She's such an embarrassment."

As soon as Umbriel was settled in his car, the caravan moved forward. We drove down the same fountain-lined road that I had first traveled as a caged prisoner. People cheered and waved as we passed. It was exhilarating. Some held up the dolls that looked like me and waved them at me. They held up banners of congratulations, and they threw confetti on our car. Several times the caravan came to a standstill as the soldiers cleared a path for us. Each time we stopped, a few people managed to break through the line of soldiers and press close to the car's glass wall, which separated us from them. They held their hands up to the glass and wanted us to press our hands next to where theirs were. The soldiers firmly pushed them away, but the people seemed hardly aware of soldiers.

When we finally got beyond the city walls, the crowds were thinner for a while. Our route was a shortcut that required us to go outside the walls for a couple miles and enter at another point farther west.

After a few minutes Hamlin told us we should shut the curtains on the car. "Why?" I asked.

"We're coming into a bad section of town. You might be safer if they don't see who's in what car."

Tracian shut the curtains as he spoke. I wanted to see, so I pulled aside one small section of drapes at the front of the car so I could look over the heads of the camucks.

"Shut it, honey," said Tracian. "Hamlin is right. I can't believe they're making us ride through here. It's horrible."

Hamlin said, "But we knew we had plenty of soldiers to protect us, so we thought we'd save a little time going this way."

Ahead of us I saw a cluster of white plaster buildings like those I had seen on the night of my arrival in the Utturies. The crowd around the buildings was enormous. The people were still at a distance, but they moved toward us in one loosely connected mass, like a slithering sea creature, first one section surging forward, then the next section catching up.

"There are so many of them!" I said. "How can the soldiers ever hold them all back?"

"The soldiers can handle it," said Hamlin.

"Shut the curtain," said Tracian.

I did not shut it.

Soon our car pushed into that undulating mass. I watched the wall of soldiers try to hold the mob back. The shouts of thousands of voices were so loud we could barely hear ourselves talking to one another. Hamlin shut the curtain. Tracian buried her face in my chest.

The crowd pushed the ring of soldiers closer and closer to our car. We could hear the mob just a few feet away. Our car stopped. We felt it shake back and forth, as if someone were trying to overturn it. We heard the crackle of the fire pellet guns of the soldiers. Suddenly, at our back, we heard—and felt—the crash of something against the window. The whole car rocked. I flung open the curtain behind me as Tracian screamed. Smashed against the window, staring at me, was the face of a scraggly-bearded man who was hanging onto the top of the car by the decorative tassels and cords. In an instant, a soldier behind the man pulled back a whip and brought it crashing down on his shoulders. The man's eyes snapped painfully shut and his teeth bared in a grimace of agony. He fell from the car, still holding a tassel in his right hand.

"It's those stupid decorations they're after!" said Hamlin, who had knelt on the floor. A large crack wound its way along most of the window behind us. Hamlin said, "Shut the curtains and get down on the floor. One more hit and that window will shatter all over us."

We sat on the floor and put the seat cushions on top of our heads. Tracian was complaining about why we had been brought through that section of town, but the mob was so loud I could barely understand her. Our car continued to lurch forward and then rock from side to side until those who had attached them-selves to the car were knocked away.

My curiosity would not let me just sit there, so I got up on my knees and lifted the curtain at the bottom of the window. "I'm not going to open it," I said, "I'm just going to peek out."

What I saw was astonishing. A middle-aged man, stumbling in a drunken rage, spit pouring out of his mouth, flung himself at the soldiers to distract them while his friends tried to slip past them to get to the car. The soldiers flung the man back at the crowd, striking him with the whip, and then the crowd flung the man back. The man's white shirt was in shreds and was covered with blood.

I saw a young woman screaming because the men around her had ripped her blouse from her and left her exposed in the crowd.

I saw a teenage boy, skinny and dirty and wearing nothing but short pants, get hit with a fire pellet in his face. The fire scorched his cheek into a nauseating red pulp, and then he fell down and disappeared from view.

I hunched back down on the floor with Tracian and Hamlin. We endured another half hour or so of screaming and shooting, and then we were out of it.

"Someone's going to lose their job over this one," said Tracian, as she got up off the floor and arranged herself on the seat.

I said, "Not Hamlin, I hope."

Tracian scowled. "Oh no," she said. "Hamlin's too good at covering his tracks. I'm sure that by now he has thought of a way to convince my father that his most ingenious servant Hamlin was against this whole idea of traveling through the Utturies to begin with."

I looked over at Hamlin, but he merely grinned, lowered his head, and resumed reading some papers he held in his hands.

—◯—

We left the barbaric fringe of the Utturies and entered into the world of stone-paved roads, unbroken sidewalks, well-kept shops, and polite, cheering crowds who waved signs and flags and never once pushed past the soldiers. All signs of poverty were gone—no raggedy gangs of underfed children, no apartments so overcrowded that trash and old furniture were simply set outside on the streets with an occasional discarded man or woman. Here the apartment buildings had flower boxes hanging outside each window, and the neighborhood smelled not of garbage and urine but of the spicy meats being sold at street-side carts. Children dressed in matching suits and hats held their parents' hands and waved signs of congratulations to the new prince.

When we reached the stadium, the drivers parked our cars in dark, cavernous rooms underneath the seats. We could hear the rumble of the crowd above us as we lined up to begin the procession. It was here that I met Shellan for the first time. She had seemed so eccentric before, her movements so jerky and erratic, that the warmth of her greeting surprised me. I had expected a quick, cold nod and maybe an icy handshake, but instead she took my hand in hers, looked carefully into my eyes, and said, "How nice to finally meet you. I have wanted to talk to you for a long time, but they've managed to keep me away."

Before I could respond, Umbriel had his arm around her and swept her away toward the procession.

Umbriel was first in line, followed by Cashmel and Shellan, followed by Tracian and me, followed by the Councilors and other dignitaries.

As we emerged from under the seats and stepped into the arena, I heard a voice introducing first me and then Father-King Umbriel through a tinny and echoey public address system. The crowd was an exhilarating blur of waving arms and streamers and banners and confetti. We walked around the perimeter of the seating area and waved like newly elected politicians, occasionally getting close enough to the crowd to shake someone's hand. The crowd sustained a deafening roar of approval. The people tried to shower us with confetti, but the soldiers, fearful of more harmful things the crowd might throw, blocked most of it before it reached us.

I saw commemorative shirts and hats and dolls and banners by the thousands. Whenever I stepped close enough to the people to touch them, they screamed as if I were a movie star or a famous rock musician. I was amazed at their adulation. I marveled that they cheered so wildly for someone who had never done a thing for them nor had even existed in this place just weeks ago. I was exhilarated, but also strangely embarrassed. What would they expect from me in return for this devotion?

When we were about halfway around the stadium, Umbriel stepped back to stand beside me. He put one arm around me and waved to the crowd, while I did the same, sending the people into new spasms of cheering. Later, as we neared the stage, Tracian leaned over and kissed me on the mouth, which also sent them into an uproar.

As we got closer to the stage, I felt dizzy. When I looked directly at the crowd, they looked like characters in an early silent film, their motions disconnected, jumpy. For several seconds at a time they blurred together in a colorful mass. My head buzzed with a roar that was deeper and slower than the roar of the crowd.

My body felt suddenly heavy, just as it had felt the first several days after my arrival in the Utturies. I tried to keep walking at a normal rate, but I must have slowed down because I felt Tracian practically drag me, her arm around my back. She said something to me, but the power of my new language had vanished from me in the first moment of dizziness. She kept speaking and I kept not understanding. Hamlin came from out of nowhere and stood on my opposite side, chattering away the whole time and helping Tracian push me toward the stage. In English I said, "I can't understand you. I've lost the—"

They spoke to one another and then stopped talking, finally understanding my predicament. I climbed the stairs as if I were climbing a mountain. Once or twice, when I felt too heavy to take the next step up right away, I managed to turn and wave to the crowd, hoping to cover up my problem.

The seats at the back of the stage were divided according to the delegations from the various countries. In the midst of the delegation from the Rock of Calad stood a woman wearing a dress that looked brighter and more stylish (in the Amian sense of style) than the other Caladan women were wearing. Her back was to me at first, but she turned toward me as I crossed the stage. She had brown hair to her shoulders, pale skin, and eyes that—

"Anne," I said.

Tracian said, "What?"

But in the next instant I saw that it was not Anne. The burst of energy the sight of her had given me evaporated, and I nearly collapsed. Fortunately I was allowed to pass up the handshaking. I walked directly to my chair, which was wide and plushly cushioned, and sank into it. My mind was a mess. Not only was it afflicted with the vision of Anne, but as the buzzing slowly disappeared, it was replaced by vivid hallucinations of music. In Tarius Arc's voice, the music pressed into my head from all sides. The sound was thrillingly beautiful, but scary, because I knew Tracian and anyone else around me could see in my face that something was happening to me. I felt as if the music were squeezing out my very breath. I could not shake it away as it swirled round and round. Tracian held tightly to my hand.

I was only dimly aware of what happened next. In the arena seven hot air balloons were being inflated, each one bearing one of the seven logos of the House of Umbriel. The balloons were colorful and magnificent, but my mind was such a blur that the balloons seemed in that moment just a minor part of the storm that was sweeping across my brain. I could not distinguish between the reality I knew and the reality those around me knew. I thought the balloons were *mine*. It took me a while to realize that everyone around me saw the balloons too.

The balloons filled quickly and floated into the air. Everyone pointed up toward the balloons as they ascended, and in a few minutes everyone gasped as a man tumbled out of the basket of his balloon and parachuted into the arena, nearly landing on some people at the far side.

The next part of the ceremony was like a circus, with scantily clad women leading animals of every exotic sort to do tricks in the center of the arena. The animals jumped through boxes of fire and did flips and stood on their hind legs and jumped over one another. One set of animals, which looked something like small bears from where I sat, stood on top of one another to form a pyramid. After the animals came athletes who did tricks of their own, waving streamers and jumping and flipping and even swinging through the air and catching one another on trapeze-like devices.

Throughout this performance my body began to lose its heaviness, but my mind was still gripped by the raging storm of Tarius Arc's music. I tried as hard as I could to force the sound from my mind because I knew my part of the ceremony was coming and I did not want to ruin it. I loved the music, but it was like a rhythmic beating of my conscience, exposing me as a fraud for taking part in Umbriel's gaudy spectacle. In the music was Spirit. In the music was Truth.

I could not argue the music away. But I had come too far. The athletes were performing their finale, and then the speeches would begin. I felt trapped. There was no turning back.

My body gradually became lighter. I understood most of the words. The music wound itself less tightly around my brain. Councilor Spence, the senior member of the Council of Ministers, so old and feeble he could barely walk up the five steps to the podium, had the honor of introducing Umbriel. After he did so, it took Umbriel five minutes to quiet the cheering crowd enough to give his speech. His delivery was passionate but controlled, hindered only by the tinny and echoey sound of the pitiful public address system. He told of the struggles Persus Am and the rest of the world had faced since the War. He told of the bloodshed in the Territory of Ur and explained that at this very moment the world stood poised once more on the brink of war.

And then he turned around, pointed to me, and said, "But that young man right there proves that God in His grace will not let us slide into the abyss of war!" Everyone cheered wildly, and I had to stand for a moment to wave and smile. "God sent us a man named Jeremy," said Umbriel, not even bothering to wait for the crowd to quiet down. "God sent a humble man. God did not plop him down in the palace, with a company of soldiers to announce his coming. No. God sent him into the humblest of our towns, at night, unannounced. Jeremy met the people, learned their language, worked among them. Gradually he rose from those beginnings—he rose not because of wealth or flash or connections but because of the simple truth and power of his message. He rose because he had a vision of the way the world could be. He rose because he had a vision of a new world. A world not of unending hatred and poverty but of happy, productive, loving people. A world where mothers don't have to fear all day whether their children will be struck down by the evil hand of terrorists. Where fathers don't—"

He continued on in this vein, never mentioning the fact that when I arrived in his humble town my arrival was accompanied by a stunning display of light and music or that his own people imprisoned me and voted to execute me as an Emajian spy. My initial imprisonment had long since been brushed aside as ineptitude on the part of his subordinates. And as for the near execution—well, Umbriel in his wisdom had stepped in and straightened out that problem too. Where would Persus Am be without Umbriel overseeing things and keeping his subordinates from making fatal errors?

The crowd was nearly in a frenzy by the time Umbriel told them that this was the day my billion-mile search for my mission in this world had been fulfilled. This was the moment I was born for.

He called me to the podium for my speech. I could walk, but I felt slow and shaky. Tracian told me later that my slow ascension up the steps looked deliberate, as if I were giving the crowd time to show their appreciation for Umbriel's speech. I could have said anything at that point, and the crowd would have loved it. I delivered the words that had been dictated to me. I had written it in English letters, since the written Amian language still gave me trouble. My voice did not carry well over the pitiful speakers, and the crowd drowned most of it out anyway. My speech was shorter than Umbriel's; even on my coronation day, I was not allowed to upstage the Father-King. My speech was full of clichés about peace and a new world. The music raged in my head through the whole thing, but I managed to say every word. My body was heavy from standing. When the speech was done, Umbriel and I stood arm in arm again and waved to the crowd. I managed to smile for the shadow-camera pictures. When I got back to my seat I fell heavily into the chair.

Tracian said, "You did great. Are you still feeling bad?"

"Yes," I managed to say.

"Well, just keep smiling. The crowd can't even tell. We'll be out of here before long."

In fact, it seemed a pretty long time to me. Battalions of soldiers marched around the arena, displaying their guns and cannons and weapons I could not even identify. It was a dazzling display. Tracian said, "Daddy brought the soldiers in as a warning to the Damonchokians not to do anything to try to block our control of the Territory of Ur. But it won't do any good. They didn't show up."

"What?"

"I just heard that the Damonchokians pulled their delegation from the coronation at the last minute."

"Pulled their delegation? Why?"

"I guess they're thinking about fighting us for the Territory. But don't worry. We've got the Rock of Calad on our side. The Damonchokians would be crazy to try to stop us now. We'd slaughter them."

She said this gleefully, like a college student talking about a football game.

"Don't worry, honey," she said, seeing my concern. The soldiers marched around and around the arena.

—◯—

Jank came to me late that night, actually just a couple hours before dawn, just after Tracian's servants had carried her away to her own room. My body had recovered from the heaviness shortly after the coronation ceremony, and the music that had seized my brain had gradually faded throughout the day, until the evening vapors knocked it out altogether. Coronation parties were held all over Persus Am all day and all evening. Tracian and I made appearances at eight of the more fashionable parties during the afternoon. At night Umbriel threw a party of his own in the palace. Afterward we lost ourselves in the vapors.

Exhausted though I was when Jank showed up, I was glad to see him because I wanted to see if he could explain what had happened to me at the coronation. I was afraid to tell anyone else about the music.

Jank hid in the closet of my bedroom. He came out as soon as my servants left.

"I've been in there a long time," he said. "I didn't know it would take so long for you to tell the princess good night."

"We sort of fell asleep on the couch. Lots of vapors tonight."

"Ah."

"What are you doing here?"

"We have problems. Tarius Arc is supposed to be released tomorrow under the terms of the agreement between Umbriel and the Rock of Calad."

"I know."

"Big ceremony in the formal gardens. All the dignitaries there waiting for Tarius. The photographers with their shadow-cameras ready to record the event."

"What's the problem?"

"Tarius is going to refuse to leave the prison."

"Refuse to leave! Every leader on the Rock of Calad has been working day and night to set him free!"

"You know how he feels about this deal with Umbriel. He wants nothing to do with it. He thinks it will bring the overthrow of the Rock of Calad and the end of Emajianism."

"That's ridiculous. They'll force him to leave. This could scuttle the whole plan."

"He said they'll have to kill him to get him out. He is a determined man. He is not afraid of anything."

"They won't have to kill him to get him out. It wouldn't be that difficult to take him out by force."

"They've trained you well. You're starting to sound just like Umbriel. You're right that they could force him out, but he could force them to cancel their public ceremony or face lots of embarrassment." Jank sat back in his chair and took on a serene, self-satisfied expression. I could tell there was more to the story than what he had told me.

"What is it, Jank? Whenever you get that smirk on your face, I know you're up to something."

"It's not a smirk, I assure you. This is a very serious matter. But Tarius Arc did say one other thing you ought to know."

"I thought so."

"He said he would consider—I underline *consider*—leaving the prison under one condition."

"What?"

"That you take him to see his daughter Ona."

"Umbriel's mother?"

"That's the only daughter he's got."

"And *I* have to take him?"

"Yes. No one else. If you don't take him, there's no deal."

"So. He *is* willing to leave the prison. This is just a ploy to get a chance to see his daughter."

"He wants to see his daughter. He may or may not leave the prison. I would take him at his word."

"I don't like this. Why should I be the one to take him? And how is Umbriel supposed to find out about this? I can't tell him you told me."

"Tomorrow, when they come to get him, he will refuse to leave. They will be in a panic, and you will offer to intervene. You will talk to Tarius and then go back to tell Umbriel that Tarius wants to see his daughter. Then the two of you will see her, and then Tarius will do whatever he decides."

"All right. Fine. I guess that's the way it will have to be. I don't know. I'm tired, Jank. I've got vapors crawling around my brain. I can't even think straight. I wanted to ask you about something, but maybe it can wait—"

"Hang on. We have one more problem to discuss."

I fell back on my bed and covered my eyes.

Jank continued, "Have you checked into getting Pannip transferred up here to be your servant?"

"I mentioned it to Umbriel, but he said it's not a good idea. He said the palace servants are carefully chosen. He doesn't want them moving from one household to another."

"But you told Pannip you'd bring him with you."

"I told him I'd like to. I told him I'd try."

"Well, find a way. I'm afraid of what he'll do. He's threatening to tell about our visit to Tarius Arc, not to mention my visits to you, those music portraits you painted, and who knows what else he might make up. I really believe they'd kill me if they knew I took you to see Tarius. They let me get away with a lot, but that would be stepping over the line."

"That's not what you told me before. And I thought you trusted Pannip."

"I did. It would be suicidal for him to betray us. He would be ostracized. Nobody would trust him. And nobody would want to hire a servant who was known for telling secrets. But he's ambitious, and foolish enough to think he could cut a deal with Vanus or one of those guys. Just find a way to get him up here with you. That will at least give us time to deal with him."

"All right. Now let me tell you what happened to me today."

I described how the music had overtaken me at my coronation. He listened with great interest and then asked, "You're certain the music was in Tarius Arc's voice?"

"Yes. What does it mean? Have you ever heard of something like that happening before?"

"The minds of Emajians are often filled with the Lord's music, but the fact that it was so strong it blotted everything else out—that's unusual. Tarius has been praying day and night that the Lord would wrap His Spirit around you. Maybe that's what the Lord is doing. Maybe He's trying to prevent you from joining with Umbriel to destroy the music."

"Umbriel just wants peace in the Territory of Ur, Jank. That's all I'm helping him accomplish."

"Spare me your coronation rhetoric, Jeremy. This is a sick and perverted kingdom, and you are its prince."

—◯—

Umbriel carefully guarded his image so that he never appeared frustrated in a crisis. Every public function he attended was carefully choreographed to present him as a positive, successful leader who had everything under control. Never did he attend sessions of the Assembly, where issues were sometimes rancorously debated. Never did he submit himself to question-and-answer sessions unless the questions were screened in advance and the answers carefully rehearsed. His underlings had to deal with the complainers, the doubters, the debaters, the malcontents. In the informationals Umbriel was shown opening grand new public buildings, announcing treaties and agreements, unveiling new military hardware, launching bold new programs, and welcoming heroes to the palace. The face of the invincible leader was the only face he ever showed to the world, even to those in government as high up as the Councilors.

The only people before whom Umbriel would unmask himself were six close advisers virtually unknown to the public. Even I knew only one of them, Hamlin. Known as the "inner-circle" advisers, these men were responsible for doing anything necessary to assure that Umbriel's image was never tarnished. They got revenge on his enemies, lied for him, covered up embarrassments for him, and gathered information to use against anyone who questioned his policies or insulted him.

On the morning Tarius Arc was to be released, Hamlin summoned me to the Dome. In the center of that magnificent room sat Umbriel behind his desk, surrounded by five of the six inner-circle advisers. All formalities were dropped. Umbriel, who normally greeted me with a formal handshake, merely said hello and told Hamlin to bring me a chair. Umbriel's advisers, who normally would have been expected to stand when I entered the room, merely smiled and nodded. The tone was not unfriendly, but merely casual, as though we all knew each other too well to bother with protocol. For one brief moment I felt the pleasure of being an insider.

Umbriel said, "Jeremy, we've got problems. The Rock of Calad was offended by your coronation yesterday. They seem to think we made it look too much like you're just a personal representative of me rather than a leader who is going to rule the Territory in a partnership between Persus Am and the Rock."

Never once had anyone mentioned the word *partnership* to me. In Persus Am I *was* treated as if I were nothing more than Umbriel's representative.

Umbriel continued, "Damonchok knows how unhappy the Rock of Calad is, so the Damonchokians are now threatening to fight us for the Territory, because they think they can get the Rock to break our agreement. Not that we couldn't defeat them, of course, but we want to do whatever we can to resolve this peacefully. Jeremy, we need you to go to the Rock of Calad. Hold their hands. Reassure them that you're their leader too. And if we can work out the details, I also want you to visit Damonchok. The government may hate you, but we hear you're enormously popular with the people there. A few cheering crowds might convince the government that it's not in their interest to mount a war against us. Can you do this?"

"When would I leave?"

"Soon. Within the week. Just as soon as we work out the details with the ambassadors."

"I'd be glad to go reassure them. I don't want anyone to be suspicious of me. The only reason I'm in this is to bring peace and stability to the Territory of Ur."

"That's exactly how I want you to talk to them. Don't make new promises. Just reassure them that we have no hidden agenda beyond avoiding war and bringing peace to the Territory."

"I'll do it."

"Fine, then. I guess we'll see you later at Tarius Arc's ceremony."

The advisers had not said a word, nor had anyone introduced them to me. They were there to judge my commitment to the cause, to assess my ability to carry out their schemes. I had been invited there not as an insider, and not as prince, but as one of their hired servants. Hamlin stood and escorted me out.

─○─

Tarius Arc did not play his hand until the very last minute, after everyone else had gathered in the formal gardens, after refreshments had been served, after the preliminary speeches had been delivered. Dozens of well-dressed guests sat in a courtyard amidst the meticulously manicured rows of flowers, shrubs, and trees. The women wore wide-brimmed hats that trembled in the breeze. We ate sandwiches on little plates and drank punch from delicate china cups. Umbriel smiled as he surveyed his garden party. I sat beside him on the platform. The problems that had afflicted me the day before had vanished. No music filled my head. My body felt light, and the sun seemed to fill me with energy.

Then came the climax of the afternoon. Tarius Arc was to stroll through the formal archway and step up to the platform to be greeted by the Amian leaders and by Umbriel and me. We were to celebrate our agreement once again and pledge ourselves to cooperation and peace in the Territory of Ur. Tarius allowed the guards to clean him up, trim his hair, give him a new set of clothes, and feed him a big meal. But when the time came for him to leave the prison, he walked back to his cell and shut the door, locking himself inside. To Hamlin and the Amian ambassador who were to accompany him to the garden he said, "I thank you for the new clothes and the trim and the shower and the meal. However, since I hold contempt for everything your leader Umbriel stands for, I choose not to take part in his plan to eliminate the music of Emajus from the world. I choose to remain in my cell."

Tarius refused to say another word. He sat in his cell and stared straight ahead, as if no one else were in the room with him. Occasionally he sang part of a song, just as he did when he was alone.

When I saw Hamlin whispering to Umbriel, I knew Tarius had carried out his threat. In a few minutes, two of Umbriel's inner-circle advisers, who had not been guests at the ceremony, appeared and joined Hamlin in a huddle around Umbriel. No one said anything to me. In a short time Umbriel sent the men away and approached the podium. His face showed no sign of worry or anger. He apologized to the crowd for the delay and said that, unfortunately, the excitement and pressure of the day's events had made Tarius Arc ill and that he was being attended to by the doctors. Umbriel assured the crowd the illness was not serious. He thanked them for joining in this display of goodwill and coopera-tion among the two nations, and he said Tarius would be released as soon as he felt able to leave. Then the ceremony ended. Umbriel shook hands with the necessary dignitaries and disappeared into the palace, the men of his inner circle following close behind.

I, of course, was not invited to sit in on the discussion of how to handle the Tarius Arc crisis. Instead I sat with Tracian in one of the few rooms in my part of the palace that was not full of carpenters and scaffolds and dust and paint and noise. Despite

Tracian's advice not to get involved in the crisis ("That's what the 'inner-circle' guys are hired to handle," she said), I sent a servant to summon Hamlin, who let me in to see Umbriel.

On our way to the Dome I got Hamlin to tell me that Tarius was not sick but that he refused to leave the prison.

All talk stopped when I entered the Dome. Despite Umbriel's attempt that morning to make me feel like "one of the boys" by bringing me into his meeting with the inner circle, this was a real crisis, and their wary silence made it clear they did not think I belonged there. I existed to be shown off at public ceremonies, not to interfere with their handling of problems. The men were huddled around Umbriel's desk, just as they had in the morning. Umbriel tried to be polite.

"Jeremy, what brings you down here?"

"I was hoping I might help get Tarius Arc out of prison. Hamlin told me he refuses to leave. I met him, as you know, before I came here, and I think that maybe if I talked to him, it might do some good."

The inner-circle men looked suspiciously at one another and said nothing. Finally one of them said, "We appreciate your interest, Prince, and your willingness to help, but I think we have it under control."

"Do you?" I asked. "Have you figured out a way to get him out without forcing him out?"

"Not exactly," said Umbriel. "What do you propose to say to him, Jeremy?"

"I would find out why he is refusing to leave, and then try to show him why it's to his advantage and to the advantage of his people that he cooperate with you and go home."

"He hates my guts. That's why he won't leave," said Umbriel. "He doesn't want to do anything to make it look like he's going along with an idea of mine. We might just have to throw him out."

"That wouldn't do much to help relations with the Rock of Calad, though, would it?" I asked.

"No," said Umbriel. "They're already blaming this whole thing on us."

"It would be much less embarrassing if he left on his own. If you haven't thought of a way to get him to do that, I don't see what harm there could be if I talked to him."

Condescendingly, one of the inner-circle advisers began, "Prince, these matters are very complex and—"

"Maybe it wouldn't do any harm," said Umbriel, shutting up his aide. "Give it a try. If you can get us out of this one, Jeremy, we'll turn the whole mess over to you."

—◯—

When I stood before Tarius Arc in the prison, I said, "Well, you've got us all playing your game. But what I can't figure out is, are you trying to make me look good, or are you trying to make me look bad?"

"I'm trying to see my daughter."

"Somehow I knew you wouldn't answer that question."

"Let's go, Jeremy."

—◯—

Umbriel agreed to let Tarius Arc see Ona, and he agreed to let me be the one to take him to her. Jank met us at the door of Ona's residence. "She's had a bad day," said Jank. "I told her you were coming, Brother Tarius, and she's been quite flustered. She cries for a while and screams for a while and then she's quiet. She has not been in good health. I don't know what to expect when she sees you. I hope you understand—"

"Yes, Jank. I know she is not the Ona I knew. I am prepared."

I was not prepared. The whole place was eerie. Candles filled every room because globe lights made Ona nervous. Jank decided to take us to her one at a time, so that it would be less of a strain on her. I offered to stay in the hall and let Tarius see her alone, but he insisted that I meet her. I went first.

Her sitting room blazed with candlelight. Ona sat on the opposite side of the room from us, curled up on a couch, apparently reading something. The candlelight behind her shone through her thin, frizzy hair and made it glow. She looked older than Tarius Arc, wrinkled and bent. She seemed not to notice us at first, even though Jank whispered, "Ona, Ona."

When she did see us, she jumped, as if we had sneaked up on her; she screamed and jumped up from the couch, letting the pages fall from her lap onto the floor. Her eyesight was not good, and she refused to wear glasses. She stood partially behind the couch and squinted furiously, as if she expected us to lash out at her at any moment and wanted to be prepared to run.

"It's all right, Mother," said Jank.

"There's somebody with you," she said. "Who have you brought in here, Jank?"

Jank did not have time to answer. By the time her question was finished, he had led me close enough to her so that she could see my face. She screamed loud and long, though her voice was somewhat hoarse, and she pointed her finger at me—pointing, pointing, and she wailed, "I remember him! I remember him! I remember that one!"

Fast as he could, Jank ran to her and clutched her from behind, his arms circling hers to prevent her from knocking over the candle stands or brushing through the flames.

"No, Mother, it's not him," said Jank. "It's not him. It's not him." He swayed back and forth with her and hummed a tune, soulful and deep, hummed as loud as he could while her ranting grew softer and then stopped. He took her back to her couch, where she fell in a heap, practically on top of Jank. She panted in exhaustion. Jank said, "This is a new man, Mother, a Visitor from the Bright World. His name is Jeremy. He's the one they made Prince."

"Oh!" she said. "Oh!" And then she laughed uproariously, hoarsely, and buried her head in the couch. When the couch extinguished her laughter, she became suddenly serious, turned to me, reached out her hand, though I was too far away to touch, and said, "I am sorry for being so hysterical when you came in. It's just that I remember things. I remember so many things that happened, and I even remember things that didn't happen." Her hand now stretched upward, and she looked toward the ceiling as if she were addressing me there. "Or that's what they try to tell me at least. 'No, Mother, it wasn't that way at all. It could have never happened that way.' And yet I remember it as vividly as if it was yesterday. But, 'No, Mother, you're just a senile old bat who's off your rocker, and the world doesn't work the way you think it does.'"

"Mother, you know no one ever—"

"Don't Mother me, sweetie. I get worse every day. I know that. But there are a few things I'm right about."

"Of course there are."

"Don't patronize me! I know there are."

Jank began to strum an instrument I had never seen before. It looked something like a ukelele, but it had a deeper, richer tone. Ona relaxed back into the couch at the sound of it. She said, "But Jank knows. Jank remembers things too, and he is not afraid of them. He remembers before the War, just like the crazy people, but he is not crazy. And he remembers the music we played then, but he is not afraid of it."

For a few minutes we listened to Jank's music, but then the woman sprang up and said, "Why don't you cover your ears, little prince? Aren't you the heir to my son? Aren't you afraid of the music too?"

"No, I'm not afraid of it."

"Don't you want to stamp it out like he does?"

"No."

"He is my son's prince and yet he doesn't want to stamp out the music. It sounds to me as if he's a liar from the pit of hell rather than a Visitor from God."

"Mother—"

"That should make him a good heir for my son, though. Was it lying that got him the job? Or does he know how to murder? Is that it, he's a murderer? Have you told him, Jank, that part of being prince will be that he has to murder his father, just as my son murdered his father? Tell him! It's a family tradition! Have murderers been provided for our new prince?"

"Mother, stop this please."

"He must have murderers. Why, they're more useful than servants! I'm afraid you'll have to tell him the other murderers have already been killed, but I'm sure he can find some of his own. Or maybe he'll just do the deed himself. Is that it?"

"Mother! We can't talk about this now. I have—"

"Oh!" The old woman put her hand over her mouth and smiled, as if she had accidentally let out a little secret. "Was our little prince not supposed to know how one Father-King succeeds another? Was he supposed to figure it out on his own and think himself quite original?"

"What's she talking about, Jank?" I asked.

"She believes Umbriel had his father assassinated and then made it look as if he died from natural causes."

"Is that true?"

"Probably. But let's not get into it now. Mother, your father is here to see you—"

"Not probably!" cried Ona. "Jank knows for a fact that it's true. And he's probably the only person besides me in the kingdom that's brave enough to mention it to you. And I'm a crazy woman. And the ones who did it are dead."

"Mother, your father is waiting to come in."

"My father."

"I didn't want to bring both of them in at once because I was afraid it would startle you. I'm going to bring him in now. Are you all right?"

"I look a mess."

"You look fine. I'm bringing him in now. You be good for him."

Jank left me with her while he went to the other room to get Tarius. She pulled her legs up against her face, curling herself into a tight ball, and swayed back and forth. By the time they came in she was swaying hard and making a high-pitched "hoo" sound, long and loud, on the same note.

When Tarius said, "Ona," she sat quiet for a moment, as if listening intently for a distant sound. As he got close to her she looked up and squinted to see if it was really her father. When the spark of recognition flashed within her, she bolted off the couch and ran toward the other room. Jank and Tarius both started after her, and when they did she wailed in fear. She put her hands straight out as if to stop them. They stood still. Backing up, crying, she knocked over a candle stand. I hurried to put out the candles that had fallen to the ground while Jank and Tarius ran to restrain her.

As soon as Jank had his arms around her, Tarius also reached her and knocked Jank aside. "I will take care of her," Tarius said. "Just leave us alone." He held her not from behind, as Jank always did, but put her head on his shoulder and drew her close as if to comfort her. In a moment she stopped fighting him, and the screaming stopped, giving way to mighty sobs. "Ona," he said, over and over. "Ona. My child."

"Will you leave us?" asked Tarius.

I moved toward the door, but Jank hesitated. "Brother, maybe I should stay to play—"

"No," said Tarius.

"She sometimes gets—"

"Please, Jank, I'll take care of her."

We sat in silence in the next room. Occasionally we heard a few words of an Emajian song Tarius sang, but otherwise we did not know what went on. Our agreement had been that he stay with her for an hour, far longer than any visitor had stayed with her in years, but Tarius stayed for nearly two hours.

Tarius charged out of the room in a rage, swinging the door back so hard it crashed against the wall. He said nothing to either of us. He headed for the door that led out of the residence. I ran to the door ahead of him and stood in his way.

"What are you going to do?" I asked.

"Get out of my way before I kill you right here on the spot for what you've done to my daughter."

"What are you talking about?"

"You saw her!"

"But I didn't—"

"You're one of them, Jeremy! You did it to her just as much as they did! You sicken me. How can you look at my girl and not realize the kind of people you've gotten involved with? How can you not see that Umbriel and his kind do nothing but sap the life out of others for their own benefit? How can you go along with this and even pretend that you are a man of God? Get out of my way. I can't stand the sight of you."

Tarius pushed past me and stormed out into the hall. Jank went after him, but I stood still. In the other room Ona wailed one high-pitched, painful note, held it until her breath ran out, and then was silent.

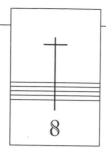

8

Tarius Arc went back immediately to his prison cell. He refused to discuss his decision with me or anyone else. The ambassadors from the Rock of Calad blamed Umbriel and said they had been tricked into believing Tarius Arc would be released. Umbriel was afraid his whole plan was unraveling before he could even get the Territory of Ur under control. He insisted that his aides hurry up their preparations for my trip. He said, "We know for a fact that the people on the Rock of Calad and in the Territory and even in Damonchok support you. We've investigated it. There's a sort of cult built up around you. Many of the people are Emajians, but we won't worry about that. We can use that to our advantage. You just go and let these governments see the crowds surround you and love you, and they won't dare back out of our agreement." I was to leave in just two days after Tarius Arc's meeting with Ona.

Tracian did not want me to leave. All afternoon we argued— the first time we had ever done so—about whether or not I should go. Like Jank, Tracian was worried about what would happen while I was gone. "Daddy never leaves," she said. "He has a beautiful home by the sea, but he almost never goes to it. When you leave is when people work against you behind your back. You've got enemies, Jeremy. You've got to be careful."

"I know that," I said. "But if I don't go, the whole agreement might unravel. I can't just sit here and let that happen. Besides, the whole idea of making me prince was so that I would rule the Territory of Ur. Eventually I'll have to move there permanently."

"Then wait till they build your palace. Wait till our army is so entrenched in the Territory and your own power is so firmly established that nothing can stop you."

"Those things will never happen unless I go and gain the people's confidence."

"I'm not worried about the people. I'm worried about Vanus and how he's trying to work against you. If you're not here to defend yourself, he could poison people's minds against you. And there's Bortius."

"What about him?"

"He blamed you for the fact that I broke off my relationship with him. He is a Councilor's son and he knows everybody. He's very vindictive. He's out to get you. And who knows how many others there are who are upset that an outsider suddenly has so much power."

"Why can't your father put a stop to these people?"

"Oh, Jeremy. You don't know how things work around here. That's why you've got to trust me and stay here. For now."

"I'm sorry. I have to go. If you're so worried, why don't you talk to your father?"

"He won't listen. He's more stubborn than you."

All afternoon Tracian pouted, harangued, reasoned, and begged until she finally became so angry with me that she walked out of my residence without a word of good-bye and told her servants she was not to be disturbed. I ate dinner that night alone.

———○———

I caught Jank crawling in my bedroom closet to hide just after dinner.

"Jank!" I called. His body whirled around and smacked hard against the door, his face more contorted in fear than I had ever seen it.

"Shut the door!" he whispered hoarsely.

I shut it and said, "I didn't mean to scare you."

"No! No. I'm getting too careless. I've never been caught up here. I didn't think you'd be here. I thought you were with Tracian."

"She's mad at me."

"Why?"

"She doesn't want me to take my trip to the Rock and the Territory and Damonchok. She's afraid Vanus and the others will try to sabotage me while I'm gone."

"She may be right, of course. I'm still worried about Pannip. Have you worked it out to get him moved up here?"

"It can't be done. Umbriel just doesn't like to switch servants around like that. He's suspicious about why I'm pushing for it so hard."

"Prince of the most powerful nation on earth and yet you can't choose your servants."

"I'm just trying to get through this the best I can, Jank. I never wanted to be involved in all this in the first place."

"I know. So what did you think of Ona?"

"I was amazed at how far gone she is. Does Umbriel know she's that bad?"

"Yes. But Umbriel's not too good when it comes to dealing with the women in his life. His wife is so addicted to vapors that she can hardly function, his mother is out of her mind, Shellan will probably follow in her footsteps, and Tracian—I won't even say anything about Tracian."

"But Umbriel seems very devoted to his mother in a way, doesn't he?"

"Yes. But he has destroyed her."

"Why? How has that happened?"

"I know you don't want to hear my explanation, but there is a rottenness in this place, Jeremy. It devours people from within. You're fighting on the wrong side."

I said nothing. I did not want to have that discussion again.

Jank said, "But Ona hasn't always been that bad. She's taken a turn for the worse lately. I'm worried about her. She can't go on like this much longer."

"Are you afraid she'll—"

"Die? Yes. And then that's the end of me too."

"No, Jank. I won't let it happen. I'll insist on taking you with me to the Territory of Ur."

"You can't even get Pannip moved upstairs."

"This is different."

"No, it's not. But let's not talk about it. I came up here to tell you something. I'm glad I don't have to wait for hours in that closet to do it. Have you talked to Dakin lately?"

"Not really. At the coronation party for just a little bit. Why?"

"I hear he's acting very strange. Hardly eats. Stays in his private office for hours on end. Sees no one. Miriaban is really worried about him. I'm not sure it has anything to do with you, but you might want to see him before you leave."

"I will."

"Take no chances, Jeremy. Tracian is right. I'm sure Vanus and others will try some tricks while you're gone. But you're traveling to the land of the music of God. Maybe there's still hope for you."

—————○—————

Before I had time to go down to check on Dakin, one of Tracian's servants brought a note from her asking me to come to her residence.

One of Tracian's attendants was waiting for me in the main hall. I followed the echo of her choppy steps as she led me through room after room to get to the one Tracian had chosen to receive me in. Every room we passed through blazed with globe light as if ready to receive hundreds of guests, but the rooms were all empty.

When the woman opened the double doors to the sitting room, I saw Tracian through a cloud of purple haze. She lay on a white couch bigger than a king-sized bed, dozens of cushions surrounding her. Around the couch were vases stuffed with flowers, not carefully arranged the way Miriaban's flowers always were, but crammed in, as many as would fit. The room smelled like vapors and flowers and perfume. She lifted her head from a pillow as I entered, and her hand reached up to motion the attendant away.

She sat up slowly, but before she could make an attempt to stand, I was beside the couch. "Sit down here with me, darling." Her voice was as hazy as the air.

I sat next to her and eased back into the cushions. She took my hand. "Just look at you," she said. "You're my darling shining prince." I held her close while the vapors filled my brain. We lay together silently for an hour or more. The vapors washed over us and filled us with the most amazing sense of satisfaction and well-being. When Tracian finally spoke, she said, "Don't go, Jeremy."

"I have to, honey. You know that. Let's not argue."

"I love you," she said.

"I love you too."

I had one last moment of clarity when I should have left, but I let it pass. Tracian brushed her fingers through my hair.

—◯—

I opened my eyes to a room cleared of vapors. I could feel that I had slept for a long time. I lay on my side beside Tracian, who was still asleep. I felt a hand on my shoulder and turned to see Tracian's attendant hovering over me. Startled, I sat straight up, waking Tracian.

"Get out of here!" Tracian screamed at the servant. "What's the matter with you!"

"I'm terribly sorry," said the servant, appearing not the least bit sorry. "I didn't want to come in, but your father insisted on having Prince Jeremy called. He needs to see him in one hour in the Dome."

"Get out of here!" snarled Tracian. The attendant bowed and left.

"What now?" I asked, quickly rearranging my clothes.

"Probably nothing," said Tracian, not at all alarmed. She lay sprawled on the couch and stared at the ceiling.

"Then why would he send somebody in here—like that—to call for me? What am I even *doing* here?"

She laughed and put her hand out to me. "Come here,

sweetie." I took her hand. "Daddy loves to do this kind of stuff. He likes to get control over people. Now he has something on you."

"Doesn't he control me already? Why this?"

"This is different. This is personal."

"This place is sick," I said, heading toward the door. "I wish I had never come here."

"Just one more thing, Jeremy. Come here."

"I'm in a hurry. I want to clean up before I see him."

"Come here, darling."

I went over and sat down next to her.

"I have an idea," she said.

"What?"

"I think we should get married."

—————⊖—————

I swirled in the hot water of my bathtub filled with my favorite soap. Four glasses of a fruit drink that helped quench the incredible thirst a night of vapors always caused were lined up at the side of the tub. I guzzled two of them and leaned back into the soothing water. The water lulled me into one of my most vivid dream-visions of Anne. In the vision I was lying beside Tracian just as I had been that morning; but instead of being awakened by her attendant, I opened my eyes to find Will hovered over me, bearded and brawny in his winter coat, smelling like cold and winter.

"What are you doing?" he demanded. "Anne is here. She's waiting for you just outside. Who is this girl? Anne is—"

Just then I saw Anne peer through the opening in the door and then disappear.

My servant's voice broke through the vision and shattered it. "I'm sorry, sir, but the Father-King demands to see you right away."

"All right. Send word that I just need to get dressed."

"He's here, sir."

"Here!"

"His servant told me the Father-King will see you in the sitting room next to your bedroom immediately."

"Don't I have time to get dressed first?"

"No, sir, I don't think so."

I had only a towel to wrap myself in. Standing in my bedroom was Umbriel's servant, who opened the door to the sitting room before I managed to find my robe and put it on. I did not recognize the woman who stood there at first, not just because her clothes were so subdued and she wore no hat, but because for the first time I saw her smile. It was Shellan.

"I hope I didn't catch you at an inconvenient time," she said.

I did not see the situation in the same humorous light that she did. Water from my hair dripped on the floor. A servant brought me a towel. Shellan asked her servant to shut the doors and leave us alone.

"I was told the Father-King wanted to see me," I said.

"No. That was a lie. I wanted to see you."

"Did you just want to embarrass me?"

"Are you embarrassed?"

"Yes."

"Go put some clothes on, then."

"Was there anything in particular you wanted to say to me?"

"Yes, there were several things in particular. But I'm not sure I want to say anything at all if you're going to be rude."

"You're the one who tricked me to get me here. Why didn't you just let me know you wanted to see me?"

"Would you have come? Have you been ordered not to come if I call?"

"I haven't been 'ordered' to do anything."

"Why do you think they never let me near you?"

"I don't have the slightest idea."

"Oh, come on now. I think you do. You surely listen to the palace gossip, don't you? Go ahead and tell me why they don't want me around you. I won't tell them you told. They don't listen to me anyway."

"All right. I think it's because you're considered eccentric. And it might have something to do with the fact that your—attitude—toward your father, and toward what we're trying to accomplish is—less than supportive."

"'Less than supportive'? That's a sweet little phrase. Did they teach you that one? 'Less than supportive.' The fact is I hate his guts, and I hate what he's trying to do to this country and the Emajians."

"He was planning to make you heir to his throne at one point. Do you want to be the heir?"

"Yes."

"Then you must be unhappy that your father named me prince."

"Don't get cocky, stepbrother. He didn't name you heir to the throne of Persus Am."

"No, but that's a possibility."

"Don't count on it. He thinks he's going to live forever. I wouldn't be surprised if he died without having named an heir. Or maybe he'll be overthrown first. Either way, don't let anyone fool you into thinking that I'm obsessed with becoming heir to the throne. I'm not like my sister. I wanted to be heir to reverse the crimes my father has committed. But there is more than one way to fight him."

"Then you don't believe in his goal of bringing peace and stability to the Territory of Ur?"

"Jeremy, in the palace of Persus Am words are just flowery containers made to hide the garbage inside them. My father's goals are not the same as the words he has taught you."

As she spoke, someone in the bedroom knocked on the door. "We're busy! Come back later!" shouted Shellan.

The voice in the bedroom said, "Shellan, let me in. I need to talk to you." It was Tracian.

I turned to open the door. Shellan grabbed my arm and whispered, "Wait! Just one more thing. I didn't come here to argue with you. I want to be your friend. I wanted to tell you there is one way I can help you that no one else can."

"What is it? We've got to let her in. She'll be furious."

"Yes, she certainly will." Shellan could not suppress a quick smile. "What I wanted to tell you was that your musical instrument has been rebuilt and I know where it is."

"What? I saw them demolish it."

"Yes, but they've put it back together. It works. They have played it."

Tracian pounded on the door.

"Why did they fix it?"

"They were looking for clues as to where you're from. Even though they made you prince, some of them still think you're an Emajian spy. They're trying to prove that your instrument is from the Rock of Calad."

"Can you let me see it?"

Tracian was yelling at Shellan.

"Yes, I can. But only if you keep it strictly between us. If you tell Tracian or anyone else, it's off. Nobody wants you to know about it. I'll deny the whole thing if you tell anyone."

"All right. We have to let her in now. You will get back to me soon? I leave tomorrow."

"Yes."

I opened the door, and Tracian was leaning against it so heavily she practically fell inside. Her lips were thin with anger. Her pale face and the splotches of red on her neck, signs that had become familiar to me, also displayed her rage, but I concentrated on that tight sliver of lips, like rubber bands that were stretched to the breaking point. She said nothing for a moment.

Shellan could barely restrain from smiling.

Tracian said, "I see now why you didn't want to open the door for me."

"Your sister wanted to speak to me, Tracian. She just got here a few minutes ago."

"Well, you certainly wouldn't want to get dressed before you talked to her."

"I was taking a bath when the servant came. He said your father wanted to see me. I thought it was an emergency."

"But the emergency was my sister."

Shellan laughed. "It sounds a little far-fetched to me too, Trace. But really, hon, no harm's been done. What do you need?"

"I came to talk to Jeremy."

"Well, then, I'll be off. Nice to see you, brother. Sister."

Shellan nodded to us both and left.

Tracian's anger had not subsided. She kept her voice barely under control. "Don't ever see my sister behind my back. That is one thing I cannot tolerate."

"She tricked me. She sent the servant to your room this morning. Your father didn't want to see me at all."

"Why wouldn't you let me in when I knocked?"

"We—she grabbed my arm and was still talking. I let you in."

"What was she talking about?"

"Nothing. Just political stuff. The Territory of Ur."

"I am so sick of living with liars!" screamed Tracian. "You make me sick."

She stomped away and slammed the door behind her. I went back to the swirling hot water.

———⊖———

Miriaban looked regal and enormous in a blue gown, her stature emphasized by the cylindrical pile of gray hair on top of her head. She waited for me in the garden.

"Just look at you!" she said. "I remember how skinny you were the first time I saw you when Dari brought you out of prison. Now you look so handsome."

"Thank you, Miri. And you are stunning as usual."

"Oh, they've taught you how to flatter old women too. How delightful. Sit down and let's talk. I was so glad to get your note saying you were coming down. I figured they had you so busy running the government that I wouldn't get to see you much anymore."

"You might think so, but really I don't have much to do with it. They just haul me out for public ceremonies and that kind of thing."

"Well, enjoy it," she said, putting her hand on my arm as she used to do. "At least this way they can't blame you if things go wrong."

"Who knows? Maybe they made me prince just so they *could* blame me if things go wrong."

"Oh my. What a shocking thought. You're getting far too cynical, Jeremy."

"But you don't deny the possibility."

"I would like to remain diplomatically noncommittal on the subject of the motives of the politicians of this country."

"Well, I didn't come to talk about politics, anyway. How is Dakin doing these days? I haven't seen him lately."

"Hardly anybody sees him. I'm very worried about him. He leaves the house only to do the things that are absolutely required of him, and then he spends the rest of the time here in his study. Not his public office—he hardly ever goes there—but his study where he keeps all the pictures and books and files and things from before the War. He has trouble sleeping at night—sometimes he gets up and wanders down to that study. I don't know what he's doing. He looks through all these old papers all the time. When I ask him, he just says he's doing research. He used to tell me all about his work. It's always been that way between us. But now he keeps to himself. He's losing weight. He almost never eats."

"Can I see him?"

"He's down in his study right now. He won't let anyone disturb him in there. I could send him a message you want to see him."

"Why don't you take me there and see if he'll let me in. I don't have much time left. I leave for the Territory of Ur tomorrow."

"We could give it a try. After all, you're the prince. You're one of the few people who outranks him. But if he lets you in, you'd be the first."

Miri took me to Dakin's study and asked me to wait outside while she went in to talk to him. In just a few minutes she came back out and said, "He wants to see you. He didn't hesitate at all. This is a good sign."

The room was windowless and not half the size of Dakin's public office. Along one wall was a worktable with a chair behind it. That was the only furniture in the room. Three of the four walls were covered floor-to-ceiling with shelves crammed with books, folders, and loose sheaves of paper. Some wooden boxes were scattered on the floor. Crowded on the wall behind the worktable were shadow pictures in battered old frames. Several of them contained the image of a young and self-assured Dakin, a stark

contrast to the shriveled old man who stood before me needlessly
straightening his shirt and then curling the hair at the back of his
neck around one finger.

"Come on in, Jeremy. I'm sorry I don't have a chair for you.
You can use my chair. No one ever comes in here, so I never need
more than one chair, and hardly more than that will fit."

"That's all right. If you don't mind I'll just sit here on top of
your table. Will it hold me?"

"Oh yes. Sit right down. It's from before the War, when
everything was made to last forever. Most everything you see in
here is from before the War. See these globes?" He pointed to two
lights on gold stands at opposite ends of the table. "These lights
have been burning since many years before the War. I'd be willing
to bet that almost all of these globes that survived the destruction
of the War are still burning. They last much longer than the new
kinds of globes made in the factories. But they take much longer
to make."

"Who are these people in the pictures? I didn't even know
they had shadow pictures back then."

"Of course! Tarius Arc helped invent them." Pointing to one
photo he said, "There's Miri and me not long after we were
married."

"You were a good-looking couple." Next to this picture was
one that showed two couples standing side by side. There was
Dakin, Miriaban, Tarius Arc, and a woman I had never seen.
"There's Tarius Arc," I said.

"Yes. We've all aged some, haven't we."

"Is that his wife?"

"Yes. As sweet a woman as ever lived. Got caught up in the
Emajian movement. Followed Emajus out to the desert and died.
But you've heard all about that. It's hard to believe she's the
grandmother of Umbriel, isn't it? Who ever could have predicted
how things have turned out? Who ever could have looked at the
two young couples in that picture and foretold all the things that
would happen to them?"

Dakin sat down and ran both hands through his hair.

"How have you been, Dakin?"

"I have not been well, as I'm sure Miri must have told you. Did she call you down here to check on me?"

"No. It was my idea. What are you doing in here?"

"I'm not sure, really, but I think I've been reading about you."

"What do you mean?"

"I've been going through old Emajian songs written at the time of the War. It's my specialty. Emajian propaganda. That's what we call it. To the Emajians these things are prophecy. They're part of Emajian holy scripture. By now you know that the most famous song, written by the prophet Jolanan, one of Emajus's closest followers and one of His best friends, says that a servant of the Lord will be sent one day, when the people's salvation has been accomplished, and that servant will bring the Lord's people back from the mythical Caladria, where Emajus took them."

"And the Emajians hope that person is me, and you think so too?"

"Well, there's no proof of it in that song. There's not much evidence to say *who* it will be. And besides, you claim you're not an Emajian."

"Right. And I don't have the vaguest idea where Caladria is. I've been told it doesn't exist, because where the Emajians think it is is a desert, and even if it existed, there couldn't be any people there, because you found the Emajians' skeletons in the desert."

"Right you are. That is certainly our version of things."

"You saw the skeletons yourself."

"Indeed I did. But the Emajians don't believe our skeletons and they don't believe their friends died and they don't believe Caladria is a desert. But none of that proves anything. So I've been going back through some of the older, almost forgotten songs from the immediate post-War era to see about this prophet. The term *prophet* is never used, first of all. But the term *servant of the Lord* is used many times, and even in Jolanan's Song, that's the term that's used. Now it's always been assumed that different songs were talking about different people, and in some cases we know that's true, because 'servant of the Lord' referred to specific persons alive during the time of Emajus. But what if these things are also prophecy, and what if they all refer to that same person?

We've got one song here that said the servant of the Lord was 'Shrouded in the Light of the Lord God/ And spoke with His voice./ Angels hovered about him/ They joined in his praise.' How does that compare to the night of your arrival?

"And here's one that tells about the servant of the Lord being imprisoned, and his song being trampled underfoot, and the servant being prepared for slaughter. Exactly what happened to you. And there are scattered references in a number of songs to the servant of the Lord wearing the robes of his enemy and sitting in his house of splendor and such things as that. The Emajians have always assumed that would happen *after* Emajus returns, but it could refer to what's happening to you now."

I said, "But to believe all that you'd have to believe in Emajianism."

"Yes."

"Are you saying you believe in it?"

"I would be executed if I said that. I am a scholar. I am talking to you about the Emajian songs."

"But do you believe it? Do you think I'm this 'servant of the Lord'?"

"My only answer can be no. But many things trouble me. Many of the scriptures you translated sound much like Emajus. Things about love, forgiveness, the bread of life, the light of the world, the salt of the earth, the vine and the branches. All those are phrases that Emajus liked to use."

"But couldn't many religions share those concepts?"

"Perhaps."

"Why are you telling me these things?"

"The Emajians will look at these songs as I have eventually. They may have already done so. They may confront you with it. You should be ready to answer them. You need to decide what you're going to do. Everybody wants to use you for their own benefit."

"But you weren't doing all this research just to warn me, were you?"

"No. I am searching for reasons of my own."

"Miri is very worried about you."

"No one need be worried about me. Not Miri. Not you. I am an old man with few choices left to make. You still have many decisions confronting you. If there's anyone you should be worried about, it's yourself."

———⊖———

Tracian punished me that night by refusing to see me. She left the palace and went to the theater with some friends. I hoped that Shellan would use Tracian's absence as an opportunity to take me to see my guitar, but she did not come until late at night. Because I was to leave the next day, I spent a good part of the evening going over my itinerary with Hamlin and directing the servants in packing my things. Shellan came so late that I had already gone to bed and given up on her. She woke me up herself rather than sending a servant in.

"Shouldn't we do this tomorrow?" I asked. "How can we get away with roaming through the palace at this time of night?"

"I took care of that for you. I brought your instrument to you."

"You did? Where is it?"

"It's out there hidden in a large jewelry case. But we can't bring it in here. We don't want the servants to hear the instrument or even see it. Is there a part of your residence where we can go to be alone?

"Let's see. There's a room they're going to turn into a rogno court. It has only one small door. The walls are thick."

We went to the unfinished rogno court. Shellan got the servants to stay put by telling them a few more cases would be coming soon. If anyone (such as Tracian) found out that Shellan had been there with a jewelry case, my explanation would be that in the morning Shellan had promised to let me borrow some of the jewels for my jacket that her grandfather, Umbriel I, had left her at his death.

The guitar was absolutely flawless, even better than it was before they smashed it, the wood perfectly shaped and polished, the strings made of a slightly different material but producing the same sound as before. I played slowly at first, my fingers getting used to the feel of it again. I began to play the song that I had played—or that had been played through me—on the night of my arrival. This song had nearly driven me crazy in my dream-visions, and as each note hit my ears I felt surges of relief and joy. What pleasure it was to feel this sound wrapping itself all around me! The music seemed to multiply, each note rising straight up and bursting outward in a flourish. It was not like music at home, where the sound is heard and then is gone. Instead, the notes took on an energy of their own and weaved in and out of the music I played. It's almost impossible to describe this, but the music carried not just sound but *meaning*, as if it were a language beyond words with which God Himself were penetrating my spirit.

On and on I played, for how long I don't really know. A few times the light leapt from the guitar as it had done on the night of my arrival, but mostly there was just sound and spirit. For a time I lost track of all reality except the music. Finally I glanced over to see Shellan crumpled up in the corner of the room. She had her head down and her ears covered. I stopped playing. It took several minutes for the music to stop.

When it stopped, Shellan stood up but leaned hard against the wall. She was pale. She lifted her hands to her face. Her fingers trembled.

"Shellan, will you be all right? I didn't know you would have such a reaction."

"It's all right. I am not opposed to the music philosophically. But physically—only true Emajians can—"

"Why don't you come over and sit in this chair?" I said, leading her across the room. She collapsed in the chair and tried to recover her breath, which seemed to have been knocked out of her.

When she was breathing normally again, I asked her, "If this is so painful for you, why did you bring this instrument here for me to play?"

"Because I want to stop you if I can from becoming like my sister and my father."

"And what are they like?"

"Please listen to me, Jeremy. I do not say this lightly. I was once in your position. I once hoped I could work with my father without losing my integrity. But it can't be done. You can only be his enemy. You can only be like Tarius Arc, and like the other Visitors before you, who sacrificed their lives. Otherwise he will twist and pervert you and make you do things you never dreamed you would do. And he'll make you smile about it and say words that justify it."

"What will he get me to do?"

"He'll get you to betray the people of the Rock of Calad, crush Emajianism in the Territory of Ur, crush the Rock, eventually overthrow Damonchok, and finally push into Wilmoroth. His appetite for power knows no bounds. Neither does the ambition of the men around him. They won't let him stop until he has done those things, and if he does try to stop, they will replace him. He is vulnerable. He is afraid. The only way he can stay in power is to keep conquering. These are the things I learned when I was educating myself to become his heir. These things and many other ugly things. He killed his father. I know it for a fact. His other maneuverings have been more subtle, but just as deadly. Look at my mother. Look at my grandmother. He's destroyed them both. *He* did it to them. Look at my sister. At first she thought she could use you to score points with my father. Then you one-upped her by being named prince. Now she wants to trick you into marrying her so that her victory over me is complete and irreversible."

I stayed quiet for a moment.

Shellan said, "You don't have to answer. You owe me nothing. You have your own decision to make. You cannot play music like I just heard and be the son of my father. Sooner or later, this will all come crashing down."

9

I left Persus Am the following night. We traveled at night because the military men in charge of escorting me thought we would attract less attention from onlookers or terrorists. The announcement of my trip had been temporarily withheld from the informationals for the same reason. Before I left I spent two unpleasant hours with Tracian listening to her final appeals about why I should not go. I had little patience with her. After my incredible encounter with the music the night before, I felt guilty about all my entanglements in Persus Am. I felt like a traitor to Tarius Arc, to Jank, to Shellan, to myself, and to the Spirit in the music. My relationship with Tracian seemed dirty and cheap, though I must admit that at the same time I felt attracted to her and close to her and I did not want to lose her. I felt manipulated by Umbriel, but at the same time I knew resigning my position would have meant death. This trip was a welcome escape, and I was eager to go.

Hamlin drilled me over and over about what I was and was not to say to the officials I met in Damonchok and on the Rock of Calad. The agreements that had been made dealt not only with the status of the Territory of Ur but also with very detailed aspects of trade between Persus Am and the Rock. For many years Persus Am had boycotted trade with the Rock because it was an Emajian nation, and the boycott had made life on the Rock rather difficult economically. Under the new agreement trade would open up considerably, but not completely. I had to master all these details. Another part of my mission was to persuade the reluctant Damonchokians to sign on to the plan, in hopes of avoiding any military confrontation in the Territory. In exchange for Damonchokian cooperation in the Territory, Persus Am would agree to send its military to help secure the border between Damonchok and Wilmoroth. Wars between Wilmorothian tribes, which apparently were almost unceasing, had been known to spill over into Damonchok, where entire villages had been ransacked. Persus Am was thought to have influence over these tribes. I was assured that Damonchok would believe me when I told them Persus Am could bring peace to the Wilmorothian border.

My main objective, however, was not to rehash the details of the agreement, which had been interminably discussed among the government officials. My objective was to show the governments of Damonchok and the Rock of Calad that I had tremendous support among their people. Umbriel wanted them to see the kinds of cheering crowds that had greeted me in the stadium on Coronation Day. I was said to be a cult hero already in the Territory of Ur and in much of Damonchok, where young people pestered their parents to buy them Coronation Day dolls in my likeness and where they cut my pictures out of the informationals and hung them up on their walls. Umbriel hoped this enthusiasm would translate into huge crowds at my rallies that would persuade the reluctant governments that the wrath of the people would be too great to risk turning against me.

The landscape of Persus Am was barren. I could understand Umbriel's desire to expand his kingdom into more fertile lands. As we rattled along the bumpy roads hour after hour, I often fell asleep, or partially asleep. During these times I was again assaulted by visions of Anne, sharp images of her standing just out of reach. Sometimes she stood in familiar places, like her grassy front lawn. I wanted to run to her, but I could not move any closer. Other times I would see Will first, and he would tell me she was just in the other room, or just outside, waiting for me. Usually I would catch a glimpse of her, but each time she faded into a fuzzy cloud of black and white, and I woke up.

I could hardly wait to get to the Rock of Calad, where the other Visitor was rumored to be. I prayed desperately that the Visitor would be Anne, that I would finally see her again in the flesh.

Persus Am is separated from the Territory of Ur by a range of mountains. At one point along this range, in the southern part of Persus Am, is a gorge that cuts through the mountains, though even that dip in the mountains is quite a climb from the flatlands of Persus Am. The only road between the two nations was built at this point, and all travelers had to pass through government checkpoints to go from one country to the other. A line of more than a hundred people waited at the checkpoint on the Amian side of the mountain. Our group, which was made to look like a purely military convoy in order not to attract attention—I even wore a military uniform—was quickly allowed through that crowd and through the checkpoint. Then we made our way through the gorge, with mountain cliffs towering magnificently on either side of us. The road was rough and sometimes frighteningly narrow, but I was glad for the change of scenery. Gone was the tan-colored flatland with only an occasional scrawny bush to break the monotony. Here was a scene of majesty, the cliffs looming above us so high that it seemed at any moment each side would collapse and erase the little gap that was our road.

As we reached the other side of the mountain, the forests of the Territory of Ur came into view. It was a magnificent sight. Mile after mile of majestic trees covered the hills and valleys. An occasional farm or village was carved out of part of the forest. "This is amazing!" I said to Hamlin. "I can't believe this beautiful place is full of terrorists and poverty and all the other things I've been sent here to solve."

"The view is deceiving from here. It's every bit as bad down there as you've been told. Not that it isn't beautiful. It is. That's one reason everybody wants it."

After we went through the checkpoint at the bottom of the mountain, we plunged into the forest. For the first time since we had left the palace, I felt lighthearted. "Let's get out and walk around a little bit, Hamlin."

"But, sir, they're expecting us in Ofeen at—"

"I know. I just mean a few minutes. Just to walk among the trees. This reminds me of where I'm from. This is better than your desert, don't you think? When was the last time you walked through the woods and heard the leaves blowing? When was the last time you stood in the woods and looked up to see the sun filtering through the leaves?"

"Never, sir, but we're very concerned about your safety—"

"Never? You've never walked through the woods?"

"No, sir. I've been to the Territory, but we never go outside the protected buildings. There are terrorists out here who don't believe Amians are fit to live. It's very dangerous to—"

"Yes, I know. But just for a few minutes. We won't go very far. The soldiers might enjoy it too. I need some fresh air."

"Sir—"

"I order it to be done."

Hamlin pulled the cord, and the driver stopped. Within moments, the whole caravan stopped. We got out, and Hamlin told the military commander what I wanted to do. "Tell them to stay here," I said. "I don't want a crowd."

As I stepped off the road and walked among the trees, my spirits soared out of all proportion to the small pleasure I was enjoying. More than anything else I had seen, the woods triggered memories of home, which, except for my visions of Anne, had grown frighteningly dim. I remembered the sight of the trees clipping past me on the highway as I headed toward work. I remembered skiing past the trees with Will. I remembered my last night with Anne, skating on the lake surrounded by trees. I remembered the trees that had grown so large they brooded over my parents' home. The memories came in short bursts, like someone flashing a picture in front of my face and then taking it away. I could not concentrate on the memories for long. The images faded into the real woods that were before me.

As we walked farther into the woods, Hamlin complained that his clothes were getting snagged with thorns. I looked up to see the sun lighting up the leaves, a sight I always loved. When we were far enough in so that we could no longer see the road, I stopped and sat down against the trunk of a tree, pulling a leaf from a branch and running my hands over it. Many of the trees in this world had leaves that were much bigger than those at home. They gave the forest a primeval look.

"Sit down, Hamlin. Enjoy this." This blonde-headed, well-dressed college boy looked out of place in a forest. He looked as if he would feel more comfortable on the tennis (or rogno) court with his rich friends or in a fancy restaurant eating delicacies nobody else had even heard of. Still, I was determined to teach him this pleasure.

"Sit down there and lean your head back against a tree trunk, and for heaven's sake, relax."

"Bugs are crawling all over the place."

"They won't hurt you."

He sat down and leaned warily against the tree.

"Now breathe it all in. Look up at the leaves. Watch how the sun filters in. Watch how it lights up all the leaves at the top. When I was a kid, we used to start somewhere and try to count the leaves. You can never do it, of course, but it makes you realize how many there are. It makes you realize how marvelous this is."

Hamlin looked at the leaves, trying to enjoy it, and for several minutes we were silent.

"Listen, Hamlin."

"What?"

"Just listen. Listen for every sound you hear. That's part of it. Try to figure out what every sound is. Can you hear the birds? How many different kinds are there? Can you name them? They're all new to me, but you must recognize some of them. Can you hear the other animals? Can you hear the wind as it touches each leaf?"

Hamlin tried to listen. He leaned back and tried to relax, though he did so in a studied way, like a schoolboy trying to learn to "appreciate" a piece of abstract art that means nothing to him. He picked up a twig and broke it apart. I wanted to close my eyes and take a nap with the forest all around me, but I knew Hamlin would not have the patience to stay for more than a few minutes.

He said, "Just think, sir, you're now the ruler over this forest for as far as your eyes can see. This place is yours."

"It seems hard to believe, doesn't it? Do you really think things will ever fall into place enough so I can actually lead?"

"Yes, I do. Events have moved faster since you got here than they had for years. I think we're just working out the details now."

"I hope you're right. I do like it here. This is better than any palace, don't you think? We used to love to just walk and walk and walk through the forest. We should go hiking while we're in Damonchok, Hamlin. You don't know what you've been missing."

"It is beautiful. They'll be wondering what's keeping us, sir."

"I know. I guess we'll leave."

On our way to the Amian fortress we saw not only forests but also farms that stretched for acres and acres. I saw farmers in some of these fields standing behind their camucks and gripping in their hands the plows that cut through the dark soil. I saw houses made of real wood, built sturdy and square, unlike the chaotically shaped plaster buildings so common in the Utturies. I saw men walking along the road wearing their wide brimmed hats and brown coats with big buttons, a Damonchokian style that was common in the Territory of Ur. Most women wore scarves if they were working outside, but when they were relaxing or just walking along the road they took them off and let their hair flow freely. Many of them wore slacks that looked just like the men's, and if they wore a dress it was of a simple cut, always ankle-length and long sleeved. Whereas the women of Persus Am had great variety in colors and styles of clothes, these women showed little variation in their clothes or hairstyles.

"Why do they dress so much alike?" I asked Hamlin.

"I don't know. They have funny ideas about that sort of thing. I've heard if it gets too flashy, people accuse them of trying to be too Amian, which means to them the women are trying to show off or be snooty. They're very suspicious of anything that's too Amian. They like to come to Persus Am once a year to blow their money in our shops and hotels and to gawk at us and make their sacrifice in the Temple, but they don't want to be like us. I don't mean to give you a bad impression, but there's still a lot of suspicion and bigotry."

"I see."

"It's just like those farmers. Did you see them with those plows? We have machines we could sell them that would make their job much easier. But some of those guys won't buy them just to spite us. And some of them are Emajians, so they're not allowed to buy from us."

"Even Emajians here in the Territory aren't allowed to buy farm equipment? I thought that was only on the Rock of Calad."

"No. Trade is very closely controlled in the Amian sector of the Territory. We can't condone Emajianism in any way. It's what has brought us most of the problems we're facing now. Anyone caught selling restricted items to an Emajian faces jail."

"But that's going to loosen up under our new agreement, right?"

"Yes. Just like it will in the Rock of Calad."

"Umbriel made the Territory sound so horrible—poverty-stricken, full of violence—to me it looks pretty peaceful."

"It's really along the borders of the sectors that it gets bad. We're in the middle of Amian sector. Along the borders and in the bigger towns there's more violence and poverty. But occasionally you get terrorists even here. We're going to keep you away from the really bad parts. It's too dangerous."

———◯———

Government officials from the Rock of Calad and Damonchok waited for us at the Amian fortress near Ofeen. They were to follow us to most of the rallies because they were in fact our intended audience. The rallies started the next day, and we had scheduled one a day for six days as we worked our way north to Damonchok.

The rallies took place at local fairgrounds, which the people made use of when times were peaceful enough. An army of Amian planners had arrived a few days ahead of us to plan each rally with the local people. To attract as big a crowd as possible, they made each rally an all-day extravaganza, with food, contests, gifts, acrobats, magicians, and other entertainment. Mid-afternoon, when the crowd was at its largest, I appeared, ready to receive the adulation of the well-fed, happy audience. The first two rallies, which were in the Amian sector of the Territory, went perfectly according to plan. There were no terrorist attacks of any kind, which was unusual for any public event in the Territory of Ur. The Damonchokian and Caladan officials, most of whom had not been able to attend my coronation, were amazed by the size and enthusiasm of the crowds. In private discussions they seemed optimistic that stability might finally come to the Territory. To Hamlin I said, "I think we're winning them over. I don't sense any opposition at all."

He answered, "It's easy for them to talk this way now. The real test is what happens when they go home and vote on our plan and start to put it into practice. We've heard kind words for years. We need to see action. But you're doing well. Let's just keep going."

On the third day, when we left the Amian sector of the Territory and entered the sector loosely controlled by Damonchok, the rally took a much different turn from what we had expected. Several thousand more people than we had anticipated showed up, overwhelming not only the fairground facilities but also the members of the Damonchokian army who were in charge of controlling them. It took us nearly an hour to get my car through the crowds to the platform. The Amian army, which had strictly controlled the first two rallies, was allowed to bring only a few dozen soldiers to this event because we were in the Damonchokian sector. Hamlin, normally dignified and cool, spent much of the day nagging the Damonchokian officials about security arrangements that were not up to his expectations.

The crowd roared and cheered from the moment the government officials and I walked onto the platform. The public address system was even worse here than the others I had used—they were all bad—so the people in the crowd who could hear my speech at all heard mostly a metallic squeak. When I was about halfway through the text, I noticed that in the midst of the crowd a group of young men, standing on barrels or something, were unfurling a huge banner, and just beneath that banner was another, held by a group on the ground. The top banner read *Child of Emajus*, and the one underneath it said *Come to Set Us Free*. These were lines of a well-known Emajian song. The words were forbidden, of course, in Persus Am, and the Damonchokians had agreed to keep all mention of Emajus out of the rallies while the Amians were present. Much of the crowd turned their attention from me, whom they could barely hear anyway, to the banners, and many of them cheered. I turned for a moment to see the reaction of the officials behind me. Hamlin had lost all decorum and was openly shouting at the Damonchokian official in charge of the rally. The man said he had tried to control the Emajians, but the crowd was so large and chaotic that the soldiers couldn't arrest every person who held up a banner. I saw no indication the soldiers were even trying.

As I continued my speech, two more banners appeared, emblazoned with the words *Child of Emajus, Come to Set Us Free*. Then in the distance I heard what sounded like a trumpet. I looked in the direction of the sound and spotted the man who played it. Just as I found him in the crowd, five or six other instruments appeared around him. People had hidden them under cloaks or in bags. They joined in the man's song, and by this time the music was too loud to ignore. Many people in the crowd fled as soon as they heard the first notes, creating chaos for a few minutes. But others began to clap with the music, and many began to sing. Instruments sprang up all over the crowd, from trumpets to stringed instruments to drums and tambourines. The Damonchokian soldiers stood at the edge of the crowd and did nothing. I turned to see Hamlin's reaction, but he had left the platform to try to find my car, which was nowhere in sight. No one in charge of the rally remained on the platform; in fact, I did not know where they had gone. I stopped my speech and listened to the singing. The song, once it caught on, rose strong and clear over all other noises. Music-starved as I was, I felt a thrilling surge as I heard the singing and the clapping and saw the people sway back in forth in joy. It was all I could do to keep from joining in. The crowd was not content to see me stand by and watch. People crowded along the edge of the platform to scream, "Sing with us! Sing! Sing!" I knew that to do so would be a crime, especially since the chorus of that particular song said, "Emajus reigns/ Sweet Lord of our lives/ Emajus reigns/ Praise His name/ Praise His name."

I did not sing, but not knowing whether clapping was exactly against the law, I finally got so caught up in the music that I stood at the edge of the platform and clapped to the rhythm, which encouraged the crowd to sing with even greater intensity. It was a joyous moment. The music in this world was more penetrating than any music I had ever known at home, and hearing it multiplied by hundreds upon hundreds of voices was overwhelming. Later I was told that I began to sing as well as clap, but I do not remember whether I did or not. I just remember that one second I glanced to see my car beside the platform, and the next second I was grabbed by three Amian soldiers, dragged off the stage, and thrown into my car.

In the chaos Hamlin did not end up in the same car that I rode in. With me was Eornus, one of the ambassadors from the Rock of Calad who had been going with us from rally to rally. He was beside himself with happiness as we rode past the singing crowd. He pulled the curtain aside and waved at them, shrieking, "Whoo! Whoo!" every so often. When we finally got beyond the crowd and onto the open road, Eornus shook my hand and thanked me for showing support for the Emajians. "You have taken a stand today that could turn the world upside down," he said.

That was exactly what I did not want to do.

Hamlin rode back to the Damonchokian fortress in a wagon made for hauling barricades. He arrived just moments after we did, and we arrived just moments after the Damonchokian officials. When Hamlin crawled off the wagon he unleashed his fury on the Damonchokians, screaming about the incompetence of their soldiers in the face of the crowd's disruption and raging about how we had been tricked into attending an Emajian worship service instead of a rally for the new ruler of the Territory. The Damonchokians listened in silence.

Finally, the man in charge, whose name was Petralkis and who was dressed in the somber Damonchokian brown suit and wide-brimmed hat, calmly said, "We did not trick you, Mr.

Hamlin. We did not plan it this way. We are not believers in Emajus, as you know. But how can we possibly know whether someone is going to hold up a banner at a rally? What are we supposed to do, kill them for it? Is that how the Amians would handle such things?"

"The Amians would never have let things get to that point in the first place. How did those banners get inside the fairgrounds? How did those instruments get there? What were your soldiers doing?"

"Damonchok is not Persus Am, sir. We do not bash someone's brains in just because they happen to think a thought that is different from our own."

—◯—

We communicated with Persus Am by way of a crude telegraph system that linked many parts of the Known World. There was no direct link from Persus Am to where we were. Messages were relayed from station to station, and the system often broke down. It normally took nearly a day for a message to reach the Territory of Ur from the palace, unless the terrorists had destroyed the lines, in which case it took longer. When we got back from the rally, some day-old messages from Persus Am were waiting for us.

Hamlin walked into my room and plopped down in a chair, the messages in his hands. "More bad news," he said. "Umbriel's mother, Ona, has died."

"Oh no!" Immediately I thought of Jank. I wondered what danger he might be in. It was a question I could not ask, since I was not even supposed to know him. "What else did they tell us about it?"

"Not much. It says, 'Gossip and uncertainty swirling about.'"

"What does that mean?"

"I have no idea. They normally don't like to get into details in these messages because too many people have access to them along the way."

"Gossip and uncertainty. Is that all?"

"It says, 'Return as soon as mission complete.' I think Ona's death might be just the excuse we need to return now. I'm sure the

Father-King will plan an elaborate funeral to honor her. It's natural for us to be there. The news will be in all the informationals. People will expect us to be there. I just don't see how we can continue with these rallies after what happened today."

"I don't see why you're reacting so negatively to what happened today. The people had a great time. They turned out in record numbers. They loved me. Isn't that what these public appearances are all about?"

"Prince Jeremy, do you realize you broke Amian law today by joining in that music? You have humiliated the Father-King. He'll be furious."

"I am to be the ruler of the Territory of Ur. That Territory includes a significant number of Emajians, who will also be my people. The agreement that put me in charge of this Territory is between both Emajians and non-Emajians. No harm was done today."

"Well, you'll just have to try to tell that to the Father-King yourself. I don't know what to tell him. This rally has been a disaster, and he'll be in a rage. If I may give you one piece of advice, I wouldn't say to him what you just said to me."

"I agree with you that it's time for us to go back."

"Good. We'll leave in the morning."

More bad news awaited us at one of our stops on the way back to Persus Am. Somehow underground Emajian information-als in the Utturies and in Damonchok had gotten hold of my scripture translations and had published them. They presented them as being "the words and deeds of Emajus in the land of Jeremy, the Visitor from God." Hamlin got a copy of one of the informationals and read parts of it to me. In every place where *Jesus* should have appeared, they had written *Emajus*.

"Those are my scriptures," I said. "But I never wrote *Emajus*. They made that up themselves."

"Well, the stuff sounds awfully Emajian to me," said Hamlin. "Let me ask you something, sir. The first thing they're going to want to know when we get back is, did you give those scriptures to the Emajians?"

"No! I don't even have copies of them."

"Only Dakin had copies?"

"I don't know who had copies."

"I understand that you want to protect him, sir, but if he is guilty of helping the Emajians, by now they have certainly found it out."

"Well, I just don't know if Dakin was the only one. Many other people were interested in those scriptures. They were the very reason I was not executed, so that I could translate them. Dakin could have given copies to many different people. Why would Dakin have done it? I don't believe it." I thought about Jank. Would he have done it?

—◯—

The only person I looked forward to seeing when I got back to the palace was Tracian. Despite our difficulties, I missed her, and I hoped she would be waiting to welcome me when I arrived.

She wasn't. Instead, when our caravan pulled into the palace grounds, only some servants and soldiers waited in the courtyard. When I stepped out of the car, a servant that I recognized as one of Dakin's came up to me, bowed, and said, "Prince Jeremy, Councilor Dakin asked me to tell you that he wishes to see you as soon as you arrive. A servant has gone to fetch him. If you please, he would like you to wait here for him."

"I will."

But before Dakin got back, a dozen or so soldiers, led by one of the top generals, named Borgard, came out of the palace and approached me. Borgard said, "Welcome home, Prince Jeremy! The Father-King asked me to apologize for not greeting you himself, but he has been quite busy and distraught, with the death of his mother and other issues weighing on his mind. He sent me to escort you upstairs."

"Why you? Why with all these soldiers?"

"His other aides are quite busy, sir."

"Well, thank you, but Hamlin and I know quite well how to find our way to the Dome. You are dismissed, General."

"But, sir, the Father-King insisted—"

"And I am telling you I don't need an escort. I am not going to be led through the palace like some prisoner. Now go. I've had a long trip."

"I assure you, sir, we are here strictly for the sake of courtesy and protection."

Hamlin said, "Why don't we just walk up with them, Prince?"

At that moment Dakin came running out to the courtyard.

"Hello, Dakin! I am glad to see you."

"Welcome, home, Jeremy." Dakin did not smile. He looked thinner than ever, his cheeks sunken, the skin under his eyes dark and puffy. His voice was thin. He said, "I see that someone already has come to greet you."

"Yes, but I was just sending them away. I'd enjoy walking up with you if you're headed in that direction. And maybe we can stop off at your place for a few minutes for a cool drink with Miriaban."

"Splendid. She would love to see you."

"Fine. Gentlemen, thank you, but I will find my own way to the Father-King shortly. Please tell him."

The general cleared his throat and said, "Prince, I am afraid we have received direct orders from the Father-King to escort you to him as soon as you got here. I am afraid we'll have to carry out those orders."

Dakin, who had already turned toward the palace, wheeled back around, his frail body shaking with anger, and said, "General Borgard, it has come to my attention that we're going to need some good military commanders to cover the border of Wilmoroth. Would you like me to suggest your name to the Council of Ministers?"

"No, sir. Are you trying to threaten me, sir?"

"Are you trying to threaten the Prince of Persus Am? I've never heard such insolence in all my life. Now he's told you you're no longer needed. I'm certain the Father-King did not intend for you to take the Prince by force, like a criminal, did he?"

"No, sir."

"Well, then, get out of here!" Dakin bellowed. I had never heard him shout that way before. I could hardly keep from smiling as the general nodded and marched his men away. Hamlin followed them, but Dakin and I took a separate door into the palace.

When we were alone, Dakin said, "I'm glad I got to you first. Things are bad, Jeremy, very bad. I guess you know that already."

"I'm not sure how much I know. Tell me."

"First of all, there's a threat of war now with the Rock of Calad; it looks like they might back out of the agreement in the Territory even though we released Tarius Arc."

"He's released?"

"Yes. Umbriel bound him up and forcibly turned him over because he was afraid they would use Tarius as an excuse not to go along with us. It was a big mistake, I think. Umbriel has no idea how dangerous a free Tarius Arc really is to him."

"Why?"

"Because he's the only one left in the world who knows how to make the kind of bombs that destroyed Persus Am in the War."

"Well, I've heard rumors that Umbriel's scientists are close to perfecting that kind of bomb themselves," I said. "Umbriel once told me that he doubts Tarius even has the capability anymore. Umbriel said Tarius would have used those bombs by now if he could still make them."

"Well, I don't think Umbriel is being completely truthful with you. I think Umbriel believes that now that the Rock is willing to deal with us, that just might prompt Tarius to build his bomb again as a precaution. I think Umbriel hopes to steal it. We have spies everywhere. But back to the immediate problem. Since Damonchok is resisting unifying the Territory with you as the ruler, the Rock is afraid Damonchok will fight them, and the Rock doesn't think this whole idea is worth fighting a war over."

"But maybe Damonchok will agree to go along with this whole plan. They seemed pretty positive toward me when I was there."

"Well, maybe, but their people here are telling a different story. And that's not all. Pannip has betrayed you. I'm pretty sure he was bribed by Vanus. At any rate they've taken him away from me, and he has been telling them some pretty damaging things if they're true."

"I'm afraid they're probably true."

"He tells of late-night visits to Tarius Arc?"

"Yes."

"Arranged by Ona's servant Jank, of all people?"

"That's right."

"Oh Jeremy, how could you have risked that? They're just sure you're an Emajian. And then we got some kind of report that you started singing with the Emajians at one of the rallies."

"Not exactly. I was just clapping to one of their songs. The whole crowd was—"

"Oh, just clapping. As if that makes any difference. You might as well have played a trumpet and taken requests. Jeremy, they're out to get you. If this whole thing with the Territory falls through, you're going to be the scapegoat. It would be easy for them to kill you now."

By the time Dakin said this we were in his residence. He took me to his private office and locked the door. I sat on his worktable like I had before. I asked, "So what about my scriptures in those Emajian informationals? Did you give them to the Emajians?"

"Of course not. I assumed you did."

"No. They must have been stolen. But you still have your copy of them?"

"Yes. There were no other copies as far as I knew. I've let a few people see them, but I didn't know anyone copied them."

"Well, obviously somebody did. You may remember that they were missing from my room one time, and then someone brought them back?"

"Do you think it was Pannip?"

"I don't know."

"Well, it's just one more nail in your coffin. I don't mean to be so pessimistic, Jeremy, but I think things have gone too far. I think you're going to have to go into hiding before they put you in prison. You could always come back once things get straightened out. If they ever do."

"Where would I hide?"

"I have connections in Damonchok. I could send you there until it's safe for you to come back. I have done this sort of thing before, especially when Umbriel's father was still alive. I have a friend who could disguise you. He's very good—he works in the theater. I've talked to him about the possibility of doing this—I didn't tell him I was talking about you, of course—and he is ready whenever I call for him. He's in the palace right now."

"What would I do in Damonchok? Even if I'm disguised, wouldn't people figure out—"

"We would tell them you are an Emajian fleeing from the Utturies trying to escape religious persecution. That happens frequently, and it would give you a good excuse to be secretive and say nothing about your background. You would stay with a family there that I know."

"You've worked this all out, haven't you?"

"Yes. Honestly, I don't see any other option for you. And the truth is, Miri and I might have to escape too eventually. Many people are suspicious of me and my connection with you. But Miriaban says she won't leave, so I'm not sure what will happen to us."

"I'm sorry to have put you in so much danger."

"Don't be. Besides, I can stall them for a good while yet. I know how this place works."

"If I agree to your plan, when do you think I should leave?"

Before he answered, a servant knocked at the door. Dakin opened the door and said, "What is it?"

"I'm sorry, sir, but Princess Shellan is waiting in the entry hall and demands to see Prince Jeremy."

"What on earth does she want?" Dakin asked me.

"I don't know."

"Tell her he'll be there in just a minute," said Dakin. He shut the door and continued, "I think you should leave tonight. I don't know if they've told you, but the public memorial service for Ona is tomorrow. I think you'll be safe until then, because Umbriel will want everything to look stable and normal for the informationals. But after that, it's hard to tell what they'll do."

"There are a few things I'd like to take care of before I leave."

"Jeremy, I don't know what this business is with Shellan, and I don't know what it is that you want to take care of, but I think

I should tell you, your relationship with Tracian is over. They have poisoned her against you, and you will not be allowed to see her. So just in case you were thinking of going to her, it can only make matters worse."

"Thank you for telling me. I'll go see what Shellan wants."

"I'll get my friend here as soon as I can. Come back early this evening, all right?"

"I will."

Shellan waited alone in a sitting room. When I came in she whirled around and said, "You're a dead man, dear brother. You're next on the list."

"Shellan, why don't you sit down and—"

"No! Jeremy, you don't know how far things have gone. You've got to see for yourself. I came to take you to see for yourself. They're going to try to hide it from you, but I won't let them do it!" Her tone was frantic.

"What am I supposed to see?"

"Just follow me."

I followed, but she was headed toward Umbriel's residence, where I did not want to go. I said, "Shellan, stop. I'm already in enough trouble as it is. I need to know where you're taking me and what we're going to do. If this is some scheme—"

"It is no scheme. This is the only way. Please be quiet and follow."

We went past Umbriel's wing of the palace and down a now-darkened hallway toward Ona's rooms. "I don't want to go down here. What are we doing, Shellan?"

"You'll see."

She kept walking, her stride stiff and unwavering, like a soldier. She took out a key and unlocked Ona's door. She did not step in.

She said, "You go in. I have seen this. You need to see it."

My stomach was already churning. I walked in, went through the entryway and into the sitting room. The sight was devastating. Shellan came in after me and put her arm around me. In the center of the room, hanging from a rope that had once held a globe light, was the body of Jank. Shellan cried as she saw the body again. I was too stunned to speak or cry or move. His neck was broken, his face horribly contorted, his body bloated, his skin an eerie gray color.

I heard myself say "Jank!" in a thin, dead voice. I was dizzy. My body was numb.

"My father ordered it done."

"Why?"

"Because my grandmother was dead and he could get away with it. And because he found out that Jank had been visiting you and had taken you to see Tarius Arc."

I turned away from the body. "You people are insane."

"Yes, we are. And Daddy is blaming what happened here on you, because you dabbled in Emajianism. He brings people here to warn them about how bad Emajianism can be. Emajianism means death."

"I should have stayed in prison with Tarius. What have I done?"

"Tracian blames you too. She has turned against you completely. All the rumors that have come out against you she believes. She believes you are an Emajian, a filthy Emajian. She has ordered that you not be allowed to see her."

We heard the door slam back against the wall. A voice yelled, "Who's in there?" Then we heard the sound of soldiers' boots. About a half dozen of them ran in, as if ready for war, their guns pointed toward us.

The commander said, "No one is allowed in here. You'll have to leave at once."

"Do you know who you're talking to?" I screamed.

"Yes, Prince Jeremy, but the Father-King has ordered that absolutely no one, with no exceptions, be allowed in here without his permission. You'll have to come out."

The commander stepped forward. With a force I did not realize I had left in me, I smashed him in the face with my fist. It felt good to feel the force of it, the release of it, to see his head smack against the wall. I wanted to hit him again. Because I was the prince, none of the soldiers would have resisted me. In that moment of rage I understood Umbriel. I understood that he had killed Jank because of the thrill and the beauty of wielding that force and of knowing there was nothing they could do to stop him.

"I'm sick of being spoken to like a criminal!" I yelled. One soldier stood close to me and kept his gun pointed at me. I turned to him and said, "Are you next? Would you like to end up like my friend Jank? If we can hang honest men like him, do you think I won't hang a piece of filth like you?"

"Prince, we were only—"

"What? What! Do you want to see what *I* can do with these little fire guns you have? Do you want to feel what it's like to have a fire pellet or two pierce through your face and burn out your eyes? Or do you plan to shoot them at me? Has it come to that? Do you carry those around in order to shoot the prince and princess?"

"Sir, we mean no—"

"Shut up!"

I pushed past them and went out into the hall. Shellan followed. We headed in the direction of the Dome.

"Why are we going this way?" she asked.

"I don't know."

"Let's go back to your residence. You're too upset."

When we got to the door that opened to the reception rooms for the Dome, Shellan took hold of me and said, "Don't try to go in there, Jeremy. He won't see you now anyway. He doesn't see anyone unannounced. You're too angry. Wait and talk to him later. You can only hurt yourself now."

I kept walking. The guards at the door of the reception area snapped to attention as I passed through. "What are you going to do when you get in there?" Shellan asked.

I did not answer because I did not know. My rage was carrying me forward. I felt perfectly calm, but my rage had blotted out all restraint. Several of Umbriel's aides hovered around a table just outside the Dome. "Prince Jeremy!" said one of them, as they all stood. "Was the Father-King expecting you now? And you, Princess Shellan? I thought he was meeting with—"

"I need to see him right away," I said, walking past the table to the guards, who opened the high double doors with ceremonious solemnity. Shellan stepped to the door but did not go past it. It remained open so that she could hear but not be seen.

Umbriel sat casually on a couch in front of the fireplace. Tracian stood near him, leaning on the couch. Hamlin, Vanus, and two other Councilors sat in chairs around him. Vanus was speaking. Hamlin saw me first. Surprised, he stood and said to Umbriel, "Have you called the prince here already, sir?"

Umbriel stood and faced me. I stood on the opposite side of the couch from Tracian. Umbriel smiled and said, "Hello, Jeremy. It's good to have you back home. They must have called you by mistake, though. I'm sorry. I'm not quite ready for you yet. Could you come back in a little while?"

"There is no mistake. I have come on my own."

"Well, as you can see, I'm busy with this meeting right now."

"Gathering some more evidence, are you? Have you picked out a good place to hang me?"

"You're an idiot," said Tracian.

"Jeremy, I will deal with you later," said Umbriel.

"You will deal with me now."

Hamlin said, "Prince, perhaps it would be better if—"

"Butt out, Hamlin. I have come to talk to Umbriel."

Umbriel said, "I don't know what's wrong with you, Jeremy, but if I were you, I would keep in mind that you have done enough already to put yourself in great jeopardy without another little outburst. Some of the things you have been accused of just might be considered criminal acts punishable by—"

"Don't talk to me about criminal acts! I think we're all aware that you are a murderer. I'm here to find out why you killed Jank."

"Oh? Was he a friend of yours? Are you afraid you won't have anyone to help you sneak around the halls to see the Emajian criminals anymore?"

"What kind of lunatic are you to kill an innocent man, who never did anything to harm anyone, who took care of your mother—"

"He was an Emajian, a sneak, a criminal of sound, and several other things I could list. If you have come here to defend him, then we really do have a problem here."

"Oh yes, we have a problem all right. I've put up with one indignity after another since I've been here, but I have no intention of standing silently by while you murder a friend of mine."

"So he is your friend. If you don't stop talking, young man, you are going to build the case against you yourself, something your enemies have been trying to do the whole time you've been gone. I'm not interested in listening to a whole lot you have to say right now. Not until you explain why you have visited Tarius Arc repeatedly since we let you out of prison, why you translated your scriptures into Emajian propaganda, why, of all the outrages in the world, you sang an Emajian song in the rally—"

"An outrage? After what you've done, you can call singing a song an outrage? You can murder an innocent man, make a sideshow attraction out of his corpse, and then call singing some words an outrage? What kind of insane place is this? Do you know what words I sang? Do you want to hear them?"

The room was deathly silent. Everyone hoped I did not really intend to sing the words. At any other time I would have been more cautious and kept silent. But I was beyond that now. After a deep breath, I opened my mouth and began the chorus, "Emajus shall reign/ Praise His name/ Praise His name." As the sound flew around the Dome, every face was frozen in disbelief. Even Umbriel seemed paralyzed from the sound. I turned and left the Dome as quickly as I had come, with Shellan running after me.

"Oh Jeremy, what have you done now?" she said.

"I don't know. I had to do it. I could kill them all."

"You're a dead man now." She took hold of my arm. "Wait. You can't go back to your residence. You know they're going to be coming for you."

"You're right. Let's go to Dakin."

As soon as we found Dakin, Shellan blurted out the whole story as quickly as she could while Dakin shook his head in silence. Then he said, "Thank you for your help, Princess. I think you've done all you can for Jeremy now. I'm sure they'll be coming to question you. Maybe it would be good for you to be in your rooms. Maybe you could think of a good story to tell them."

"Yes, of course. So you'll hide him, then. Of all of my father's people, I never expected that you would—thank you, Dakin. I'll never forget this. If I'm ever in a position where I can help you—"

"Thank you, Princess. I am honored."

After Shellan left, Dakin said, "Well, it looks like we'll have to move up your escape by several hours. I just hope I can find Dwinkzer."

"That's your friend from the theater?"

"Yes. He's going to disguise you and try to get you out of here. For now we'd better get you out of my house. This is probably one of the first places they'll look."

Dakin took me downstairs to the theater wing of the palace, where the wealthy came for entertainment. He locked me in some sort of storage room and went to find Dwinkzer. He came back with a middle-aged man who wore a silky multicolored suit and had a thin black mustache and a goatee. He bowed low when Dakin introduced him. He walked all around the chair I was sitting in, as if I were a piece of stone he was about to sculpt.

"Can you do it?" asked Dakin.

"Of course I can do it. First the hair." My hair had grown to a fashionable shoulder length. Dwinkzer took out his scissors and began to clip it.

"Is this really necessary?" I asked.

"I am afraid so," said Dwinkzer. "This long hair might look good in Persus Am, but it won't work in Damonchok. We are making you into a servant from the Utturies who is escaping to Damonchok."

"You have extra servant uniforms, don't you?" asked Dakin.

"Yes. Everything is ready." After Dwinkzer cut my hair, he rubbed an oily lotion all over my head. When he finished and gave me a mirror, I was astonished to see that my brown hair was now black, short, and slicked back. Then he carefully glued on a beard, not a fashionable goatee like his own, but a fuller beard like the Utturans were fond of wearing. Then I put on a blue servant's uniform.

"That's good," said Dakin. "I would never recognize him."

"Thank you very much," said Dwinkzer. "From now on,

Prince, your name is Pryce, and you are a servant. Can you drive a camuck, Pryce?"

"No, I've never done it."

Dakin said, "We don't want him out in the open anyway, Dwinkzer. Let's don't push our luck."

"All right, then, you may ride in my van and I'll sit up front and drive the camuck. I just thought it would be more fun to have the Prince of Persus Am drive out of this palace right in front of their faces without them even knowing it. Driving a camuck and pulling a theater van. Wearing a beard and servant's clothes. It would be great fun, wouldn't it? Just perfect."

"Let's don't worry about fun," said Dakin. "Let's just get him out alive."

"Alive and well, I assure you, friend. Have I ever let you down before?"

"No, Dwink. You have done brilliantly. Jeremy—Pryce—is in good hands."

Dwinkzer said, "I'll go down and get everything ready, and then we'll leave. I'm going to have to miss tonight's performance, Dakin. I'll have to charge you extra."

"I'm paying you plenty as it is."

"Is that so? Well, maybe Pryce will only make it halfway there."

"And maybe you'll be putting on plays in the Utturies when you get back."

"You're lucky to be getting out of here, Pryce. The government officials are awfully corrupt."

"Get going," said Dakin, "or we'll all have to finish this conversation in prison."

As we waited, I said to Dakin, "You and Miriaban should go with me. It's no good here anymore. They're murderers."

"I know that. I've known it for a long time. But I have to stay and face some things, and Miri refuses to leave. So you go, and do what you know you should do."

"I have no idea what I should do."

"Well, you can follow your conscience now. You're free."

10

I was in no sense free. I was stuck in the back of a small, stuffy van filled with costumes and cases and boxes. The van was dark, the only light coming from three slits on both sides of the car that let in a little air. At first I was glad to be away from everyone, hidden in the darkness. The chaos and rush of events had until that moment let me avoid my grief for Jank, but once I was alone and settled into this long journey, the horror of his death overwhelmed me. I sat scrunched in the corner, my arms wrapped tightly around my knees. The image of his dead body hanging from the ceiling replayed itself again and again in my mind. It filled me with terror, made me numb with grief, made me pull closer into myself to try to shut it out. I was outraged at Umbriel for murdering him and at Tracian for condoning it. But I also felt horrible guilt, as if my friend's dead body were the ultimate result of the mistake I had made and the sin I had committed in believing Umbriel and in going along with him in order to save myself from danger. I thought of Umbriel's paralyzed gaze as he heard my song, as if the music were unmasking his evil. Dakin was right, at least, that I was free of Umbriel. For I had determined that no matter how completely the controversy blew over and no matter what kind of appeal Umbriel might make, I would never follow him again. There in the darkness of the van I renounced the title of Prince of Persus Am. I abdicated the throne.

After we were well past the Utturies and into the desert of Persus Am, Dwinkzer felt we were safe for the time being and invited me to ride up front with him. This made the trip a little more bearable, and a few hours later we reached the inn where we were staying that night. It was a crummy place, with sticky, cold food and bumpy mattresses. The inn was apparently a regular stop on Dwinkzer's Emajian-smuggling underground railroad because he had a key to our room before we arrived and some of his theatrical equipment was already there.

"The theater is a great cover for the work I do for the Emajians," said Dwinkzer. "Nobody gets suspicious when I travel, because I serve theatrical companies in Persus Am, the Territory, and Damonchok. Nobody gets suspicious when I bring servants with me, or so-called actors, or other theater people, because that's quite common. And nobody gets suspicious at all my equipment and makeup, because that's quite natural for me to have too."

I was deathly tired and wanted only to sleep. I was surprised and unhappy when Dwinkzer told me he wanted to put more makeup on me that night.

"I thought we finished that at the palace," I protested.

"Oh no. You're just an Utturan servant right now. That was good enough to get you out of the palace, but we've got to make you into a Damonchokian to get you across the border. The pass I had forged is for a Damonchokian."

"But I thought I was going to Damonchok as an Utturan servant."

"You are. But you're going as an Utturan servant disguised as a Damonchokian. That's the beauty of it. Lots of people in Damonchok will figure out you're not really a Damonchokian. But underneath that mask, we want them to see an Utturan. Nobody would suspect that you are an Amian Prince disguised as an Utturan posing as a Damonchokian. It's too convoluted and absurd. It's beautiful!"

I was too tired to see the beauty of it.

In the center of the room was a huge vat, and after Dwinkzer poured bottles of chemicals in it and then filled the rest of it with water, he told me to take off my clothes and get inside it. The water was black. When I got in and sat down, the water was up to my neck. Dwinkzer pulled off my beard, stinging my face in the process. I was glad to have the beard off, though, because it was itchy and uncomfortable. Dwinkzer said I would not need one as a Damonchokian. Dwinkzer gave me a washcloth that I had to keep dipping into the water and rubbing all over my face to make it the same dark color as the rest of my body would be. I got tired of sitting in the tub, but Dwinkzer made me stay in the water for more than three hours.

When I finally got out and looked in the mirror, I was amazed to see a man with a dark brown tan. Dwinkzer said, "Now you look like a Damonchokian farmhand who has spent some time in the sun. No one will recognize you now, especially considering how idealized they made those pictures of you in the informationals. You really don't look much like those pictures, I'm sorry to say."

"How long will my skin stay like this?" I asked.

"For several weeks. And I'm going to give you several more bottles of this stuff for you to use when you start to fade. It's very easy to maintain that color."

"Well, I hope this works."

"You'll be just fine. None of my people have ever been caught. Well, two of them were caught actually, but they were unusual cases. And another one got caught once he got back to Persus Am, but I'm not responsible for that. But the point is you won't be caught, so just put your mind at ease."

—◯—

Dwinkzer took me only as far as the mountain pass, which took us four days to reach. In a house near the border checkpoint we met a Damonchokian man named Jipsum, who was to take me the rest of the way. I changed into a brown Damonchokian suit with big brown buttons, an outfit that looked exactly like Jipsum's. He was a dark man, about sixty years old, and he said not one word more than absolutely necessary to communicate the information he was paid to bestow. I was to pretend to be his son traveling with him in the back of his wagon. Jipsum did not know who I was. He thought, as everyone else was supposed to think, that I was an Emajian from the Utturies escaping persecution.

Before Dwinkzer left us, I asked him, "How can I get in touch with you or Dakin if I need to?"

"You can't. But I'm sure Dakin will contact you as soon as he can."

"When?"

"I don't know."

"Well, do you mean a matter of days, months, years, or what?"

"I have no idea. You just wait there and be patient."

"What am I supposed to *do* while I'm there?"

"I don't know. You don't have to do anything. I mean, as far as making a living, you'll have plenty of money."

"So I just sit?"

"You don't have to. Do anything you want, just so you don't make people too curious about your past. If people try to press you, just tell them you don't want to talk about it. They'll drop it. There are all kinds of people with hidden pasts and strange stories in Damonchok, especially near the border of the Territory, where you'll be. People in Damonchok believe in minding their own business. So if you want to get a job or something, I see no reason not to. You're well-disguised. You don't have to hide out in a room or something."

"I don't like this. Tell Dakin to contact me as soon as he can."

"I will. I'm sure he won't just abandon you."

As Dwinkzer drove away, I crawled into Jipsum's open wagon, which was heavily loaded, and sat down between two trunks. Jipsum said, "Your clothes and things are in the trunk there by your head. There's food here in this basket. Help yourself. When you need to stop, let me know. At nightfall we'll pull over for the night."

That was the longest string of sentences I ever heard from Jipsum. We made it over the mountain that day and rested in the magnificent forests of the Territory that night. Over the next two days we traveled through some of the very places where the crowds had cheered me at the rallies just days before. The crowds were gone now, and no one paid any attention to me at all, not even Jipsum. In a way I missed all the excitement, all the adulation, the good food, and the comfort, but in another sense it was good to finally be able to look at this place from the perspective of a citizen who belonged there, who was just traveling through conducting everyday business and attracting no attention. Whenever we stopped at inns, to feed the camucks or take a shower or get something hot to eat, I enjoyed the simple pleasure of engaging in small talk with the innkeeper or guests who happened to speak to us. For the first time since I had been in that world I did not feel like an object of curiosity who was being inspected or manipulated or tested.

On the morning of the day we arrived at my new home, I woke up sick, either from something I ate or from some native virus in the air that my foreign body had not learned to combat. I vomited repeatedly, daylight made my head throb, and most frightening of all to me, the inexplicable heaviness that had overtaken me at my coronation and on my night of arrival in the Utturies overcame me again and made it almost impossible for me to move. Jipsum made me drink two different kinds of vile tasting medicine that only made me feel worse. After those didn't help me, he said not another word about my illness but let me suffer alone in the back of the wagon while he kept driving as fast as he could. When we reached the house where I was to stay, I jumped out of the wagon but almost immediately blacked out from the pain in my head. I clung to the side of the wagon, hearing some vibration that I came to understand was Jipsum's voice. The only words I caught were, "I'll go up and tell them you're here, then."

The house was built of wood, with a wide front porch across the front and one side. Several additions had been put on the house so that it sprawled in a number of directions. But it looked homey and sturdy and well-built, which was typical of the houses of Damonchok. On a grassy area just in front of the porch sat a little girl who stared at me while she absentmindedly pulled up clumps of grass. Her stare embarrassed me into letting go of the wagon and trying to walk toward the house. The closer I got to her, the faster her grass-pulling rhythm became. As I approached the porch, Jipsum and a woman came out of the house.

"Here he is, then," said Jipsum.

The woman was drying her hands with a towel. Her face flushed with embarrassment, and she tried to push hair off her forehead with her arms. Her hair was tied back, but several strands had broken free and were stuck in the sweat on her forehead. She was in her forties and rather fat, with wide, rounded hips. "My name's Goldaw," she said. "My husband ain't here."

"His name's Pryce," said Jipsum.

"I hope you ain't feelin' too bad," she said.

"I'm really not feeling very well at all, to tell you the truth. Is there somewhere I could lie down for a little bit?"

"Sure! Come on in. Your place is all ready."

"Can your boy come and get his trunks?" asked Jipsum.

"He ain't here either. Just set 'em out in the yard and I'll keep an eye out till he gets home."

"No, I'll bring them on in, then," Jipsum said with a weary sigh.

Goldaw said, "Pryce, we better get you in your room 'fore you fall down. What kind of junk has Jipsum been makin' you eat? You're lookin' kinda puny."

She led me to the end of a hallway in one of the additions to the house.

"We gave you the room at the far end where it's quiet. My kids get kinda noisy sometimes. Can I get you somethin' to eat? Or some medicine or somethin'? I've got some stuff that—"

"Oh, no, thank you. This will pass. Just something cool to drink would be great."

"I'll bring it right away. Now if you want anything, you just holler. We're nothing fancy around here. Once you learn your way around here, we'll just let you help yourself. We keep plenty to eat and drink, I can tell you that. But you lay down and rest now. I bet Jipsum gave you somethin' that wasn't fit to eat. Or maybe it's just the Utturan air. Ain't fit for a Damonchokian to breathe, my husband says. But you stay here, and you'll be better in no time."

My room had a bed, a dresser, and a nightstand. It was a

small bed, but the mattress was thick and soft. For much of the next three days I was ill and confused. I slept most of the time, and whenever I woke up I could not remember for several minutes—once as long as half an hour—where I was. I would awaken with a strong sense that someone had called to me, and I would be alarmed to find myself in such a small and unfamiliar room in the palace. Once I called for a servant over and over, and finally Goldaw came, embarrassed and alarmed, asking if there was something she could get me. The visions of Anne continued too. In one vision I was walking up to Goldaw's front porch, and Will was there. "She's here," he said. "She's been waiting for you." He opened the door for me and there stood Anne, dressed in the humble dress of a Damonchokian woman.

During the times I was awake, my head felt as if some grinding force were trying to crush my skull. I often had to run across the hall to the rather primitive bathroom to vomit. Only during those several minutes after vomiting did I have complete mental clarity. Besides suffering from my illness, I was also terribly afraid of being caught. Every time I heard footsteps outside my door, I imagined Umbriel's soldiers preparing to come crashing through the door to drag me away. My fear was increased by the fact that I had no way to communicate with Dakin or anyone else that I knew. I was stuck in this place, just waiting to be caught and executed.

Goldaw brought me a tray of food five or six times a day. Most of the time I was either too sick to eat any of it, or else I let it sit and get cold while I lay there asleep or confused. She also brought me some medicine, which did not taste as bad as Jipsum's and which seemed to do some good. She told me later that she also brought a doctor in to visit me, but I have no recollection of that.

Finally, by the afternoon of the third day, my appetite began to return, and I gobbled down the meal that Goldaw brought me. She asked me if I wanted anything else, and I told her I would like to take a bath. A bath in Damonchok was not nearly as luxurious as one in the palace of Persus Am. There was no swirling water, no servants to bring me drinks, no fragrant bubble baths, no huge, soft towels to step into once I was finished. In Goldaw's home there was a black metal vat, which she filled with buckets of hot water she heated up for me. Even so, the tingling hot water felt good to me, as if it were stinging out the last remnants of sickness from my body. Goldaw gave me some gooey stuff that looked like toothpaste. It was shampoo. I rubbed it through my hair until it felt gloriously clean. Goldaw gave me a bar of soap and a spongy washcloth that I rubbed hard over my body, my strangely dark body, until I tingled with cleanliness. Then I leaned back against the rim of the tub and relaxed, wide awake, strong.

After the bath I took out one of the brown Damonchokian suits that had been packed for me and put it on. It was not a new suit (Dwinkzer said that would be too suspicious), but it fit me perfectly. As I was buttoning the coat, Goldaw came in.

"Well," she said, "you look like a new man."

"Well, thank you." As I looked at myself in the mirror, I *did* look like a new man, a dark Damonchokian man.

"Will you come in and eat with the family tonight? They're all wonderin' who I'm hidin' back here."

"Yes. I'd be glad to. Goldaw, have there been any messages for me?"

"Nope. Are you expecting somethin'? We only get the mail every other day usually, but if you're expecting somethin'—"

"Oh no. I'm not. I just wondered."

"Do you want to send a letter or anything?"

"No thank you." I shrugged. "No one to write to."

"Well, I just bet there is. And I bet it's a she. And I bet you won't tell me nor nobody else a thing about her."

I only smiled.

"That's just fine," said Goldaw. "One thing about stayin' here is you don't have to answer no questions. Don't let anybody bug you about things either. The family knows they're s'posed to leave folks alone who stays here."

At the time I moved into Goldaw's house, she lived there with her husband, Rothter, their three children, and Rothter's older sister, Mettie. This was the fewest number of people that had lived in the house in several years, Goldaw told me. It seemed that nearly half the county was related to Goldaw or Rothter, and most of the time two or three or more relatives were staying at Rothter's, who was a relatively well-off farmer who had plenty of rooms and plenty of hospitality. Also, there were usually at least a couple of paying guests like me. But for the time being all the relatives outside the immediate family except for Mettie were living elsewhere, and the last of the paying guests had moved on before I got there.

The table in Goldaw's kitchen/dining area could seat fifteen comfortably—twenty if you wanted to squeeze that many in. Like just about everything else in Rothter's house, it was built solidly, of wood, so that even when the children bumped against it, nothing spilled. Goldaw brought out the food in huge bowls and great platters. The children were already sitting at the table when I walked in. The boy was about eighteen, and was introduced to me as Dubov. The oldest girl, sixteen or seventeen, was named Taron, and the youngest girl, who had pulled up tufts of grass and stared at me on the first day, was named Cresha. She scooted closer to her sister when I walked in and whispered to her as I passed. Aunt Mettie, a middle-aged woman with black and gray hair, sat at the end of the table. Rothter came in from the living room when he heard Goldaw introducing me. "I thought we never were going to get to meet this guy," said Rothter, putting out his hand. "I thought maybe Goldy's food had killed you."

"Watch it, buddy," said Goldaw. "Ask him whose food put that fat gut on him, Pryce."

"I hope she hasn't treated you as bad as she treats me," he said.

"She's been wonderful. I wouldn't have gotten well without her."

"It's nice to be treated respectful for once," said Goldaw. "Well, sit down, everybody. Taron, get me a spoon to dip this out with."

When Goldaw told the children to do something—like "Slide this down there by your dad," or "Go put the rest of that meat on this platter"—they did it without comment. Goldaw was clearly in charge of every move made in the house. It was equally clear that Rothter was in the house to rest from his labors and would not be called upon to do any of the little chores that the children or Goldaw did. He had the look of a man who had worked much and said little. His face was stubbly, weatherworn, with sagging pouches under his eyes. He chewed on a brown stick that I first thought was a thin cigar, but there was no such thing in Damonchok. The stick was some sort of compressed meat-and-plant mixture that the men of Damonchok—never the women—chewed while they relaxed. Rothter rarely smiled, but he liked to tease his wife with gruff little jokes, and whenever he did so his lips showed the faintest smirk of mischief. He said, "I was beginnin' to wonder if we was ever gonna get dinner this evening."

"I don't want to hear it. I've had lots of work to do today. It ain't that late."

"Oh, I know it. The rest of us just sit around all day long." Rothter winked at Cresha.

"We all do our fair share, I reckon," said Goldaw. "Taron, you let Pryce sit in that chair. He's too big a man for this one. Now, you met everybody, didn't you? Did you meet Mettie? This here's Aunt Mettie. That's Rothter's older sister."

"No need to tell him I'm older, Goldy. I'm sure he can figure it out for himself. How-do."

"So start dippin' it out. Go ahead, Dubov."

"Mama, we should let the guest go first," said Taron.

"Well, now, Pryce is going to be treated just like anybody else in this family. We're not going to go around acting fancy all the time. This is not some Amian hotel, Pryce. I hope you don't mind being treated just like one of the family."

"Not at all. I'd feel funny being treated any other way. I'm not used to being fussed over," I said, thinking how surprised they would be if they knew about the dozens of servants I had left behind who were there for the sole purpose of satisfying my every whim.

Mettie said, "Your talk sounds kinda fancy, boy. Where you from?"

"Mettie, you be nice," warned Goldaw.

"I've lived in the Utturies for quite some time. I'm originally from Damonchok."

"You learn to talk like that in the Utturies?"

"Mettie, now you just get off his back," said Goldaw. "You know we don't nib into our guests' business. Now he told you where he's from. He didn't sit here with us to be pestered to death with questions."

"Well, he's got that sound in his voice I ain't used to hearin'. Pardon me for saying anything at all. I'll just sit here and keep my mouth shut."

Rothter said, "Don't let her kid you, Pryce. Ain't a woman in this family ever knew how to keep her mouth shut."

"That's enough outta you," said Goldaw. "You can tell him and Mettie are brother and sister, can't you? They're just alike."

"Ain't nobody in my family like me at all," said Mettie.

"That's for sure," said Rothter.

Mettie said, "I been standing on my own all my life. Not waitin' for anybody to take my part in anything, 'cause it won't never happen. You just have to stand up for yourself. It's the story of my life."

"And it is one sad story," said Rothter.

"Let's not get it started, Papa," said Goldaw.

Cresha said, "Mama, why's he sittin' in Taron's chair?"

"That other little old chair ain't big enough for him, honey."

Mettie said, "The only person in my family like me was my mother. That's why she wanted me takin' care of her when she got bad. I's the only one could understand her. Roth, you were more like Daddy."

"You interested in workin', Pryce?" asked Rothter.

"He don't have to work, Papa, now, he's all paid up."

"Well, for heaven's sakes, I didn't ask him to pay his bill. I know he's all paid up. Did I say one thing about payin' up? I asked if he was interested in workin'. I thought maybe he would want to earn some extra, or at least get away from you chatterin' women all day long. That'd be enough to get me outta the house even if I had all the money in the world."

Dubov said, "There's work with Mr. Ranejun. That's who I'm workin' for." Smiling at his father, he added, "He pays better than Dad."

"See how my family treats me, Pryce? My own boy works for somebody else."

"I work for the highest price, Dad. I can bring in more money for this family from him than I can just workin' for you. You don't need that much help anyway."

"See what I mean? Let Dad do it all. Let him carry the load." His tone was casual, as if he had presented this bit of banter dozens of times before.

Mettie said, "You don't know what carryin' a load really is, Roth." Turning her attention to me, she said, "He was too young to remember what it was like when we first moved into these parts. He was just a baby. It was our daddy that carried the load. Times was tough back then."

"Have some food here, Pryce," said Goldaw. "You need to build up your strength. You've hardly eaten anything these last three days. I was almost afraid you was going to die on us."

"It's that Utturan air," Rothter said. "It's not fit for a human being to live there, all them factories. You was probably sick about half the time, I bet. It ain't natural. You stay here for a while and I bet you won't be sick a day. I've never been sick a day in my life."

Dubov said, "If you want to work, I could ask Mr. Ranejun if he could use you. He needs all the help he can get this time of year. I bet he'd let you work if you wanted."

"What sort of work would I do?" I asked.

"You just never know from day to day. It could be anything, fixing fences, hauling stuff to town, anything Mr. Ranejun wants. It ain't all farming stuff."

"Ain't nothin' wrong with farming stuff," said Rothter.

"Yeah," said Dubov, dismissing him. "You never know what you'll be doin' one day to the next. It don't get boring. It's kind of hard, but not too bad. He lets you take breaks ever' once in a while."

"Yeah, I'd like to know how many hours a day that 'once in a while' ends up bein'," said Rothter.

Goldaw asked, "Do you think you should rest up a few days first? You just started feelin' better today. You overdo it and you'll be right back in that bed."

"He didn't have nothin' wrong with him that some good Damonchokian air won't cure," answered Rothter.

"I think I'd like to try working," I said, not at all sure that I was making the right decision. But I had to find a way to avoid doing nothing but sitting in my room all day and worrying that every sound at the door was Umbriel's soldiers arriving to take me to my execution. I had to face the prospect of spending weeks, maybe even months, here without any contact with Dakin or anyone else I knew.

Goldaw said, "Well, you don't need to work all day long if you don't want to. You work till you're tired and then you come back here. You're all paid up. There's no need for you to go out there and kill yourself."

"Woman," said Rothter, with a wink, "I believe I could choke down a little more of that meat."

—⊖—

Mr. Ranejun needed workers, and he hired me on Dubov's recommendation. We started early the next morning. Our project for the entire day was "shovelin' spread." In his barns Ranejun had huge mounds of a powdery yellow fertilizer called "spread" that farmers mixed with water and sprayed on their fields. Ranejun sold it to them in big sacks, and our job was to shovel the spread into the sacks, staple the stacks shut, and stack the bags where the farmers could pick them up. Whenever someone stopped to buy some of it, we helped load his wagon.

It was hard work, and after the ease of Persus Am, I was not used to physical labor. The most exercise I had managed to get at the palace was occasionally playing rogno and even less frequently swimming. But those activities had not prepared me for the workout this job gave my back and shoulders. Though the work was exhausting, it created a steady, physical rhythm to accompany my thoughts, which were filled with rage and bewilderment. Over and over again I saw Jank hanging from that ceiling. Over and over I saw Umbriel's terror-stricken face as I sang to him—a face unmasked by music, to reveal deceit and horror. I saw Tracian's cool glance of betrayal as I entered the Dome to confront her father. She stood in his presence, in his inner circle; she had what she wanted. I was no longer necessary. I was as expendable as Jank. I pictured Pannip whispering his secrets, pretending to be reluctant, pretending to be ignorant of the implication of what he said, as Vanus, fat-faced and eager, coaxed him along with promises of money and position and respect. I heard the voice of Tarius Arc sing like a throbbing conscience, berating me for having rejected the voice of God and having, like Pannip, accepted Umbriel's bribes. As always, I pictured Anne, so vivid, so elusive, the one clear memory from my former life, which had faded into gauzy images of unreality, as if it had not been my own life at all but just an elaborately detailed book I had read long ago. I imagined Umbriel's soldiers fanning out over the countryside, offering big rewards for my capture. I pictured them crashing through Ranejun's barn doors and kicking me to the ground. At times I got so caught up in the intensity of my thoughts that I found myself shoveling like a madman, until Dubov said, "Hey, take it easy, Pryce. You're gonna wear yourself out before lunchtime. You're attackin' that spread like it's your worst enemy in the world."

When we took breaks outside, Dubov liked to sit close to the barn, where it was shady, but I sat out in the sun. It felt good to feel its rays blazing against me, as if it were purging something rotten out of me, as if the heat and the light and the exhausting work had the power to restore to me something pure that I had lost. Dubov was a good companion, easygoing and friendly, but he did not understand me. He thought I worked too hard and enjoyed pain far too much. "You'll be lucky to last a week at this rate," he said.

Every night we came home, washed up, and enjoyed one of Goldaw's plentiful dinners. After dinner was finished and the dishes were washed and put away, everyone gathered on the front porch, which was the center of social activity not only for Goldaw's family but for many of the neighbors and relatives as well. Rothter's porch was wide and long and held about twenty chairs. At the corner of the porch stood a cauldron that looked much like the ones we took baths in. Beneath it was a disc-shaped stove powered by some kind of liquid fuel. An orange glow shone from the edges of the disc, burning day and night. In the cauldron Rothter brewed a drink called flagoon. Rothter was the flagoon maker for the whole community, and each night neighbors and relatives brought pitchers and jugs to fill with the fresh drink. To me it tasted like apple cider with too much cinnamon or some other strong spice in it. I did not particularly like it at first, but after several days I got used to it and didn't mind finishing a mug of it. It wasn't alcoholic, but it did have some ingredient that relaxed my body and gave my head a slight tingling feeling. On most nights the children played in the yard while the rest of us drank flagoon and gossiped on the porch.

Within a week of my stay in Rothter's home, Goldaw decided that I might be a good match for her daughter Taron. Goldaw never mentioned this to me herself, but Dubov, who overheard many things as a result of the fact that nobody thought he was interested in such gossip, told me everything he overheard the women saying about me. Even though I was a stranger and my background was mysterious, Goldaw thought I was hardworking, handsome, and most important, she thought I had a great deal of money that I was keeping secret. She based her suspicions about my wealth on the fact that my bill had been paid for two months in advance. Jipsum had also told her something when he dropped me off that made her think I was wealthy, but Dubov was unable to find out what Jipsum had said.

I was not pleased to become Goldaw's intended for her daughter. For one thing, I did not like being the object of so much attention. Also, I did not find Taron particularly attractive. Her figure was lanky and boyish. Her face was fairly pretty, but her hair was often in a rather unflattering tangle. The only thing that saved me from being placed in an awkward situation at first was that Taron already had one boyfriend named Keech and was flirting with another. Taron's love life was a frequent topic of conversation on the porch.

One night, when Taron walked out onto the porch, Goldaw said, "Lally is coming over."

Lally was one of the aunts, Goldaw's older sister, whose opinions held great sway in the family.

"Did you talk to her today?" asked Taron.

"Yes."

"What did she say about me?"

"Well, she asked about you."

"What?"

"Well, she asked about Keech. What you're going to do about Keech. That's what everybody wants to know. Everybody likes Keech."

"Well, I like him too."

"Well, you—"

"Now wait, Mama. Don't start sayin' things. Let's hear what other people think first."

She looked toward her father and Fornd, a friend of her father's whom she normally could count on to be on her side in a discussion.

But before they could say anything Goldaw blurted out, "You like Keech, but as soon as Dalin comes swaggerin' by you decide you like him too. Everybody's worried you're gonna do Keech dirty."

"What do you think, Daddy?"

"I just think you should be honest with both the boys," said Rothter, the diplomat who knew better than to delve too deeply in the women's arguments.

"It's not that we don't like Dalin," said Goldaw. "We barely even know him. But Keech is a nice guy. You should think about his feelings too."

"I know Keech is a nice guy. But that ain't everything. I know he's a nice guy."

There was a pause then while everyone looked at her, and Fornd ladled out another glass of flagoon. We could see Lally's figure on the horizon as she made her way down the lane toward the house.

Taron said, "Last night when Keech came over I was sittin' in the living room workin' on my dress and I had all those towels that needed to be folded sittin' in the other room, and he went in there and folded them all and I didn't even know he was doin' it." She let her audience think about this for a moment and then finished with a flip of her hand and said, "I was workin' on my dress," as if that were somehow a crucial part of the story that needed to be repeated.

"See now?" said Goldaw. "What about Dalin? Would he ever do that? Is he—does he—have you ever seen him do anything like that?"

"But Dalin sent me a card in the mail today."

"What kind of card?"

"Just a card. I don't know. With flowers on it."

"Well, don't go by that kind of stuff. Sometimes it's those guys who'll do ya the dirtiest. That's why when I see too much of that—cards and flowers and things—I think, now what's he up to? A guy can send you flowers every day and still mistreat ya. That's what those kind of guys do lots of times. They'll beat ya and then send flowers to make up for it. That don't mean nothin' to me."

Lally stepped onto the porch then, and Taron said, "We're arguing about me, Lally. I'm a wild woman."

Goldaw interjected a "No-o-o-o!" of protest while Rothter laughed.

Taron continued, "I'm doin' Keech dirty. And they don't like Dalin 'cause he's either beatin' me or sendin' me cards. I'm steppin' on everybody's feelings. I'm a bad person."

"Well, Dalin better not be beatin' ya," said Lally.

"Nobody's beatin' anybody," said Goldaw. "See how she does? You can't tell her anything."

With a smile, Lally said, "Taron, honey, are you twistin' her words?"

The whole story was repeated once again for Lally's judgment.

Among the women no one's opinion was as important as Lally's. I don't know how or why she had gained such influence, but no controversy was ever considered settled until Lally had her say. She was Goldaw's older sister, but there were few resemblances between the two women. In Goldaw there was no delicacy at all. She blurted out whatever she felt, she yelled when she was angry, she cried when she was sad, she worked hard and let the sweat pour down her body. Whenever there was action she was in the middle of it, clumsy, large, and earnest.

Lally, on the other hand, preferred to stand just outside the fray. On the porch she sat with her prim arms folded firmly against her, the most appropriate position for watching and judging, her favorite activities. For her the world was a parade that passed by, and she had only to sit with folded arms and a knowing smile and judge each participant to see if they were "normal" or "friendly" or "sneaky" or "no-good" or "strange." She collected notes as each player passed, sometimes asking questions but never signalling her judgment until the proper time. Any act or attitude that fell outside the sphere that constituted normalcy for her would be duly jotted down, and gradually a case against the person might begin to emerge. She never announced her judgments on the porch—this was a place for watching and noting—but at the appropriate time, usually when she was in intimate conversation with only one or two of the women, when they felt she trusted them supremely and would tell no one but them what her verdict was, she would spew out her volumes of evidence in remarkable and passionate detail. The other women would sit back in amazed admiration as they watched Lally in her full glory, her face pink with conviction, and they would invariably agree that there could be no doubt about the validity of her judgment, no doubt at all. Over the next several days the judgment would become known throughout the entire community, even to us outsiders on the fringes of Rothter's porch, and the condemned person would be flung from the realm of acceptability with no chance for appeal.

For Lally the sphere of normalcy was small. Amians were automatically excluded since they were the ones who lived in the mansions, bullied the poor, had odd habits of dress and food and entertainment, and generally kept all the splendor and glory for themselves. Physically unattractive people had a hard time meeting her standards, even though she, in her late fifties, enormously overweight, with a bulbous nose and a few missing teeth, was no beauty. Some unattractive people were able to redeem themselves because they were "friendly," which meant nothing more than they liked and approved of her. She did not like people who were overly ambitious or who were more intelligent than she was. She did not want others to do things to draw attention to themselves or to their actions. She offered herself as an example to follow. She had grown up, found a husband, raised her children, and then sat back, folded her arms, and judged the parade. The only appropriate action for her now was engaging in little activities that gave her frequent access to the women of the community. She made things, like homemade dolls that she could show to the women to hear them say, "Oh, now them are cute. You could sell them and make some money if you wanted." She collected and made other little things, like napkin holders and centerpieces for the table. The women loved to go to her house, which was forever bustling with all this creating and collecting and judging, stuff piled on top of stuff, with cute new curtains replacing the old ones, a new picture on the wall—"Now ain't that purty"—new carpet and candles, and "Oh, ain't that a sweet little box to hold bread in."

Taron's case was poured out before Lally as she sat noncommittal, smiling.

As Taron told her story to Lally, Mettie, who sat on the fringes of the group, pulled her chair a little closer to mine and told her own story.

"Let me give you a little warning right now," she said. "Don't let yourself get tangled up with Lally. She's always stickin' her nose in other people's business. She's been like that since she was a little girl. I remember years ago when me and my husband moved here and he was gonna work for Kothter. She was not much more than a kid but she decided she didn't like my husband and she was gonna do all she could to hurt him. She started spreadin' tales that wasn't true. I can tell you I didn't put up with it for a minute."

Mettie was seized by a wheezing, body-shaking cough that interrupted her story and left her red-faced and quiet for a moment. She said, "When they turn that fire up like that, that smoke or whatever it is makes it hard for me to breathe and I start coughin'." I felt uncomfortable and hoped she would not resume her story. Lally sat close enough that she was bound to pick up bits and pieces of Mettie's whisper.

But as soon as her breathing returned to normal, Mettie took a big swig of flagoon and picked up where she had left off. "She was stickin' her nose into my business, and I let her know right off that I wasn't going to be one to sit back and take it. I told her, 'You're a person who likes to carry tales, and they don't get repeated the way you heard them. You been sayin' things about my husband, and you been tellin' people he said things that he never said. Anybody that misquotes my husband or me is gonna pay for it.' But I didn't have anybody on my side, you see—the story of my life—even Rothter wouldn't stick up for me. He said, 'Mettie, now Mettie,' like he does, and acted like I was makin' the whole thing up. But he knew as well as I did what she was doin'. He didn't try to stop her and neither did Goldy or anybody else. When my own brother kicks me around, see, they feel like they can get away with it too."

Just then the whole porch erupted in laughter at some comment I hadn't heard, drowning Mettie out. When the laughter died down, Lally turned to me and said, "Well, Pryce is a man. Let's hear what he has to say. What do you think Taron should do about her man problem?"

"Oh, I think I'm the wrong person to turn to for advice. I say follow your heart."

"Good answer," said Rothter. "Don't let these women suck you into their traps."

—◯—

Each day I expected some kind of message from Dakin, but nothing came. It was hard to get any news from Persus Am. The Amian informationals were usually a few days late, and I still had great difficulty reading the Amian language. Rothter did not subscribe to the informationals, but usually someone brought one to the porch and passed it around and discussed it. These discussions were far from complete summaries of the news, though, and they were so fraught with condemnations of the Emajians and other exaggerations that I didn't learn much of substance from them. I didn't want to draw any suspicion to myself by asking what the informationals said about the Prince of Persus Am. But I did learn one important fact from the informationals; at least for now, Umbriel had decided not to make my escape public. This was clear because his writers included me in stories about events that happened after I was already gone. For example, I was reported to have been present at Ona's funeral, and I was even quoted giving words of condolence. I was also supposedly present at later high-level meetings concerning the Territory of Ur. How long Umbriel could keep up this deception I did not know, but sooner or later it would be obvious I was no longer in Persus Am. Maybe by then Umbriel figured he would have captured me. I still lived in constant fear of being caught.

While the informationals from Persus Am tried to give the impression that the world was calm and Umbriel's peace plan for the Territory of Ur was on track, the informationals from Damonchok gave a much different impression. They told of attacks on Damonchokian villages in the east by Wilmorothian tribes thought to be tied to Umbriel. They told of almost daily terrorist attacks in the Territory, mostly against workers trying to transport raw materials from Wilmoroth to Umbriel's factories in Persus Am. They told of the suspicions the Damonchokian and Caladan leaders harbored about Umbriel and his peace plan for the Territory, despite the new Prince's popularity with the people. The clear message was that the world was poised for war against Umbriel. And all I could do was sit anonymously and quietly on Rothter's farm, "shoveling spread" during the day and drinking flagoon at night, all the while hoping no one would ask too many questions.

The hard, physical labor I did every day was the only relief I had from my worries. In Persus Am I had grown fat. But in the sunshine of Damonchok, lifting and loading and shoveling and walking and running every day, my body became firm again, my stamina increased. Dubov liked to make up little games at work, like who could lift the most sacks and load them on the carts. Sometimes, after a day of strength-sapping work, Dubov would challenge me to race him all the way home. We ran as hard as we could until we collapsed exhausted on Goldaw's front porch. Hearing the commotion, Goldaw would come out, shake her head, and say, "Look at you two! Sweatin' all over my porch. Runnin' up here like a couple idiots. Ranejun must not work you very hard if you've got enough energy to run all the way home every night."

Dubov stood up, walked toward his mother and said, "Thanks for welcoming us home, Mama. Let me give you a hug."

"You touch me with that sweaty body and I'll knock your head off!" she wailed. "Get in there and get cleaned up. If you're late for dinner, you'll just have to do without."

—⊖—

After I had been in Damonchok for four weeks, a crisis took place in Taron's love life that drew me closer into the life of the family. Taron's boyfriend Keech, jealous of her increasing flirtation with Dalin, dumped her and turned his attention toward one of Taron's cousins. Dalin, the charming, card-writing dream date, vanished from Taron's life days later, apparently having snagged another dream woman of his own. All this left Taron without a man, and I was the most eligible bachelor on the porch. Dubov had already told me that his mother approved of me, but as far as I knew Lally had not yet made her all-important judgment. Goldaw took steps right away, however, to help ensure my rise in status. Up to that time I had been given a chair on the outer edge of the porch, beyond the family, who got the best seats closest to the flagoon cauldron, and even beyond the neighbors who were the closest friends of the family. I was out on the fringes with the neighbors who were there just out of politeness. I sat next to Mettie, who, although she was technically a family member, was doomed forever as an outcast.

After Taron's love crisis, Goldaw immediately saw to it that I was given a seat near the family, right next to Taron and just across from Lally. No longer did I have to ladle my own flagoon; when I stepped onto the porch, a hot mug was immediately held out to me. While Taron was not a treasure I wished to seek, I did not want to draw attention to myself and risk the family's hostility by insisting on resuming my normal place on the fringes. I played along, hoping that something would happen to get me out of the predicament without undue embarrassment.

For the first several days, Taron said little or nothing to me, and I felt no pressure to turn my attention toward her. But then at work one day, Dubov, ever silent with the women on these matters but ever vigilant to their schemes, said, "You're in trouble now. I think they've decided you're the right man for Taron." When I tried to press him on what he meant, he refused to explain any further. "You know what it means," he said. "They've decided."

To turn Taron aside with a polite "no thank you" would have been considered not only a slap in the face to Taron, but open rebellion against the family, against the order of the community. While that order might never have intruded so far as to coerce me into marrying the girl, if I had simply shunned her and insisted on staying on the fringes with Mettie, I would have been banished there for good.

Taron was a restless girl, a trait I had attributed to flightiness or even mindlessness. Even before I was in the picture, she never liked to sit on the porch for very long. So after only one mug of flagoon, before the sun had quite set, she asked me if I would like to take a walk with her before it got too dark. I found this option preferable to sitting there and having everyone on the porch examine my every word and gesture toward her, so I said I would go.

We walked down the lane for a while and then toward the setting sun, in a wooded area behind the house that we both liked. The trees were high and thick with leaves. It was like the first forest I had ever seen in Damonchok, the one I had forced Hamlin to experience, the one that filled me with such peace. I would have liked to sit under the trees and look toward the sunset, but Taron kept moving, rifling through the forest as if we had to get to the other side by sundown.

"We'd better not go too far since it's getting dark," I said.

"We won't. We'll turn around soon."

"Do you ever just sit in the forest and enjoy it?"

"I like to walk," she said. Now that we were alone, she seemed nervous to be with me.

The setting sun made the sky orange, but on the other side of the sky dark storm clouds gathered. Through the leaves we could see orange light reflecting off the heavy gray clouds.

"We're going to get rained on," I said.

"We'd better turn around then."

"Let's do."

As we started back, she stopped, turned to me, and said, "Pryce, I know we're not supposed to ask you stuff about where you're from and all, but can I just ask you one thing?"

"What?"

"I know you're s'posed to be Damonchokian, but to tell you the truth, nobody believes that. They say you're an Emajian and you ran away from the Utturies—or maybe Persus Am City—because you were afraid to get caught. Is that true?"

"Well, why are you asking?"

"The part I want to know is, is it true you are an Emajian?"

"Well, I don't know if I should get into that."

"If I tell you something, do you promise not to tell it to anybody?"

"Oh, Taron—"

"Do you promise? I'll trust you if you just promise."

"All right, I promise."

"You promise not to tell anybody, no matter what?"

"Yes. I promise not to tell anybody."

"Well, I am an Emajian," she said. "I believe Emajus is the Son of God and that Caladria is real and that Emajus is not dead but that he went away to gain our salvation."

"And you're not allowed to let anybody know that?"

"No. Dad would kill me if he knew I told you. He could lose his trading license if the Amians found out anyone in our family was Emajian. He practices the Amian religion so he can keep the license. But he really doesn't care about religion at all."

"And he doesn't know you're an Emajian?"

"I think he knows I go to the Emajian celebrations, but we never talk about it. He wants to pretend not to know."

"So you go to Emajian services where there is music?"

"Yes. All the time. You could go too—if you're interested."

"I am. I would like to go."

She took me in her arms and squeezed me for a moment and then let go, embarrassed. "I knew it! I could just tell. You'll love the celebration. There's singin' and dancin'. And the music! The Spirit of God is in that music. That's why I started to believe. Dubov is Emajian too."

"He is?"

"Sure. We've talked about whether you might be. He said you never said nothin' about it, but I said you haven't told us nothin' about anything! Dubov will be glad you're gonna go."

We felt tiny sprinkles on our faces. Taron took my hand and we ran out of the woods. By the time we reached the clearing it was raining hard. Realizing we would never make it back to the house dry, we stopped running and let the rain cool us off. Steamy mugs of flagoon waited for us on the porch. I was the last one to leave the porch that night, and when I finally went to bed, I slept more soundly than I ever had in Damonohola.

———◯———

When Dubov and I got home from work the next day, Goldaw met us on the porch and said, "There's a fella here been waitin' for you all afternoon. Says he has a message. Wouldn't leave it with me. Says he has to see you hisself."

"Where is he?"

"Waitin' in your room. Hope you don't mind I let him in there. He didn't wanta wait out here or in the living room. Nervous fella. He's dressed like a Damonchokian, but I don't think he is."

In my bedroom was a man dressed in brand-new Damon-chokian clothes. Though his face was painted dark, I recognized him immediately as Dakin's servant Cleopus. I wondered if my own attempt at looking Damonchokian was so transparent.

Cleopus said, "Prince—Pryce, I have a message for you from our friend. I'm so glad you're finally here. I've been a nervous wreck. I know my costume is terrible. It's a miracle I haven't been arrested and thrown in jail."

"It's good to see a familiar face. You're brave to come. What is the message?"

"I don't know. I haven't read it, sir." From a concealed pocket in the lining of his coat he pulled out a small envelope and handed it toward me, but I told him to read it to me.

Cleopus read:

Dear Pryce:

I am afraid my letter brings little good news. The situation here is not as calm as the informationals would imply, if you have chanced to see them. The Father-King is in a rage over your disappearance. Your method of escape remains a mystery (thank God), but accusing fingers are being pointed everywhere, including at me. Princess Tracian is reviling you with great zeal (she whines that you made a fool of her), and it will not surprise you to find out that Vanus spends night and day trying to persuade everyone that you should be publicly executed once you are caught. Rumors about you are rampant, and soon, maybe by the time you get this, Umbriel will go public with your escape. What story he will tell has not yet been determined. Only the truth has been ruled out.

One detail you might be interested in is that your singing episode in the Damonchokian rally is being blown all out of proportion. It is now widely believed that you not only sang, but you *led* the crowd in songs, and some rumors have you delivering a message to the crowd in favor of Emajianism.

As is already obvious to you, then, your return right now would mean certain disaster, and I think we should face the fact that you may never be able to return. No one seems to have any inkling of your whereabouts yet, and for that I am grateful. Let me stress to you that you should confide in no one and should take no risks. I have sent you my most trusted servant. Besides him, me, and the one who arranged your trip, no one knows you are there.

I have not been well since you left. I feel as if the Lord is torturing me. Do not try to reach me. I have indirect ways of finding out how you are, and I will keep monitoring your situation.

One final thing. I do not know why you were brought to this world, but I am certain it was not to sit and do nothing in the wilderness of Damonchok. I am going to take certain actions soon. I am making contacts that may be quite a surprise to you, and that, I am afraid, will cause you even more risk and trouble. But that seems to be your lot. Within a month, maybe sooner, you will hear from me again, and things will start to move. It is unsafe to be any more specific. I tell you this only so that you hang on to hope. You have not been abandoned.

"That is all," said Cleopus. "He did not sign it. He told me not to have you write back to him because of the risk, but if you want to give him any message, I am to memorize it."

"Tell him I am fine. I am treated well here. I thank him for the message. I appreciate what he has done for me with all my heart. I look forward to whatever he has planned for me to do next."

"Very good, I will tell him."

"Thank you for coming, Cleo. What will you do now?"

"A man is waiting who will take me across the border, and then someone else will take me to the Utturies, and then someone else will take me back to the palace. None of them knows that I'm a servant of Dakin's. If I'm caught, I have evidence on me to show that I am engaged in illegal activities related to smuggling."

"Do you want to stay here for the night?"

"No. I am overdue already, since I stayed to wait for you. Good-bye, sir. Be careful, sir. They're going to be searching every village in the world. May God protect you."

———◯———

That night Taron and Dubov and I went to the Emajian celebration. I knew it was unsafe to go, but the music was too powerful a temptation to pass up. Besides, if they were going to catch me, I'd rather be caught singing and dancing than sulking in my room. The Emajians had their own church. The sanctuary, if you could call it that, did not have pews or a pulpit. There was a raised platform in the middle, where those playing instruments sat and where the Keeper, their version of a minister, spoke. Otherwise the room was bare except for a few chairs in the corners. The room held a couple hundred worshipers, and by the time we got there it was crowded and the music had already begun. In a room next to the sanctuary, tables of food were set up for after the celebration. We added two pies and a jug of flagoon to the feast, and then we joined the worshipers. They were singing an Emajian song I had heard before, a song with many verses and with a chorus that translated, "Blessed be Emajus/Son of God/Drown us in your love/Prince of Peace/Wash away our sins/King of Kings/Bring us on home." The platform was covered with instruments of all types, one which sounded particularly like a saxophone but looked nothing like it; it was made of dark wood and strangely twisted. Men and women played various kinds of stringed instruments, no two of them exactly alike. Some looked like guitars, others like various kinds of harps. There were horns, which sounded something like trumpets and trombones except that the sound was more muffled. Blending in with all these instruments were the voices of the people, free and loud. I was caught up immediately into the energy and the joy of it. No one sang halfheartedly. People danced and clapped as they sang, the whole crowd bobbing up and down in rhythmical unity. It was as if the song were singing the people, as if the music had come alive in the room and the people were merely riding in the flow of it.

We celebrated song after song, with the Keeper leading the musicians from one to the next. The music did not stop for more than two hours. Occasionally someone would get tired and would have to sit along the wall or go outside to rest. Even those sitting along the walls usually clapped and sang while a brother or sister, as they called one another, brought glasses of water or flagoon to refresh them.

Finally the Keeper wound down the music so that he could speak. As the last strains of the song faded and people shouted "Amen!" and "Thank the Lord!" the Keeper, a dark, burly man with a piercing voice, held an Emajian informational above his head and shouted, "Brothers and Sisters! I hold here in my hands the words of the Lord Emajus!"

"Amen! Tell it!" shouted the crowd.

"Some of these words is what we heard all our lives, what the Lord himself spoke among us so many years ago."

"Glory!"

"But some of these words is new to us. The Visitor Jeremy

translated 'em to us, and some say he's God's prophet and some say he ain't, but either way God used him to translate the book brought here by the Visitor Elaine years ago 'fore they chopped off her head. Some of you read these words on this page, but I'm afraid it ain't yet sunk into your *hearts*!" he said, his voice rising. Then he shouted, "I'm talkin' 'bout Emajus's words now!"

"Hallelujah, brother! Amen!"

"Last time we met, Brother Chidiock read you a parable of the Lord Emajus. He told the story of a son who was lost. He told of a son who asked his father for his share of the estate and then went off and squandered it all away in wild living."

"Preach it!"

The Keeper's mighty voice gradually took on a rhythmical quiver. "He told how when the son's money ran out he was destitute and hungry and had to get a job feedin' pigs!

"And he was so poor and hungry that even the pigs' food looked good to him. He had hit rock bottom, do you hear what I'm sayin'? He had betrayed his father and spoiled his life. Are you listenin' with your hearts?" The Keeper walked about the platform. He mopped his face with a towel.

He looked at us again and said quietly, "But finally he came to his senses."

"Glory!"

"Finally he came to his senses and he said, 'Well, I'll just go back to my father! I'll just go back to my father! Why, his servants are better off than I am. I'll go back and be one of his servants. I'll tell him I'm not worthy to be his son! I'm not worthy to be his son! But I can be a servant.'

"So he went back, but brothers and sisters, did he go back as a servant? Did he go back to the scorn and punishment of his father? No! Bless God, his father met him on the road! Met him before he even made it home! And he gave him new clothes and a ring, and he threw the biggest celebration you have ever seen. Why? Because he said, 'My son was dead and now he's alive again! My son was lost and now he is found!'"

The crowd showered him with *Amens and Thank the Lords*.

The Keeper paced back and forth across the platform. The

musicians were restless. They held onto their instruments, ready to play.

The Keeper continued, "Brothers and sisters, this story is from our own Lord Emajus. We would have known it was His even if they hadn't told us. And it has been given to us, brothers and sisters, to call us back."

"Amen!"

"He's calling us back to Him!"

"Yes, Lord."

"Because some of us have drifted away."

"Yes, Lord. Help us, Lord."

"Some of us have drifted away because our Lord has been gone a long time, and our faith just couldn't hold out."

"Help us!"

"Some of us have drifted away because we're scared to follow Emajus. Because we're scared of the price we might have to pay if we stand up and declare, 'I am an Emajian!'"

I felt a sudden sting of conviction. This shouting, strutting preacher, who a moment ago had been nothing but a curiosity, an entertaining interlude in the music, suddenly sounded like my own conscience. It was like listening to Tarius Arc.

He said, "We drifted away because we could not see the Lord with our eyes. We drifted because He seemed far away from us, and we were left alone, and the voice of the Evil One whispered in our ears and said, 'Emajus is dead. He done led His people into the wilderness and they all died.' But deep down we knew he was lying, brothers and sisters."

"Yes!"

"We knew he was lying, but it's awful easy to doubt when it seems the Lord's beyond your reach. The Lord has taken His people to the paradise of Caladria, and He has gone on to finish our salvation, and deep in our hearts we knew it, but we were still here all alone. We couldn't *see* it. All we could see were the doubters and the scoffers. So we went off and spent our inheritance in foolish living."

"Help us, Lord."

"We didn't mean to. We didn't really know we were doin' it,

but we just sort of drifted on out there. And now our hearts have turned cold. Our hearts have turned cold and we don't want to think about Emajus. But let me tell you something. We may have drifted away and turned our back on Him, but He's callin' us back anyhow!"

"Glory!"

"He's not just sitting there waiting on us to come back. No! He has come out to meet us on the road!"

"Hallelujah!"

"His arms are open wide, and He's ready to take us back in! Not as slaves. No! He wants us back as sons and daughters like we were before."

"Well, thank the Lord."

"Do you feel His Spirit tuggin' on your heart? Do you feel the Spirit when we sing the songs? Do you hear Him callin' you back? Why don't you just come on home? Come on home to forgiveness. Let Him wash all the darkness away. Wash it away. Let His love and forgiveness just flood right on over you."

"Do it, Lord!"

"We're gonna sing now, brothers and sisters, and you just let the Spirit do some talkin' to you. You've heard our Lord's story. Now is the time to turn back to the Father, for His arms are wide open and He wants to take you in. You don't have to wallow in the sin and guilt and lies anymore. You just come to the Lord Emajus and put your trust in Him, and He's gonna see us through. Let's sing, 'We don't know what the future holds/but we know He'll see us through.' Start us off, brother."

We sang his song, and when we finished, we sang a song that said, "Take me back, Lord Emajus/Enclose me in Your sweet love again." The music was soulful and rich. The Holy Spirit swirled in the music. I felt myself wrapped in Spirit.

The Keeper said, "The Father's callin' to you, brothers and sisters. Can't you hear His voice? Whoever would come back to the Lord, do it now. Come now and let us pray with you. Let us lift you together in prayer to the Lord. Let the Lord's Spirit return to your soul today."

I was wrapped in Spirit. I prayed, "Father, Father, Father.

Forgive me for betraying you. Forgive me for what I have done."
The prayer screamed within me. It repeated itself again and again
and would not stop.

"Step forward and let me pray with you, brother. Step
forward, sister. The Father's arms are wide open."

I prayed and prayed. And while the slow and rhythmic,
"Take me back, Lord Emajus/Enclose me in Your sweet love
again" filled everything around me, I stepped out into the music
and walked toward the minister, who said, "Bless you, brother.
Bless you. Come on back to the Lord."

The minister put his hands on my shoulders and said, "What
is your name, brother?"

"Pryce."

"Do you want to come back to the Lord?"

"Yes."

The Keeper prayed as the music played on. He prayed,
"Restore him to You, Lord. Forgive him, Lord. Take him back.
Amen! May the Lord be praised."

—◯—

In faith—in my mind—I believed the Lord forgave me that
night, but for the next week I was still not satisfied. I did not sense
the closeness of the Lord's Spirit that I once had known. I was still
tortured by many things—the memory of Jank, my anger at
Umbriel and Tracian, my own guilt, the words of Tarius Arc, my
fear of being caught, my concern for Dakin and Miriaban's
safety—these and other worries kept me in constant turmoil.

Then one day Ranejun let us off work a couple hours early,
and we decided to go swimming at a nearby lake. We often raced
home, so feeling a new burst of energy after being set free from
the day's work, we decided to race to the lake. The road took us
only part of the way, and then we had to take a path through the
woods.

As we started down the road, I ran faster than I ever had.
Dubov usually got ahead of me early on, but now he was far
behind. "Whoo!" he screamed. "You're not gonna be so easy to
beat today."

I felt good running. I loved the rhythm of the pounding of

my feet and the sound of my breath and the energy pulsing through me. During work my thoughts had followed their usual tortured course, but now the only thought that rang out to the rhythm of each stride was, *I have made a mess of this thing. I have made a terrible mess.* I felt the guilt crawling inside me, and I wanted to run and let it seep out like sweat.

To the rhythm of the pounding feet, letting it seep out like sweat, running faster and faster, through my mind beat the words I had translated, *"Do you not know that in a race all the runners run, but only one gets the prize?"*

I wanted to run faster and faster still, as the breath began to hurt. *"Run in such a way as to get the prize."* Wanted my guilt to seep out like sweat, like sweat . . . *I have made a terrible mess—*

"I do not run like a man running aimlessly; I do not fight like a man beating the air." By the time we reached the path Dubov was too tired to run anymore and yelled, "Pryce! Pryce! Stop!" And by the time I was halfway to the lake, he was too far away for me to see or hear.

Running for the prize. How can I stand still when I have made such a terrible mess of . . . seeping out like . . .

My breath hurting, my chest pulling—*Run, run, run in such a way as to get the prize . . .*

And then there were no words. No words at all, but it was just like when I had stepped out, stepped toward the white sweltering altar at my church at home with Pastor Fletcher saying, "Come home to Jesus," stepping to the purge like sweat seeping out and praying, *Jesus, Jesus, Jesus*—the Keeper saying, "Come on home, brother, the Father's arms are open wide."

I stopped running but the trees kept hurtling by on either side of the path; when they finally stopped, I raised my arms and felt the gasping air. There were no words anymore, but a gasping of air, and when there was enough of it I yelled a wordless, inexplicable yell—yelled to no one in particular in those woods. Only Jesus heard it, for even Dubov was far behind me on the path. And after I yelled, I dropped to the ground, and I knew the Lord had returned to me in that moment. I knew the Lord had returned and

I could not stay there on the ground, so I stood and jogged lightly down the path toward Dubov, my sweat cold now in the breeze.

When we got to the lake, we dipped ourselves into the water. It was gripping, cold. When we got out, we found a patch of sun and lay there in its warmth. We sat back silently, and I let words pile up around me, images in slow motion, words in a stream that dumped images on the bank, where I picked them up and rolled them over slowly in my head, until at last I was asleep.

—◯—

Late that night, alone on Rothter's porch, after everyone else had gone to bed, I said out loud, "I am an Emajian."

—◯—

One tradition at the Emajian celebrations was to let the new believers lead the rest of the worshipers in some songs as a testimony to their faith. This opportunity was given to me at the next celebration, so I led the crowd in a song I had heard Tarius Arc sing in jail, the first verse of which can be translated, "When our waiting is done/Mighty Emajus will come/Bearing our redemption in His hand./He'll fill us with light/He'll restore His own kingdom/Then Emajus shall reign/Praise His name/Praise His name." In the original language this is one of the most powerful and energetic songs ever written. It has eight verses, and the first time through it the other worshipers let me sing them alone, while they joined me in the chorus, "Emajus shall reign/Praise His name/Praise His name."

Just as in the other celebration, the song filled the room with joy, and the Spirit of the Lord seemed to speak through the voices and the stringed instruments and the horns and the tambourines and the dancing and the clapping. Once all eight verses were finished, I intended to step off the platform and let the Keeper take over again, but the instruments kept playing the song, so we started again from the first verse. By that time I could hardly be said to have been leading the song, for it had taken on a momentum of its own. But as I sang the song with all my heart, something strange happened. In front of me I saw strands of blue light, and as I continued to sing, I sang strands of green and yellow and red. The light swirled around the room, dancing to the beat of the music. It took me a few minutes to realize that the light was coming from my own voice. It sprang from my own voice just as it had from my guitar on the night of my arrival. The light gradually filled the room and wrapped itself around people as they sang and praised God. The light, like the music, was filled with Spirit. We sang and danced in it nonstop for nearly two hours, though we could not calculate the time until afterward. While the light filled the room, time ceased to exist.

Gradually physical exhaustion slowed us down, and then the light faded away. When it was all over, people crowded around me in amazement, but I was too awed and confused to try to reduce what had happened to words. I felt an overwhelming need to be alone to think rather than talk. In the commotion I managed to slip through the crowd and I ran toward home. When I could hear no one behind me, I stopped running and walked the rest of the way home. I abandoned words altogether, even in my thoughts, and enjoyed the silence and the tiny lights that were millions of miles away in the sky.

The next night, after dark, as I rested with the others around the glow of the flagoon kettle on the porch, Taron took my hand and said, "Do you want to go for a walk? I need to talk to you."

"Honey, he's restin' right now," said Goldaw. "I think he was just about to doze off. He don't need some girl a-pesterin' him this late in the evenin'."

Rothter said, "Get used to it, Pryce. I ain't had a nap in twenty-five years. Women just won't let ya."

Goldaw said, "If you ain't had a nap in twenty-five years, then I'd like to know who does all that snorin' in the living room ever' night before dinner."

"I never snored in my life," he said, and the whole family laughed. Goldaw swatted him with a towel.

I got up and went off with Taron.

She said, "There's lots of rumors goin' around about you."

"Like what?"

"People tryin' to figure out who you really are."

"What are they saying?"

"Some thinks you're just a Damonchokian like you say, but others say you sound kind of Amian. Some thinks you're a spy from Persus Am tryin' to find out who the Emajians are so you can take away their trade permit."

"That's ridiculous."

"I know it is. After hearin' you sing last night and after seein' that light in your music, I know for a fact you're an Emajian through and through. So some people say if you're not an Amian spy, you might be an Emajian from the Amian government who's escaping Persus Am so you won't get caught. I know Mama has told us over and over that we're not allowed to ask you anything about where you came from."

"That's right. That's one thing I can't tell you anything else about."

"Anything *else*? You haven't told me nothin' as it is. Do you know how amazed everyone was by what happened last night?"

"I was amazed too."

"You didn't know that was gonna happen?"

"No. I had no idea."

"Pryce, what have you come here for?"

"I just don't know how to answer that. There are so many things I'm not even sure of myself."

"I've got to talk serious with you. I know Mama and Lally and everybody thinks I'm just tryin' to get you to marry me, but I know that ain't gonna happen. I can see that in you, that that's not what you want. I'm not askin' that at all."

"Taron—"

"Wait a second. I intend to say this. I don't know who you are or what you're here for, but I know you are something special for Emajus. I know you probably won't hang around here very long, because the Lord will call you to your work, and it ain't gonna be on Ranejun's farm. And what I want to tell you is that whatever your work is, I just want to be a part of it and help you with it. I believe that's what the Lord wants me to do."

"Taron, you just don't understand—"

"Please don't put me off with some answer. I don't want any answer. I know you can't tell me anything about why you're here.

But you just think about what I said. I'm askin' you to make me a part of whatever it is. When the time comes. I love the Lord with all my heart, and I'm willing to do anything, no matter how dangerous, no matter what it takes. You just think about it, and you pray about it. Now don't say anything. I'm walking back alone. Good night."

—◯—

A couple weeks later we suffered a thunderstorm so violent that it swept water onto the porch and forced us inside to finish our flagoon. We sat at the windows and watched the lightning flood the entire outdoors with daylight for a split second at a time. After one flash Taron said, "Look there down the lane. Somebody's standin' by the side of the road."

"What?" scoffed Goldaw. "I don't see nothin'."

"He's down there on the right-hand side of the road."

"You can see him now?" asked Goldaw.

"No," she said. "But he was there when the lightning flashed."

Ever paranoid about being caught, I went to the window to look for the man. I could see nothing, even when lightning flashed.

"Prob'ly just a tree," said Rothter.

"No it wasn't," Taron insisted. "There was a man out there just as plain as day. Should we go out and see?"

"No!" said Goldaw. "You're not goin' anywhere in a storm like this. For heaven's sake, Taron."

"He's prob'ly drowned already by now anyhow if he's out there," said Roth.

Taron kept her eyes on the spot where she had seen the man, but everyone else dropped the subject.

The storm still raged when I went to bed that night. I was not yet asleep when I heard the thud at the front door. I heard Rothter's voice, but I could not hear who had come in. Moments later I heard footsteps coming down my own hall. I got out of bed and put on a robe.

There was no knock. When the door opened it crashed against the wall. "Careful with the door," Rothter started to say, but before he had finished his sentence the figure who had opened the door shut it in Rothter's face and stood dripping before me. I turned on the globe light, and as its glow brightened, the figure peeled off layers of wet black clothes. His face was covered by a hood. He flung his coat against the wall, and then he took off the hooded cape.

"Dakin!"

"Be quiet! We mustn't let them know."

"Here, let me help you with those wet clothes. What are you doing here? Is everything all right?"

"No. Everything is not all right. I could stay no longer. Do you have something warm to drink?" He was shivering. He ran his fingers through his wet hair and drops of water flew everywhere.

I stepped outside the room, where Goldaw and Roth stood not far away in the hall.

"We wanted to make sure you was all right," said Goldaw, blushing with embarrassment at being caught eavesdropping.

"I'm fine. An old friend. Could we get him some warm flagoon?"

"Sure. Will he be wantin' to stay the night?"

"I don't know. I'll ask him."

"Kind of a nervous guy, ain't he?" said Rothter.

This required no answer. I shut the door and listened to their footsteps fade away. In a few minutes Goldaw brought the flagoon and some pastries. I took them without letting her into the room to see Dakin.

"Thanks, Goldaw. He's not staying. You can go on to bed if you want. I'll see him out."

She stood at the doorway, hesitant.

"Thanks again," I said.

Reluctantly she walked away.

Dakin told me he could stay only a few minutes because someone was outside waiting for him and they were going on that night.

"Somebody's out there in the rain waiting on you?"

"Unlike me, he is dry and safe in our van. I walked because I didn't want to attract any more suspicion than absolutely necessary. I waited outside for a couple of hours until your guests left the house. This is a miserable business, Jeremy. I'm too old for this."

"So what are you doing here?"

"I have left for good. They were getting suspicious of me. Everybody's paranoid. More terrorists have attacked our soldiers and civilians in our sector of the Territory of Ur. Damonchok is threatening war if we make any attempt to set you up as ruler of the Territory. The Rock of Calad is getting very nervous. They're urging that we put off the whole plan for a year or so until things cool down. Umbriel is furious. He feels betrayed and humiliated by you and the Rock and nearly everybody else. He's threatening the Rock that if they don't live up to their agreement, it will mean all-out war."

"Where is Miriaban?"

He leaned back against the wall and sighed. He looked old and utterly weary. "I am sorry to say that Miriaban still refuses to leave. We've gone round and round about it, and she is very stubborn. She told me to go if I had to and to come back when I finished what I had to do."

"Do you think she's safe?"

"No one is safe anymore. But relatively speaking, yes, she's probably safe. They will probably watch her constantly and try to use her to find me—and you. But I don't think they'll harm her. Umbriel is unpredictable, though, especially now. He's trying to keep things under control, but he's in a panic. Vanus and his crowd are pushing for war. If Umbriel can't solve this crisis, he may not survive as Father-King."

"And if he doesn't, do you think you might be able to return like Miriaban said?"

"There may be circumstances someday that would allow me to go back, but Umbriel's demise would not be enough. If he fell right now, Vanus and his crowd would probably take over. And they are even more hostile to me than Umbriel."

"So under what circumstances could you go back?"

He hesitated, tugging absently on his hair. "I really shouldn't get into that yet. You'll see when the time comes. You might even be able to go back someday yourself."

"What is Umbriel doing about me?"

"The latest idea when I left was to say that you were kidnapped by Emajian terrorists probably connected to the Rock of Calad."

"Kidnapped?"

"Yes. Absurd, isn't it? Kidnapped right out of the palace. That's how desperate they're getting. But the kidnapping story does two things for Umbriel. One, it spares him the humiliation of having to admit that you fled from him and tricked him after he had invested so much in you by making you heir. And two, it gives him another reason for declaring war against the Rock. They were working out the details when I left, so that story might even be out in the informationals by now."

"So what are you going to do now? What are you here for?"

"I can't tell you everything. You're just going to have to trust me. Many things could still go wrong, and the less you know, the better for us all." He pulled a pouch out of his pocket and took an envelope out of the pouch. "I'm here to arrange a few things. I am going to give you this envelope. It contains a map. One day a messenger will come to you with a box containing a new hat. You will simply tell everyone that you ordered the hat. That is not unusual. On the day you receive the hat, you must go to the place on this map at midnight. Don't tell anybody what you're doing."

"And then what?"

"Somebody will be waiting for you."

"I understand, but what then? What's the ultimate plan?"

"Let's just take it one step at a time."

"Dakin—"

"I know it's frustrating to wait and to be kept in the dark, but I and other people are risking our lives for this. It's the only way. Now I'd better get going. Do you understand the plan?"

"Yes."

He put on his wet clothes and stepped toward the door.

"By the way," I said, "I am an Emajian."

Breaking into a rare smile, Dakin replied, "So am I."

———○———

The map Dakin had given me led to storage barns on a farm that was about an hour's walk from Rothter's farm. I kept the map with me at all times. My room at Rothter's was not very secure since Goldaw went in and out and the room was never locked.

The day after Dakin's visit, no one said a word to me about him. There was a time when I would have been naive enough to have taken comfort in this silence, but by now I knew it only meant they thought the visit of such importance that they could not confront me about it directly. Their gossip and speculation would take place out of the range of my hearing.

The days after Dakin's visit were tense. A group of Amian officials came into the area just a few days later. They were there for an annual visit to renew the trade permits with the area farmers. Damonchokians do not like Amians. Most Amian citizens were not allowed into the country, and these officials were allowed in only reluctantly, only because the trade permits would not be issued any other way. Uniformed Damonchokian soldiers accompanied the Amians around the clock. The soldiers were assigned not only to restrict the movement of the Amians but also to protect them, for Damonchokian terrorists had murdered Amian officials on three previous occasions.

Persus Am had a policy against doing business with any member of the Emajian religion. The Amian government did not need absolute proof that one was a follower of Emajus to deny a trade permit. If it merely suspected that a farmer were an Emajian, it could deny the permit. Even if a farmer were not an Emajian himself, he could lose his permit if there were any evidence that he had sold Amian equipment or other goods to farmers without permits. Trade permits not only allowed farmers to buy superior Amian equipment and other goods, but it also allowed them to sell their crops to the huge Amian market. Some Damonchokian farmers without permits tried to get around the law by paying farmers with permits to sell their crops for them. A farmer would lose his permit if he were caught selling another farmer's crops. The Amian officials interviewed farmers, family members, and neighbors in their quest to uncover illegal behavior. People cooperated with them only to the extent that was absolutely necessary to retain their own permits and to protect their friends. To inform against a fellow Damonchokian was considered a disgrace. Still, the Amians relied on paid Damonchokian informants and its own spies to gather information. They also inspected homes and barns in search of Emajian musical instruments or literature, possession of which was grounds for the loss of a trade permit.

Many farmers patriotically defied the Amians by refusing a trade permit and by refusing to have anything to do with the Amians. Some terrorized the Amians at every opportunity. But most played along, engaging the Amians in a subtle psychological game of cover-up, lies, and appeasement for the sake of good business. My presence, particularly because of all the rumors about me, caused problems for Rothter. He had housed questionable characters before, so the Amians already were suspicious of him. They pressed him for details of my background, and he told them the necessary lies. He had worked out for me a detailed life history, including a birthplace in a remote region of Damonchok, the names of my parents, a work history, and other details. Dakin had already given me a fake personal history, of course, before I arrived in Damonchok, but Rothter believed his sounded more plausible. I did not even bother trying to convince Rothter that what I told him about my background was true. No one in his family believed I was really Damonchokian. He was confident I could fool the Amians, however, if I kept my story straight and if I talked with more of a Damonchokian accent, which I was learning to do.

My presence also caused problems for my boss Ranejun, whose business relied heavily on his trade permit. After the Amians visited Ranejun one day, Dubov picked up the rumor that Ranejun planned to fire me to appease them. He did not fire me, but after his meeting with them, it was not uncommon for them to come to wherever I was working and just watch me for an hour or two, as if my Emajianism would show in the way I shoveled or lifted or rested. One night they even showed up at Rothter's porch, causing everyone to excuse themselves early and go home.

What worried me most was not knowing exactly what it was

they suspected. Through which layer of deceit had they cut? Did they simply suspect that I was not Damonchokian, that I was instead a fugitive from the Utturies? Or was it possible they suspected the truth? I prayed every day that my signal from Dakin would come, so I could get myself and everyone else out of danger. I told Goldaw and Rothter that if they thought they were going to lose their permit because of me, I would find somewhere else to stay. Rothter, who hated the Amians, said he was not willing to make one more concession to them. "They suspect everybody," he said. "You will stay put."

On one of our days off during the second week of the Amians' relentless harassment, Dubov, Taron, and I went swimming at the lake. As was customary in Damonchok, we walked fully clothed to the lake and did not strip down to bathing suits until we were ready to jump in. Late in the afternoon, Taron grew tired and rested on the bank next to our clothes while Dubov and I swam.

As my head came up out of the water, I heard Amian voices talking to Taron. Dubov had already heard them and was halfway to shore. I thought immediately of the map folded tightly and buttoned up in an inside pocket of my jacket, where I always kept it. When I reached the bank and saw the Amians going through our clothes, my stomach tightened. I began to work on a lie that might explain the map.

By the time Dubov and I stood dripping on the bank, however, the search was over, and the Amians held nothing in their hands. I knew that Dubov usually carried a book of Emajian scriptures in his coat, but the Amians found nothing.

One of the Amians said, "Strange that young men carry nothing at all in their pockets."

"Why is it strange?" asked Dubov. "We're goin' swimmin'. What do you want? We're not doin' nothin' wrong."

The men stepped away and whispered to one another. One came back and said, "Have a nice afternoon," and then they left.

We said nothing at all until their voices were far away, and even then we whispered. "I hid the stuff in those leaves," said Taron. "I heard them coming."

"Thank God," said Dubov, as she took out his scriptures and handed them to him. "Thank God," he said again.

As Dubov dressed, Taron slipped my map into my hand and smiled. Though neither of us said one word about it, I knew she had seen it and that she had at least a vague idea what it was for.

———◯———

I was working in Ranejun's barn when the signal came. Taron brought the man with the hat box into the barn just an hour before it was time for us to quit. She had never interrupted us at work before. Dubov said, "Why'd you bring him all the way down here? He could've just dropped it off at the house."

Taron answered, "The man insisted on giving it to Pryce himself."

"What is it?" asked Dubov.

"Looks like a hat box to me," said Taron. "Messenger's awful particular 'bout deliverin' a hat."

I opened the box and took out the hat. I thanked the messenger, and he left without saying another word.

"Who's it from?" asked Taron.

"An old friend of mine."

"Mighty peculiar."

"There's nothing peculiar about an old friend of mine sending me a hat."

"All right, if you say so. Do you want me to take it back for you?"

"No thanks. I'll take it." I was afraid the box might contain some other message that Taron should not see. When I got off work and was alone in my room, I searched the box and the hat for messages, but there were none. Since I did not have to meet Dakin—or whoever else might be there—until midnight, I ate dinner as usual and sat out on the porch. I followed my usual pattern in order to avoid any suspicion, but I was so distracted that I could hardly eat or keep up my end of the conversation on the porch. I wanted to get Taron aside to tell her a veiled good-bye—I couldn't let her know what was really going on—but she left right after dinner. When I asked Goldaw about this, she shook her head and said, "She's goin' out with some other boy. I reckon a girl gets tired of sittin' on the porch every night." Goldaw was irked with me for not pursuing her daughter. If only my life could have been so simple, I thought, that my biggest problem was figuring out which girl to date.

I was the last one to leave the porch. It was not unusual for me to sit out there by myself an hour or so after everyone else had gone to bed. After Goldaw cleaned away the last of the cups and dishes, she asked, "You stayin' out here a while?"

"I think I will."

"Well, I'm goin' to bed."

"Good night, Goldaw."

"Taron's prob'ly gonna be late gettin' in tonight," she said.

I only looked at her and smiled. She shook her head and went inside. After it grew quiet inside, I stepped off the porch and left Goldaw's house behind. I packed nothing. If I were caught on the road, I did not want to have to explain why I had a suitcase. I felt sadness and guilt for walking away from my friends without a word of explanation. I felt afraid. Still, there was something liberating and hopeful about being in motion again. My long wait was finally over. I jogged down the road and daydreamed about Anne, home, and the music of Emajus.

———◯———

I did not have a lantern, so I had a tough time finding the right barn door. I heard all kinds of noises that sounded like footsteps, but no one was there. When I found the door, I pushed it open and stepped silently into a black, cavernous room.

"Pryce?"

It was Dakin's voice. "Yes. It's me," I said. He came into view, though he had to move quite close to me before I could see him. He fiddled with a lantern, an old-fashioned Damonchokian model, trying to light it.

The next words I heard were not from Dakin.

The words were in English.

"Hi, Jeremy."

I could not see. Dakin could not get the lantern lit.

"Jeremy," said the voice.

It was a man's voice.

Strong hands gripped my shoulders. "Jeremy, don't you recognize me, man?"

I was too stunned to answer. The lantern flickered a dim, surrealistic glow. He said, "It's me, Will!"

"Will!" The beard, the bulky frame, the voice, the grip— memories from a million years ago. Will. "Will! It's impossible."

"Speak English, Jer. Don't you remember it anymore?"

The lantern glowed brighter, making Will real before my eyes. He said, "You didn't suspect me? They told me you might have heard rumors that I was here."

"I heard *somebody* was here, but I thought—"

"What?"

"To tell you the truth, I thought it was Anne."

"Anne. What made you think so?"

"I have these memories of her that are so vivid—more like visions, actually—and you are in them sometimes too. Everything else about home is so hazy, but Anne is sometimes so clear in my mind that I feel like I just talked to her a few minutes ago. But Anne isn't here?"

"No. I haven't seen anybody else. The memory of home is pretty hazy for me too. Anne seems like somebody I knew thousands of years ago."

From the corner of the barn, near one of the vans the group had traveled in, came a voice that said, "What a beautiful language you speak, Brother Jeremy."

"Tarius?" I said. "Is it possible that Tarius Arc and Dakin and Will are all in the same room together?"

"It is possible," said Tarius. "God works in strange ways, and those ways are getting stranger all the time."

He came over and clasped my arm. I said, "It looks like they're treating you well on the Rock."

"Oh yes. They have fed me, they have given me plenty of rest, they have cleaned me up, they've given me new clothes. And now, just when everything is going so well, I guess you're going to send me back out on some wild adventure."

"Am I? I don't really know."

"Well, here is your friend Will. Ask him."

I turned to Will and said in English, "What's going on, Will? What part do you play in this?"

"I was hoping you would tell me that. All I know is, I came here knowing just a few things, and one of them was that I was not to make myself known to you right away, but when the time came for me to see you, I would remember how to do it."

"Remember?"

"Yeah, it's hard to explain, especially to those guys on the Rock—especially since I can't speak the language as well as you can—but it's like I've seen it all before—all of what's going to happen to us—and at certain times I remember what I'm supposed to do next. Just like when ol' Dakin came to the Rock all squirmy and nervous. I remembered right away that he was the one who was supposed to take me to you. But I never knew it before even though I'd seen his picture in the informationals a hundred times."

"What are you supposed to do once you've found me?"

"I'm supposed to help you get to a place that nobody else knows how to get to."

"Caladria?"

"That's it."

"So it's true, then! Caladria is a real place. The Lord has sent you to take us to Caladria. I can't believe it." In Amian I said to Dakin and Tarius, "He has come to take us to Caladria!"

Will said, "Hold on, Jer. In the first place, the Lord did not tell me a thing. I just remember this stuff, like I told you. And I haven't even remembered all about Caladria yet. It's just vague in my mind. I expect I won't get it till we're on the way. At least I hope I get it."

"So what do we do now?"

"We're on our way. You were our first stop. We're going through Damonchok now to Wilmoroth, and then across Wilmoroth into the Gray Desert, and from there I don't know what we do."

"Amazing. Just the four of us?"

"No. We brought four drivers with us, two for each van. We have one van to ride in and the other for supplies. And we're picking up some other people in Wilmoroth. So we'd better get started. We can talk in the van. Dakin is pretty nervous about hanging around here."

The vans looked like windowless stagecoaches, pulled by camucks. The only light and air available to passengers came through a series of small slits that could be opened in the sides. Our journey would likely be hot, cramped, and bumpy.

After making sure everything was secure, Dakin, Tarius Arc, Will, and I—the most unlikely group of traveling companions in the world—boarded our van and started off toward Caladria, which we did not know how to get to and which all known evidence told us did not exist.

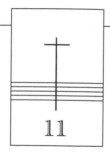

11

We left the barn right away and headed east toward the Wilmorothian border. It would take us several days to get to the border if all went well, and before we got there we were to meet a guide who would get us across the border and who would be our translator throughout Wilmoroth, since the people there spoke a different language. If we made it through Wilmoroth, a nation known to be hostile to outsiders, we would cross the Dead Mountains into the Gray Desert, an uninhabited place where no one, not even the hardiest Wilmorothians, ever went. It was in this forbidding place that the bodies of the Emajian pilgrims to Caladria had supposedly been found years after their deaths. The Amian government had paid high salaries to explorers to search the area to prove that Caladria did not exist. More than half of the exploration team had died, mostly because of strange diseases spread by the horrible hard-shelled insects that thrived in that desert.

The most frightening part of our trip was that even if we made it to the desert without being killed, Will had no idea what we were to do next. Earlier explorers had already proven that the place he marked was not Caladria. Would we wait there for some miraculous rescue? Would we all eventually die there and discover that Caladria was really another name for heaven? I asked Tarius these questions, and he replied, "Caladria is not heaven. It is a real place that exists somewhere on this planet. We are going to it. We just have to trust Will and the Lord to show us the way."

Will had not adjusted well to this new world. He understood the language, but he did not speak it very well and said no more than he had to. With me he insisted on always speaking English, which by this time was less natural to me than Amian. Will said, "Since the day I got here, they've been pumping me with questions I don't know anything about. I came only knowing that I was to take you to Caladria when the time came, but every little move you made after you were taken prisoner in Persus Am they asked me about. 'What should we do now?' 'Why did Jeremy do that?' 'Why do you think they released him from prison?' On and on. 'How am I supposed to know?' I said. 'I never understood him back home, let alone now when he lives in a palace and is pretending to be a prince and has money and women all around him. How am I supposed to know what he's doing? Making the best of it, I guess.'"

"But did you have anything to do with the people on the Rock making the deal that would let me rule the Territory of Ur?"

"All I finally said was I don't know anything about politics. It's not my department. I told them I thought it would be safe to trust you and do whatever you thought best. I told them you probably knew what you were doing, and I was just waiting here to play my part of this whole thing, so that hopefully I could get it over with and go home."

Will did not particularly like Emajian music, and he wanted nothing to do with the Emajian religion. On the Rock of Calad he had been surrounded by music almost constantly; there were nightly celebrations with Emajians singing and playing more kinds of instruments than existed anywhere else in the world. But during these times, which for me would have been a spiritual feast, Will hung back and refused to participate. From the way he described his stay on the Rock, he was not always a welcome guest. He loved the vapors, and from what I could piece together from his story, he often got so intoxicated on them that he made lewd and, to his Emajian guests, shocking advances toward the young women. In the vapors he found ecstasy and escape, but the music left him cold. He said he found the sound "interesting," but as far as sensing the voice of God in it, he didn't; he thought this was just one of my religious delusions like those I had indulged in at home. Though my friendship with Will had survived my conversion to Christianity, he had always held a barely concealed contempt for it. It was a subject he never wanted to discuss. My embrace of Emajianism did not surprise him. He just figured I was prone to that sort of thing.

We rode all night with only a few short stops. When it had been daylight for a couple of hours, we stopped along the side of the road to eat breakfast, switch drivers, and give the camucks a chance to rest and eat. As I stepped out of our van, I saw two of the drivers scuffling with someone in the back of the other van, which was supposed to contain only supplies. From where I stood I could not tell who they were fighting; I could see only kicking feet. One of the drivers yelled, "Keep her in there! Don't let her get away!"

Their cries brought us running because we had told everyone to stay quiet to avoid attracting the attention of people passing by. When I came around and looked inside the van, I saw, scrunched up among the boxes and other supplies, the slender, frightened form of Taron. "Pryce," she begged, "don't let them hurt me." The drivers already had their fire pellet pistols pointed at her, weapons that would have killed her in an instant. "It's all right, men," I said. "I know her. She won't do us any harm. Come on out, Taron."

By now Dakin, Tarius, and Will were also standing by the van to watch this stowaway teenager crawl out and stand sheepishly before us, her head bowed in fear and embarrassment.

"Who is she?" asked Dakin.

"She's a girl in the family I lived with," I said. "Taron, how in the world did you end up in that van?"

"I had to do it," she said. "I want to be part of your work for Emajus."

"How does she know you work for Emajus?" asked Dakin.

"She doesn't know anything," I said, "not even my name.

She knows I'm Emajian because I went to the celebrations with her."

Taron said, "And because the Lord's light was all over the music when he sang. Not very many people have ever seen that before. The light was flashing everywhere. Fantastic. I know he's not just some Damonchokian farm worker. I'm not stupid."

"Did you follow me to the van?" I asked.

"No. That day you was swimmin', I saw your map, and I just knew it had somethin' to do with your work. I went home and wrote down what it said. I waited for the day when you'd go there. Then when that guy brought that hat in the box, I knew somethin' was up. He acted awful funny to just be bringin' a hat."

"So you followed me to the barn?"

"No. I got there before you did. When it got dark, I slipped inside the van."

"Well, that was a very foolish thing to do, young lady," said Dakin. "We'll have to send you home immediately."

"Who else knows about the map?" I asked.

"Nobody," she said. "I promise. I did not tell a soul."

Tarius asked, "What is your name?"

"Taron."

"What is it that you imagine we're doing?"

"I don't know. Something for Emajus."

"Who do you imagine Pryce is?"

"I don't know. But I know he isn't what he says he is, or what everybody else says he is."

"What do they say he is?"

"Some thought he was a criminal, some thought he was an Emajian, some thought he was a spy. But I heard him sing. I know what he is."

Tarius and Dakin exchanged glances. Later they told me that Taron's list of who people of her village thought I was duplicated almost exactly the lyrics of an Emajian prophetic song.

Tarius asked, "What do you think we should do with you, Taron? You are young. You are far from home. You are involved in something that does not concern you and something you know nothing about."

"I want to go on with you, sir. I think you're doing something for Emajus, and I believe He wants me to do something for Him too. You tell me what to do, and no matter how hard it is, I'll do it. I just want to be a part of this."

"You have no idea what you're saying," he said. "This trip might land us all in prison. It might cost us our lives."

"I'd give my life to go, sir. I love the Lord Emajus with all my heart."

"I think our group needs to discuss this alone, Taron. Why don't you go get something to eat with the drivers."

When we were alone, Dakin said, "I don't see what there is to discuss, except the quickest way to get her back to her home. She's a child. She has no business here."

Tarius turned to me and asked, "What is your sense of it, Jeremy? Do you believe her story, or do you think she's up to something?"

"I believe her," I said. "She worships Emajus at great risk to herself and her family. I think she's totally trustworthy."

"Should we send her back," asked Tarius, "or should we consider taking her with us?"

Dakin stopped twirling his hair and pounded his hand on the van. "I knew that's what you were thinking when you told her to step aside. It's ridiculous! She's just a kid. It's just too dangerous to get outsiders involved in this."

"For heaven's sake, Dakin, we're all outsiders," said Tarius. "Who is Jeremy? Who is Will? Who am I? Where are we all from? We're all from the outside, trying to get to a place that most people don't even think exists. Who are you? You are a refugee from a foreign land. Where are we now? We're in Damonchok. And who is the only native in our party? Taron!"

"And this is exactly where she should stay," said Dakin. "What if she's a spy?"

I said, "If she had meant to do us any harm, she would have turned the map over to somebody and they could have arrested us all at the barn. Besides, if she was a spy, it would be too late now to just send her back home where she could tell everyone about us. I say we take her with us."

"I agree," said Tarius. "What is your vote, Will?"

"Well, I don't know that I'm entitled to a vote."

"Everyone is entitled. What do you say?"

"I say anybody who's willing to practically suffocate in that van all night just for a chance to go with us deserves the chance."

"I agree," said Tarius. "We might need that kind of courage somewhere along the line. I'm afraid you're outvoted, Brother Dakin. Taron is the newest member of our band of outlaws."

So Taron became one of us that day, but to placate the worried Dakin, we agreed that we would not divulge our identities or our plans to her until we were in Wilmoroth, where it would be more difficult for her to run home or turn us into the authorities if she happened to be a spy. She rode up front with the drivers. In fact, she became a driver, insisting that her training on the farm in Damonchok made her perfectly capable of working an equal shift with them. We traveled for three more days in Damonchok, until we sighted the border of Wilmoroth.

—⊙—

Because the Wilmorothians were suspicious of outsiders, we could not get past their checkpoint without help. Tarius Arc had arranged for one of his Wilmorothian contacts, a woman named Danuta, to meet us in the Damonchokian town of Mogas. Danuta was originally from the Rock of Calad and was called a Rememberess, a sort of Emajian missionary to one of the few Wilmorothian tribes that allowed the religion to be practiced in their territory. Her main task was to translate the Emajian songs into the tribal language. She also was a historian of Emajianism, and Tarius wanted her to join us to record our trip for future generations.

We waited for her in Mogas at an inn, the only public place we dared to stop in Damonchok. We had to wait for nearly two days for her to arrive, so we had plenty of time to take baths and to wash our clothes, luxuries I had missed during our days on the road. Danuta was late because she was at another Wilmorothian checkpoint many miles south of us helping another group of Emajians from the Rock of Calad cross safely into Wilmoroth. The group she was helping was to join us several days later at a town called Bornigo. Tarius Arc and the others thought that it would be safer for us to go to Wilmoroth in small groups to attract less attention. There were three groups in all, and when we came together, we would have almost thirty people, many of whom were trained soldiers. Danuta also hoped to get about twenty soldiers from Ek Phalot, the town where she lived deep in the jungle, to join us, swelling our number to about fifty. By that point in our journey, our main concern would not be secrecy, for Amians rarely if ever went to the wilder sections of Wilmoroth. The dangers we expected to face at that point would be roving bands of robbers and warriors from rival tribes.

But at the inn in Mogas we wanted only to keep to ourselves and not attract any undue attention. We had rented our own sitting room, where we ate and socialized during the day, so that we did not need to have any contact with other guests. Dakin sat at the window by himself most of the time, fidgeting. He had sent word to Miriaban before he left the Rock of Calad that Mogas was the last place she could hope to meet him if she changed her mind and agreed to go with him to Caladria. She never came. He sat and fretted, watching the road.

Dakin was not the only one waiting for a miracle in that strange collection of individuals. We were all waiting for something, hoping for something. What had we staked our lives on? For what had Dakin abandoned his wife and his comfortable position in Persus Am? For what had Tarius risked a return to the hellish prison? For what had Taron left her family and everything familiar to her?

For belief in a Spirit that inhabited sound that was music. For belief in a Spirit that could inhabit people and create them anew. For belief in a Spirit that was a Person who had led His followers to a paradise called Caladria, and for the belief that we could find the place even though all objective evidence said it did not exist.

We all waited and hoped for something. Dakin hoped for his wife to join him, I hoped for my vision of Anne to come true, Tarius hoped to find his wife and child alive in Caladria, Will hoped to be freed from this whole mess and go home, Taron hoped for a chance to do something big for her Lord Emajus.

Will seemed to brood most of the time, and that worried me. At home he was always brash and uninhibited. He said whatever was on his mind, he made everyone laugh, he was the center of attention in any crowd. Here he spoke hardly at all, unless it was to me, in English. His beard, which had grown even longer than he wore it at home, looked like a mask behind which he hid from the strangers. He was taller and brawnier than anyone else in the world. No one knew quite how to treat this imposing figure. Mostly they left him alone.

I could not look at him there in Mogas without wondering why he rather than Anne had ended up with me in this place. Will knew nothing of the Spirit that filled the music. He had always been suspicious of anything spiritual. Anne, I thought, could have understood the voice of God that lured us toward Caladria. Though Will had often entered my visions, Anne was the center of them. What a comfort she would have been to me. How I needed to see her and touch her and speak to her. Every day I prayed the Lord would send her, but she did not come. If she was not going to come, I prayed, let me understand why, and let the visions stop. But as with most other things, I received no explanation. The visions did not stop. Every day I sensed she was just beyond my reach. Every day I came achingly close to the sight of her face, the touch of her hair, her lips, her skin. But for me, as for Dakin, each night there was nothing to do but turn away and bury the loneliness.

—⊖—

Danuta did not come to the inn but sent word for us to meet her a few miles out of town, which was just a couple hours' ride from the border checkpoint. I did not see her until we were already in Wilmoroth. When we left the inn, we were told that we could not get out of the van until we were safely across the border. If the border soldiers opened the van and tried to question us, we were to remain silent and let Danuta handle it.

"This woman is brilliant," Tarius told me. "She's gotten me across the border a number of times. I don't know any of the

Wilmorothian languages, so I don't know exactly what she tells those soldiers, but it always works. She won't tell me her secret. I'm just glad she's with us. I'd hate to try to get through Wilmoroth without her."

As we sat at the checkpoint, we heard Danuta's blizzard of words just outside, and occasionally we heard a soldier squeeze in a response. They opened the door of the van and looked in at us, but Danuta remained hidden from view, talking the whole time, sometimes laughing. A Wilmorothian guard took a long, thin cane and poked at us a few times, grunting in response to Danuta's tirade, and then he laughed and shut the door. In a few minutes, we were allowed through the checkpoint.

"Amazing," said Tarius. "You have no idea how hard it is to get into Wilmoroth. I don't know how she does it. She just wears them down with whatever that spiel is she gives them. I'd love to hear a translation."

Wilmoroth is separated from Damonchok by a mountain range, but it is much less formidable than the mountains that separate Damonchok from Persus Am. At points along the Wilmorothian range, including where we now rode, there were only low hills with a fairly wide and easy road. Danuta wanted us to be quickly and safely out of reach of the border guards, so she did not let the vans stop for a couple more hours.

Danuta looked nothing like what I expected. For some reason, after hearing her voice commanding and cajoling the guards the way a crafty politician woos an eager audience, I had pictured a tall, striking woman, brash and self-confident. But Danuta was just over five feet tall, with round hips, a beautiful fair-skinned face, and wavy hair of a subdued reddish tint. She dressed in the bright, loose clothing of the Wilmorothians, a wraparound dress with colorful geometric shapes on it, and a scarf on her head. She called Tarius Arc "Papa," hugging him and laughing with him as soon as we got out of the van. She seemed as carefree as if we were all on a vacation together. I felt I knew her instantly. Unlike most of the people I had met, she had no sense of reserve in her whatsoever.

When we were in the van together, Tarius sang Danuta's

praises. "She knows more about the Wilmorothian languages and culture than probably anybody in the world. The cause of Emajianism in Wilmoroth would be lost without her. She's a Rememberess, as I already told you. She's going to record this trip so that one day all believers across the world will read about it and thank God for what we're doing right now. She was born for this moment. All of us were."

Danuta's presence, combined with the fact that we were out of Damonchok with its abundance of Amian spies, brought new energy and optimism to our group. Danuta loved to sing, and like everything else she did, she sang fervently, seriously, her eyes closed to concentrate on the music. It was on the mountain road into Wilmoroth that I first heard Dakin sing. His voice was hesitant at first, distant, as if his mind were elsewhere and he did not even realize he was singing. But soon a clear and flawless baritone emerged, a voice that had once been used to singing for hours on end, a voice that understood the music. When I heard Tarius and Dakin together, I could imagine them years ago, with their wives, singing in the innocent land of Persus Am where the Spirit of the Lord was no more unusual a presence than the wind. Whenever a song ended, they grew quiet. They remembered. They knew they risked their lives for the slim chance that those days of innocence could be recaptured.

We estimated that our journey to Bornigo, where we were to meet the rest of our group, would take five days. The land we crossed was mostly flat and rocky, with dirty little mining towns all along the route. Here the Wilmorothians mined the minerals that fed the factories of Persus Am. Even so, we did not expect to see many Amians because the Wilmorothians hated them and did not make them welcome. Rather than letting the Amians come to get the minerals themselves, the Wilmorothians hauled them to a city called Aroshomot far south of us, near the border, where the Amians picked them up and carried them across the Disputed Territory and into Persus Am.

Surprisingly, however, we came across several small groups of Amian soldiers in the towns we passed through. Danuta quietly inquired what the Amians were doing there and found that they were offering assistance to various tribes to fight the Damon-chokians, who were said to be secretly preparing for an attack against Wilmoroth. As Danuta explained, "I don't think the Damonchokians are planning any attack at all. I think the Amians are preparing for their own war, and they want Damonchok to have to worry about the Wilmorothians attacking them from the east and the Amians attacking from the west."

I agreed with her, and so did Dakin. Umbriel, we believed, might have already given up on negotiation and compromise. I had not delivered the Territory of Ur to him, so he was ready to take it by force. Unfortunately for Umbriel, most of the Wil-morothian tribes were not buying the Amian rumors that Damon-chok was preparing to attack. Danuta found out that two tribes had killed the Amians that had come to talk war with them, and others were skeptical. If war came, it was clear that at least as many Wilmorothians would fight against the Amians as for them. Umbriel would take on the world without even one dependable ally to support him. Everyone expected a bloodbath even worse than the first War. Even the Wilmorothians, who needed little excuse to fight among themselves, knew that such an all-out war would leave no corner of the world unchanged. If Persus Am defeated Damonchok and the Rock of Calad, how long would it be before Wilmoroth, with the richest mines in the world, fell also? Persus Am was discovering that although a few tribes might fight on their side in the short term for their own reasons, in the final analysis the Wilmorothians fought for no one but themselves.

Because there were so many Amians around, Dakin, the most cautious and perhaps the most paranoid member of our group, insisted that we not reveal our identities or our plans to Taron until we reached Bornigo. I thought this unnecessary and unfair to Taron, but she took it without complaint. She seemed not to mind riding with the drivers, and they were grateful for her help.

Danuta was everything Tarius praised her to be. She got us out of one jam after another during our five days on the road. When the wheel on one of our vans broke and had to be repaired, she bargained with a nearby farmer for the parts we were missing and had us back on the road in an hour. When suspicious men lurked around our campsite, she not only confronted them to make sure they meant no harm but even talked them into bringing us hot meals for a very reasonable price. Even though Wilmorothians hated outsiders, one night she managed to talk an innkeeper into letting us stay with him. In just a few quick conversations in each town she managed to pick up all the information and warnings we needed to avoid areas where tribes were fighting or where highway robbers were known to strike. When we were in the van, she never slept or sat quiet and bored like the others. At those times she became a Rememberess, recording our journey. When she was not writing, she was either reading, singing, or talking. Usually she did not talk to the whole group but focused on one person, listening intently and talking in quiet tones as if the two of us were the only people in the van. She wanted to know every detail about what had happened since my arrival in this world. I told her many things, but I omitted many too, such as my relationship with Tracian, which I glossed over while Dakin shook his head and scowled.

Bornigo was the last town we would pass through before we reached the tropical forests, where Danuta's home Ek Phalot was. Bornigo was the center of commerce for a large province. The products of all the mines in the province were brought there and loaded into camuck-drawn trucks before they were taken west, toward Aroshomot. Those first few days in Bornigo were the last happy and peaceful days we were to have for a long time. Bornigo had one Emajian church, and the believers welcomed us lavishly, giving us comfortable beds in their homes and cooking us three huge meals a day. For safety reasons we could not tell them who we were or what we were doing. They knew only that we were "missionaries" gathering large stores of provisions before we would head into the jungle toward Ek Phalot. Somehow a rumor got started that our trip had something to do with Caladria, so the people were full of questions we could not answer. The Emajians in Bornigo revered Danuta; she was considered one of the pillars of the Emajian church in Wilmoroth. She had sent word ahead asking them to prepare provisions for our journey, and the church had almost everything ready by the time we arrived. They had food, medicine, clothing, blankets, tents, weapons, and all sorts of other supplies. Much of it was paid for by the church on the Rock of Calad, which had taken the responsibility for financing our trip, but the Wilmorothians donated extra supplies. Danuta said we would have enough to last a couple of months. If we had not found Caladria by then, God would have to provide.

Bornigo, like so many other towns we had visited, had more than the usual number of Amian soldiers in it. The Amians in Bornigo were having no better luck convincing the Wilmorothians they needed Amian "assistance" than they had enjoyed in any of the other towns we had gone through. The Amians worried us, though, because more people knew about us in Bornigo than in any other town, and we were afraid the Amians would get suspicious. For an Amian soldier to capture me or Dakin or Tarius would mean fame and glory back home, not to mention a big promotion and lots of reward money.

We wanted to get packed and head into the jungle as soon as possible. No Amian dared go there for any reason. Tree People, which is what the people of the jungle were called, used Amian skulls as bedposts—or so went the legend in Persus Am.

After two days the provisions were almost ready to go, but we still waited for a group of eight soldiers from the Rock of Calad. We had heard nothing from them at all. But the alarming news we received on our third day in Bornigo made us stop waiting and head for the rain forest as fast as we could travel. Danuta had picked up the news that Umbriel had promised a reward for the capture of Dakin, who had been condemned as an Emajian collaborator. He was thought to have fled to the Rock of Calad or beyond. Though the official story was that I had been kidnapped, there were rumors that I might have been moved off the Rock, perhaps to Wilmoroth. Danuta said the Amians were curious about our group and had been asking the townspeople questions about us. The Amians held no authority in Wilmoroth, and plenty of Wilmorothians would have been willing to fight the Amians if they had tried to take us by force; even so, we did not want to take any chances at being caught and hauled back to Persus Am, and we did not want to risk drawing any more attention to ourselves. Besides, we did not know which Wilmorothians we could trust. Many of them would have been happy to collect the reward for our heads. We decided to leave that afternoon and let the stragglers meet us at Ek Phalot.

Bornigo was on a huge, rocky plateau, so most of our trip was a gradual descent toward the jungle. We took only one van, filled with our original group—Dakin, Danuta, Tarius, Will, Taron, and me—the drivers, and enough provisions to get to Ek Phalot, which was two and a half days away. Because the rest of our group was not at as much risk from the Amians as we were, they stayed behind to finish getting the provisions together, and they planned to leave in a day or two.

We reached the edge of the jungle by mid-afternoon of the second day, and it was nearly sundown of the third day before we encountered anyone. As we rode through the jungle at the end of that day, we were no more than a few hours drive from our destination. As we listened to the screaming of the birds and the incessant buzz of the insects outside our van, a new sound hit our ears, the crashing of limbs and bushes. Danuta sprang up, banged on the front wall for the driver to stop, and said to us, "Stay in the van until I tell you, and then come out with your hands raised high in the air. And smile and nod."

Danuta opened the door and got out. Through the door I could see men rushing toward us—and there were even a few women and boys in the group too—with fire pellet guns and spears and hatchets glinting in the sun. Danuta waved her bandana in the air and shouted a flurry of Wilmorothian phrases, the same sounds over and over, almost wildly, as the Tree People slowed down and held their weapons ready to strike. They were villagers, not soldiers, and their age ranged from children of no more than eight or nine to men so old and fat they came puffing along nearly ten minutes after the rest of the group had encircled us. Baggy shorts were their only uniforms. Even when the Tree People halted at the command of a leader, Danuta kept right on shouting. Finally one of them spoke to her, and during their conversation some of the others came to the van and peeked in at us, hesitantly, as if they were afraid of a trap.

Danuta's tone of voice calmed down. She told us to get out of the van. We stepped out with our hands in the air as she had told us to do. "Smile," she said. "Nod." So as dozens of guns and spears and hatchets lay poised in the hands of an entire village ready to slice us to shreds or shoot us to death, we smiled and nodded idiotically, our arms growing tired in the air. They searched our van, but we had brought no weapons. The Tree People fought so well in the jungle, Danuta had told us, that it would be foolish for us to try to fight them. Our best protection, she had insisted, would be to prove our peaceful intentions by being completely defenseless. As I looked at the ragtag band of "soldiers" that surrounded us, I doubted her advice, but Danuta now looked perfectly calm, as she leaned against the van and spoke quietly to some of the leaders of the Tree People.

After the search of the van, Danuta told us to get back inside. "Bad news," she said, as she crawled inside with us. "It seems that the Amians have figured out who we were and have followed us into the jungle. They're just a few hours behind us. The Tree People stopped us because they thought we might have been Amians too. But they know me, and I told them we were the ones the Amians were after."

"Will these people stop the Amians?" Dakin asked.

"Yes, they'll try to eventually. But first they prefer to let the Amians get well into the jungle, where the Tree People can more easily outmaneuver them and tear them to shreds. The Amians will be too far into the jungle to retreat, and no reinforcements will ever reach them."

"So what do we do now?" Tarius asked.

"We wait. The Tree People are going to take care of the Amians, and then they'll escort us to Ek Phalot. It's the best way. We really don't have much choice."

"That group of hick soldiers take on the Amian army?" scoffed Dakin. "Most of them are little boys or fat old men."

"They may look that way to you, Dakin, but this is not Persus Am. This is the jungle, and nobody knows it or can fight in it like these people. If all you see are boys and old men, that's because the other soldiers are so well hidden in the trees that you wouldn't notice them until they were slicing you to pieces. You Amians know nothing about fighting here. It will be a massacre."

"So we act as bait for the Amians," I said.

"Exactly. You might as well sit back and wait for the show to start."

We pretended to set up camp in the jungle. The Tree People even helped us build a fire by our van, where we cooked our food and sat around as if relaxing. The Tree People hid in the jungle all around us, ready to swoop down on the Amians and kill every one of them. They did not expect a single casualty among themselves or us.

Danuta argued with them, trying to convince them to attack the enemy farther away from us, but they just told her not to worry, we would be safe.

We waited nervously for hours. We strained to distinguish each new sound, and there were dozens of them—the buzzing, chirping, clicking, crackling sounds of the jungle. After several hours I grew tired and began to think the Amians would not come at all that night. When they finally charged down on us, I was staring at the fire, daydreaming. The Tree People allowed the Amians to get dangerously close to us to make it easier to trap them and kill them. The first sound I heard was the war cries of the Tree People; then immediately the jungle was bright with the flash of the fire guns. The blazing balls of fire that sprayed through the trees like fireworks would have been beautiful had they not been so deadly. Not far from me I saw one of these fire pellets smash into the leg of an Amian soldier. For a moment I saw his dazed face in the firelight, and then he stumbled into the brush, his whole body engulfed in flames.

Those of us without weapons headed for the van, but just before we shut the door, we realized Taron was not there. I ran back outside to find her, but all I could see was fire and smoke and the chaos of bodies running in every direction. Suddenly an Amian sprang from a hiding place in the trees and ran toward me, to get a better aim, I suppose, with his fire gun. In the next instant, though, one of the Tree People jumped down on him from a low tree limb and buried a knife deep in the man's chest. The sight nearly made me sick, but I watched the struggle in fascination, as the men wrestled on the ground, the Tree man stabbing the Amian again and again until he was dead.

Danuta screamed for me to get inside the van. Seeing no sign of Taron, I hurried back to the van and slammed the door.

"They let the Amians get too close!" I yelled. "I don't see Taron anywhere."

Danuta said, "It's so strange. I thought I saw her run toward the van, but in the confusion I lost her. Did you check underneath the van? Maybe she's hiding there."

"I didn't look there. Maybe you're right. It's a miracle we weren't all killed as close as those Amians got."

"We may not get out alive even now," said Dakin, who watched the battle through a crack in the door. "I can't tell who's winning and who's losing."

"The Tree People are winning," said Danuta. "The Amians didn't stand a chance from the moment they walked into the jungle." She was remarkably calm considering the scene of horror that surrounded us.

The fighting went on for more than an hour, though it seemed much longer as we crouched there listening to every shout and every explosion and every moan of the wounded. When it finally grew quiet, I wanted to go out immediately and look for Taron, but Danuta stopped me.

"It's too quiet out there," she said. "It's not over yet."

"It's quiet because it *is* over," I said.

"No. If it were over, you'd hear the Tree People whooping and shouting. Some of the Amians must still be missing. They're probably hiding in the brush. Just wait a while. It won't take the Tree People long to find them."

Just as Danuta predicted, in less than twenty minutes there were some more shots, and then all over the jungle we could hear the war whoops of the Tree People celebrating their victory. I got out of the van immediately to look for Taron, but as soon as I did one of the Tree People saw me and let loose a barrage of words I could not understand but I knew were not kind. Danuta, close behind me, said, "They want us to stay in the van. They're going to take us to the camp they've set up not far from here. He says we look too much like Amians, and we're likely to get shot."

"What about Taron?"

"They can find her easier than we can. Don't argue with them, Jeremy. There's nothing we can do."

The forest was dotted with smoldering fires, dead bodies, cheering Tree People. The look of the fire and the ancient trees and the bloody horror was surreal, frightening. I hated the thought of leaving Taron alone in that chaos, but with the Tree People jabbering away at me trying to get me back in the van, I knew I had no choice but to trust them to find her. Danuta, calm as ever, invited me into the van with a sweeping gesture of her hand, as if she were inviting me into her parlor for tea. She was as businesslike and cheerful as she had always been. The nightmarish quality of the scene seemed to be lost on her. "Now that that's over," she said, "we can make it to Ek Phalot by tomorrow. The others should join us by the day after tomorrow, and then we can leave the jungle and head for Caladria."

—◯—

The Tree People brought Taron in from the field later that night. She was alive, but she had been hit in the leg by a fire pellet. As soon as Danuta got word from the Tree People that Taron had been found, we went to see her. She was in a tent lined with mattresses for the wounded female soldiers. Her eyes were closed when we came in. Her face was puffy and red. Drops of sweat gleamed on her forehead.

I sat beside her and took her hand. She opened her eyes. She rose up and hugged me tight. "Thank God," she said. "I haven't been able to find anyone who could speak our language who could tell me what was goin' on."

"How bad does it hurt?" I asked.

"I'll survive," she said.

"We looked for you in the jungle, but they made us come back to the village. We were so worried—"

"I got hit when I was running to get into the van, and then I crawled into the brush to hide. When the Tree People found me, I thought they were gonna kill me. At first I think they thought I was one of the Amians. I'm not hurt as bad as some of the others. The guy was pretty far away when he shot me, so it didn't hit me as hard as it could have, but it burned me. They put some kind of cream on it, though, and that made it feel better. They gave me some kind of medicine to drink too. It makes me drowsy. It makes me hot too."

"We'll let you sleep. We just wanted to see how you were. Taron, we can make arrangements for you to go back to Damonchok if—"

"No, I'm staying right with you. We discussed this already, remember? I knew what risks I was taking. I'll be better in no time. I'm in it till the end, Prince Jeremy."

"What did you say?"

"Prince Jeremy." She smiled, and then reached up and hugged me again. "I may not be the smartest girl in the world, but it doesn't take me forever to figure things out. I know now that's who you are, so you can stop playin' games. I know you and I know Dakin and I know Tarius Arc."

"How did you figure it out?"

"I pay attention."

"We were getting ready to tell you anyway. Dakin is very cautious—"

"That's all right. I understand. Maybe now that I'm injured he'll realize I'm ready to make any sacrifice for the cause."

Danuta said, "I'm glad we don't have to hide it anymore, Taron. You've been very brave, very patient."

I asked, "Have you also figured out what we're going to do?"

"I think we're going to Caladria," she said.

I nodded.

"So you know where it is, then?"

"No. I wish I did. We only know that the Lord is leading us into the Gray Desert. We know where to go to wait for Him, but we don't know what will happen once we get there."

"That's fantastic," said Taron.

"Well, the Gray Desert is a pretty horrible place, they say."

"Oh, I know it is. Anyone would be crazy to go there. But if that's where the Lord wants us to go before He shows us Caladria, then at least we know we won't have to worry about our enemies following us there."

"You're right about that," said Danuta. "We haven't been thinking about it that way, but it's true. Once we get into that desert, only time can kill us."

"Only lack of faith can kill us," said Taron, and she settled back comfortably into her pillows.

—◯—

We took the three-hour journey to Ek Phalot the next day. Danuta's people had been told of her return and of our battle, so they prepared a joyous celebration for her and for us when we arrived.

We could hear the music from far off. The music was much different from what I had heard anywhere else. The beat was fast, at times almost frenzied. The Tree People rarely put words with their music. According to Danuta, they felt that because the music was the very voice of God, to interrupt His singing with words of their own was sacrilegious. The Tree People had all kinds of drums and pipes and horns, very few of which looked like any other instrument. Danuta said the Tree People took great pride in creating instruments that had never existed before. They felt each instrument was a new channel through which a different part of God's voice could be heard. The blending was extraordinarily beautiful, one of the richest sounds I have ever heard. When we heard the music, Danuta and I got out of the van and rode up front so that we could better hear the sound. I will never forget the joy that filled me as we sliced through that lush forest, the music of Emajus getting louder and louder. As always, the Emajian music brought me a sense of hope and power far beyond what our circumstances seemed to promise. For the first time in many days I felt confident about our journey. I believed that beyond this jungle there must really be a Caladria.

The Tree People mobbed Danuta as we approached Ek Phalot. They threw garlands of flowers over her and hugged her and kissed her. The music was almost frenzied by this time, the drums keeping a furious rhythm. The air was filled with smoke that came from a hut nearby (whose roof had been taken off and set aside) where three pig-sized animals were being roasted over a fire. After everyone greeted Danuta, they turned toward the rest of us. None of the people spoke our language, but that did not stop them from talking to us. They chattered away as if we could understand every word they said. Each of us was surrounded by a group of ten or twelve people who put garlands around our necks and gave us blindingly strong drinks in large wooden mugs. They took us into the hut to see the meat they were preparing for us, and they let us smell the vegetables grilling over a fire outside. Before dinner they separated the men from the women and provided large tubs of hot water for us to take baths in. After our baths the women doused our hair with lotion that smelled like flowers. Danuta said this lotion was reserved for the most cherished friends.

That night we enjoyed the best meal I had eaten since I left Goldaw's table. The thick slabs of meat were more tender and delicious than any steak I had ever tasted at home, and the grilled vegetables were spicy and crispy. The Tree People filled our plates time after time, and we ate ravenously, grateful to get a break from the rations we carried with us on the van. After a long, relaxed dinner the people returned to their musical instruments, and we all stood to dance and celebrate. It was a joyous night. The instruments were set up near the fire pit where the vegetables had been cooked. When darkness fell, the pit became a bonfire to light our celebration. Those of us who did not have instruments sang, though we did not form our sounds into words. The Spirit of God filled the sound. At times I could hardly keep singing, so overwhelmed was I with ecstasy that enveloped me when the music filled up with God's voice.

Late in the night, when most of us were exhausted with celebrating and sat quietly by the fire listening to the subdued strains of music, some men brought out wooden bowls filled with what looked like sand. Several people in the crowd stood up at the sight of this, and a few even applauded. The men took the bowls to the fire and threw handfuls of "sand" into it. The fire sputtered and smoked, and at first I thought the men were trying to extinguish the flames. But then the smoke changed colors and hovered over us, turning purple and green and red as it washed over our faces. This was the Tree People's version of vapors.

As soon as the vapors rolled over us, Dakin and Tarius got up to leave the circle and go back to our tents for the night. Vapors made Dakin nauseous if he got too many of them, and Tarius Arc objected to them because he did not want anything but the Lord's music to alter his consciousness. Taron, still not feeling well, had already gone to bed for the evening, and Will had not joined in the music because he did not like it. That left only Danuta and me to enjoy the vapors with our hosts.

The scene was beautiful. Through the rainbow of smoky colors we could see, off in the jungle, individual fires and individual lamps burning in the windows of the Tree People's homes, many of which were literally built in the trees, straddling the mighty branches. The vapors were calming at first, and I felt a dreamy sense of well-being. I sat relaxed against Danuta, who rested her hand on my head and looked out onto the lights with me.

The second phase of vapors, after the euphoric sense of calmness, is always a burst of energy, and Danuta and I felt it at the same time.

"I'd like to take a walk," said Danuta.

"So would I. I was just thinking that," I said. "Why don't you show me around this village? I'd like to see those houses in the trees."

We walked along the path lit only by the light from the homes above us. The trees in this part of the jungle were ideal for supporting homes. Their trunks were sturdy and wide—sometimes fifteen or twenty feet in diameter—and the lower branches were thick and strong. The houses were supported not only by the branches of the trees but also by wooden poles extending from the ground. The rooms were narrow and wound around in all different directions, depending on where the branches could support them. Some of the homes were connected by walkways between the trees. Many of the Tree People were outside on their walkways talking and laughing, shouting from tree to tree.

"I feel really good tonight," I told Danuta. "I feel better than

I have in a long time. I mean, here we are, just one step away from the Gray Desert, where the Lord is going to find us and take us to Caladria. I just feel like maybe the hardest part is over. I've been through so much confusion since I've been here, but I finally feel like it's leading somewhere. I just have to believe we're going to get to that spot on Will's map, and then we're going to find Caladria, and then I'm going to get some answers from the Lord about what this is all about. Why He has put me through all this. What we're supposed to accomplish."

"I hope you're right. I hope the worst is behind us," she said. "But everything that's happened to you, even though I know it seemed like confusion to you at the time, is right in line with the prophecies of the Emajian songs. They show the prophet as a prisoner, a prince, a farmer—none of us who knew the scriptures could ever reconcile all those things before. But here you've done them all."

"And done them all by accident."

"Yes, maybe. But I'm beginning to believe few things— maybe nothing—is accidental. It just takes us a long time to piece it all together."

The path went deep into the woods, the settlement being much bigger than I expected, and the farther out we got, the fewer houses there were and the darker it became. After a while the energizing effects of the vapors began to wear off, and we grew tired.

"Let's sit down and rest," said Danuta. "I'm wiped out."

As we sat down I said, "I can't believe how loud it is out here! Those animals make so much racket." We heard the screeching of birds, the buzzing of insects, the howling of we knew not what, various rustling sounds in the leaves and bushes.

"It's to get away from some of those animals that the Tree People build their houses above the ground."

"So there are dangerous animals out here?"

"Of course. Horrible animals."

"Then why are we sitting here?"

Danuta stood. "Because those vapors make us think we have all the energy in the world and nothing can harm us! We'd better get back. It's crazy to be walking around out here so far from the settlement."

The vapors gave us the energy to walk into the woods, and fear gave us the energy to get back. By the time we got back to the relative safety of the camp, I was ready to crawl in my tent and go to sleep. I was to share a tent with Will, but he was not there. Figuring he could take care of himself, I went on to bed. Right after I got to sleep, though, I was awakened by the strong hand of Maddel, one of our drivers, who shook me repeatedly and said, "Sir, sir, please come quick. It's Brother Will."

"Has he been hurt?" I asked, immediately thinking of the horrible creatures Danuta and I had imagined we heard rustling in the bushes near the settlement.

"No. But he's gonna be hurt if you don't come quick. He's had too much of the vapors and—well, some of the women, the Tree People women—they had a little too much too—and he went into a building with a few of them—"

"A few of them?"

"Yes, sir. Two at least. And a couple of the men grabbed me and starting making a big fuss with me, but I don't speak their language, and none of them speak ours, so they took me over there, and they took me inside the building where Brother Will was, and I saw him with one of the women sort of—holding her—and he yelled at me and slammed the door, and those men were screaming their heads off at him."

I was already up and outside the tent by this time. "Show me where he is, and then go get Danuta," I said.

"We already got her. She's the one who told me to get you. Come on. He's over here."

A crowd of about fifty Tree People had now gathered outside the building where Will had barricaded himself with the women. I pushed my way through to the door, where Danuta stood yelling at Will.

"Jeremy!" she said, turning to me, her back against the door. "You've got to talk some sense into him. He's in there with two women, both of them married. And they're married to two men who have been out hunting with the Ranekee, and he is expected back tonight."

"Who is the Ranekee?"

"He's the leader of Ek Phalot! And the husbands of these women are his advisers. This could really cause us problems."

I banged on the door. "Will! Let me in right now. You're putting us all in a lot of danger." I spoke in English, and Will answered in English.

"Go away now, Jer. We're doing something private." His voice had a hint of laughter in it, the same way his voice sounded when he used to get drunk at home.

"Will, they could kill us for this. Come on out of there now. The party's over."

"Jeremy, I can't hear you very well."

"Those women have husbands!" I shouted. "Big, jealous, powerful husbands."

"Oh really? Well, maybe that's what these ladies have been trying to tell me."

"Let me in, then."

I could hear the barricade of furniture inside being moved away from the door. "Only you, Jer. I don't want any of those other guys in here. This little gal is for you."

I told Danuta I wanted to go in alone, and she agreed. She tried to get across to the Tree People that only I should go in, but when the door opened, the crowd surged forward. Will and I leaned against the door with all our might, even to the point that we heard the door splinter, but finally we got it shut and locked.

When I turned around, directly in front of me stood a girl in her late teens, wearing Will's enormous jacket, who greeted me with a kiss on the lips and then stepped away in boisterous laughter at my surprise.

"Be more friendly, Jer. She's laughing at you." Another girl sat among some pillows on a mat in the far corner of the room.

"Let's get out of here, Will. You've put yourself and the rest of us in a lot of danger. These girls have husbands. That crowd out there is just waiting to bust in here and kick your head in and kill you or maim you or who knows what."

"The girls here told me their husbands wouldn't mind."
Addressing the girl standing near the door, he said, "Didn't you
say that to me, honey? Didn't you?"

Both girls seemed to think the English language was hysterically funny, and whenever Will spoke it to them they melted in
laughter. After her outburst of laughter the girl in the pillows
answered him in Wilmorothian, to which Will replied, "Booga
booga gloobala to you too, sweetheart," another sentence that put
her on the verge of hysterical tears.

"Come on, Will. We'll talk about this later. Let's just get out
of here."

"Jeremy, this was their idea completely, I promise you."

"Just come on, before I go ahead and let these guys in to take
care of you their own way."

"It's just all a misunderstanding. They just invited me in for
a cup of coffee. The welcoming committee. That's all."

As Will tried to retrieve his jacket from the girl, I shouted to
Danuta outside, "We're coming out. Can you get those people to
back off until I get him away from here?"

"I'll try," she said.

"Should we wait a while then?" I asked.

"No, get him out of there. But when you open that door,
run!"

Danuta tried in vain to talk the people away. Most of them
were merely curious, but a good number were angry and eager for
a fight. As soon as the door opened and Will appeared, the crowd
surged forward and one of the angry men in front smashed Will
in the face with his fist, knocking Will against the building's
outside wall. Recovering almost instantly from the blow, Will,
hulkier than any of the comparatively slightly built Tree People,
crouched down like the football player he once had been, and
charged through the line, growling ferociously and leveling men
and women, fighters and bystanders alike, most of them drunk,
with equal abandon. I had only to follow close behind Will and
walk through the hole he created. We were out of the crowd in
seconds, and then we ran with all our might, not saying a word.

Some of the men followed us at first, but by the time we

reached the tents, they had dropped away and we were alone. Will stopped at our tent at first, but I pulled him into the van, which was nearby and which had the advantage that we could lock it from the inside. As the globe light inside the van heated up and began to glow, it revealed Will's bleeding lip and the battered right side of his face. In spite of his wounds, he laughed hysterically once the door had locked out our pursuers. He yelled "Whoo!" over and over, slapped me on the back, and looked happier than I had seen him since the trip began. "We almost didn't make it out of that one, did we, Jer?"

"Will, don't you realize what you've done?"

"I wish I had a picture of your face when you walked in and saw those girls. I haven't seen you look like that since that time in college when we—"

"Shut up, Will. We're counting on the mercy of these people to get us out of here. We can't afford incidents like this. This is not some college prank. These people are counting on us, don't you see that?"

He stopped laughing then, wiped the blood off his lips, and said, "Jeremy, we are not part of these people. This has nothing to do with us. I never asked to come here."

"It's too late to think that way, Will. We are a part of this. These people are staking their careers and families and their entire lives on the idea that we came to bring them to Caladria. You can't just say, 'We're not part of these people.' We are. This is our life too."

"No it isn't. I don't care about Caladria. I don't care about their music. I don't care about their religion. I just want to do whatever I have to do to get out of here and go home."

"I want to go home too. I'd give anything in the world if I could step out of this van right now and be at Anne's front doorstep, and she would come to the door and welcome me like nothing had ever happened and this was all a dream. But we're not at home, and there's no way we can get there. These people are my friends, and I'm not going to let them down."

Will held his face in his hands, wincing at his bruises.

"If we can just get to Caladria," I said, "maybe we can get

some answers. But for now let's not stir up any more trouble with these people. I don't know how this is all going to end, but I certainly don't want it to end out here in the jungle with some brawl over women."

"All right, all right." Will leaned back and sighed. "Those were a couple of gorgeous ladies, though. You can't deny that."

—⊖—

Within four days of Will's indiscretion our company stood at the base of the Dead Mountains, the final barrier between us and the horrible Gray Desert.

Though Danuta had stayed up most of the night after Will's escapade to calm down the angry Tree People, his actions had caused us no lasting damage with their leaders. The rest of our company arrived the next morning, and the Ranekee, Ek Phalot's ruler, got back from his hunting trip the next night, one day late. Within a few hours of his arrival he invited Danuta, Tarius Arc, Will, and me to his office, a lavish structure in the trees that was filled with cushioned couches, tapestries on the walls, and modern globe lights (imported from the hated Persus Am, a fact the Tree People would not have acknowledged). He was a large man who looked as if he were in his fifties, though I had learned that many people in this world were much older than they looked. He had the bulkiness of a man who had once been strong but had turned rather flabby through the ease of rich living.

Our identities and the exact nature of our journey were still supposed to be secret, but he clearly suspected who we were. He spent most of our meeting trying to talk us out of going to the Gray Desert, which he said no one ever went to and survived. He spoke of horrible animals there called farks, overgrown insects the size of a man's fist that had strong teeth that bit into a victim's skin and brought about certain death. We had been warned about these creatures at every step in our journey. He said that beyond the physical dangers, the Gray Desert was pervaded with an inexplicable aura of evil, unlike any other place on the planet, and that no one who went there ever survived it. His own people were strictly forbidden to go beyond the Dead Mountains, the final barrier between the jungle and the desert. It was a law, he said, that needed no enforcement, since the legends of that horrible place were enough in themselves to keep people away.

Danuta explained to him that we were aware of the horrors of the desert, but that we had no choice but to go. The Lord was leading us there, and He could lead us safely out.

"Do you seek Caladria?" the Ranekee asked.

Danuta responded, "Though we mean you no disrespect, sir, that is a question we cannot answer."

The Ranekee smiled. "Sometimes, Danuta, the best way to publish the news is to make it a secret. Though you will tell no one why you are going into the desert, thirty-seven of my best warriors have volunteered to join your mission. They seem to believe your friend here is a prophet of God, and that he is taking you to Caladria. They want to go."

"Ranekee, we serve the Lord Emajus. We believe He sends us into the desert. We welcome your warriors. We would be grateful for your permission for them join us."

"Ah, now this poses a dilemma for me. Shall I give my warriors permission to disobey my own law?"

"I would not presume to tell the Ranekee how to guide his warriors. I only know that the laws of the Ranekee are intended to lead people into God's will, not to keep them away from it."

"You speak wisely, Danuta. And cleverly. So be it, then. May God's will be done. You have all shown great courage to come so far and to risk so much. You have shown yourselves as fellow warriors against the demons of Persus Am, which is the devil's own kingdom, and its leader Umbriel, who is the devil's own slave. We honor you. Though I will not order any warrior to go to the Gray Desert, I grant permission for those who feel the Lord's calling to go there. Furthermore, I hereby order that three wagons full of supplies be given to you to help sustain you in the desert. May the Lord Emajus be glorified."

Danuta thanked him profusely for his help. His offer was indeed generous, for the jungle was difficult and dangerous, and his thirty-seven warriors got us through it twice as fast as we could have managed by ourselves.

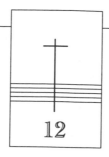

12

The lush jungle of the Tree People turned thin and gray as it approached the Dead Mountains. The trees were scrawny and bent, as if they carried some invisible weight. There was an ashen look to the forest there, as if a volcano had scorched it many years before and only a few stubborn remnants of life had bothered to push their way through the dust to stand ugly and defiant against the barren mountains. The mountains looked like something transplanted from an entirely different planet, like an astronomy book picture of some rocky, dusty moon that had never known life.

It is not easy to describe the change in attitude that came over our group as we faced those desolate hills. The jungle had brought challenges of its own—vicious animals, enemy warriors who might attack, millions of insects that afflicted us, the enormous task of slicing a hole through the wall of brush and trees big enough to squeeze our people through. But we took comfort in our numbers—more than seventy strong—and we were buoyed by our victory over the Amians and heartened by the fact that our real journey was finally under way. We sang bold Emajian songs as we slashed our way through the tropical web, our voices somehow more vivid in the jungle than inside a building. When we stopped after long hours of work, we ate big meals from the generous store of provisions we had brought with us, as well as the fruit and meat the jungle itself provided. We felt—I certainly felt—that the Lord's own hand was guiding us to Caladria. We could see the jungle being sliced down right in front of us. We half expected, I think, to chop through one final wall of brush and find the sparkling city standing there in its splendor before us.

But then those awful rocky mounds loomed in the distance, and the jungle became a grove of twisted trees, standing as gray warnings of the life-killing force that lay ahead of us. No one in our group, not even the Tree People, had ever crossed the Dead Mountains. They would be easy to cross, since they were smooth, their slope was slight, and they were not nearly as high as the Amian or Wilmorothian mountains. But that was little comfort to us as we drew close to the Dead Mountains' base. The silence was eerie. We had grown used to the thousand different noises of the jungle—hundreds of insects, birds, and other beasts in a constant chorus. But at the base of the mountains, no living thing grew and no animal made a noise. As we made camp facing the mountain, Danuta said, "It will be easy to cross here. By tomorrow night we'll be in the Gray Desert, farther than any of us have ever gone. Farther than any law allows us to go, and farther than common sense tells us we should go."

Only Taron's clear and worshipful soprano voice cut through the silence that night. No one else felt like singing. Some said they were tired and wanted to get plenty of rest for the next day's journey across the mountain, but the silence sprang from more than just weariness. Our mood was apprehensive. Everyone knew this was the last night any of us could turn back to avoid the evil that lurked in the desert. As I watched some of the Tree People huddled in quiet circles near the fire, I imagined that some of them were debating whether or not they should return to their homes.

That night for the first time our company was attacked by the horrible black insects called farks that the Tree People had been so worried about. They did not get into my tent, so I did not find out about the problem until the next morning, when someone showed me one of the dead bugs. It was about the size of a quarter and had a hard, rounded shell. They had bitten three of the Tree

People who were sleeping on the perimeter of our group. I was
told that about thirty of the bugs had crawled on and around the
men while they slept side by side. When the first man was bit, he
yelled, sprang up, and lit the torches, which scared the bugs away.
Before he could get all the insects off him, though, he was bit four
times on the legs and arms. The other two men were bit twice each.
The Tree People had brought medicine to treat the wounds, and
the men were not seriously hurt. But the farks were the main topic
of discussion the next morning, particularly among the Wilmorothians and Tree People. If the dreaded bugs attacked even
before we crossed the mountain, they wondered, what kind of
horrors might we expect when got to the Gray Desert itself?

—◯—

Our trip across the mountains was relatively easy, but we did
not make it all the way across in one day. We stayed on the
mountain one night, and by mid-afternoon of the next day we
were in the Gray Desert.

We were surrounded by deadness, enveloped in it. Grayness.
Dust. Rocks piled needlessly on top of rocks. For the first time I
understood why the Tree People feared and loathed this place.
What I had not understood until that moment was that the
Grayness of this place was more than a physical phenomenon
caused by the barrenness of the land or the color of the rocks. It
was more than a feeling of gloom that you might feel on a cloudy
day. This Grayness existed apart from all its physical manifesta-
tions. It was not tied to subjective emotional reactions. The
Grayness was an entity unto itself, an almost palpable, almost
physically observable presence.

Danuta spoke of the Grayness not as a presence but as an
absence, the utter absence of the Spirit of God in that place. She
explained, "This is not like Persus Am, where the Spirit of the Lord
withdrew from the music when sin brought about the War and
destroyed the Temple. In those days the people knew that something had gone out of the world, that the voice of God no longer
spoke to them in the same way it once had, but in reality His Spirit
did not abandon the world completely. Even in its sadness after
the War, the whole Known World was infused with and upheld by

the silent and invisible presence of God. Even though only the Emajians could hear His voice faintly in the music, all people still enjoyed the benefits of His blessings—the living abundance of the land, the orderliness of the seasons, and a thousand other good things—though they did not know the Lord who had provided them. So it was then, and so it is now.

"But in the Gray Desert," she said, "unlike anywhere else, the presence of God is totally absent. The place is utterly abandoned, a wasteland. Not one living thing is known to grow here. There is no known source of water anywhere in it. No one knows where the desert ends. And besides the physical desolation, a horrible feeling of emptiness and hopelessness abounds here. The only presence of God that exists here is what we bring with us inside ourselves. Most of the people who have come to the desert for more than a few days have either died or gone mad. That's why when Emajus led His people into this desert and told them they were going to Caladria, it was assumed that He was leading them into mass suicide."

I asked, "But what caused it to be like this? Why did God abandon this place?"

"We don't know. As far as all the nations of the Known World know, it's always been this way. We can only speculate."

"What do you think it could be?"

"Maybe there was a whole thriving world here once; maybe they turned to evil and either God destroyed them or they destroyed themselves, much as we would have done in the War if it had continued, the bombs killing and killing and killing until there was nothing and nobody left. Perhaps God just sadly walked away from it forever."

"That's horrible!"

"Well, it's just a guess. But think about it. If Umbriel gets his way and has his war, what will the Known World look like when he's done? It could be a wasteland just like this."

———◯———

We followed Will's map through the desert. The leader of the Tree People had guided us through the jungle and over the mountain, but as soon as we reached the desert, Will took command without a word ever being spoken. He led us as if he were taking us through his native region. It was eerie to hear him give accurate, detailed descriptions of rock formations or craters or hills that we would come to in a few hours, even though the maps we had indicated none of these landmarks. The only map worth anything, in fact, was the one in Will's head. Because the Gray Desert was a wasteland where no one in normal circumstances wanted to go or was even allowed to go, no one had bothered to make very good maps of it. What maps did exist Will had refused to study, to the consternation of his hosts at the Rock of Calad, who wanted him to pinpoint exactly where he would take the group to find Caladria. "Those maps are no good," he had told them. "That desert looks nothing like those maps."

"Have you ever been to that desert?" they had asked quite reasonably.

"Nope. I've never been to any desert in my life. But I know exactly what this desert looks like. Just get me right here," he had said, pointing to the place in the Dead Mountains where we would eventually cross over, "and I will get you to the place you want to go." He then had reluctantly marked the approximate spot on the map where they would end up, and after that he had refused to look at or discuss maps any further. The Caladans simply had to take the word of this burly, bearded young man who could barely speak their language, who refused to answer their questions, who was from a place that was just as impossible to locate on a map as Caladria was.

Will looked grim, almost mean, as he led us through the desert. I had never seen him this way. At home he had always been the liveliest person in any crowd, always laughing, or bear-hugging someone, or talking too loud, or accidentally saying something he shouldn't. With his smile comfortably nestled in his beard, which was always neatly trimmed, he looked completely carefree. But here in the Grayness, with his hair and beard bushy and filled with dust and with his eyes intently studying each sand dune and rock formation, he looked like the wide-eyed, eccentric prophet that most of our company thought he was. Almost no one tried to talk to him except me, and I could interest him in no topic other than the desert. I was still having my dream-visions of Anne, and I wanted to talk to him about them, since only he knew her and knew our home, where the dreams were set. I thought he would want to talk about home, but he might as well have been from a different planet entirely for all the interest he showed in home. For Will home was now nothing more than some vague idea of a place he wanted to go once he had finished his task in the desert. He thought of home the way people think of heaven; he knew nothing about the details of it, but he knew that it must be a nice place and that he wanted to go there. I admired his single-mindedness, but I worried about the strain the trip was putting on him. Maybe he would have to bear it only a few more days, I hoped, and then we would find our spot in the desert and our answer to the mystery of Caladria.

—◯—

On our second night in the desert, as I lay sleeping in my tent next to Will, I was awakened by clicking sounds, like a fingernail scraping over the teeth of a comb. I heard what I thought was someone brushing against the tent outside. Assuming someone was still just walking around outside, I tried to ignore the sounds and go back to sleep.

What happened next, however, was impossible to ignore. I felt a hard tug on my hair, as if someone had grabbed a clump of it and was pulling as hard as he could. I reached up to grab whatever it was, and my hand gripped what felt like an egg, soft and rounded. As soon as I pulled it out of my hair, the creature's jaws bit into two of my fingers, and I screamed and flung the thing across the tent.

Will sprang up and yelled, "What are they, Jer? Aaaaaaaah! There's one on my arm!" He knocked it away and clicked on one of the globe lights, which slowly illuminated to reveal five or six of the shiny black pests scampering to hide from the light. "What are they?" he asked.

"Let's get out of here," I said, scrambling to work my way through the door of the tent. "They're those farks."

"They can't be. They're too big! That one's the size of a

baseball. Those things we saw before we crossed the mountains looked more like beetles."

"I know. But they're the same creature. They just grow bigger out here, I guess."

The farks must have attacked the entire company at about the same time because when Will and I got out of the tent, we saw people all over the camp springing out of their tents, lighting torches and globe lights, yelling, tending to their wounds.

Almost immediately Danuta came. "They're all over the place," she said. "I just came from Dakin's tent. He's been bit pretty badly, on the face and arms. I'm worried about him. Were you two bit?"

"I was," I said. "On my hand."

"Let me see."

Two of my fingers were gashed and bleeding. "Oh, that's nothing," said Danuta. "You'll be all right." It didn't feel like nothing. It hurt quite badly.

"You should see Dakin," she said. "They really bit into him."

"Let's go see him. Is he being taken care of?"

"Yes. The Tree People have medicine that they say counteracts the poison of the bite. You'd better take some of it too."

On our way to Dakin's tent I stopped and said, "Listen."

"What?"

In the midst of people talking and scurrying around, I heard the same scraping noise I had heard in my tent. "I can hear those things chewing somewhere."

"Are you sure it's—"

"Yes, listen. That's the sound I heard before they bit me, that scraping sound. It's awful. They're all around us, chewing everything up."

Will walked up to an empty tent and kicked around the base of it. Two fist-sized farks fell at his feet and then scrambled away. "Those things are getting in by chewing through the tents. There's holes all over this one."

"Isn't there any way to get rid of these things?" I asked.

"Not that we know of," said Danuta. "Light is the only thing they're afraid of. We could keep the globe lights and the torches going all night long. That's the only thing I know to do."

"Where do they come from? What could they possibly live on out here in the desert?"

"No one knows. The Tree People say they're the devil's own children and he feeds them evil."

Will said, "The Tree People blame everything on the devil or God. These overgrown bugs live on idiots who come out into the desert to commit suicide. They've probably been sharpening their teeth for us for years."

This from the man we were trusting to lead us to the right place in the desert. Danuta, ever tactful, said nothing. I kept quiet too.

Dakin looked horrible. The bites on his arms weren't too bad, but the entire right side of his face was a swollen, bleeding blotch of red. The rest of his face was so pale and gaunt that the wound stood out all the more dramatically. He was as fidgety as ever while two of the Tree People, who did not know his language, tried to treat his wound.

The whole night was miserable. The company, already exhausted from the day's travel, had to tear down and rearrange the tents so that our torches could be placed efficiently. Once we finished that and treated the wounded, we went back to bed, leaving guards to watch for farks that might get past the circle of light. Tired as I was, I could not get to sleep for a long time because I kept thinking I heard the creatures chewing outside my tent, and I kept remembering what the awful fark felt like when I had grasped it in my hand. The medicine I had taken left a thick, metallic taste in my mouth, but because I had already drunk my water ration for the day, I could not quench my thirst. *Rescue us quickly,* I prayed to the Lord again and again. *Rescue us quickly.*

But when I awoke to the gray dawn, I saw only miles and miles of desert before us.

—◯—

We limped through the desert another day. Will remained in black despair, but he kept his wide, staring eyes focused on the sand, as if there were more to that desert than the monotonous grayness that the rest of us saw. He spoke only to me and, to my surprise, Taron, who rode next to him and tried to encourage him.

At Danuta's urging, I mingled with the company and tried to reassure them that all was well and to remind them that we knew this part of our journey would not be easy. Danuta said, "The company knows that it's Will's job to get us through the desert, but they're looking to you for leadership. They know who you are. They've risked everything for Emajus, and you're the one who represents Him out here." The people responded well to my simple words of encouragement. I decided that for several hours each day I would break away from my inner circle—Danuta, Will, Tarius, Taron, and Dakin—to talk to the rest of the company. Some of them, I learned, had left their homes in spite of frantic pleas from their family and friends not to get involved in such a dangerous venture. One man had been married only a few months but told his wife he felt the Spirit of the Lord calling him to Caladria. Another was an Emajian who had been persecuted in Persus Am for playing Emajian music in the Utturies. He told me, "I suffered in Umbriel's prison just like you, brother, and I would have been killed in it except for a miracle that got me released by mistake. But I think the Lord released me so I could help you find Caladria. If you and I can survive that prison, there ain't nothing this desert can throw at us that we can't handle." I heard one story after another of courage and determination. They had put their very lives on the line because they believed in a Spirit, whom they called Emajus, who inhabited the music and filled their souls. They had taken the risk; now they expected me to deliver Caladria to them. All I could do was throw myself at the mercy of the Lord. *Rescue us quickly,* I prayed.

Dust blew into our mouths all day. We were hungry and thirsty most of the time, but we had to strictly ration water. The Grayness so enveloped us that it was hard to sing. Though it is difficult to describe, the sound of the music clashed with the emptiness of the gray absence of Spirit in the desert and made the music seem not only annoying and out of place, but actually painful to our ears. I understood for the first time the discomfort the nonbelievers in Persus Am had experienced at the sound of an

Emajian song. I remembered the way Shellan had grimaced when she had heard my guitar. Our company was dismayed to find that the music that had always been the source through which they reached out to God had become painful and ugly to them. Danuta and Tarius and I spent long hours reminding them that the ugliness of the music was a distortion of the desert, not a sign that their faith was weak. We urged them to dig deeply into their reserve of faith; we urged them to follow what they knew to be true and not to be deceived by what the Grayness made them hear. We had come too far, we told them, to be defeated by the tricks of the desert. Taron was determined to sing no matter how much it hurt her. Every few hours she would step away from Will and the rest of the company and sing as confidently as she could into the Gray, which curdled the sound and then gobbled it up in empty silence. Sometimes the music hurt her so much that she would lose her breath and collapse to her knees. I told her the Lord would not expect her to keep putting herself through that pain, but she answered, "I won't turn against the Lord's voice, no matter what. Even if it never stops hurting. Even if it kills me."

—◯—

On our fourth day in the desert, I noticed that Will was especially vigilant, his eyes staring out from his wild mass of hair and straining to see as far as he could into the horizon.

"What do you see, Will?" I asked.

"That rocky place up in the distance. That flat hill. See it?"

"Yes."

"I think that might be the place."

"Could it be so soon? I thought we had at least one more day, according to the map."

"The map is worthless. I think that's it. But I won't know until we get there."

Because Taron was beside him, Will had spoken Amian. His words were overheard, and before long word had spread through the entire company that the end was near, that the final spot on the map was in sight.

The rocky place was farther away than it looked, and we did not reach it until almost dark. The hill sloped gently upward and would be fairly easy to climb, but the company was exhausted by that time of day. The wind had picked up too and was blowing dust all around our heads. I decided to leave the company at the bottom of the hill and take Will and Danuta up with me to check the place out. From the perspective of the top of that hill, our company was a sad and forlorn sight. They sat on the ground, huddled close together, their heads covered with blankets to protect them from the dust. Where had we brought them? To a pile of rocks in a land of death.

"This is it," Will said. "End of the road."

"Are you sure, Will? We can't afford mistakes."

"I'm absolutely sure. I knew it the minute we got up here."

"But there's nothing here!" said Danuta.

"That's right," said Will. "The place I am supposed to bring you to is a piece of nothing in the middle of nowhere. This is it."

"Well, then, our rescue could happen at anytime," I said.

In English, Will said, "What if it doesn't, Jer?"

"It will. That's what this is all about."

"But what if it doesn't happen? What if we just sit here and absolutely nothing happens?"

"I just don't believe—"

"But *what if*, Jer?"

"Then we'll die."

"Nope. Not me. I'll give this thing a little more time, but then I'm getting out of here while there's still time to make it back alive."

"Don't even think about that, Will. We've come to far to abandon our mission now. If you left the company, it would be a disaster. People are already having doubts as it is. We've got to stick it out. We will be rescued."

"My part was to bring you to this place. I've done it. Now I'm free. I've served my purpose."

"The purpose is to get to Caladria. Will, do you really think that you and I would have been dragged this far from home, been given these visions, and been put through all the stuff we've been put through if the end of it was going to be that we would die in the desert? Come on now. I'm discouraged too. But an answer will come. But if you leave, others might follow, and then we could lose it all. As your friend I'm pleading with you not to do that to me."

"You say an answer will come. If it comes there's no problem. But this place is already killing me. I'm not just saying that, either. I feel like I'm literally dying little by little each day. I can't promise you I'll stay if it means dying."

Danuta asked, "What are you two talking about?"

I answered, "Brother Will is having a moment of discouragement after seeing what a wasteland we've been brought to. I don't blame him. It looks pretty awful to me too. But at least we made it. Now we just wait on the Lord. Let's go down and tell the others that this is the end of the road."

—◯—

At the base of the mountain the company gathered around me. I said, "We should thank the Lord, for he has brought us to the end of the map. We have fought evil every step of the way, but we have accomplished our mission. We are here, and now we must simply wait upon the Lord. I know we are tired. I know we are hungry, and thirsty, and lonely, and that some of us are in pain. I know that the place the Lord has taken us to seems barren and hopeless. But I plead with you as brothers and sisters in Emajus not to falter now. The Lord has worked too many miracles to get us here for us to give up now in discouragement. We have overcome the armies of Umbriel. We have joined together from every nation—Persus Am, the Rock of Calad, Damonchok, Wilmoroth—and we have survived against mountains and jungles and deserts and farks and soldiers. Now the Lord has brought us to the edge of victory. For all we know He might rescue us today. We may wake up in the morning in the Lord's own paradise, Caladria.

"The Lord has made us totally dependent on Him. We are powerless now. We are in His hands. We wait on Him, even though that is sometimes the hardest thing to do. If we can only overcome this final obstacle—waiting—we will see glorious days, and everything we have suffered will be worth it."

Tarius Arc and some others shouted, "Amen!"

By mid-afternoon the next day our camp was set up on top

of the hill, which we named *Shabalay,* the Amian word for "waiting."

———◯———

At times the Grayness was so overwhelming it felt like a physical force squeezing in on us from all sides. Moving through the desert had at least given us something besides the Grayness to think about, but once we set up camp on top of Will's hill, we had absolutely nothing to do but wait to be rescued.

Nothing to do but let doubts creep in about whether or not we had made a big mistake. Could we really trust Will, who had become this wild-eyed, scary-looking creature who never spoke, who never sang, who was not even a believer? Why would the Lord make him the messenger to lead us into Caladria? Will made no secret of his lack of enthusiasm for our journey. Is it possible he was only saying this was the place because he did not want to go any farther into the desert? Was he stopping here because he planned to abandon us and knew that if he went much farther he would never make it out of the desert alive?

And I could only imagine the doubts the company had about me. After all, hadn't I served Umbriel, the archenemy of the Emajians? In the relentless gloom of the Gray Desert, suspicion and paranoia flourished.

The only thing besides sheer stubborn faith that held our company together was two miracles—I will call them miracles—that occurred during our first two days on the hill. On our first day we sent some of the soldiers to explore the hill and the area surrounding it, hoping that we might find some clue as to why we had been brought there. There were a number of caves on the far side of the hill, and in one of them a soldier found a spring that gushed sparkling pure water. The Gray Desert was thought to have no sources of water, so we were astonished and delighted. Of all of our provisions, water was what we most feared running out of. After the soldier reported the water to me and after I went to the cave myself and filled a large pitcher with it, I immediately called the company together to share the good news. I began by pouring the water over my head, which brought gasps of amazement. "Don't look so upset, friends! Not one drop of the water I just drenched myself with comes from our meager provisions. No, I just drenched myself with water given to me—given to us all— from the Lord Himself. In those caves on the other side of the hill we have found a spring gushing the best-tasting, coldest, most refreshing water you've ever tasted."

"Water!" shouted Tarius, amidst the rest of the chatter that broke out after my announcement. "There's not supposed to be any water in the Gray Desert."

"There's not supposed to be a Caladria, either," I answered, loud enough for everyone to hear. "And we were never supposed to survive more than a day or two in the desert. Nevertheless, the water is there, and it just keeps pouring out, as it probably has for years and years, maybe since the first pilgrims to Caladria came this way and drank from it. Gallons and gallons of it every hour, every day, more than we could ever use. And you're all welcome to drink it and bathe in it and play in it. But let's thank God for it! The Lord has shown us by this sign that we're in the right place. There's probably only one water hole in thousands of miles of desert, and it's ours!"

Just about everybody spent the rest of that afternoon at the water cave, splashing each other and drinking as much as they wanted and washing their filthy hair and smelly bodies. The gloom seemed to lift a little bit that day, but by nightfall, even the good fortune of the water brought doubt to some in the company. Some wondered whether the water was a sign that the Lord intended to keep us there for a long time rather than rescue us soon. I had no answer for them. I said only, "Let's just survive one day at a time and not lose faith. Just be glad that this day the Lord has given us an infinite supply of water. Tomorrow, maybe He'll surprise us with another good thing."

The next day did bring another miracle, but like the miracle of the water, there was a dark side.

Taron continued to sing to the Lord every day, despite the pain each note brought to her and those around her. No one else sang in the desert; even Tarius Arc, who had insisted when the journey began that he would sing every day as he had done every day of his life, finally gave it up because it seared his body with pain to the point of collapse.

Only Will ever asked Taron to stop. The rest of us, as Emajians, did not like the idea of stopping God's song for any reason, no matter how much it hurt us. But Will had no such compunction. He told her, "There's no use putting yourself and the rest of us through that. We're suffering enough as it is."

"God's voice, His music, has always been my strength. I won't forget Him just because it hurts," she said.

The day after we found the water Taron sang as she did every day. She stood at the edge of the camp, but close enough that everyone heard her. Will walked away from her, and then her song began: "Praise to the Lord God Almighty/ To the King of Kings may my praises rise." Her soprano voice, so beautiful in normal circumstances, pierced through us that day, even causing some to cover their ears. Will doubled over and covered his head with his arms. Others went inside their tents.

It took us a while to hear the miracle. Her voice seemed unusually loud, as if the surrounding mountain magnified it and held onto it. Then it sounded as if two people were singing, the second voice a vague and haunting response to Taron's. I got up and walked closer to where she sang. I listened as each note she sang hung in the air, then took on a life of its own, creating the effect of a second singer. Everyone concentrated on her now, amazed. The music grew not only louder but more penetrating and absolutely clear, blocking out all other sound. Taron slumped to her knees and leaned forward, as if every note stabbed her. But not once did she shrink back from her singing. The notes she released stayed in the air and blended into a mighty chorus; it sounded as if the whole company were singing with her. Taron was a tiny speck on the mountain, dwarfed by the sound that came out of her.

The sound finally reached an intensity that Taron could not bear, and she collapsed in a heap. Immediately the sound—in physical form, a ring of multicolored light as piercing in its intensity as the music had been—swallowed her up for a moment so that we could not see her. Will jumped up immediately and ran toward her, afraid the strange force would kill her. The light held him away. When he tried to break through it, he fell backward and was knocked unconscious.

From the center of the light, where Taron knelt, swirling circles of light, like rings of water on a lake, issued forth in blue and red and yellow bands. The circles of light shattered and dispelled the Gray as they pushed outward toward us. I walked toward the bands of light, and as each one touched me, the Gray emptiness of my spirit was filled with the music, and I was flooded with joy. The music no longer hurt; I wanted to drink it in, feel it wash over me. The sound was electrified with life and with the Spirit of God. Later some said it sounded like thousands of voices, but others thought it sounded like instruments. I heard voices and instruments of every kind. I got as close to the center as I could, but only Taron could inhabit the core of that column of light. Like a powerful wind, the light held the rest of us back.

I don't know how long the music played; none of us could agree on that later. The sound obliterated time as well as the Grayness. Judging by the afternoon sky and our timepieces, the music could not have lasted for more than a few minutes. But it seemed much longer than that to me, as if we had been taken out of time for several hours and then returned to approximately the same spot where we had left it. However long it lasted, the light gradually disintegrated like mist and took the music with it. Taron was left kneeling on the ground, her head down, clutching herself and crying with joy. Will ran to her and put his arms around her. She hugged him but was too overcome to speak.

As the light faded from view, one of the Caladan soldiers who had suffered the worst of the fark bites in the big attack came up to me with tears in his eyes, shouting, "They're gone! My wounds are gone!" Sure enough, when he lifted his shirt and ripped away the bandages, his skin was as smooth as if he had never been bitten at all.

"Where were you standing?" I asked.

"Just behind you. In the light."

I immediately thought of Dakin, whose horrible face wound had hardly healed at all. But when I made my way through the rest of the company and found him near his tent, I saw the same ugly scab covering almost half his face. Three people were healed that day, but no one else was, for reasons no one could explain.

When the music and light disintegrated, the Grayness quickly enveloped us again. The Grayness seemed to push us together into a huddled mass, for comfort. Everyone gathered around me for an explanation of what had happened.

I pulled Taron aside and asked, "Can you explain what happened?"

"No. The Lord's Spirit just swept over me and then the angels were singing and then He was gone, and everything closed up again and the ugliness was all over me like before."

Danuta stood beside us, listening. She said, "What is the Lord up to? What's going on?"

"I don't know," I said. "It's a sign of something. I don't know what."

Already we could feel the oppression of the Grayness. It seemed to press in on us even heavier than before. All eyes were on me. I had to say something. "I can't explain all that has just happened, brothers and sisters, but all I know is that the Lord has revealed Himself to us today. He has not abandoned us. He has not forgotten us. Yesterday He gave us water, today He has spoken to us with His own voice. He has healed some. He has touched us all. We've got to hang on just a little longer. We must never give up on Him. He'll save us if we are patient."

For the rest of that afternoon we stayed huddled together, talking about the light and the music, our only shield against despair. If He were going to send such a powerful sign, I wondered, why did He not go ahead and rescue us? Why drag out this misery? What was He waiting for?

—◯—

The miracle, as I have said, had a dark side. Not only did the temporary joy of the music make the Grayness seem even more desolate by comparison, but the music made the farks more ferocious than they had ever been. Ever since the fark attack during our second night in the desert, we had managed to keep them out of the camp by placing our tents close together and surrounding the whole camp with a ring of torches and globe lights placed low to the ground. We left the supplies and the camucks outside the circle of light because the farks did not bother them. We did not know why camuck blood was not as appealing as our own, but the farks ignored everything but human beings. Every night we heard the low hum—actually a scraping sound—as the farks encircled our camp. The sound kept me awake the first night, but after that I learned to ignore it.

There were no more fark attacks, and most of those who had been bitten were slowly beginning to heal. The one exception was Dakin, who worried us very much since the bite on his face only got worse. The poison from these creatures could, of course, kill people, and Dakin showed two signs that the poison had taken hold: weakness and hallucinations. He was becoming so frail that he could not get out of his tent by himself. All day he reclined in a chair by his tent and stared into the desert, toward home. In one of his hallucinations, he thought the farks were all over him. He slashed at himself so wildly that two men had to hold him down to keep him from hurting himself. In a few minutes the hallucination passed, and he lay there speechless, exhausted, seemingly unaware of the people around him. During another episode he thought he saw Miriaban walking across the desert toward our mountain. He ran toward her, screaming her name. Before we could catch him, he fell face forward into the dust and rocks, causing his wounds to gush open again. We gave him medicine every day, but it had no effect.

Now the music and light from Taron's worship filled the farks with rage. By the time we went to bed that night, the scraping noise had reached a furious intensity, like thousands of knives being sharpened at once. I could not sleep.

"How can that noise be so much louder?" I asked Will. "I can't stand it. I can't sleep with it."

"It's not that much louder. Don't think about it. It's no worse than crickets."

"Crickets can't bite your face off. These things can." I knew Will did not believe what he said. He had lapsed into a depression so deep that he pretended nothing had any effect on him. He pretended to be immune to suffering. I said, "I keep remembering what it felt like when I reached up and grabbed that fark on my head. That hard shell. And then those teeth biting into me. It was horrible!"

"Well, there's lights all around, Jer. So don't worry about it. Go to sleep."

I did go to sleep. But I was awakened by the most horrible pain I have ever felt. Two farks, one egg-sized and one the size of a man's fist, clasped onto my face at once, digging their teeth in. I lurched upward, screaming, and tried to tear them away. They growled as they chewed. I was hysterical with fear. My hands tugged furiously at the creatures, even though Will was yelling, "Don't pull them, Jer! Don't pull them! They'll rip your skin off!" It was true that there were better ways to get them to release their bite, but at that moment I wanted them off at any cost. I ripped the smaller one off my face. I heard my skin tear. Blood was everywhere. The pain was so searing I thought I would pass out. Will poked at the other one with a knife, as it growled and chewed until finally after several minutes later it dropped to the floor. Will jumped on it with all his might. I heard the crunch and saw its entrails squirt across the tent. I was dizzy with pain. I stumbled out of the tent.

The next minutes were a blur. The farks had an uncanny ability to attack the whole company at the same time so that we could not warn one another that the creatures were in the camp. People were screaming and bleeding and crushing the farks under their feet. Some of the black creatures were the size of a grapefruit, bigger than any that had ever been reported. I was in too much pain to be of any help at all. It was all I could do to keep from collapsing in the dirt, where more farks might bite me. Will, who was not bitten, did his best to treat my wounds, and eventually, maybe half an hour later, Danuta caught up with me. I was lying down just outside the tent by then. Things had quieted down. Dead farks dotted the ground. She leaned over me, but I was so overcome with pain that I said nothing. The skin around her eyes was dark with exhaustion. Her red hair was matted in places with other people's blood. She looked worse than I had ever seen her.

"We're out of medicine," she said. "There's nothing we can do but clean your wound and hope for the best."

"How did this happen?" I asked. "How did they get past the light?"

"It seems there just isn't enough light to keep the big ones out. They just charged right through."

"How many people were bit?"

"Probably half the company."

"And we have no more medicine?"

"No."

"Why didn't we bring more?"

"We brought all that exists in the world."

"Well, what do we do now? How are we going to keep this poison from killing people? How do we keep it from killing *me*?"

"There's nothing else we can do. Some people's bodies can fight off the poison without the medicine. We can hope. We may have to face the fact that some people are going to die. The Lord is going to have to rescue us soon. There's no other way out."

—◯—

Two of the Tree People died the next morning, within two hours of each other. Their bodies were prepared for burial right away, and the funeral took place that afternoon. The company was despondent. My greatest fear was that Will or somebody else would decide to give up the mission and head back. I was certain that if Will, whom they considered a prophet, left, many people in the company would follow him. But that day Will did nothing but shut himself off in the tent and talk to Taron. At the funeral Taron sang one short, painful chorus, and Tarius Arc spoke a few words, since I was too injured to do it.

Much of my face was covered with bandages, and it was horribly swollen. I also felt the first effects of the poison. Midway through the day I noticed that everything I looked at seemed to quiver slightly. I would shut my eyes and rub my temples to try to make everything stand still, but when I opened my eyes the world still shook. The endless motion made me nauseous, as if I were on a trampoline that barely bounced but never stopped. By nightfall I was worse, the dizziness turning to a throbbing pain in my head.

At times I felt quick, rhythmic pounds that made me feel as if my whole head must be expanding, as if anyone who saw me must wonder why it was so huge and why it pulsated and bulged in so many directions. Then the throbs would ease and the focus of suffering would be my stomach, which churned and threatened to erupt. All these symptoms were in addition to the pain of the wounds themselves. When the bandages were removed from my face, the sight was horrifying—a bloody, pulpy mess.

Near the center of the camp was a supply tent that we used as our headquarters that day. Danuta, Tarius, Taron, and I stayed there most of the day, and Will came in for a while in the morning. Dakin, despite the fact that his wounds were not healing and that he had received another small bite the night before, had a few hours of relative clarity that morning, and he also joined us in the tent. Seeing how injured I was, Dakin immediately came to me. "Jeremy, I was hoping you would be spared this suffering. You don't deserve it. Why did God bring you here to suffer with us? My own wounds I deserve. But not you."

"No," I said. "You have sacrificed as much as anyone for Emajus. We don't suffer because we deserve it or escape suffering because we don't deserve it. We suffer because we're in a war, and we have to endure to the end."

He shook his head. "I doubt that I'll make it to the end. That is my punishment."

"Of course you'll make it. Why don't you sit with us, Dakin. We're talking about where we go from here."

"I have no advice to give!" he said, throwing his hands in the air. "I have nothing left to say."

"No one knows the Emajian songs and prophecies as well as you do, Dakin. What do they say about this part of the journey? Do they give any clue about how long we'll have to wait? Or what we're waiting for?"

"Some songs mention a desert, and suffering in a desert, and being swept to Caladria. But these songs are about the believers who went with Emajus to Caladria. Of course, they could be prophetic. Most of the prophecies are about two things at once."

"Well, if the songs talk about believers suffering in the desert and then going to Caladria—"

"Being 'swept away' to Caladria," corrected Dakin. "That's how it's described in the Song of Ramon, isn't it, Brother Tarius?"

"Yes, that's right. They wander around, they doubt, they question the Lord, and finally they're swept away. It's been a long time since I've heard or read that song. It gets very poetic at the end. Makes you wonder whether it's literal. Something about swept away to the Lord's paradise on a river of His mercy."

"River of His *love*," corrected Dakin. "But we don't know that the song has anything to do with us."

"Well," I said, "the closest thing to a river in the Gray Desert is our little spring. We can't float away on that."

Danuta said, "Maybe the Lord miraculously created a river in the desert. Maybe our spring will erupt into a mighty river and we'll float to Caladria on it."

I shook my head. "This is no help at all. We don't even have anything to float away *on*. And it doesn't tell us anything about *when* this is going to happen."

In English Will said, "Maybe it's like Noah, and we're supposed to build an ark."

I ignored him. I said, "Maybe we're at the wrong place. Maybe there's a river out here, and we're supposed to find it."

"We are in the right place," said Will. "That's the one thing I am sure of. I don't know why we're here, but I know this is the place. There was nothing about any river."

Quietly Tarius said, "There is no river in the Gray Desert, Jeremy. Not unless the Lord creates one."

"We didn't think there was any water here either, but now we have a spring."

Dakin took hold of my hand, squeezed it, and then wandered out of the tent.

———○———

That night I got horribly sick. I vomited repeatedly. I could barely stand. My mind was so muddled that I could not make sense of most of what people said to me. I could hear their words and I could understand the words individually, but I could not form thoughts with them. When Danuta brought a meal in for me and asked me whether I was ready to eat, I understood *meal* and *eat* and other words, but I could not put it all together to realize that she wanted me to eat the food she had just brought in. She repeated herself several times, but it was as if she were reading a story about someone else. I made no connection between the words and the food. Eventually I ate the food she sat next to me, but even then I did not make the connection to what she had been saying.

I slept in the headquarters tent, and late in the night I had a vision of Anne. She walked through the door of the tent, dressed in bright Wilmorothian slacks and a wraparound blouse, like the clothes Danuta wore. She was part of our company. I was not surprised to see her. "What is that on your face?" she asked, and she came and sat down next to me on the reclining chair. Her hands touched my cheeks, and as they did, pieces of something dry and white, like dried paint or plaster, flaked off my face. Anne brushed the flakes to the ground. She brushed everything away until my face was smooth and tingly, the way it feels right after I have shaved. Her face was close to mine.

The smell of her hair.

Her fingertips on my face.

I awoke to weary gray daylight. Danuta hovered over me, crying. Even with all we had been through, with all the burden we had put on her, I had never seen her cry before.

"What?" I managed to say.

"Dakin," she said. "He took a turn for the worse last night."

"No!"

"He died this morning."

I lifted my head. The world became fuzzy and gray and then cleared again. Hot, sharp pains raced through my head and body. *Dakin. No!* How much more were we supposed to take? *How much more?*

"Just lie still, Jeremy. There's not a thing anyone can do."

I was numb with grief and pain. "He seemed better to me yesterday. Didn't you think so? He talked about the prophecies.

He seemed more worried about my condition than his own. I thought he was coming out of it. Mentally at least."

"He lapsed into a coma last night. There was nothing we could do." She began to cry again. "Nothing we could do. All these people are suffering, and there's not a thing we can do to help them. Jeremy, even for you, I'm afraid that—"

That I might die too. She did not finish her sentence, but the words were in the air just as clearly as if she had shouted them. Strange as it may sound, I had never considered the possibility that I could die of my wounds. But they were at least as bad as Dakin's had been. Why should I be spared if he was not? The mission had seemed so inevitable, so right, that the thought of death intervening to stop it had not taken shape in my mind. I held out my hand to Danuta, and she sat down next to me.

"We can't think about that," I said. "We can only get through one day—one hour—at a time. We've just got to hold the company together."

"Why is this happening, Jeremy? You're the prophet. Do you have any idea why God is doing this to us?"

My own mind screamed, *Why? Why! We have followed every leading of the Spirit. We have sacrificed everything. Why bring us out to a desert to slaughter us?* I answered, "No one has an explanation. We just have to keep on going no matter what the cost, until He rescues us."

"Or until we die."

I said, "It's better to die obeying the Lord than to live even one moment running away from him."

But as waves of rage and grief for my friend washed over me, I was not so sure.

———○———

We buried Dakin that day, just before dark. Just before the ceremony, Tarius Arc came in to speak with me. "Dakin's death has hit the company very hard," he said. "I'm afraid we're losing them."

"What do you mean?"

"There's talk that some of them are planning to desert."

"They can't! We knew it wouldn't be easy. We knew we might have to suffer."

"Nevertheless, that's what they're planning."

"Who? How many?"

"I don't know for sure. Will's name comes up often. And some of the Tree People, since home is relatively close for them."

"I doubt if they would even make it back alive. It takes all of us just to protect each other from the farks." Ever since the fark attack, half of the company had stayed up at night and slept during the day. These guards killed a few dozen of the creatures each night. "Are they going to take our provisions? They just can't do it. We've come too far. We have to stick together. We have to see this through, for better or for worse. Backing out was never an option."

"You've got to talk to them."

"All right."

"Are you doing better today?"

"No, I'm worse. I have blacked out three times. I'm confused about half the time. My eyes don't work right; everything has this quivering motion to it."

"Have you considered the possibility that we have made a mistake, that it might be best for the entire company to go home?"

"Tarius! We have made no mistake! We have—"

"Jeremy, I will stand beside you until death if that's what it takes. But I just need to know that you're absolutely sure that we're doing the right thing."

"I am sure. Don't you abandon me too, Tarius."

"I will not."

At the service for Dakin I wanted to stand as I spoke, but I could not do it. My chair was brought out to me. I had just come through one of my episodes of hazy confusion, in which my thoughts disconnected themselves from each other and stood helpless and alone in my brain. I prayed for clarity.

After Taron sang, I said, "Brothers and sisters in Emajus, our situation is too desperate to try to cover it over with empty phrases and promises of hope. This is the worst day of my life. I pray to God only that I may speak to you with simplicity and truth. Dakin was my friend. I loved him. When I was in the horrible prison in Persus Am, on the verge of execution, he found a way, at great risk to his own standing, to set me free. He made me a guest in his home. He made it possible for me to translate the scriptures, which since have reached the entire Known World. He was a wealthy man with great power. Umbriel respected him and listened to his advice. The whole government of Persus Am held him in high esteem. His wife loved him and looked after him. He had everything a man could ask for, and he could have lived out the rest of his life in luxury and ease.

"He chose not to do that. Instead, when the Spirit of God, the very voice of God, spoke to him, as it has spoken to us all, through the songs that Dakin was supposed to only study as a scholar and as an enemy of Emajus, he chose to give up all his wealth and family and security to follow the gentle and powerful voice of the Lord. He never wavered. Despite all his suffering, he knew he had made the right choice. The voice of God was true. It was the only thing worth living for.

"All of us have at some point made the same decision that Dakin made. Following Emajus has never been the easy way. It never made sense from everyone else's point of view. But that Spirit! That Spirit. We could not get away from it. Nothing in our lives compared with it. We set out on our journey with great hope, and now we are in despair. We do not understand why God seems to have abandoned us. We do not understand why God has taken Dakin, who sacrificed so much, who wanted so much to go to Caladria. I have little strength left. I do not want to waste it. My friend Dakin suffered greatly, but he never gave up. He believed in this mission, even though it cost him everything, even though it killed him. I for one will not betray him by abandoning our journey. I will not turn away and say that Dakin died in vain. I will stand firm and believe that the Lord will see us through. Brothers and sisters, this is the most dangerous time in our journey. If we leave now, what will we go back to? Our lives will have been nothing but a contemptible mistake. Faith means standing firm in what you know deep in your heart to be true, even though circumstances cry out for you to cut your losses and run. I will not disgrace my friend Dakin by betraying his dream. I will follow Emajus."

———○———

Mornings seemed to bring the worst news. By the time I was awakened the next morning, or rather, by the time I moved from sleep to a state of confused semiconsciousness, three more men had died of fark wounds. Two were Tree People and one was a soldier from the Rock of Calad. Danuta said the only hopeful news she could give was that those three were the last members of the company in any serious danger of dying from the fark attack.

Except me. Danuta did not say that, but she might as well have. The thought permeated the air, stifling our conversation for the next few uncomfortable moments. As we resumed our conversation about the burials, the company's low morale, our shrinking provisions—all the usual topics for these dismal briefings—Tarius Arc came in with some news.

"One of the soldiers on top of the mountain has spotted a group of people far off toward the Dead Mountains," he said. By the top of the mountain Tarius meant the area just west of our camp. We had camped just east of the summit because the ground was flatter. From our camp, therefore, our view of the desert that stretched toward the Dead Mountains was blocked. We stationed guards at the very top of our mountain so they could watch in all directions for any signs of life. This was the first movement of any kind they had spotted.

"Could it be our rescuers?" I asked, lifting my head from the pillow and nearly blacking out in the process.

"I don't know. I don't think our rescuers would come from the Dead Mountains, would they?"

I kept my eyes closed to stop the dizziness. "I have no idea. They could come from anywhere. Who else could it be?"

"It could be Amians."

Danuta asked, "What all can our soldiers see?"

"They're still pretty far away to see a whole lot of detail. But there are at least fifteen people down there, maybe more, and they have camucks and at least two vans."

"I wonder if they know we're here," Danuta asked.

"They wouldn't be able to see our camp from there, unless they see the guards, which is pretty unlikely since they're hidden among the rocks. Of course we probably left a pretty good trail for them to follow. Even with the wind blowing everything, we still left a lot of trash behind. And they're coming from the same place where we crossed the mountains."

"I don't see how they could be Amians," I said. "They think it's suicide to come here. Besides, how could they have gotten through the jungle in Wilmoroth? The Tree People killed them all."

"Well, they didn't kill them *all*, they just killed all the ones who came after us. And by now the Amians probably know for certain that you are in this company and that I am in it and that Dakin is in it. Umbriel might risk sending his soldiers into hell itself to capture the three of us."

"Would he only send fifteen people against a company of fifty?"

"Well, there may be more. We can't really tell yet."

"Or maybe those fifteen or so are the only Amians who have survived the trip," said Danuta.

Tarius said, "Maybe deep down Umbriel believes we're right, and he's afraid we really will find Caladria and then come back and destroy him."

"I saw no indication that he believed in Caladria," I said. "On that point, at least, I believe he was sincere."

"So what do we do now?" asked Danuta.

I said, "Let them come. When they get closer and we figure out who they are, we'll go from there."

―――○―――

"They're Amians," announced Tarius Arc the next morning in our headquarters tent. Danuta, Taron, Will, and I huddled there to hear his report. "I saw them myself through the magnifiers," he said.

I said, "I'm still amazed that Umbriel would go to such great lengths to—"

"I'm not," said Tarius. "Deep in his heart, he knows that if our mission succeeds, it will mean the end of his reign."

Will laughed and shook his head. "It looks to me like Umbriel needn't have bothered sending someone out here to kill us. We're managing to die off all by ourselves."

"You're a cynical man, Will," said Tarius. "After the gift of insight the Lord gave you to get us here, it seems like you'd have more sense than to believe only what you see in the here and now. This thing isn't over yet."

"It's over for Dakin. It's over for five other men," said Will.

Danuta interrupted, "The thing we have to figure out is, what do we do now? Do we know now how many of them there are?"

"There are seventeen."

"Do they know we're up here?"

"Not that we can tell. But they've done a strange thing. They've stopped. Yesterday they traveled all day and then stopped at night, but they're not moving again now that it's day. It looks like they might be setting up a more permanent camp. So maybe they do know we're here."

"And maybe they're waiting on reinforcements," said Danuta. "They must realize that seventeen soldiers are not enough to stop a company of our size."

"So what do we do?" asked Tarius. "What do you say, Brother Jeremy?"

It was all I could do to keep my eyes fixed on Tarius and not drift off into blankness. I did not know how to answer his question. What *could* we do? They were of little threat to us right now. If they brought reinforcements and it did come to a fight, the best place for us would be right here on this mountain. But even these thoughts I could not hold in my mind for more than a few seconds at a time. Most of the time the mental puzzle would not stay together. Amians in the desert. I could hold that thought. But beyond that my mind would not take me except when it drifted for a few seconds into little oases of clarity.

I answered, "I think we should just trust the Lord."

Danuta said, "He's sick, Tarius. Why don't you let him rest? There's nothing we can do now about those Amians anyway. Just keep people away from the top of the mountain where they could be seen. As always, we just have to wait."

"I suppose so," Tarius agreed. "I just know that we've come too far to be stopped by a bunch of Amians now."

———⊖———

In the middle of the afternoon Tarius burst into the tent and brought what we thought was finally some good news. "They're turning around!" he shouted.

"The Amians?" asked Danuta, who was seated beside me, tending to my bandages.

"Yes! I couldn't believe it. It looks like they've given up. They're going back the way they came from."

"Maybe it's some kind of trick," said Will.

"What kind of trick would it be? They're headed toward the Dead Mountains."

"Maybe they're going back for more men," said Will.

"They wouldn't *all* go back," said Tarius. "Besides, I don't think they know we're here. They don't seem to be looking in this direction at all. I've been watching them all day."

Danuta said, "I'll bet they had a deadline of some kind—a certain number of days they had to look for us—and then they could go back before their provisions ran out or the farks got them."

"The Lord is watching out for us," said Tarius.

"Yes," said Will, "now we can go back to dying alone and in peace."

No one responded. Everyone had come to the conclusion that the best way to handle Will was to leave him alone. Only Tarius Arc occasionally argued with him. Will had even shut out Taron. Muttering to himself in English, Will left the tent.

———⊖———

"We have trouble, brother. Will is deserting. You've got to talk to him."

Danuta was speaking. Through a slit in the tent I could see that it was dark outside, but I had no idea what day or time it was.

"When is he leaving?" I asked.

"At daylight, we think."

"How soon is that?"

"In about an hour. He wants to try to catch up with the Amians so they can help them get out of the desert."

"No! How many are going with him?"

"Nine, as far as we know. We just found out about this a while ago. They tried to keep it secret. I think everyone else in the company is solidly with us. Fortunately, most of our people are so suspicious of the Amians that they'd rather endure anything here than trust the Amians for help."

"But if Will goes, some of the others, even if they stay, might lose faith. We can't afford that. Bring him here."

I wasn't sure that Will would agree to speak to me, but in a few minutes he came, his traveling gear on, his pack already strapped to his back. He looked huge in the little tent. His hair and beard were bushy and wild. He did not wait for me to speak. In English, he said, "I'm sorry, Jer. I've got to do this. We'll die if we don't. Just say the word, and I'll take you with us."

"Don't do this to me, Will. Just a few more days. God will rescue us. I ask you as my friend to wait just a few more days."

He came close to me and knelt down beside the bed. "Jeremy, you could be dead in a few more days. Don't you see that? You are going to die here. That group of Amians turned around yesterday and has started back toward the Dead Mountains. They looked strong. They seemed to have plenty of provisions. They no doubt have medicine that could save you. Leaving now is our only chance for survival."

"If you leave, many others will lose faith."

"They've lost faith already. It's time to give up. This is not my struggle, and it shouldn't be yours either. We're not from here. We're not part of this. I just want to get out of it alive."

"How can you have spent so much time with these people and experienced so many things and still say that you're not part of it. You are part of it. Just think, Will. Everything we did in our lives before we came here prepared us for this moment. And who knows what kind of future we're preparing for now? You can't just walk away. You were the messenger spoken of in the prophecies. You brought us here, though God only knows why He entrusted that task to you. You refuse to believe, in spite of all the things He has let you know and see."

"I see that we are dying, and I am going to fight to live."

"If you go to those Amians, they may come back for us. You may single-handedly destroy the mission you were chosen to accomplish. As your friend, Will, I beg you not to do that."

"I promise you this one act of friendship: I will convince those Amians that we are the last survivors, and that your dead bodies are lost in the desert too far away to ever retrieve. I'm sorry, Jeremy. I have to go." I felt his burly arms embrace me for a moment, and then Will walked out of the tent without another word.

—◯—

Ten members of the company deserted with Will. As if to make up for their desertion, they did not take their allotted portion of the provisions but took only what they thought they would need to reach the Amians. Some suggested that we not allow them to take any provisions at all, but I rejected that idea; we would keep no prisoners.

Early in the evening on the day Will and the others deserted, I slipped into unconsciousness, and nothing anyone did would revive me.

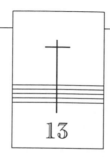

13

I felt the swaying of a boat beneath me. I was leaning against someone. Her arms were draped over my shoulders, cradling me, and her hands rested on my chest. I reached up and took hold of the hands. They were Danuta's.

She said, "Jeremy."

I could not answer. I was awake, but after a flash of clarity my mind grew dark again and I could not speak. We were in a room, small and wooden, with one light in the corner. Several others were in the room, Tarius Arc and Taron, I think, and others. It was a room on a boat, for it rocked, and rocked, and rocked. My hands slipped away from hers. She reached down and squeezed them.

"Jeremy," she said again. To the others in the room she said, "I think he's coming out of it. He looked so aware for a minute. He reached up and squeezed my hands. I could have sworn he started to say something." I heard others draw close. I could not open my eyes. I tried; they would not open. "We're safe, Jeremy. We're on our way now. We're safe."

I could not feel her hands anymore. The room seemed to buzz and break apart, and then I faded into darkness.

———⊖———

Music in high and slow strains—music in slow motion—

music that blended with the rhythms of a man at rest—penetrated my consciousness. I lay still and kept my eyes closed. At first it seemed the soft strains must be inside my head, they were in such harmony with my awakening mind. But as I became more and more lucid, I realized that the music was outside me; it was real. My eyes were still closed and I did not want to open them, for the music had made my mind so peaceful and at rest that I did not want to jar my senses with whatever I might face when I opened my eyes.

I was lying on something soft, and the sheets that surrounded me were silky and luxurious. My face, which I last remembered as swollen and sticky and stinging with pain, felt clear and clean. My scalp felt tingly too, not greasy and itchy as it had for so long. I lifted one hand from under the covers and ran it across my face. I felt one grooved, painless bump on each cheek. Otherwise the skin was undamaged. I spoke out loud: "Thank God. Thank God." I put both hands on my face and opened my eyes.

I was in an enormous bed in a darkened room. Daylight peeked in at the edges of the blinds that covered the window. That was no Gray Desert light. That was real sunlight. As I contemplated the sliver of light, a woman opened the door to the bedroom, letting in a flood of light behind her.

"Please come in," I said.

"He's speaking again," said the woman to someone outside the room. *Again?* These were the first words I remembered saying since . . . whenever it was that we were waiting for rescue in the Gray Desert.

She came to the bed and said, "Brother Jeremy, can you hear me?"

"Yes. Where am I?"

"You are in the home of Amandan and Rickeon."

"In Caladria?"

"Yes, Brother, Caladria. Did you not even know that?"

"No, I've been—"

"You seemed to be somewhat aware when they first brought you off the boat. We talked and talked to you, but then you slipped away from us again."

"I don't remember anything. Last I remember, we were in the Gray Desert, waiting to be rescued."

"Yes, you've been rather incoherent. We had to feed you with tubes for a while, but lately you've been eating and talking now and then, mostly in a language we don't understand."

"How is the rest of the company? Was everyone rescued?"

"They're fine. All of your company were brought here safely."

"How did it happen? We waited so long. I seem to vaguely remember being on a boat, but maybe I was just dreaming."

"You were not dreaming, but I'd rather let your friends tell you all that has happened. My name is Leander, and I have been your doctor since you've been here."

"My face. It has healed so quickly. So completely. I can't believe it."

"Yes. Just a few scars where the actual bites occurred, but those will fade eventually, I think."

"How long have we been here?"

"Ten days. We had to give you massive doses of medicine to heal those bites. The medicine had the side effect of reducing your sense of awareness, I'm afraid, but it worked beautifully. It's all experimental. We don't have much experience with farks. We don't have them in Caladria, as you might imagine. Not since the believers came here from Persus Am many years ago have we even heard about such creatures. But tell me, how do you feel overall? This is the first time I've been able to hear from my patient."

"I feel fantastic," I said, touching my face. "All the pain is gone. And my mind is so clear. It's so good to be able to think a thought clear through. It's so good not to feel the Grayness pressing down on me. I'm incredibly hungry."

"I'll have someone bring food right away. There are lots of people who have been waiting to see you. I'll try to keep your flow of visitors under control until you're rested and have regained your strength."

"I've had enough rest to last me for months. I'm ready to get up and see the world that's behind those drapes."

———⊖———

After the ordeal of the Gray Desert, I took enormous enjoyment from even the smallest pleasures of Caladria. The meal that Leander brought back for me was rather simple—a tray of fruits and bread and cheese and some sort of sweet, fruity drink. She apologized that she could not bring me more. I had woken up in the afternoon, and except for herself and the nurses who were there to take care of me, the whole household had gone to town. They were expected back by supper, she said, and then they could fix me a proper meal. But to me this meal was extraordinarily delicious, the fruits juicy and sweet, the bread soft and tasty. I ate each bite slowly, with great pleasure. Then a nurse prepared a bath for me, and I luxuriated for a long time in the great tub full of soap bubbles and hot water. Then I put on a new set of clothes. Leander was amused by the pleasure this gave me, but I enjoyed the feel of the clean shirt against my body, the crispness of the fabric, the fresh smell of it. Only those who had suffered the deprivation of the Gray Desert could understand my taking so much pleasure in such minor details.

I was feeling human again. I was well fed, well dressed, clean, clear headed, free of pain. When Leander and I went outside the house so that I could see Caladria for the first time, I could hardly keep from crying for joy. The house was surrounded by a wide lawn, beyond which was a cluster of towering trees. What is absolutely indescribable about the place is the light. In the distance, the green leaves in the cluster of trees lit up so brilliantly that they looked almost liquid. Every color in my view was absolutely vivid, almost shimmering.

Leander, a tiny woman no more than four feet tall, kept her eyes on me as I gazed at the light. "You're looking just like the rest of them," she said. "This is just the backyard of a country home, but all of you gaze about as if you're looking out on heaven itself."

"But that light!"

"I know. The others say the same thing."

"Especially after being in that Grayness for so long. I just want to run out into it. I feel like I have so much energy."

"Yes, the light has strengthening qualities. We've walked you out here every day."

"I wish I could remember."

"I must admit, you had me worried those first few days. The first night I thought we were going to lose you. The poison was just eating you up. It's probably best that you weren't very aware of what was going on. The medicine we had to use to kill the poison was not very pleasant. There was a war going on inside your body. It was not immediately clear that you would win that war."

"Well, I feel good now. I feel very, very good. Thank you, Leander, for what you did."

"My pleasure," she said. "It's worth all the effort just to see how happy you are looking out toward those trees. Shall we take a walk out there?"

"Yes!" I felt better than I had any time since my days in Damonchok, when walks in the country were the best form of relaxation after a hard day's work. I took pleasure in every step. We walked to the trees whose leaves were so brilliantly lit by the sun. I took the leaves in my hands to feel the reality of them. On the way back to the house I lay in the grass to feel it against my skin. I stared into the blue sky. I heard music far away. Leander did not rush me. Each time I stopped she sat quietly and rested until I was ready to move on.

After our walk Leander and I sat on the patio in the backyard, and I drank a milkshake-like concoction that she said would revive my strength. Before long Leander heard noise inside the house, and she smiled and said, "Someone's home." I stood up, but before I could even get inside, Danuta had run out onto the patio, shrieked, and then caught me up in a hug. "I thought you'd never wake up!" she said.

"They cleaned you up," I said. Her red hair flowed in soft waves about her face. The weariness was gone from her eyes. She wore a dress of brilliant red and blue. She had the same look of barely contained energy that she had when I first met her.

"Look at you," she said. "You can barely tell the farks even bit you. Isn't Leander a miracle worker?"

"She's fantastic."

"How do you feel?"

"I feel great. Like I could run and run and never stop. Are the others here too?"

"No, they're in town. I was over at Flotwinder's farm, just down the road from here, learning to play a new instrument. The nurse came and got me."

"Ah. Then it must have been your music I woke up to. The first thing I was aware of was the most beautiful music."

"It may have been our music. But it may have been something else. There are some things about the music in this place that you just won't believe. I have a lot to tell you."

"Well, the first thing I want you to tell me is how we got here. Leander saved the story for you to tell."

"I will tell it. But let's don't sit here. I want to show you around. Will you set your patient free, Leander?"

"Yes, as long as he doesn't stay out too long. I know he feels totally cured at the moment, but I want to watch him carefully. He's come so far, I don't want to risk a relapse now."

"We won't be gone long," she said. "I want to go to Rickeon's lake and back."

We started off toward the woods where Leander and I had walked. Danuta said, "Rickeon is going to build a house by a lake beyond those woods. Leander told you whose house we were staying in, didn't she?"

"She said the names, but I don't—"

"Amandan and Rickeon. Amandan is Tarius Arc's wife!"

"Of course. His wife."

"And Rickeon is his son. He was just a little boy when the Emajian pilgrims left Persus Am for Caladria and Tarius was left behind looking for their daughter. But now Rickeon is a grown man. Tall, blonde-haired, good-looking. Tarius is so proud of him. I wish you could have seen it when Tarius first saw his wife. As soon as he stepped off the boat, she was there to meet him. After all these years! She was crying and hugging him and kissing him. And he was crying too. All of us were, we were so happy for them and so happy to have made it out of that Gray Desert alive and to be in this wonderful place. I so wished you were aware of it. But you don't remember any of it, do you?"

"No."

"Even those last couple of days in the Gray Desert, I could tell your mind had wandered away. You just stared and slept and mumbled things in your other language. Sometimes you would eat the food we brought you, other times we would have to feed some of it to you before you would start eating. Sometimes you got up and started walking around and we'd have to lead you back. A few times I thought we were going to lose you like we lost Dakin. I was so afraid. But now look at you!" She squeezed me close to her, and we walked arm in arm across the lawn. "But God has brought you back to us, and we're in Caladria! I can't get over it. Look at this place. It's everything the songs said it would be. The light. The music. Can you hear it? Everything we've worked for and suffered for has paid off."

"What about Will and the others who left us? Are they with us now?"

"No. They were nowhere to be found. The last time we saw them they were walking across the desert chasing after the Amians."

"So we don't even know whether they caught up with the Amians."

"No. We may never know. Their chances of making it out of the desert were slim either way, I'd say. But we can pray for the best."

We went through the woods and came to another clearing, where we could see houses and lawns and lush farm fields for miles around. The sight was dazzling, not because the houses were especially impressive but because the light made every detail—each blade of grass and leaf and roof shingle and every fence and barn door and windowpane—blaze with clarity. It was as if my sense of sight itself had been transformed, as if before I came to Caladria I had seen everything through a haze that had now been burned away.

We walked for about a mile across some fields until we reached a grassy hill dotted with trees and bushes. The grass was almost up to our knees. As we walked up the hill, I said, "We've walked a long way, but I'm not tired at all. The strength must come from the light."

"Yes. And the air. Notice how rich it is to breathe. And wait till you hear the music—I mean really hear it. Incredible."

"You know who I keep thinking of?"

"I think I might know, if it's the same person I keep thinking of. Dakin."

"Yes. If only he could have hung on a few more days! If only God had spared him long enough to get here and be healed. I keep thinking he *deserved* to survive."

"I know. I don't understand it either. I only hope he's in a Caladria of his own."

At the top of the hill was a clearing, and in the clearing was the foundation of a house made of blocks of stone. Danuta told me this was Rickeon's house, the construction on which he had abandoned in all the excitement of his father's arrival in Caladria. On the other side of the hill was a gorgeous tree-lined pond that would provide Rickeon a magnificent view from his home. Danuta and I sat on the blocks of the foundation of the house, and she told me of our rescue from the Gray Desert.

"Do you remember nothing?" she asked.

"I remember just a few moments, waking up on what seemed like a boat. I was lying against you, and you tried to talk to me. I couldn't answer. I tried to figure out how we could possibly be on a boat, and then everything went black."

"We *were* on a boat."

"How? Where did the rescuers come from?"

"At first we didn't know. A couple days after you faded out, a group of people, almost fifty of them, suddenly appeared on the mountain. They were dressed in these bright clothes like the Caladrians wear, only they were dirty. These people nearly scared us to death because we had not seen them come from the desert on any side of the mountain. You know we watched that desert carefully for any trace of anyone. We thought maybe they just appeared suddenly from heaven or something. But they had not

327 SONG OF FIRE

come from the desert or from heaven. They had come from the mountain itself. From those caves."

"Caves!"

"Yes. You know the spring where we got our water?"

"Yes."

"Well, it's in a cave. And if you go farther into that cave and keep going down, you'll find vast caverns and a river. And that's where they came from, that river underneath our mountain."

"I can't believe it."

"Neither could we. But it's there. I don't know what ancient evils happened in that Gray Desert centuries ago, but the more I learn about it, the more I realize that more than any place else in existence, it has been abandoned by God and turned over to evil. One thing they told me when we got here was that the Gray Desert was once a thriving world that looked a lot like Damonchok, with trees and fields and rivers. That world is buried now underneath the gray rocks and dust. If you dug down far enough, you would find the remains of homes and farms and cities. And underneath the mountain where we waited—a gray mountain that did not exist in the ancient world—is a river called Urgamom. When the gray rocks and dust covered the whole region, because of explosions of great bombs or meteors from space or we're not really sure what, the Lord preserved this one river in caverns underneath the ground. It is hidden to all but those to whom He shows it. And He has chosen to show it only to the Lord Emajus and His followers years ago, and now He has shown it to us."

"So how did they know to come for us?"

"The same way we knew where to go to wait. They have their own prophecies and visions."

"Was it another Visitor like Will who came and told them?"

"No. It was one of their own people."

"So there's no chance that—"

"No, Jeremy. Anne, the woman in your visions, is not here. I'm sorry. I asked about her as soon as we came. Are you still troubled by memories of her?"

"Yes, but it's more than just memories. Her presence is as real as if I had just been with her a few minutes ago. I thought maybe I could find the answer here."

"Maybe you will."

We walked down to the lake and waded in the warm water up to our knees. "This place is paradise," I said. "Did you ever lose faith, Danuta? Did you ever think we really were just going to sit out in that desert and die?"

"It crossed my mind."

"But the cost! To lose Will. And Dakin. And the others who died. And now what? What happens now?"

"Well, there are a lot of people who want to ask you that very question."

"As if I know. As if I've ever known anything since the day I was flung into this world against my will."

"But you have led the Lord's people to Caladria. You have confounded Umbriel and the enemies of God. You have translated the scriptures of the Visitor Elaine and brought word of the Lord's gift of salvation for His people."

I laughed and said, "Is that the way Danuta the Rememberess will write it in her book?"

"Yes, I will. It's the truth."

"But all the mistakes. The dead ends. The wrong turns. The confusion. The frustration."

"I'll manage to get some of that in the book too, but the important thing is you have followed the Lord and obeyed His leading. Now we go back to Persus Am and finish it."

"What would I do without you, Danuta? How would I have made it through all this?"

"None of us could make it without the others. We weren't meant to."

We watched white swanlike birds glide across the lake. My whole body drank in the health of the light from the sun. My head tingled with alertness.

After a while Danuta said, "The others will have heard by now that you're awake. They'll want to see you. We'd better get back. There are still many things I haven't told you. You'll be amazed by what you see."

———○———

I was the center of attention at dinner that evening as I sat
with Danuta, Taron, Tarius, Amandan, and Rickeon in Amandan's dining room, where the walls were decorated with her own
paintings of the Caladrian landscape. I was not particularly
pleased with the picture of myself that emerged of my first ten days
in Caladria—a staring, mostly silent invalid who did nothing but
eat and sleep and occasionally utter a few unintelligible phrases,
presumably in English.

I was amazed by how different everyone looked compared
to the way I had last seen them in the Gray Desert. Taron had
changed the most. She wore a bright Caladrian robe that swirled
gracefully around her, and someone had pinned her hair in loose
waves on top of her head, taking away the tomboy look that was
so characteristic of her. Tarius Arc looked twenty years younger
as he sat with one arm draped casually around his wife's shoulders.
His white hair and beard seemed almost to glow in the slanted
Caladrian sunlight that filled the room. He was different around
Amandan than I had ever seen him. His intensity—that force in
him that had always made his eyes bore through my soul like a
searing conscience—seemed toned down when he was with her.
He seemed as at home as if he had always lived in Caladria.

Amandan put everyone at ease. She reminded me of Miriaban
in this way, but Amandan looked much younger and prettier, her
figure still very attractive and her blonde hair pinned gracefully
on top of her head in the Caladrian style. She had hardly changed
at all from the way she looked in the picture I had seen of her in
Dakin's study in Persus Am. I was amazed that she had aged so
little.

Noticing my gaze, Amandan said, "Jeremy, is there something else I can get you? You've hardly eaten."

"No thanks. I'm just not used to such big meals yet. It all
tastes great."

The truth was that I had trouble concentrating on my food,
delicious as it was. My mind was so unused to its acute state of
awareness that I was more restless than anyone else. Our meal-
times in the Gray Desert had almost always been crisis meetings

in which we discussed nothing less important than our very survival, so now I had trouble simply settling back and enjoying dinner. I was eager to discuss what would happen next, where we would go from here.

The others, however, had had ten days to unwind and to get used to the good food and good music and leisurely pace of Caladria. They were casual about the future, as if we were going to stay here forever. When I interrupted the conversation to ask what everyone thought we should do next, Tarius said, "There are some people on the committee who want to talk to you after the celebration tonight to discuss it." He said this as if he were reminding me of a haircut appointment, but his tone also made it clear that this was not a subject for dinner conversation. My friends had learned to relax. I had to catch up with them.

What they mostly talked about at this meal was the past, the glorious days in Persus Am before the War, when knowledge exploded like the bombs Tarius and his friends so innocently built, when he and Amandan walked carefree and in love down country lanes that would later become a wasteland, when miraculous light and music flowed from the Lord's temple every day, feeding their spirits like nothing else they had ever known.

And they talked about Dakin. Not the jittery old man I had known, but the young genius in pre-War Persus Am who had made discoveries in science and music and agriculture, who married Amandan's best friend, who was witty with a dry and clever but never mean-spirited sense of humor. I was astonished at how easy it was for them to speak of him, while with every story they told I ached with grief for him even more.

Amandan, who had the uncanny ability to respond not only to what you said but also to what you were thinking, said in a hushed tone to me, "Jeremy, none of us can believe he's gone. We think of him every day, what this place would have meant to him, and to Miri too. We don't understand it. We just trust the Lord and hang on. But it helps us to talk about him." They had had time for their grief, and once again I had to catch up. I thought of Dakin. I thought of Anne. I thought of Will. I thought of Jank. So much death and separation, and there was nothing to do about it but to try to make the pain go away.

Yet there in front of me sat Tarius Arc and his wife Amandan, reunited, against all logic and expectation, after years of separation. And there sat Taron in the Promised Land, who weeks ago was a farmer's daughter to whom Caladria was only a name in the songs. I had given up trying to predict my own destiny. Nothing ever turned out as I expected.

———○———

As I said, I was catching up, and the night still had many surprises in store. The celebration took place in an outdoor theater built for that purpose at the side of Amandan's house. The place was called a celebration field, and it was just one of dozens of such places throughout Caladria. It looked like a crater, with a round stage at the bottom and terraced landings extending up the sides. The field was dimly lit by globe lights on top of poles spaced at regular intervals around each terrace. People worshiped at these places every night, and because it was widely known that my friends and I were staying at Amandan's house, an especially large crowd of more than two thousand people had gathered at Amandan's field every night since we arrived. I was relieved to find out that I had not been put on display at these celebrations, though I had sat near the window closest to the field to receive as much benefit from the music as possible.

The music did not begin until after dark, but by the end of dinner, with the sun still low in the sky, the people began to arrive. It was then that I realized once again that Caladria was a much different place from the one we had left. I heard a motor outside somewhere, though I could not see anything from the windows in front of me.

"Do the people here have motorized carts?" I asked.

"Better than that," said Danuta, and she stood and led me outside. To see the motorized vehicle I had to look not across the lawn but up into the sky. There, flying over the house and toward the celebration field, was the strangest machine I had ever seen. It looked like a giant pillow, about the size of an automobile. On all four sides of the pillow, jutting out on poles, were whirring propellers enclosed in metal rings. The propellers were so small that they apparently were not what kept the craft airborne, but I could not tell how the machine worked. There was enough room for four people in the compartment on top. The machine was quiet, its only sound a high-pitched whir. The bottom of the contraption was painted in a colorful pattern, and it was thrilling to see three or four of them suddenly appear together from behind the grove of trees at the edge of Amandan's lawn and head toward us, like magic carpets materializing out of the sunset.

"Isn't it amazing?" said Danuta. "These people can actually fly like birds. What do you think the folks back home will think of that?"

I still remembered—vaguely—airplanes from my own world, of course, but in this world the sight of a machine in the air still brought a rush of awe. All of us non-Caladrians stared transfixed as the machines landed gracefully on the lawn. Inspired as I was by the beauty of this sight, I also could not help but think what a great military advantage these flying machines would give us if we were to go back and take Persus Am by force.

But this was no time for military strategy. The people were gathering for a celebration. Many came by aerocart, as the flying machines were called, but others walked, rode camucks, or came in motorized carts not unlike those in Persus Am. Rickeon wanted to introduce me to the gathering crowd, and he wanted me to begin the night's singing. I told him I would rather see and hear one of these celebrations from the background before I took such a public role. He reluctantly agreed but added, "I at least want you to come down to the center later in the evening and sing with me. I won't tell them who you are if you insist." Rickeon was the leader of the music on most nights in Amandan's field. He was known as one of the best musicians in Caladria and had built many instruments with his own hands.

The music began even as we stood and watched the people arrive. We moved to an open second-story window that looked out over the field. I could have stood there all night and let the sound wash over me. We heard mostly stringed instruments at first, and the first melodies of the evening were slow and subdued.

But as Rickeon knew, this was only the prelude, and the truly amazing sound was yet to come. He paced restlessly behind me, eager to get out to the music. His mother said, "You don't have to wait on us, Rick. Go on out there and get started. We'll be along."

I watched Rickeon as he descended each terrace of the crater toward the center. He had the naturally confident, almost regal air of Tarius. He was tall, well built, with striking shoulder-length blonde hair. He possessed Tarius's enthusiasm and energy, but he did not have his father's dark intensity born of years of pain. He greeted nearly everyone in his path on the way down. They all seemed to know him. When he reached the center, he glanced up toward us and smiled, as if to invite us into the sound.

In the center of the circle at the bottom of the crater was a cylinder composed of long black plastic strips that looked something like window blinds hanging from a gold metal frame. The cylinder was three or four feet in diameter and about eight feet tall, large enough for a person to stand inside. Rickeon pushed back some of the black strips and stepped inside the cylinder. At this time the music was still slow and soothing, mostly instrumental, with just a few voices humming the wordless song.

What Rickeon did with the music is hard to describe to someone who has never been to Caladria, for music there is subject to different laws of nature than music anywhere else. Before Rickeon went into the cylinder, about twenty instruments located in all different parts of the field played the song fairly harmoniously. But when he stepped into the cylinder, he pulled a cord that turned over each of the black strips, revealing silver surfaces to the crowd. This alteration of the cylinder had a dramatic effect on the music.

The cylinder seemed to draw every musical sound to it instantly, and instead of twenty separate instruments scattered around a field, there was suddenly a unified sound emanating from the center of the crater. For the person in the cylinder, that sound was like clay that could be molded into a sculpture. By moving his arms and body inside the cylinder, Rickeon could shape and change the music, slowing or increasing its tempo, pulling forward the sound of some instruments, breaking long notes into smaller bits of sound. As I learned later, when I stepped into the cylinder, the movement inside was a dance, a motion based entirely on one's instincts of the music, a gift that could never be taught.

Rickeon's music amazed and comforted me. It was as if healing water were being poured over my spirit. I closed my eyes and let the sound wash over me. It was full of strings and flutes and muted drums. After a while Rickeon began to sing inside the cylinder, and his beautiful tenor voice could be heard all over the field. It melted into the music, never overwhelming it. I could have stood there all night and enjoyed the sound, but when it was completely dark outside, Danuta put her arm in mine and said, "Let's go out there before the splitting begins. You'll want to experience that close up, not inside the house."

Splitting, as the Caladrians call it, is when the music reaches such an intensity that it breaks apart into dozens of fragments of sound far beyond what any musician humanly would be able to play or sing, like a single beam of light splitting into a burst of fireworks. The Caladrians say that this phenomenon is the closest communication human beings are allowed with God while they are in the mortal world. For when the music splits, what really happens is that the Lord Himself takes up the music His people are playing. The people are speaking to Him through their instruments and voices, and He is talking to them through the language of song.

The music had not split by the time I stepped onto the celebration field. But many more voices and instruments had joined it, and the tempo had picked up considerably. The crowd sang Emajian songs that were familiar to me. The mood was joyous, with families and friends packed close together on each terrace, clapping and singing and swaying to the sound. The music washed over me like magic healing water. Only Danuta and Taron were with me. Tarius and Amandan were in the center with Rickeon. We stopped about halfway down, mostly because I wanted to concentrate on the music rather than on pushing through the crowd. Some people invited us into their cluster of worshipers, but none of them seemed to suspect who I was. People concentrated only on the celebration. We accepted their invitation, and soon I was singing with the rest of them, feeling the music deep within me, feeling it wrap itself all around me.

When the music split, I was so overwhelmed at first that I had to stop singing and dancing and stand completely still to keep the force from knocking me down. Danuta was not surprised; she had been just as overcome during her first celebration in Caladria. The sound of the splitting, first of all, was unlike anything I had ever heard, even in other Spirit-filled celebrations. Even though we were outdoors, the sound was so rich that it seemed to be all around us, yet it was not loud or blaring. The sound was brilliantly clear. There was a purity to it that no music I had ever heard had achieved. But beyond the sound itself was the personality that inhabited the sound, the feeling that Someone real and loving was making contact deep within me. I was amazed that anyone could stand up to this every night, but soon I learned to move in the rhythm of the sound, not just musically but spiritually and psychologically, as if I were not simply making music but having a conversation with the musician himself.

For a few hours I enjoyed the music in the obscurity of the crowd, but then Danuta drew close to me and said that Rickeon wanted me to come down to the center of the field. We worked our way through the crowd to the circle where Tarius and Amandan stood just outside the cylinder where Rickeon was.

Tarius said, "He wants you to take his place inside the cylinder."

"Will it stop the splitting of the music?" I asked. "It's so beautiful, I wouldn't want to change it."

"No, no. The music has a life of its own now. The Lord is singing it. None of us could stop Him even if we wanted to."

Rickeon pushed aside the panels of the cylinder, stepped out to where I was, and said, "Brother Jeremy, why don't you go inside and lead the music for us?"

"I'm so overwhelmed by all this, I wouldn't know what to do."

"Just sing to the Lord, and remember that you can move the

music with your body as well as your voice. Just talk to the Lord. Let it come naturally."

With great hesitation I stepped inside the cylinder and sang the song that had already begun. The power inside the cylinder was amazing. I felt as if the music followed not just my voice and movements but my thoughts as well. With a stroke of my hand in one direction, I could bring out the sound of trumpets that were barely audible before. With the sweep of one arm, stringed instruments added a beautiful rush of sound to the music.

The miracle that happened while I was in the cylinder was unprecedented in Caladria, but because *everything* that night seemed so miraculous to me anyway, I did not know it. At the beginning of a new song, I suddenly heard a sound that I had not heard before and that I had not directed into the music. It sounded something like the crash of cymbals followed by a *whoosh* of air. I stepped out of the cylinder. As I looked across the terraces, I saw that every globe light had shattered and the poles shot fire straight up in the air like blow torches. Everyone else looked as amazed as I was, and some people had dropped to the ground.

Directly above the cylinder whirled a white light composed of thousands of thin strands that made loops to the rhythm of the music. As we watched, the strands multiplied, and the light expanded to cover the whole field of celebration. Blue and red and green strands emerged and shot to the ground, where they disappeared. Before long, rings of shimmering color descended and began to encircle three or four of the worshipers, who danced in the joy of the light. After I saw several others wrapped in the light, I was also encircled by it. It was just like the light that had surrounded me in the Utturies on the night of my arrival, like the light that had enwrapped Taron in the Gray Desert. It was as if the Lord's own Spirit had descended in physical form and greeted us one by one. I felt greater joy, greater love than I had ever known, folding itself all around me.

The light stayed for hours, and when it finally faded, the sky was filled with its own light. Dawn had come to Caladria. The people huddled in tight little groups, awestruck, exhausted, but not quite ready to leave that place.

———◯———

I slipped away from the crowd at the first sight of dawn. I hoped to avoid lots of attention, which I did not feel ready for, and I wanted to sit alone and contemplate the amazing things that had happened during the night.

Unfortunately, by avoiding the crowd I invited attention and speculation. Because I was in the cylinder when the miracle of light occurred, most people assumed I had something to do with it. Then suddenly when the light and sound evaporated, I too disappeared and gave no explanation for the miracle I had helped to trigger. In fact, I was just as amazed as everyone else by what had happened, and I had no explanation for it whatsoever; I only "disappeared" by walking straight through the crowd and into my room in Amandan's home.

I was not to have much time to myself. The leaders of Caladria wanted to meet with me right then, before they went back to their homes. This was the meeting Tarius had mentioned at dinner the night before, but that was before he knew the celebration would last all night, a rare occurrence. In spite of our lack of sleep, all of us were wide awake. The physical letdown would come later, once the energizing effect of the music and light had worn off.

We met in Amandan's dining room, after all of us helped to prepare a breakfast (there were no servants in Caladria, or as the people there liked to say, everyone acted as a servant to his friends). There were twelve men and women at the meeting, counting Tarius, Amandan, and Danura, the only people I knew. It was an informal group, not a governing body. A few were government officials, some were church leaders, others were leading musicians and "explorers," as their scientists and inventors were called.

All of them treated me with great reverence, the night's events enhancing my already special status. Tarius began the meeting with an elaborate introduction of me. He praised me for having stood up to Umbriel even though I had forfeited incredible wealth and power in doing so and had risked my own death. He told them of my weeks in hiding, toiling as a farm laborer and living every moment in the knowledge that I could be caught and killed. He told of my courageous and unwavering leadership through the Gray Desert as I pressed on in faith in spite of all the odds against us. And now, he said, I had been the instrument of the Lord in one of the most miraculous celebrations anyone had ever seen.

To me, of course, this was all exaggerated, since I knew that every step of the way I had wavered and bumbled and made many mistakes for which I still had great regret. But they were building a legend, a leader around whom they could rally in the coming difficult days when they would be called on to make great sacrifices of their own.

After introducing me, Tarius then introduced the oldest person at the table, a man named Lemel, whose exact age remained unclear to me but who evidently had lived in Caladria for many generations. Lemel was, among other things, a historian of Caladria and an expert in prophecy, and he told us a great many things that I, at least, had never heard before. Caladria, I learned, was not founded by the Emajians who had left Persus Am after the War. In fact, when those believers arrived in Caladria, they found a thriving city-nation who also revered Emajus as Lord. That city, with abundant land and resources that seemed to go on forever, had been prepared for the coming of the Amians through prophecy and welcomed them as fellow citizens and fellow believers.

The original Caladrians had come from, of all places, the Gray Desert. Centuries before, as Danuta had told me, the Gray Desert had been a thriving paradise much like Persus Am before the War. But gradually the people's hearts turned toward evil, and Emajus took His followers to Caladria, much as He had the believers in Persus Am. Not long after they left, the people who remained in what would soon become the Gray Desert engaged in war, battles so bloody and devastating that after several years of it not a single creature remained alive. The Lord's Spirit utterly abandoned the place, and in a few centuries it turned into the horrible place we had journeyed through. This history sounded chillingly like the future of Persus Am.

I asked, "What do the prophecies say about what's going to happen to Persus Am? Is it going to become another Gray Desert?"

Lemel sat back and paused for a long while, though his

friends, who had great respect for him and were used to his slow and deliberate ways, did not interrupt.

Finally he said, "Well, brother, as you have probably realized by now, the prophecies concerning everything in Persus Am—yourself included—are more cryptic and vague and frustrating than those about any other topic in history. The only straightforward prophecy ever given about Persus Am was that your Emajians would be brought here to live with us. And that one was given by our prophets and not yours. But I think that Tarius Arc and Danuta would agree with me—and they know the songs as well as anyone living—that the prophecies say that the Lord through His servant will bring His salvation to Persus Am and that there will be singing in the Temple again. Now that seems pretty clear in a way, except we don't know, for instance, whether a war will destroy everything and then a Temple will be rebuilt, or whether the Temple is only symbolic and stands for the hearts of believers, as some say, or whether all this will happen and *then* the war will take place. Much is prophesied about war, I can tell you that, but even that is open to interpretation, since it might just be *spiritual* war. That is my answer, but it does not answer much. But if any salvation message is to go to Persus Am and if there is to be any music again in the Temple there, I don't see that there's anyone but us who can take it."

When Lemel had finished, another man, one of the religious leaders, said, "Jeremy, Tarius Arc has shown us the scriptures you translated from the book brought by the Visitor Elaine. We are told that these are the events of the Lord Emajus in your own world, is that right?"

"Yes, I believe so, though we do not call Him Emajus where I come from."

"Now we have been given only part of that story of Emajus, and I understand that because of the turmoil you've been caught up in, you were unable to translate any more than this."

"That's right."

"Are you aware that we have had Visitors of our own and prophets of our own that have given us details of the life of Emajus in your world?"

"No. No one told me that."

"I wonder if you would tell us the end of the story as you know it. What happened to Emajus?"

"He continued His teaching and healing, and finally He was crucified by being nailed to a cross made of wood. He was buried in a tomb and for three days was dead. And then He was resurrected and was seen by many people before going back to be with the Father. And His followers believe that His death was a sacrifice to atone for the sin of people and that anyone who repents of their sins and believes in Him can be forgiven and be made right with God."

For a moment they all looked at one another and said nothing. But I could tell that my story had confirmed something with them, that it had not come as a complete surprise.

"And were you witness to these events that happened in your world?"

"Oh no. These things happened long before I was born."

"But you believe them."

"Yes, I do."

"You have told us exactly what our own prophets and Visitors have told us and what we ourselves believe. This is the salvation the Lord promised us."

A man called Governor Brant, a burly, middle-aged man with thick black hair and an impressive military stateliness about him, asked, "Do you come to us with a plan for taking our message back to Persus Am and restoring music in the Temple?"

"No," I said. "Unfortunately, I haven't been able to see very far ahead since the day I found myself unexpectedly outside my own world and in this one."

Governor Brant said, "Well, sir, as you know, in Caladria we have devoted much of our time and energy planning for this very moment. We do not have a temple of our own, as you see. We did not build one because we never wanted to forget that our real task was to rebuild the Temple in Persus Am and restore the Lord's music to it."

Lemel added, "When the first Caladrians came here long before the believers from Persus Am, they also planned to return to their former land and rebuild a temple, but war destroyed it first."

I said, "That's what I'm afraid of in Persus Am. The whole Known World was on the brink of war when we left."

"We are aware of that," said Brant. "But when we go there, we will have some advantages. One of the most important ones will be our aerocarts."

"Yes. Those are very impressive. And they could transport people all the way to Persus Am?" I asked.

"Definitely. No problem."

"And what military capabilities do you have?"

"Not much, not in the traditional sense."

"Governor, I served in Umbriel's government. I know that his war machine is formidable."

"Yes, that is what we have heard. But we have not been mandated to build bombs and guns anymore. This may seem foolish to you, but Caladria is a nation composed of people from two countries that were both devastated by war, one of them bombed out of existence. In this paradise the Lord gave us, where there is no threat to us from any outside nation, we made the decision not to build weapons of war."

"So how can you confront Umbriel? He will not give in to the Temple being rebuilt. He will fight it with all his might."

"There are two possibilities. One is that the war—if it is taking place—will topple him and that we will arrive in a place that is war-torn but not hostile to us. Tarius Arc and Danuta have acknowledged this as a possibility."

"A slim one, I admit," said Tarius.

"The second possibility is that Umbriel will be ready to fight us when we get there. He will have bombs, though not *the* bomb from the War, and he will have soldiers stationed in Wilmoroth and in Persus Am and in his section of the Disputed Territory."

"And maybe in Damonchok and on the Rock of Calad," I added, "depending on how far along the war has progressed and how well he is doing."

"That's awfully pessimistic," said Tarius. "I think we can at least count on the Rock of Calad to hold out against him."

From his briefcase Governor Brant took out a round black ball the size of a grapefruit and placed it on the table. He said, "At any rate, when we get there we would set up a base of operations, preferably on the Rock of Calad. Then, using our advantage of surprise, we would fly every aerocart available to us—and we have thousands of them—across whatever areas are occupied by Umbriel's soldiers or command centers and drop these little babies by the thousands." He held up the ball. "Have you ever seen one of these, Jeremy?"

"No. What is it?"

"Amandan, may I use your wall to demonstrate?"

"Certainly," she said.

At that word, Brant, who sat directly across from me, flung the ball just past my head and sent it crashing into the wall behind me. Suddenly music filled the room as if someone had turned on a stereo full blast. The song was a march, filled with trumpets and drums and strings. I turned around to see a small metal box, no larger than a deck of cards, lying on the floor at my feet. The music was apparently coming from this box, though I did not see how such a small piece of metal could create such a huge sound. We could hardly hear ourselves talk.

I picked up the box. "How do you turn it off?" I yelled.

"You can't!" said Governor Brant. "That's the beauty of it."

He reached out his hand and I gave the box to him. From the pouch he took a ball, this one with hinges that allowed it to open and close, and he put the metal box into the ball. As soon as he closed it, the music ceased.

He smiled at me in a very satisfied way, though I had not yet completely caught on. He said, "Well, Jeremy, what do you think of that as a weapon?"

I answered, "You mean you will fly above Umbriel's soldiers and rain these things down on them?"

"Exactly."

"And you hope that will distract them?"

"Distract them! Jeremy! It will paralyze them. They will not be able to stand up to it."

I realized, to my disappointment, that these black balls were not just a *part* of the military strategy, not just a distracting force that could be used while the real weapons could be unleashed. No, these black grapefruits with their little stereos inside represented the *entire* weaponry of Caladria. I was astounded. Generations the Lord had given these people to prepare for the coming conflict, and they wanted to throw music boxes at the enemy.

I could hardly conceal my disappointment. I said, "Governor Brant, I know that music is very disturbing to the Amians, but honestly, these people have bombs that can destroy buildings, and they have guns that can shoot pellets of fire and—"

The governor threw up his hands in frustration. "A paralyzed man cannot shoot!" he bellowed. "An army cannot advance if its soldiers are covering their ears and screaming in pain."

Tarius interrupted us, speaking quietly to derail any argument. "Jeremy, you have seen, I believe, some of the effects that music can have on the Amians. You know that it can make them sick, make them dizzy, disorient them. And all that happens just with the ordinary music of the Known World. You have noticed, haven't you, how much different the music is here in Caladria, how much more powerful it is, how much more infused it is with the Spirit of God? It is a purer sound. It is a perfect sound. Nothing like it has ever been heard in Persus Am or the rest of the Known World since the War, except perhaps on the night of your arrival or on a few other miraculous occasions. These music shells—that's what we call them—contain pure music. They are not ordinary machines. They pull the sound from the very energy that runs the universe. It sounds like music to us—it is music—but more fundamentally it is power itself, energy itself, from God, the source of energy. The Amians are not in harmony with that force, so when the music shells remove the protective layers of the world and allow pure music to penetrate these people, it will be too much for them. They will not stand up against it. As Governor Brant says, it would literally paralyze them. They could not turn off the music. Only this black material that surrounds the boxes can do that, and it does not exist in the Known World. So we have a very powerful weapon here. It is the least bloody way for us to win a war."

I said, "I am very impressed by the force of this, and I hate to seem so doubtful. It just seems to me that we should go as fully armed as possible. If Umbriel has bombs, should we not have them also, at least as a show of force? There is something I am reluctant to bring up, but the stakes are too high to avoid it. One advantage we have that no one has mentioned is that we alone—you alone, Tarius—have the knowledge to build *the* bomb. Even if we only use this as a tool to threaten—"

"No!" shouted Tarius. "Never. The bomb is not the way. There is no one left alive but me who knows how to build it, and I absolutely will not do so. It is not the way. The Lord has called us to save the world, not to destroy it."

An uncomfortable silence filled the room. The Caladrians were disappointed in my lack of enthusiasm for their weapons. But I knew how formidable Umbriel's forces were. The idea of fighting guns and bombs with paralyzing music seemed so bizarre to me that I couldn't help but be skeptical.

Most of us had been awake for more than twenty-four hours, and the energy the music had given us had begun to fade. No one was eager to debate. Lemel finally broke the silence by saying, "I am no prophet, but if I am any judge of events at all, I think that the miracle we saw last night is a sign that something big is coming that may make many things much more clear to us."

Several people around the table nodded their heads and mumbled agreement, as if they knew precisely what big something he was referring to. I did not know. But it was clear that Lemel's statement was a concluding comment, not a new topic for discussion. Whatever might be coming to make everything more clear, I welcomed it. Tarius closed the meeting with a prayer of thanks to God, and everyone went home.

—◯—

If happiness can be found anywhere, Caladria is the place. Never before had I been in a place where just by sitting on the lawn the light could penetrate my body and fill me with such an incredible feeling of well-being. Along with the light, of course, was the music, which, if I concentrated very hard, I could hear at absolutely any time, day or night. I asked Amandan, "Isn't there ever a time here when someone is not playing the music?"

She said, "Not all the music you hear is music that someone is playing. The Spirit of God so permeates Caladria that His voice can always be heard if you listen closely enough."

It was in every way an amazing place, particularly in contrast to the hell we had endured in the Gray Desert. Still, my mind was not at ease. Freed from the immediate crisis of survival, my mind, more fully aware than it had ever been, could no longer suppress certain scenes that haunted me. Over and over I saw Jank's corpse hanging from the ceiling. I felt as guilty as if I had killed him myself. I saw wild-eyed Will, his hair and beard scraggly, his expression desperate, as he stood up from my bedside, turned away from me, and walked away forever. Why, my mind screamed again and again, *why* did the Lord choose Will of all people to be the messenger? And why did Will have to leave just days before our rescue? And why did Dakin have to die on the verge of finding what we hoped for? I saw Dakin's horribly swollen face, his befuddled expression. Why? I relived scenes of splendor in Umbriel's palace, dining in his magnificent rooms, bathing in the swirling pools, speaking orders to his servants, embracing his daughter. I was filled with shame, as if every moment of luxury had been purchased with the blood of my friends.

And then, beyond all these visions, there was Anne. By this point memories of my old life were so dim that she and Will were my last vivid connections to it. My thoughts of Anne went far beyond normal memories. I did not just *think* about her. Instead, the very essence of her seemed to hover nearby. She was maddeningly just out of reach. It was as if she were just beyond a window, but no matter how hard I banged on the glass, she did not see or hear me. My brain was filled with the reality—not just the memory—of reaching across the table in an elegant restaurant and touching her hand. I could feel her pressed against me as we lay on a blanket in the grass. I could hear her voice saying my name. I could smell her hair.

I had never felt comfortable discussing Anne with anyone. My visions of her seemed too bizarre and too difficult to explain. Only with Tarius and Amandan did I feel secure enough to finally describe what was happening to me. Though I trusted Danuta with any other topic, this one I could not discuss with her. The reason I could not discuss Anne with Danuta, though I would not admit it even to myself then, was that Danuta had begun to fall in love with me. Most of the company must have picked up on this by then, but only Tarius was bold enough to say it to me. He brought it up subtly, almost jokingly at first, saying something about how he noticed the way Danuta had been looking at me lately. I dismissed it with a laugh, and he let it drop. Later, though, I asked him whether or not Danuta had said anything to him about her feelings for me.

"Of course not," he said. "You know her well enough to know that she would never bring it up, and she probably wouldn't even admit it if I asked her."

I said nothing, tracing a line in the dirt with my foot.

He said, "Many times these things have a way of working themselves out. But sometimes not. It's not exactly a secret that Taron is also infatuated with you. When the time comes that we are fighting Umbriel, you will not want to be spending all your energy sorting out your love life."

"No. I promise you that will not happen. Tarius, Anne is the only woman I love."

"I know that. But a woman does not surrender her feelings very easily for an invisible rival."

If only Anne would come, I thought. If only she could be by my side to end all my confusion. I shrugged and ended the conversation by saying, "Well, as you said, sometimes these things take care of themselves."

I usually talked to Tarius and Amandan in the late afternoons, before supper, when they invited me to walk with them in the fields and woods behind their home. It was beautiful to see how close they had become, how completely united they were despite their years of separation. They spent most of each day alone together, but by evening they usually wanted company. The three of us spent many hours together, sometimes missing dinner, sometimes taking it with us in a picnic basket. I felt a chill whenever Amandan brought up Anne's name, especially because she said the name so casually. She would say things like, "If the

Lord sends Anne to you, Jeremy, we'll invite her to walk with us in the evenings, just as we used to do with Dakin and Miriaban."

I hardly knew how to respond to such statements. Anne so thoroughly haunted me that I couldn't discuss her in casual terms. I couldn't say, "We'll do this or do that if Anne comes." I asked Amandan, "When you were separated from Tarius, didn't you ever think that maybe you wouldn't see him again? That it had been too long? That he might have died or that he would never be able to find you?"

"No," she said. "My friends talked to me about those possibilities a few times, but deep down I just knew I would see him again. I always talked about him as if he had just gone away for a few days."

"I wish I could do that," I said. "I can't get it out of my head that Anne will always be just out of my reach, so close that her memory—her presence—never fades but so far that we can never be brought together."

Amandan said, "Jeremy, I don't know that the Lord is going to answer your prayer. I don't know if He'll bring Anne to you or not. I pray that He does. Tarius and I both pray it every day. But if not, I do believe she will eventually fade away from you."

"That would kill me," I said.

Amandan answered, "When Tarius was apart from me, there were times he seemed so close that I felt I could reach out and touch him." As she said this, her eyes stayed on me, but her hand, in one of the most loving gestures I have ever seen, reached up and cupped her husband's face. "The remotest possibility of that one touch was worth all the years of waiting. I could never have given up as long as that possibility remained alive."

"Neither can I," I said. "But it's tearing me apart."

—◯—

At my meeting with Governor Brant and the other leaders of Caladria, Lemel had spoken of some big, impending event that would make everything clear to us. Strangely, it was hard to get anyone to talk to me about what he meant. Amandan, who was so frank about every other issue we discussed, told me to talk to Tarius about it. Tarius was uncharacteristically vague, saying that we should not jump to conclusions about anything and that Lemel was going only by his feelings and that feelings were sometimes wrong. "Feelings about *what*?" I pressed. "What does he think this big thing could be?" Nobody really knows, Tarius told me. We should just stay alert and see what happens, he said.

Danuta was more forthcoming, but even she held back. "What Lemel is responding to is this change in the music, this increase in its intensity, and the miracle of the light on the night when you sang with us. He and the others believe the change in the music might foreshadow a coming of the Spirit of the Lord to Caladria."

"We would know His presence even more vividly than we do now?"

"Yes, but they believe it is presumptuous and inappropriate to speak too freely about it. It is very sacred. It is a matter of faith, not of casual conversation. Just wait and see."

And with that Danuta would say no more on the subject.

Everyone in Caladria worked for a living. Rickeon, besides being a gifted musician, designed houses. After we had been in Caladria just over a month, luxuriating in the light and song and Spirit, Rickeon asked me to take a ride with him late one afternoon in his aerocart. He had just come home for the day, as had his parents, whom he also invited. Amandan had gone back to work at the laboratory that designed and built the "music shells" that had been demonstrated for me at my meeting with the Caladrian leaders. Tarius had gone to work for her company as an unpaid consultant. They were thrilled to be working with one another again as they had done in the days before the War.

I loved riding in the aerocart. It provided a fabulous view of the Caladrian countryside. Rickeon had taken me up in his machine before, showing me Caladria's sparkling capital city, with its glass and stone buildings and tree-lined parks. We had flown over farmlands, forests, and rivers. Nearly three million people lived in Caladria, and the room for growth was vast.

By the time Rickeon took me on this afternoon ride, I had found out a few more details about the Spirit of the Lord's elusive expected visit to Caladria. No one would speak of it directly, but that did not stop me from asking as many questions as I could of Tarius, Danuta, and the outspoken (by Caladrian standards) Lemel. I learned that after Emajus had brought His followers from Caladria to Persus Am, He had left His people, as the prophecy and He himself had said He would, in a cloud of light and music, just like the cloud I had first arrived in. He had gone away to finish the work of salvation, and someday He would appear again to prepare His people to return to Persus Am, where they would restore the music to the Temple of God for any who chose to accept it.

So what we were waiting for was not merely some elusive spiritual visit but the reappearance of Emajus himself. Why His followers would be reluctant to discuss this was beyond me. I would have thought Emajus's return would be our most important topic of conversation. But the Emajians had a much different sense than I did of what was sacred, of what was appropriate for conversation and speculation and what was not. My inquiries into the prophetic songs were always given cryptic and incomplete answers. Absolutely no one would speculate on how soon they thought Emajus might reappear. I got the impression it could be within days or it could be years. To some the change of intensity in the music and light at the celebrations signalled Emajus would return soon. But what did *soon* mean? No one knew. But we did know that we would not return to Persus Am until He came.

So when Rickeon took me and his parents on the ride in his aerocart, we all believed that Caladria might be our home for years while we waited to take the next step. We hovered low over the magnificent countryside until we reached the flat hilltop where the foundation of Rickeon's house was perched. He landed in the grassy area that overlooked the lake.

As we stood and watched the reflection of the late afternoon light on the water, Rickeon asked, "What do you think of that lake, Jeremy?"

"It's fantastic. Danuta brought me up here on the first day I woke up. We sat on the stones of your house and just enjoyed the beauty. When are you going to finish this house?"

"That's what I wanted to talk to you about."

"Talk to me?"

"Yes. Dad, would you hand me the drawings please?"

From the aerocart Tarius brought out some rolled-up sheets of paper and gave them to his son. "What we're going to do," said Rickeon, "is get your approval of these."

Rickeon opened the papers to reveal a drawing of a rambling, one story house of wood and stone that featured a cylindrical great room in the center, overlooking the lake. The doors from this room opened onto a wooden deck that jutted out toward the lake. This cylinder, a popular shape in Caladria, was full of large windows. The house also had five bedrooms and an enormous kitchen. Before I examined it any further, I asked, "What could you possibly need my approval for? I know nothing about building houses, but this certainly looks like a good one."

"It's a house you would recommend to someone? It's a house, for instance, that you yourself would not be ashamed to call home?"

I was beginning to catch on to what was happening, but it seemed too far-fetched to acknowledge. "It's a fabulous house, Rick. What's going on?"

"Jeremy, this house was to be for the family that I want to have someday. But as yet I have no fiancée. I have plenty of room in my parents' home. So this house has sat unfinished while I have built houses for other people. My business is good. People like my houses. So I went to Governor Brant and some of the church leaders and said, 'Our friend Jeremy, the prophet of God, the Visitor from the Bright World, has restored my family and made my mother and me very happy. He has brought Caladria to the edge of the destiny it has been preparing for all my life. I believe we should give him a gift. I believe we should make a permanent place for him among us, so that for once in this world he will have a home.' They agreed with me. So Jeremy, the reason we need your approval of these plans is that, if you accept this gift from the people of Caladria, we are going to build this home for you."

Amandan added, "Who knows, maybe for you and a future bride. Maybe Anne."

Rickeon's gift and the mention of Anne struck me so forcefully for a moment that I was unable to respond, for certainly this was a house Anne would have loved. In those seconds I could picture her standing on that deck as she looked out over the grassy slope and watched the sun set across the lake.

"This is too much," I said. "You can't do this."

"It's already done," said Tarius, as Rickeon smiled in delight at my astonishment. Tarius added, "We may be here a long time before we return to Persus Am. And even when we go back, our work there won't last forever, we hope. You have never had a home in this world. You have been tossed from one place to another. Let us honor you in this one small way."

Amandan said, "And when the Lord sees this, how can He help but send Anne to you?"

"I am overwhelmed," I said after a moment, and immediately Amandan took my face in her hands as if I were a little boy and kissed me on the cheek. Then Tarius put his hand on my shoulder and led me all over the hilltop, while Rickeon, for as long as the light lasted, shuffled through his pages and talked nonstop about my new home.

14

The work on my house started the next day under Rickeon's leadership. For me those next couple weeks in Caladria flew by in a blur, with one day sliding uncounted into the next as I enjoyed the richness of my life there. The progress on my house seemed remarkably fast as I checked on it every few days. I loved Rickeon and Amandan for the life they had envisioned for me on that hilltop—my wife Anne and I standing on the balcony of our brand-new home and looking out at the lake and forest and fields of the most beautiful country in existence. Sometimes as I stood and watched the workers lifting beams and boards into place and heard the rhythms of the pounding hammers singing my house toward completion, the life on that hilltop with Anne seemed so close that I ached for it. I stood dazed as the visions of it overwhelmed me.

We all pretended that the good life in Caladria could go on for years, but every day the signs grew clearer that a change was coming. The disturbance in the music, its increase in intensity, was impossible to ignore. People flocked to the celebrations, which lasted hours longer than normal. Amandan's celebration field became so crowded that I had to push my way through the people each night to get to the center. The believers shook my hand, clapped me on the back, cheered as if I were a general leading them into battle. They knew a change was taking place. They knew that the "something big" Lemel had spoken of was at hand, though no one said so openly. Every celebration was a miracle. The songs would start with their normal, rhythmic beauty, but after a few hours the music would explode out of all its constraints, the voices and instruments taking it in new and remarkable directions. It was as if God Himself were taking a simple melody and charging it with new meaning and intensity, as if the song as it had been written were only a rough draft that the Lord of the universe now brought to completion. The light that accompanied this sound— or rather was an inseparable part of it—was unlike anything anyone had seen. One night I saw Taron wrapped in so much light that I thought she had literally disappeared. No one doubted that the Lord Himself sang in the music. No one doubted that the light—electrified strands of blue and red and yellow, twirling and twisting to the beat—was the Lord's own breath whispering, "I am coming. I am coming."

When the celebrations ended about dawn, I sometimes walked to my house on the hill and slept in its skeleton until the workers arrived. I clung to shreds of hope for the life I feared would never be. I feared that a shell of a house is all I would ever have.

—◯—

When Emajus came, I had my back to the window and was just taking a step toward Rickeon. We were in his music room on the morning of his day off. The room, filled with all sorts of instruments, was on the ground floor, with a window looking out over the back lawn and the forest beyond. The light, incredibly bright though not at all painful to my eyes, burst in from behind me. When I turned and looked out the window into the lawn, the light was so bright that it obliterated every other detail before my eyes.

I wanted to rush out of the room and go outside to the light, but the light had so flooded the room that I could not see through it. I heard Rickeon say, "He's here," but the voice sounded far away. In a few moments the details in the room returned, but every chair and lamp and musical instrument shimmered and sparkled with light. Rickeon was gone.

I ran out of the room, out the back door, and onto the lawn, from which the circles of light seemed to emanate. The bands of light flowed in circles from a person who was not yet visible. The light contained beams of blue and red and yellow and white. It was filled with sound, and the sound was filled with a loving presence. As I penetrated each circle of light, I felt like a little boy being swept up and hugged by a loving father. When each circle of light washed over me, I was so overcome by the inexplicable sense of rescue and joy that it was all I could do to remain standing, let alone move forward toward the source. Gradually the details of the lawn became visible again. The grass was a brilliant, unearthly green.

In the center of the light stood Emajus, Jesus Christ. I knew Him as if I had seen Him a million times before. He was clothed in light. I tried to run to Him, but the light slowed me down. I kept my gaze on Him. I knew every detail of His face, the eyes that narrowed in concentration, seeing me complete, the smile that told me He recognized me and loved me.

He walked toward me, but the closer He got, the brighter the light became, until it partially obscured my sight of Him. For a moment He got close enough to me to put His hands on my shoulders. I felt a searing presence inside me. It felt like—it is impossible to describe this in the language available to me—it felt like forgiveness. It felt like something cancerous being burned out of me, followed by wave after wave of healing. Waves of forgiveness.

When I looked up, Jesus stood apart from me again behind a veil of light. I asked Him to remove the barrier, but He said that for now it had to be there; either He said it or I understood it without His needing to say it. I cannot remember. Part of what the light contained was understanding, and during this encounter many things were clear to me that are not clear now. Words that might have been necessary in normal conversation were understood, not spoken, that day. I know that we used words for much of our conversation, but I cannot remember exactly what was spoken and what was understood. I present the encounter, however, exactly as it is etched in my memory.

I believe He said, "You've done well, Jeremy. You brought My people to Caladria."

"I'm not sure how much I had to do with it," I said. "You know how I let myself be fooled by Umbriel and Tracian. And after that I mainly relied on Dakin and Will and Danuta and Tarius to get us here."

"You did rely on them. And you did not give up while you waited in Damonchok. And you did not give up while you waited in the Gray Desert, even though you came so close to dying." His love was like the light that swirled around me. My failures were swept away. He said, "You know that the next step will be to take the music back to Persus Am. Are you willing to do it?"

"Yes. I will do it. With Your help I will."

"You will have to depend on your friends again."

"I will. I am ready."

We remained there a while without words. The light and sound and the presence of each other made words unnecessary.

Finally He said, "You want to know about Anne."

I felt a charge of apprehension. "Yes. I want to know about her."

"I will take you to her."

I was too overcome to speak. I felt as if some force were crushing my body from every direction.

Jesus turned and walked toward where the light was brightest. I followed Him into the brightness until it was so dazzling that I could no longer see Him. The light moved so fast here that it seemed to lift me up and propel me forward, faster all the time. We came to a region that was not recognizably part of Caladria. The need for my physical senses seemed diminished, though I was certainly aware of the light and sound. But my primary awareness was of the ecstasy and tenderness of the Spirit. I could not see Jesus, but I knew He was close.

The first I knew of Anne was her voice. I heard it faintly at first, not from outside myself but from within. As it grew louder I heard it all around me. I tingled at the sound of her voice as she called my name again and again. She was nearby, and she was looking for me.

Before I saw her I smelled her hair, and then felt it against my chin. I felt electrified by her presence. Then I saw her face, bathed in light. I looked deep into her brown eyes, knowing, at last, a connection with her. This was no vision, no tantalizing dream. She was connected with me and I with her. The bond was spiritual, sensual. Our kissing, our touching was affirmation of that first connection. Time was all mixed up in this place—time was a virtually meaningless idea—but when I remembered this meeting later I believed that it was a long time before we spoke. We held each other close, two souls lost together in a place without time.

When nontime gave way again to time, the bright light faded and more definite surroundings came into view. We stood in the stark coldness of the park where I had last seen her, where I had fallen through the ice. We could see the bright light of the Spirit shimmering at the fringes of the scene we found ourselves in. We stood on the bank of the pond. Behind us were the mighty trees. Ahead was the icy flatness, the only movement coming from swirls of snowdust blown by the wind.

It was cold. We were dressed in our winter clothes. Anne huddled close to me for warmth, her face against my chest, her hair touching my chin. It seemed miraculous to be standing there with her in this cold park. I wanted never to leave. I wanted never to let her be separated from me.

She said, "You shouldn't have gone out there. You shouldn't have skated on that ice."

"I didn't know it was so thin."

"Are you going to come home with me now, honey? Are we here because He's going to let you come home?"

We *were* home, but the shimmering light at the edge of my vision told me, *No, no, you cannot go back. Your work is not complete. The only direction to move is forward.*

I said, "I can't come back, Anne. I'm not finished with this thing yet. I want to ask Him to let you come with me. I've missed you so much. I've waited so long. They have a house for us. It's so—"

"You know I can't go there, Jeremy. This journey was for you, not me. It was your test. All I can do is wait for you and pray and ask God not to take you away from me."

"Do you know how powerfully I have sensed you ever since I've been here?"

"I've been standing by you, praying, holding your hand."

"I know it. But I want you to be there with me. I want you to meet my friends, see the house they've built for us. They're all expecting you. And wait till you hear the music. It's just— incredible!"

"Jeremy, honey, it is not a place for me to come to. You had to go alone. I think the Lord was trying to get through to you. Now He's done it, hasn't He? The Holy Spirit burns in your heart."

"Yes!"

"Then soon He'll let you come home. Just don't lose faith."

"Anne—"

"Just trust the Lord to lead you. You'll find the right direction with Him guiding you. Finish up and come on home. Come home."

The light that had stayed at the fringes swept down on us, and I felt Anne pull away from me. "Don't pull away, honey!" I said. "Anne, don't pull away!"

"I'm not!"

"Don't pull—"

"I can't help it. I'm not doing it."

"Anne!"

She did not move, but the space between us increased. The park was gone. There was only light. She looked less real across that chasm. She stood dead still.

Frantic, I shouted, "Jesus! Make this stop! Don't let this happen, not after all the time I have waited and hoped and trusted You. Don't let her go!"

My prayer was not answered. My last sight of the woman I loved more perfectly than anyone else I have ever known was swept away in a static of red and blue and yellow shards of brightness. It was as if the light were a lamp that had shattered.

The pieces of it showered all over me, and I tried vainly to gather them together to find her.

My eyes and mind flooded with my own tears, and I could see nothing. I crouched down and hid my face against the grief that overwhelmed me. I felt motion beneath me, the feeling of taking off in an airplane. My feet were not on the ground. The light flung me I knew not where. I do not know how long this flight lasted, but when my feet were on the ground again, the ground was Amandan's lawn, and Jesus stood across from me as He had before, still shrouded in light.

I said, "The understanding in the light makes many things clear, but this I do not understand. You've got to bring Anne back to me."

He said, "Anne is helping to bring you home even now. Her prayers have helped you every step of the way."

"But I need her here with me. I miss her so much."

"You have to trust Me a little longer. You have come far, but your journey is not finished. Now, Jeremy, it is time to finish what you came here to do."

—◯—

What happened next is a blur. No matter how hard I try, I cannot reconstruct it, and I believe that for some reason I am not supposed to remember it. My next clear memory is of waking up on the lawn just outside my unfinished house on a sunny day. I sat scrunched up in a ball, my arms clutched around my legs. I lifted my head to see the hillside and the lake in the distance. I did not know how long I had been there, but it felt as if it had been a long time—perhaps several days—since I had seen Anne or Jesus. My body felt incredibly heavy, much as it had when I had first arrived in the Utturies. This time I did not mind the heaviness because I did not much want to move—except to eat, for I was terribly hungry. Near my house was a shed that served as a headquarters for the builders, and I had used it as a shelter from the rain when I had spent the night up there. The shed was stocked with nuts and fruit and other food for snacks. I managed to pull my body through the heaviness to the shed, where I found something to eat and drink.

I took my meal outside and sat against the shed, overlooking the lake. My mind was as heavy and numb as my body. My encounter with the Lord had been the most amazing experience of my life. The joy from that alone should have carried me for months. Yet I could not keep from my mind for very long the thought that Anne was lost to me again. I contemplated a half-finished house that should have been ours. A skeleton of a house. It would never be finished, not for me anyway, because my days in Caladria, as well as my dream of Caladria, had come to an end.

—◯—

Danuta found me early that evening, as the sun sank low beyond the lake. The physical heaviness had lifted, though my mind was still mired in contemplation.

Danuta had seen Him too. She had seen Him at the same time I had, even though I had been alone when I saw Him. Many others had seen Him too, each one at the same time though alone. "Time is different when you're with Him," Danuta explained. "Time does not follow the same rules we're used to. In fact, it does not exist."

I learned from Danuta that two days had passed since I had stood in the music room with Rickeon.

She said the committee of leaders I had met with before were already gathering at Amandan's home, and she had been sent to find me. "I figured you would be here," she said. "I just wasn't sure if you would be here alone."

She was asking about Anne. I felt a surge of dread at the question. In a way I wanted desperately to talk about Anne, to explain what I had seen and heard and to get someone else's reaction. And Danuta would have listened and understood. She very likely would have helped me make sense of it, as she had done many other times. But if I began to tell her, where would it end? What flood would it release? Could I tell the facts and stop? I felt the sick, sinking despair building up inside me.

Danuta sat next to me and we looked out at the lake. I heard myself say, "I saw Anne." I stopped. I felt the emotion churning inside me.

Danuta put her arm around me. "Do you want to tell me?" she said. "We've got time."

"I can't tell all of it now," I said. "All I can say is Anne is not coming. I don't know when I'll ever see her again."

I could have collapsed into her arms and cried, but I did not want to release that tide. I asked, "How about you? What did the Lord say to you?"

"It is hard to explain. It was absolutely the most fabulous experience of my life, but it was more than any words He said. It's what He made me *understand* and *feel*. It made sense of everything, all we've been through, all that's ahead of us."

"Yes." We both knew that no more explanation was necessary. "Our time is in Caladria is finished, isn't it? We're going to have to go back to Persus Am now and fight whatever battle awaits us."

"That's right. Already they're making plans. We had better go back. They're waiting on you. They were a little worried. Some were afraid the Lord had taken you away for good."

"I only wish He had."

"Nonsense," she said, taking hold of my hand. "You're right on the edge of accomplishing what you were brought here to do. It's time to finish it."

—◯—

We found dozens of people milling about outside Amandan's home, as if waiting for a celebration. They stopped us and wanted to talk about their encounters with the Lord. I listened and Danuta, reverting to her role as a Rememberess, took notes. It was not easy for people to describe their encounters to their satisfaction given the paltry language that limited all of us. They talked around the edges of their experience, as Danuta and I had done. We heard about the Lord's searing forgiveness. We heard of the Lord's crucifixion in another land, the sight of His injured hands. We heard of oneness with almighty God and His universe, salvation, restoration. We heard impassioned and carefully wrought words, yet no one said exactly what they were trying to say. Like a song, it could only be experienced, not explained.

In Amandan's dining room the familiar group was gathered—the ancient Lemel, burly Governor Brant, Tarius and Amandan, Taron, Rickeon, and the other religious and government leaders. They stopped their meeting and greeted me with hugs and handshakes, as if I had been gone for a very long time. The table was spread with folders and papers and trays of food and pitchers of drink. Their mood was jubilant. After years of waiting and planning, they were finally on the verge of the central event toward which their civilization had pointed for decades. They were ready to go to Persus Am.

Over the next few hours they explained their plan to me in great detail. We had six hundred aerocarts ready to fly to Persus Am. Some would carry two soldiers and some would carry three. Along with food and personal gear, the aerocarts would also carry a cargo of the black music shells that, when broken open, had the potential to spread music as loud and as far as a concert hall sound system. These music shells would be our only defense against Umbriel if he should have the capability and the will to resist us. I had no doubt that he would have both. Others, however, were optimistic enough to believe that because Persus Am had been on the brink of war when we had headed for Caladria, by now it was very likely that the Lord had allowed Umbriel's enemies to defeat him. The way would already be paved for us, they believed. I did not believe this. I did not doubt the Lord's power, not after all I had experienced, but my experience also had taught me that the Lord does not very often just sweep away our enemies. I knew Umbriel was smart, prepared, and determined, so I was fully prepared to be greeted by war in Persus Am. Was it reasonable to expect to fight guns and bombs with music? I probably had less faith in this idea than anyone at the table. I stayed quiet while the Caladrians talked.

The plan was that we would set up camp on the Rock of Calad. Tarius Arc, Danuta, Rickeon (our pilot), and I would leave ahead of the others to make these arrangements. We would assess the political situation to determine who held power in what places. If Umbriel were still in control in Persus Am (as I assumed he would be), we would try to keep our aerocarts secret from him as long as possible to prevent him from thinking of a way to shoot them down. Once our aerocarts were safely set up on the Rock, we would negotiate. Our goal, we would stress, would not be to overthrow Umbriel's government or any other government. Our only demand would be permission to rebuild the Temple in Persus Am and to restore the music there. We had detailed plans already drawn for this new Temple. We knew how many workers it would take to build it. We knew how much stone and wood and paint and how many nails it would require. If Umbriel would allow us to do this without war (which I thought was laughable), then we would not challenge his political power. If he did not agree, we would rain the power of Almighty God on him through our music shells until he capitulated.

The Caladrians worried me very much. Many of them had lived their entire lives in this magnificent paradise. They had not endured suffering or hatred. They had not known the desolation of the absence of the Lord's Spirit. All their lives they had been wrapped in love and in the hope of this glorious mission. Once the Lord finally ended their waiting and preparation and told them to go, they were as joyous as if the task had already been accomplished.

How would they react if they saw a friend slaughtered in combat, or if they came face-to-face with a blood-spattered corpse or the charred, stinking remains of a victim of Umbriel's fire pellet guns? How would they survive the psychological torture of the Gray Desert, where they would have to stop en route to their destination? What would happen to their romantic ideas of our mission when the teeth of farks clamped onto their faces and chewed their flesh?

Near the end of the meeting I warned them of the suffering that lay ahead. I told them we must pray diligently for the strength and protection of the Lord and that we must determine never to give up no matter how gruesome our ordeal became. They listened politely, but my warning was not in harmony with the prevailing optimism. Only Tarius Arc echoed my sense of foreboding. As for the others, they were ready for the adventure to begin.

—◯—

Those of us on the advance team left two days later. A couple thousand people gathered on Amandan's lawn to cheer as Tarius,

Danuta, Rickeon, and I walked from Amandan's house to our aerocart. I felt like an astronaut preparing to blast off from the launchpad. We were heroes. We had seen the Lord and we were on the way to fulfill His prophecy. Maybe we could get everything all wrapped up before the other aerocarts even arrived. Maybe the others would come not to fight but to start work on the Temple. Those were the hopes in the air on the day we left Caladria.

Before we boarded our aerocart, as I stood in Amandan's living room looking out at the sparkling lawn and the forest beyond, I said to Danuta, "I do not want to leave this place. I wish there was another way."

"I don't want to leave either."

"The Caladrians don't seem to mind it, though, do they?"

"They know that the prophecy has almost been fulfilled. This is what they've been waiting for and working for. They've had paradise long enough, I guess. They're ready for some action."

"Well, I imagine they'll get it."

Our convoy included ten other aerocarts, staffed by Caladrian "soldiers," as they were now called, though they had never served in any army. There were two soldiers and some cargo in each aerocart. The rest of the fleet of aerocarts was scheduled to fly out of Caladria in groups of twenty starting two days after we left. That would give us time to make arrangements on the Rock of Calad.

Our machines could fly fast, but we had to stop every few hours to place new fuel blocks into the engines. Then the aerocarts had to stay on the ground for about an hour. About every twelve hours the aerocarts had to stop for almost six hours while our mechanics drained from the engine the thick black liquid that accumulated in it and performed whatever additional mainte- nance was needed. Then they added new fuel and we took off again. The effect of the maintenance schedule was that instead of being able to fly straight to the Rock of Calad, we had to spend two nights and make numerous shorter stops in the Gray Desert.

I was asleep when we first flew into the Gray Desert. I was awakened by the sickening presence—or absence—that pervades the place. The aerocart was suffused with Grayness. Rickeon, who had not left the paradise of Caladria since he was a small child had a frozen, almost frightened expression as he flew through the desolation. Rick had been jubilant as we had flown through Caladria. He sang and playfully dipped the aerocart close to the trees and then swooped back up as fast as the machine would go. But in the desert even his skin faded and turned gray. When I asked him if he was all right, he responded with a weak smile and a nod of his head. His hands clutched tightly to the steering controls.

Day and night were equally hellish in the Gray Desert, so we flew every minute we could, stopping only as long as was necessary to maintain the aerocarts. My memory of the fark attacks was so vivid that I could not sleep while we were on the ground. When we took short breaks, the farks never found us, but we did see a few of them during our longer stops. We kept our aerocarts close together, and I kept bright flares constantly burning around them. I kept a constant vigil for farks. I had constructed a handy little spear made of a wickedly sharp knife attached to the end of a pole. Though even the sight of the smallest fark sent chills of fear through me, I derived a grim pleasure from placing my blade on the creature's black shell and slicing through the hated thing. The blade crunched its way through the creature's body, spilling its blood all over the ground. Then I lifted the corpse and flung it into the desert so that it could act as a warning to the others, or so I liked to think. I am proud to say that I killed seventeen farks in exactly this way. Not one of them got into our aerocarts. No one was bitten.

—◯—

On the final day of our journey, when we were to fly onto the Rock of Calad in machines that the people there would find nothing short of miraculous, no one in our group was happier than Tarius Arc. Even though the Rock of Calad was populated by Emajians, many people there had been skeptical of Tarius's journey into the Gray Desert to find Caladria. His arrival at his old home would vindicate his faith in Emajus and in Caladria. Not only had he survived the trip, but he was returning with the means of ousting Umbriel forever and restoring the Temple of the Lord.

We reached the Rock early in the morning, just after daylight. We had flown from a remote and unpopulated area of Wilmoroth, purposely traveling most of the way to the Rock in the dark, hoping that no one would see us. We knew we would not be able to keep the aerocarts secret for long, of course, but in case the world was at war, we did not want to give Umbriel any advance warning of what was about to hit him. We considered landing on the Rock in the dark, but we did not want them to mistake us for the enemy and fire on us. Tarius had written a note explaining our arrival and had attached it to a music shell, which we planned to drop in a very public place before we landed.

As soon as we reached the Rock's edge, however, it was clear to us all that something was very wrong. The first thing we saw was the charred remains of a row of houses. The roofs were burned away and all that remained of the houses were blackened sofas and tables and collapsed walls. For a moment no one said a word, each of us hoping that our fears were unfounded, that somehow these ruins were not signs of war but were merely the remnants of some more isolated personal tragedy.

—⊖—

But the destruction was not isolated. We saw burned-out warehouses and barns and homes. Many buildings stood undamaged, but clearly a horrible battle had been fought here. Tarius was pale with disbelief. "It's impossible," he said. "How could anyone have gotten up here to do this? We were too well protected."

Our aerocarts flew low over the countryside, and many people saw us. It was not until we flew into the city, however, that we saw what we dreaded most: Umbriel's soldiers in the streets and around all the government buildings. Tarius pushed against the window so hard I thought it would break. "Too late!" he said. "We have come too late. We've lost."

The sight of the aerocarts caused a commotion in the streets, where soldiers and citizens pointed and shouted and waved at machines they had never conceived of.

We had no plan for what to do if Umbriel controlled the Rock of Calad. We had not dreamed it could have fallen to him so soon.

Tarius was too stunned to even suggest where our convoy should go. Rickeon said, "Should we just go back to where we came from and stop to figure out what to do next?"

"I don't think so," said Danuta. "We've come this far. We might as well see what Umbriel has and what he doesn't have. I say we fly to Damonchok and see what's there."

Tarius said, "If Umbriel has taken the Rock of Calad, he must have taken Damonchok too."

"Not necessarily," said Danuta. "We can make no assumptions."

"I agree," I said. "We certainly couldn't have predicted that the Rock would have fallen, so who knows what we'll find in Damonchok. Let's go see."

Tarius said, "Where should we go?"

Danuta said, "Let's go to the Panjur. It's the capital, and it's a well-fortified city. The Damonchokians would have protected it above all. If any place has held out against Umbriel, that would be it."

The Panjur was a walled city, much like Umbriel's palace, that housed the government of Damonchok. The main building was a sprawling complex made mostly of wood and was called the Panjurion. The military establishment was centered there, the legislature met there, government agencies were headquartered there, and the Board of Governors, headed by the Chief Governor, lived and worked there. I knew all about the Panjurion from my briefings when I was Prince of Persus Am. Umbriel's spies had put together detailed drawings of the place. They knew in which of the hundreds of rooms the Governors met each morning. They knew in which bathrooms the Chief Governor relieved himself throughout the day. They knew through what offices a piece of mail would be routed before it got to the Chief Governor. They knew where the military leaders lived and worked, where the legislators lived and worked, even where the servants lived and worked. I found all this out one afternoon when one of Umbriel's aides briefed me a little more thoroughly than he was supposed to on Damonchok. When Hamlin walked in on the briefing and saw the detailed drawings sprawled out before me, he immediately shut the meeting down. He said the Father-King urgently needed to speak to this aide, but this was clearly a pretext to end the session. I never heard about the Panjurion again. But I had heard enough. Clearly Umbriel was obsessed with it and wanted it for his own someday.

As we flew north across the Territory of Ur and southern Damonchok toward the Panjur, what we saw was not encouraging. The Territory had been ravaged by war. Houses were ruined, fields were charred and trampled. We saw a pile of bodies that had not yet been buried. We saw clusters of Amian soldiers. The further we flew into Damonchok, however, the less damage we saw. We saw neither Amian nor Damonchokian soldiers. We stopped for a few hours in a remote place to service our aerocarts, and while we were on the ground we saw no one. Our next stop was the Panjur.

As we approached the city, we were relieved to see the brown uniforms of Damonchokian soldiers. They had held out against Umbriel after all. We flew our aerocarts low over the city several times. Crowds gathered to stare, including Damonchokian soldiers, but no one aimed any weapons at us or made any other threatening moves. We flew low enough that Tarius recognized two men from the Rock of Calad. "Some of our people must have fled here," said Tarius. "This is all very strange. Who would have thought that people from the Rock would be living in the Panjur."

Tarius had prepared a written message to drop down to the Damonchokians. It explained who we were and asked them to prepare a place for us to land safely inside the city walls. He attached this to a music shell, believing that the music would prove we were not Amians playing a trick. I was concerned that the music might be painful to the Damonchokians, many of whom were not Emajians, but Tarius said, "They are fighting with us now. The music will not harm them."

"Is the music really that discriminating?" I asked.

"It is the voice of God. It knows to whom it speaks."

Tarius was right. When he tossed the music shell into the crowd and the sound flooded the square, no one sprang away in pain as normally would happen with non-Emajians. But the soldiers—most of whom were not Emajians—kept their distance from the center of the music, while the two Emajian men Tarius had recognized rushed forward to retrieve the message. The music was remarkably loud and full to have come from such a small shell. It was full of trumpets and stringed instruments and what sounded like distant voices, but the melody was unfamiliar to me. We hovered while the men read the message. When they finished they looked up at us, waved, and ran toward one of the buildings, the crowd pressing in behind them. We flew off to give them time to prepare.

When we returned, they had cordoned off a large area surrounding the smashed music shell, which they had left on the ground where it fell. Soldiers held the ropes that kept the growing crowd away from our landing area. When our aerocarts touched the ground, the people actually applauded. They had witnessed the miracle of flight.

The two men Tarius had recognized were allowed beyond the ropes, and just behind them were three men, two in the formal military uniforms of officers and the third in the traditional brown Damonchokian suit, with large buttons and a wide brimmed hat. This last man was thin and stooped, with the most craggy and wrinkled face I had ever seen. "Remarkable! Unbelievable!" he said as he shook our hands. He introduced himself as Tully, one of the Governors of Damonchok. He said, "Let's get you and your people inside away from the crowd. What should we do with your ...your ... " He pointed at the aerocarts.

I answered, "Could you have your soldiers guard them and keep everyone away from them? It would be good if we could find a warehouse or something to put them in so that people don't get too curious."

"I'll see to it," he said. "Absolutely remarkable." The wrinkles of his face parted slightly to allow a smile to appear as we made our way through the crowd. That smile was the only answer Tully gave to the questions the people shouted at us. Soldiers surrounded us to keep the crowd away. Tully seemed unperturbed by all the commotion. He walked as slowly and casually as if we were strolling along a deserted beach.

We walked into a three-story building that was attached to the palace. Like most of the buildings, it was built of wood. The entire Panjurion complex consisted of various wings jutting out here and there, some of wood and some of stone, as if the place had evolved over the years without much planning. Parts of the city walls had, in fact, been torn down over the years to allow new wings to be built onto the existing buildings. It was a fascinating place, with seemingly endless hallways and staircases and court-yards. Many of the ceilings were nearly twenty feet high, and the walls were usually paneled with wood or covered with tapestries. The place did not have the splendor of Umbriel's palace, but it seemed older, more mysterious. Tully led us through a maze of rooms and hallways before he stopped in one that contained a wooden dining table that could seat at least forty people. He invited us to sit down at this table while about a dozen soldiers stationed themselves around the room.

"Who are you?" he asked quite simply.

Before I could answer, one of Tarius's friends from the Rock assured Tully that the man beside him was Tarius Arc from the Rock of Calad. "I have known him for years and years," the man said. "I am as stunned as you are. He didn't die on the way to Caladria after all! He found it! And now he's back."

To me Tully said, "And you? You claim to be the Visitor Jeremy, who was the Prince of Persus Am."

"That's right. I am Jeremy."

Tarius's friend spoke up again: "And this woman is named Danuta, an Emajian Rememberess from Wilmoroth. She has visited the Rock many times. I have known her for years. It absolutely is her."

"Why have you come?" asked Tully.

I said, "We have returned from Caladria, as we promised we would and as the Emajian songs have always said we would. We planned to go to the Rock of Calad and use that as our base of operations from which we would restore the Temple and the music to Persus Am."

"But then you found the Rock overthrown, so you came here," said Tully.

"Yes."

"Are there more of you?"

"Yes. If we can't set up on the Rock of Calad, we would like to set up here in the Panjur and help you defeat Umbriel. We have methods that may surprise you."

The wrinkled face cracked open again and Tully laughed. "I'll say! Machines that fly! There's a method for you! I must call a meeting of the Governors. I've sent messengers to notify them what has happened. But we are very busy with this war, so it may take a while to get them together. May we serve you something to eat and drink while we wait? And how about warm baths and clean clothes, too? You must be exhausted."

"Thank you. And please, if you can tell us what happened to the Rock of Calad. We were stunned to see that it had fallen."

Tully said, "The entire world was stunned. We will tell you the story. But first, let's get your machines taken care of and get you something to eat. This is the most remarkable thing I've ever seen. You just might be the miracle we've been praying for."

—◯—

For the next several hours our group split up. Tarius and Rickeon went with Tarius's friends from the Rock of Calad, who were staying in temporary quarters in the Panjurion that had been converted from government offices. Danuta went to take care of the arrangements for securing the aerocarts. Because our plans had changed, she also prepared a message to be sent to the convoys of aerocarts that would follow us. They would have to be intercepted and change their course to Damonchuk, instead of the Rock of Calad. I went with Tully, who took me to his own residence in the Panjurion, fed me, and told me the story of the fall of the Rock of Calad.

Danuta and Tarius and I all heard somewhat different versions of the fall. When we got together a few hours later in Tully's living room, we compared the accounts we had been told, and this is the history of the battle of the Rock of Calad that emerged:

The younger generation of leaders on the Rock of Calad was more willing than Tarius and his generation to compromise with Umbriel. So with Tarius gone, Umbriel was apparently able to get to some of these younger leaders and convince them that he was going to secure the Territory of Ur one way or another, even if it meant all-out war. He convinced them that all he wanted was a safe trade route from Wilmoroth to Persus Am so that his factories would always be supplied with raw materials and so that he could ship manufactured goods back to his buyers in Damonchok and Wilmoroth. At first the Rock of Calad ignored him; they had heard this all before. They were not about to give up their buffer zone in the Territory of Ur because that was all that kept Umbriel's army and everyone else safely away from them.

So Umbriel pressed ahead with his war plans at first, attacking not the Rock of Calad but Damonchokian villages near the Territory of Ur. His armies were totally successful at first, and Damonchok was clearly no match for him. The Rock of Calad prepared to join Damonchok in a full-scale war against Umbriel. But with a few impressive victories under his belt, Umbriel came back to the Rock to deal again. He insisted that he did not want war and that if he could only have his safe slice of the Territory, he would be satisfied. He pointed out that he had taken no aggressive action against the Rock of Calad and that he had no intention of doing so if his reasonable demands were met. He said he was willing to take the land he needed from Damonchok and leave the Rock's buffer zone untouched. He showed them on the map the land he wanted and pledged that he would never move beyond those borders. He also pledged an end to the trade embargo against the Rock and promised truckloads of free goods like motor carts and globe lights and other things that have always been unavailable on the Rock of Calad. In return, all they had to do was turn their head while he took the land from Damonchok. One thing that bolstered Umbriel's argument is that the Rock had never believed Damonchok had any right to control any part of the Territory. By agreeing to Umbriel's plan, they would simply be swapping one enemy in the Territory for another.

For whatever reason—maybe because they thought he could win the war even if they did fight him, maybe because they were just fools, or maybe because he offered the leaders more things than ever became public—they agreed to his deal. Damonchok pleaded with the Rock to come to their aid, which had always been their agreement if either side were attacked. But the Rock did nothing while Umbriel took the land he said he needed, annihilating thousands of soldiers and entire villages in the process. In the meantime he sent his truckloads of promised goodies to the Rock of Calad, piles and piles of stuff apparently, more than they even knew what to do with or how to distribute.

But to get all these products there the Amians had to have access to the Rock, which of course the Rock had never granted before. Amian spies now learned a great deal about the Rock's defenses, and before long they knew how to overcome them. In short, one shipment of goodies turned out to be truckloads of soldiers, who took over key defense posts, allowing a flood of Umbriel's soldiers to cross the buffer zone and move onto the Rock. The Rock government finally woke up and fought Umbriel with all its might, and for a while it looked as if the Rock might win. But eventually Umbriel prevailed, though he had to turn the Rock into a wasteland to do it. Now his biggest obstacle to conquering the rest of the Known World had been removed.

—◯—

As we sat in Tully's living room contemplating the fall of the Rock, Tarius asked, "So what is left that Umbriel hasn't conquered? Have we come too late, or can we still turn this around?"

Tully answered, "He controls most of Wilmoroth, though some of that is up for grabs still, and he controls everything else except the northern two-thirds of Damonchok. But right now he seems to have stopped his push northward, and he is negotiating with our Governors for peace. He says he has all he wants now and he wants to end the bloodshed."

"You don't believe him, do you?" I said.

"We are negotiating with him, let me put it that way. I frankly don't think our army can stop him, so we have to make our best effort at achieving peace by negotiation."

"He must be defeated," said Tarius. "I think we've seen pretty clearly how disastrous it is to compromise with Umbriel."

Tully said, "You can make that case to the Governors when we get them together. Your arrival may change everything."

"We need to hurry," I said. "Is there any way to speed up this meeting?"

"We're doing the best we can," said Tully. "Some of the Governors are away from the Panjurion right now, but by tonight they should all be back."

—◯—

While we waited for the Governors, we went to talk to some of Tarius's friends from the Rock, who lived in tiny cubicles sectioned off by temporary wooden dividers. Thousands of refugees had flooded the Panjur, and families had few resources and little privacy, sharing bathrooms and kitchens if they had been lucky enough to secure a spot inside the Panjurion.

The refugees told us that all of us who had journeyed to Caladria had long ago been declared dead. They said that the Amians, even after being slaughtered by the Tree People in the jungle of Wilmoroth, had sent a party to apprehend us in the Gray Desert. The story the Amians told was that when they made it to the Gray Desert, they found nothing but a pile of bodies that had been feasted on by farks. Our deaths were announced throughout the Known World, and the bodies were brought back and put on display in town after town throughout Wilmoroth, Damonchok, and the Utturies. The sight was frightful, the refugees said—stinking, naked carcasses with faces and limbs chewed away. Caladria, the Amians emphasized again, did not exist, and the Emajians were fools. The former Prince Jeremy was said to have been positively identified among the victims. Whether he had undertaken the journey of his own free will or whether he had been forced to go by the radical Emajian faction was not clear.

Amazingly, despite this discouraging news, the Emajians had enjoyed a revival across the Known World. One of Tarius's friends told us, "The scriptures that Visitor Jeremy had translated were spread all over the Known World, and word spread that your company had in fact made it to Caladria in spite of what Umbriel said. We could feel new power in the music, and we gained many new believers, especially in Damonchok and in the Utturies, which was alarming to Umbriel. Some say it caused him to move faster to crush the Rock."

As we talked, Tarius sat on a cot and pored over some papers he had asked one of his friends to give him. His expression was pale and drawn. He looked on the verge of tears.

"What is it?" I asked.

He held up the papers. "A list of all those on the Rock who died. Dozens of them, maybe hundreds, were my friends. All dead."

"I'm sorry, Tarius."

"We have come too late. While Umbriel was demolishing the Rock of Calad, we were in Caladria stuffing our faces and gazing at sunsets and walking barefoot through the fields. We should have come sooner."

Danuta said, "We did not come too late. We came exactly when the Lord told us to. We'll just have to do our work in a different way."

Tarius said, "What good was it for us to sustain the Rock for all those years if it is given over to our enemies right at the moment we need it?"

There was no answer to this question. For decades the people of the Rock had sacrificed their own comfort to make the world ready for the return of the Emajians from Caladria. Now, at the moment of that return, the Rock was gone. We sat silent as Tarius read from the list one name after another of his friends who had died.

---◯---

We met the Governors that evening in the dark, wood-paneled conference room of the Chief Governor of the Panjur. I asked Tully to keep the group as small as possible to lessen the chance that our plans would leak out to Umbriel. Secrets were hard to keep in the Known World—I knew that from serving as Prince of Persus Am. Umbriel had contacts everywhere, and he found out most of what he wanted to know about what the other governments were thinking and doing.

The group Tully had assembled included nine Governors and two military leaders. Danuta, Tarius, Rickeon, and I represented the visitors from Caladria. Noticeably absent were any representatives from the Rock of Calad. After their humiliating defeat, they were apparently now subordinate members of the alliance against Umbriel. One of the Damonchokian military men was named General Pons, a man in his early forties with dark skin, a goatee, and piercing black eyes. He stood apart from the conference table, as if in deference to the Governors who were seated there, but it soon became clear that during war he was more powerful than anyone else in the Panjur, including the Chief Governor. As he stood there in his uniform, with its double row of buttons and its fancy epaulets, his hat under his arm, his appearance was a stark contrast to the Governors. The Governors looked worried and weary, burdened by all the trouble that enveloped them, but General Pons was in his glory. Though he did not smile, his face somehow beamed with confidence. He looked as tightly strung as if he might spring from the room at any moment and lead his troops into battle. He reminded me, strangely, of Umbriel, supremely self-assured. I found myself directing my comments toward him.

At the Chief Governor's request I told of our journey to Caladria—our suffering in the Gray Desert, our rescue, our weeks in paradise. The Damonchokians were eager for every detail I would give them. I told of the aerocarts, which prompted a rare interruption from General Pons, who wanted to know how many of those machines we had. When I said six hundred, I thought for a moment he would bound across the room and hug me. He smiled broadly and his eyes were narrow and bright, as if to say, *The rest of your story is just detail. You and I and your six hundred flying machines can win this war!* It may seem strange to infer so much from a man's expression, but it had been the same way with Umbriel. When he was on your side, when he was *for* you, no obstacle seemed too great. The battle was yours to win, and fighting it would be *fun*.

When I told of Emajus's visit, and of our plan to rebuild the Temple, the Damonchokians were less enthusiastic. They were suspicious of Emajianism. Many of them believed that the Emajian revival in the Utturies and in Damonchok had been one of the main factors that had pushed Umbriel into war.

Tully said, "Jeremy, we respect the beliefs of the Emajians, and we consider the Emajians from the Rock of Calad our allies in defeating Umbriel. But this is a war for the survival of our nation. We are willing to fight and die to preserve it. But we are not Emajians. We are not willing to see our people slaughtered just so the Emajians can have a new Temple."

Pons said, "Still, Governor Tully, I think you will agree with me that if Umbriel is defeated, we wouldn't object to letting the Emajians build their Temple in Persus Am. They're going to be the ones building it, and they're going to build in Persus Am, not Damonchok."

"That's correct," said Tully. "A Temple in Persus Am is not contrary to our interests."

Pons said, "I think the question is, what else do these people from Caladria want? When we do defeat Umbriel, how will his territory be divided?"

I answered, "The Caladrians have prepared for decades for this very moment. Their sole objective is to see the Temple rebuilt and the music of the Lord freely restored to the Known World, so that anyone who chooses may worship Emajus."

"No political ambitions?" asked Pons. "They don't want things divvied up so that we get Damonchok, they get Persus Am—"

"General Pons," I answered, "these people live in paradise. Nothing the Known World has to offer is even a fraction as good as what they already have. They are driven by their love of Emajus. If you let them build a Temple and remove all barriers to the music of Emajus, you can do whatever you want with the government. It does not interest them."

No one responded, but I could tell that their suspicions of the Caladrians had not been laid to rest. This whole discussion assumed, of course, that we would defeat Umbriel, which at that moment looked highly improbable. When I told about the Caladrians' plan to use the music shells to paralyze and defeat Umbriel's army, the look of scorn on Pons's face was so profound that I thought he would laugh out loud. He fired one question after another at us about the music. How could sound of any kind, no matter how powerful, stand up against a bomb or a fire pellet,

or even a rock for that matter? Tarius picked up on these questions
and patiently tried to explain how powerful this music was, how
utterly different it was from anything the world had ever experienced, even though the music already heard in the Known World
was known to have dire effects on the Amians. True, countered
Pons, but that power did not stop the Amians from overthrowing
the Rock of Calad. Tarius responded that, with all due respect to
his fellow citizens on the Rock, they were fools to have been duped
by Umbriel. The music in those thousands of shells would paralyze, perhaps even kill anyone who fought against the Lord's
people. Soldiers cannot fight when they are paralyzed or dead, he
said. It would work. It was the Lord's way. If the Known World
had trusted the Lord's way before, it wouldn't be in the mess it
was in now.

Everyone listened politely to this speech from Tarius, and in
the silence that followed, General Pons whispered something to
the military man standing next to him. Then Pons asked the Chief
Governor if he might have a word with the Governors in private
before the meeting went any further. Before Pons asked us to leave
the room he said, "Even tonight we face new threats from Umbriel.
Apparently the sight of your flying machines has thrown his
generals into a panic, and there are signs that Umbriel's army may
be on the verge of attacking us again. There are certain matters I
must raise with the Governors before we make any more plans
with you."

—⊖—

We non-Damonchokians left the room for nearly half an
hour, and when we were called back in, we received the worst news
of all, news that Tully and our other sources had not even hinted
at. General Pons delivered it.

"We have information," he said, "that holds important
implications for the strategy we will use to fight this war. We have
tried to keep it as quiet as possible. Only we in this room and a
few others know about it, and we must ask that you also promise
to keep silent about it. If Umbriel knew that we had found out
about this, the life of at least one of our sources would be in danger.

We have decided to share it with you because your arrival has given us our best and possibly only hope of survival as a nation."

Pons stepped forward to the table. "After Umbriel defeated the Rock of Calad, his army turned toward Damonchok, and at first we had a few fierce battles with him at the edge of the Territory of Ur. But then suddenly he backed off. We didn't know what to make of it. He certainly had the advantage, and we would have expected him to keep attacking. A short time later we found out why he had stopped. On the Rock of Calad his scientists had finally come close to perfecting the great bomb. I am talking about *the* bomb, Tarius Arc, the bomb that you gave us in the last War, that wiped out Persus Am. They've been trying to get it right for decades, and apparently they have just about done it. Maybe something they found on the Rock—"

Tarius said, "There is nothing on the Rock that would give them any idea how to build that bomb." Then he sat back for a moment and stared at the ceiling. "Well, there may be one thing. But it wouldn't complete it for them. General Pons, I am the only man living who knows how to do it."

"But if you figured it out long ago, it is conceivable that they have figured it out by now, isn't it?"

"The world was much different long ago, sir. You are a young man. But yes, it is conceivable. I doubt it, though."

Pons said, "Tarius Arc, when Umbriel released you from prison in the deal with the Rock of Calad that later failed, we were all amazed! We wondered why would Umbriel let Tarius go after wanting to get at him for so long, after wanting him because he's the only man in the world who could build the bomb? And then our sources told us it was because Umbriel's own people were getting close to figuring out that bomb for themselves. Tarius is becoming a relic from the War. Pardon me for saying it, sir, but I am only quoting them. Umbriel apparently believed you were no longer the only key to unlock the mystery."

Tarius answered, "Relic from the War though I may be, General Pons, I do know a thing or two about what Umbriel's people were working on. I have a few sources in Umbriel's camp too. At least I did when I was still on the Rock. I know that they were nowhere close. And they had no idea how far they were. They could make powerful bombs, certainly, you have seen that for yourself. But the bomb from the War is something in a different category altogether."

Pons said, "Tarius Arc, if Umbriel does have that bomb, he could wipe out all of Damonchok with it. There is nothing we could do to him that he could not withstand. This war would be over in no time, and Umbriel would control the entire Known World. We need a weapon of our own to fight him with. Your flying machines will be of great help, but against a bomb of that magnitude, we need—"

"I know where you are headed, General, and I must cut you off right now," said Tarius. "I will go to my grave with the secret of the bomb. I will never build it again. It is not to be used as a weapon."

"But if it came to a choice of losing everything or building that bomb—"

"General, we have a way to win, and we have described it to you. The Lord has provided it. We have aerocarts, and we have music shells. These will stop Umbriel. We only need your cooperation in getting set up and launching our offensive."

Pons backed off for the moment, and some of the Governors took up the issue of where the aerocarts might be based, how they might be protected, where our soldiers would stay, how they would be fed, and so on, the very concerns we were there to settle. I thought Pons's idea of having Tarius build the bomb "just in case" wasn't bad, but I said nothing. Tarius would not be moved, and we did have the other plan. Pons kept quiet while we planned the details, but at the end of the meeting I heard him say, "This scheme is certainly worth a try. Get your flying machines here as fast as you can. But if we can't win it one way, we'll win it another."

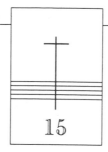

15

Our next challenge was getting the aerocarts safely to the Panjur so that we could begin launching our attacks. Tarius and I wanted to start dropping the music shells over the Territory of Ur and the Rock of Calad as soon as our first aerocarts arrived, but the Governors and General Pons were adamantly opposed to this. Umbriel's armies were still not on the move, and the governors feared that if we provoked them with a few music shells, they would launch an all-out attack and defeat us before we were fully prepared. It would be better, the Governors insisted, to get all or most of the aerocarts to Damonchok and then throw our power against Umbriel all at once, before he could think of ways to counteract our aerocarts and our weapons. We agreed to this plan.

We had hoped to have all six hundred aerocarts in the Panjur in ten days, but we were faced with disasters and delays every step of the way. Some of the aerocarts, which had been built in the perfect weather conditions of Caladria, broke down in the harsh Gray Desert. At least seven crashed there, killing their crews. Others had mechanical difficulties on the way from Wilmoroth to the Panjur, sometimes forcing them to land in regions controlled by Umbriel. Still others got lost and wandered around for hours over enemy territory. One of our worst fears was that Umbriel would capture some of the aerocarts and figure out how to use them to rain down bombs on us. As if those problems were not bad enough, violent thunderstorms delayed all flights for two days.

Even when an aerocart made it to the Panjur, our worries were not over. While Umbriel's army was nowhere near the city yet, his terrorists routinely made it into Damonchok and planted bombs in villages all over the country. Every day or two we heard reports of bombings somewhere, usually killing several people and leveling a few buildings. Though the Panjur was considered safer than most Damonchokian villages, we feared that the terrorists might make it past the local defenses and destroy our aerocarts on the ground. There was no adequate place to store six hundred aerocarts in the Panjur. The Damonchokians cleared warehouses and raised huge tents to hide the machines. Our camp was surrounded with soldiers, trenches, fences, and barbed wire, but still we knew there were points of weakness where the enemy could break through. We needed to attack quickly. There was no time to waste. Ten days after the first convoy arrived, we had just under 250 aerocarts in camp. Until that time Umbriel's army had not moved. Our sources told us Umbriel's scientists were still working frantically to perfect their bomb, and Umbriel was trying to figure out the significance of the flying machines—where did they come from? How many were there? What were the intentions of the people who flew them? Negotiations between Umbriel and the Damonchokians were at a standstill because they refused to answer any of his questions about these mysterious machines.

Taron and Amandan arrived at the Panjur together on the tenth day. Taron immediately begged me to take her to her family, whose home in southern Damonchok would not be far from the front lines of battle if Umbriel went on the attack again. I explained to her that I wanted to take her to her family as soon as we could, but that we had made an agreement with the Damonchokians that no aerocarts would leave the camp until we started our all-out assault. We had to keep our numbers as much of a mystery to Umbriel as we could, and we could not risk any of our aerocarts. If we allowed one person to use an aerocart to go to her family, hundreds would want to do it, and our whole plan would break down.

None of this satisfied Taron; she reminded me of her family's kindness to me, which I had not forgotten. The fact was I wanted to find a way to break our policy and go rescue her family before any fighting began. I put Taron off for one night, but the next day I found a way to grant her request.

On the eleventh day, when sixty more aerocarts made it to the Panjur, we learned that Umbriel's army had renewed its attack and had pushed into southern Damonchok. We learned this not from the Damonchokians but from unofficial sources Danuta had cultivated. Furthermore, we learned that the attack had not begun that day, but the day before. We were outraged that the Damonchokians had kept this information from us. I immediately sent word to the Governors, who said neither they nor General Pons were available to see any of us. I told them that our counterattack with the music shells should begin immediately. Delaying any longer, a policy we had only reluctantly agreed to, no longer made any sense.

Within an hour I received a reply that our facts about Umbriel's movements were not entirely accurate. The reply said that the attack by one small faction of Umbriel's army was unauthorized and that it had been brought to a halt. The Governors were in close contact with Umbriel's people they said, and still held out hope for peaceful negotiations. They would not agree to the commencement of our attack. They believed we should honor our original agreement to wait until all the aerocarts had arrived. They would call a meeting with us shortly to discuss all these matters in greater detail.

As I sat in a warehouse among a few dozen of our aerocarts and studied this reply with Tarius, Amandan, Rickeon, and Taron, Danuta brought more disturbing news.

"We have been lied to," said Danuta. "I have been suspicious of General Pons all along, but now I think I know what he's been up to. Pons is the one who talked the Governors into withholding the information about Umbriel's attack. And he's going to get them to lie to us now about how bad that attack was—"

"They just did," I said, holding up the Governors' reply.

"—And he's going to try to talk them into not letting us counterattack."

"They just did that too. It's ridiculous. Why doesn't Pons want to use these aerocarts?"

"Oh, he very much wants to use them," said Danuta. "He's dying to use them. But he wants to use them on his own terms. He thinks the idea of using the music shells is absolutely ludicrous. He has no intention of letting us do it. He thinks he'll be a laughingstock throughout the whole Known World if he allows it."

"But they'll work!" Tarius exclaimed.

"He doesn't think so. He's been trying to find out all he can about the aerocarts, even though our soldiers, as ordered, aren't letting anybody near them. His people have been questioning our soldiers about them, how they work, where the weapons are stored, and so on, and Pons has been preparing bombs and other weapons to use in them. That's his plan, apparently, to use the fleet of aerocarts to bomb the Rock of Calad before Umbriel finishes his own big bomb. Pons has even tried to get some of our soldiers to teach his men to fly the things, but the Caladrians won't let anyone even sit inside the machines, just as they've been told. Pons doesn't want to use any force against us until all the aerocarts are in camp because he's afraid you'll order the rest of them not to come."

"Unbelievable," I said. "So what does he plan to do when all the aerocarts are here, just take them away from us?"

"I guess so, if they can figure out how to fly them, which probably won't be that hard to do."

"As if Umbriel isn't enemy enough, we have to fight against our supposed friends."

Tarius said, "We have to get to the Governors and get them to stop Pons. Apparently he's acting on his own in this."

"Would the Governors stop him? He seems to be running the whole show right now."

"I don't know. We've got to try. Start with Tully. I trust him. And as for the meeting you've demanded with Pons, don't count on it happening. His people have been told to keep you away. We've got to go to the Governors one by one, privately."

"We've got to hurry. We don't have time for this. Umbriel's army is already moving north in western Damonchok. If they turn east toward the Panjur—"

"We can't let that happen," said Tarius. "We've got everything we need to stop Umbriel. If we have to fight Pons too, so be it."

I said, "There is one way to change Pons's mind right now."

"How?"

"Take the aerocarts up ourselves—right now—don't even tell Pons or the Governors, and show them how well the music shells work by stopping Umbriel before he goes any farther."

Tarius shook his head, but he could not completely suppress his slight smile. "That would break our agreement to coordinate all military efforts with Damonchok," he said.

"Pons has betrayed us. He has withheld information from us. He has lied to us. The agreement is broken."

"It is very dangerous."

"So is sitting here."

"We have not prepared a strategy."

"The strategy is to fly to where Umbriel's army is, unload as many music shells on them as possible, and see what happens."

Tarius laughed. "An excellent strategy, general. Beautiful in its simplicity."

"We've got to keep this as quiet as possible. We don't want any more tricks by Pons. Can you help me get together our most reliable people? Tell them only what they need to know. About twenty aerocarts should do, shouldn't it?"

"Oh yes. I think the music's going to be so powerful that even one would probably be enough."

"Well, let's take twenty. We'll leave tonight and be there by dawn."

"Good."

"And Tarius, we need to leave some room in the aerocarts."

"What for?"

"We'll be flying to Taron's home, and I want to offer her family the chance to come back here where it's safer."

"Good."

"And just one more thing. We do need to speak to the Governors about Pons. Would you be willing to stay behind and talk to them? I want to go with the aerocarts."

"I will do it. I'm glad we're finally moving, Jeremy. God didn't give us all this power just to sit on."

—◯—

We were less than twenty miles from Taron's home when we saw smoke rising from the woods. It was just past dawn, and this was the first sign of battle we had seen. Rickeon was my pilot, and Taron was also with me to help guide us through the landscape that was so familiar to her. The other aerocarts followed us. Beyond the burning woods was a small town, and as we flew over the outskirts of it we saw our first Amian soldiers setting fire to some homes. As we circled the homes, I saw an Amian soldier shoot a woman in the back with one of the fire bullets as she fled her burning house. She fell face first into the dust, screaming, turning over and over in the dirt.

"This is it," I said. "Let's hit them now."

"Look over there," said Rickeon. "There's a whole group of them standing together. Let's hit them all at once."

Rickeon flew close over the heads and let five music shells drop, one of them hitting a soldier right on the head and knocking him down.

The shells burst open as they were intended to, and the sound that issued forth was amazing. The first sound, which was like the sudden striking of thousands of drums, was so loud and powerful that it felt as if our aerocart had been hit from underneath. The machine jolted us hard against the doors and windshield, and Rickeon nearly lost control of it, swerving down toward a house and then suddenly back up. The music sounded furious, a march containing the sound of every imaginable instrument, a musical version of the anger of God. At least that's what those of us in the air heard. The music was loud and even frightening to us in its power, but at the same time we were thrilled by it; we wanted to stay in it and feel it wrapping around us.

Those on the ground reacted much differently. Several of the soldiers fell immediately to the ground and looked dead; a few lay screaming, their ears covered as they squirmed in the dirt. It was a chilling sight. The sound of the voice of God that so fed our souls was literally killing the men below us. Some of them had turned pale and stiff. I was sure they were dead.

Those who did not fall ran, though the music had so permeated the area that there was nowhere for them to go. One soldier in particular caught my attention—a boy who could not have been more than sixteen years old—and I told Rickeon to follow him to see where he ran. The boy covered his ears with his hands, his head bowed in pain, and flung himself blindly forward on the road away from the town. He was bent over so far that it looked as if he would stumble and fall at any moment.

Rickeon said, "How can he keep going like that? He looks like every step is killing him."

Taron, who herself sat pale and stiff at the sight of the screaming, suffering men, said, "He just wants to get away. I hate this! How can this beautiful music have such a horrible effect on them?"

We followed the boy-soldier for less than a hundred yards before he collapsed into a ditch along the side of the road. He lay there for a while rocking back and forth and screaming, and then he lay still.

"I know we probably shouldn't do this," I said, "but I want to go down there and get that boy. If he's still alive, I want to find out what it is he's hearing. I want to find out if he knows what is happening to him."

We landed in the road, and with a signal from Rickeon, the other aerocarts stayed in the air and circled us. The boy lay face down and did not move as we approached him. His head was completely covered with his jacket, and his hands were pressed hard against his ears. I rolled him over and pushed the jacket from his face. His body was sweaty and limp, passive, as if sapped of every bit of its energy. The boy's eyes were wide and somewhat dazed, but he seemed fully conscious.

"Can you hear me?" I asked.

The boy cried. He did not answer, only nodded.

We lifted him into the aerocart and took off again, heading north where the Amian rampage continued. Taron sat in back and cradled the boy in her lap. They both cried. She said, "It seemed like such a painless idea, fighting a war with music. It seemed so miraculous. But we're killing people. The music doesn't leave a mark on them, but it kills them."

Rickeon said, "But it can also restore them. Listen to the music. The music is beautiful and good."

Taron held the boy close and said, "Pray to the Lord. Pray that He'll let you hear the music the way it's meant to be. Pray."

The boy kept his steady and frightened gaze on Taron, and a few minutes later he closed his eyes and slept.

———◯———

We were alarmed at how far north Umbriel's army had pushed. We had expected Pons's army to have stopped them many miles south of the first village we arrived at, but they were already several miles north of it. Once again we had received misleading information from the Panjur.

The music so flooded our aerocart and the surrounding countryside that we stayed silent as we got near Taron's home. I was filled with dread because as we got closer to the more populated areas near her farm, we saw telltale smoke rising above the trees. The Amians had not only been there, but most of them had already left, pushing ever northward, leaving only a few to finish the operation. It was so smoky at first that we had trouble making out the landmarks, and we ended up flying past Taron's home. As we passed a clump of trees the smoke momentarily cleared to give us a view of the ground. The first clear sign of destruction we saw was Ranejun's farm, where smoke billowed from the remains of the house and barns where Dubov and I had worked together. Taron cried out and reached up and grabbed my hand. The sight, particularly coming upon us so suddenly, was horrifying. The once sturdy, proud farmhouse was a charred mess, with burnt furniture and clothes and stinking dead animals scattered all around. And of course the unspoken but very palpable thought that passed between Taron and me as she held my hand was that if Ranejun's farm lay in ruins, what must have happened to Taron's home? Could her own family have survived this slaughter? We rode in silence. I kept Taron's hand firmly in my own.

After finding Ranejun's farm, it was easy to fly to where Taron's was, but the area was so obscured by smoke that it was hard to know where to set down. When we came to a clear area, I told Rickeon to land.

Taron asked, "Can you see my house from here?"

"No, but there's a clear field."

"That's our field! Look—our fences. And if the fence isn't burning, maybe they didn't get to the house yet either."

Four other aerocarts landed with us. With the system of multicolored lights attached to our aerocarts, we had signalled all the others to continue north, in pursuit of the main column of Amian soldiers. Only a scattered few Amians remained here from what we could tell, apparently left to burn up everything in sight. I told Taron to leave the boy in the aerocart and to stay with me while I talked to the soldiers from the aerocarts that had landed with us. Danuta was among them, and I wanted her to go with us to Taron's.

The music swirled around us with such force that it was hard to concentrate. As I huddled with the soldiers to coordinate their activities, Taron slipped away and headed toward her house. Rickeon followed.

When our soldiers scattered out on their separate assignments, Danuta and I were left alone in the middle of the field while smoke billowed in the distance in every direction around us and the music shells belted out a melody full of trumpets and trombones and strings and drums. We were in a grassy field where camucks and other animals normally grazed, but no animals were in sight that day. I was unsure which direction to go to get to Taron's house, but when I walked to the fence and tried to peer through the distant smoke, I saw Rickeon running toward us. He ran with all his might. Danuta and I were over the wooden fence and running toward him by the time he reached us. He was so out of breath that all he managed to say was, "All dead. Come quick."

Ranejun's farmhouse had been burned, but Rothter's looked as if it had been bombed. A huge hole was blown in the porch by the front door, and the roof over the porch was hanging down, about to collapse. The heavy iron flagoon pot was turned on its side and it partially blocked the door. Smoke rose from somewhere in the back of the house, and most of the windows were shattered.

What we saw when we ducked under the roof and walked through the front door was horrifying. Taron squatted on her knees in the middle of the room, wailing, as one of the neighbor women held her and tried to pull her away from what lay in front of her. In a moment I saw for myself—it was Dubov's body, half his face a bloody mess. I knelt beside Taron and she collapsed against me.

The neighbor woman shook her head and said, "Them soldiers done it. They come through here ever' day killin' more and burnin' more. They got my husband. They'll get me too, I just know it."

"What about the rest of Taron's family?" I asked.

The woman shook her head. "Got ever' one of 'em. Rothter, Goldaw, Mettie, little Cresha."

"Too late," I said. "Always too late. Why does God send us at all if it's always too late?"

Danuta said, "Let's take Taron outside, Jeremy. She shouldn't stay in here." The smell of the room was nauseating. Cushions of the couches and chairs had burned and now filled the air with a chemical stench. Blood clung to the floor and walls. One wall was blown almost completely away. Most of the furniture was smashed or overturned. We led Taron out into the lawn, where the only unpleasant sight was the smoke in the distance. She cried in Danuta's arms and then in mine, and we cried with her. Gradually she grew quiet, her wailing replaced by a dazed stare. She swayed slightly with the music, even in grief mindful of the Lord's voice. Only after a long silence did she say, "They never even knew I was still alive. I never even got to tell them. And now—to see their faces like that. Their sweet faces. What are we going to do, Jeremy? What am I ever going to do now?"

We were not finished with death that day. When Rickeon went back to our aerocart a few hours later, he found the boy-soldier dead in the back seat.

While the rest of our aerocarts pursued the Amians north-ward, Danuta and I stayed with Taron that day and the next. We helped her neighbors bury her family, as so many others had been buried. We helped her gather her most prized possessions—whatever was not destroyed—from the house that no one would live in again. We stood with her as she said good-bye to her few friends that remained, the ones who had been spared mainly because our attack with the music shells had interrupted the Amians' plans for the total destruction of everything in their path.

Pons's army was finally of some help to us on that final day in western Damonchok. While his troops to the south had been crushed by Umbriel's onslaught, he had another army to the north that was pushing southward while we pushed north. When our aerocarts finally found the main battalion of Amians north of Taron's home and pelted them with music shells, the soldiers either collapsed or fled northward to escape the sound. Those who fled fell weakened and suffering into the arms of Pons's best fighting force, who slaughtered them.

Our work on one battlefront complete, we headed for the Panjur. I was determined that as soon as I got back, no matter what opposition I faced from General Pons or the Governors, I would order every aerocart into the air and they would stay there until the war was won. We would fight with the music that swirled in my brain and that would not let us doubt God's power any longer.

As we flew over the magnificent Damonchokian landscape toward our camp, I prepared myself for the message I would give to the Panjur. We would use the tools the Lord had provided us, I would tell them, the music shells and the aerocarts. The voice of God would be set free once more in the Known World. Those who trusted in Him, even Amian soldiers, who let His Spirit cleanse them and fill them would be energized and protected by the music, but those who clung to evil and fought against His Spirit would be overpowered and annihilated by His song. No bomb invented by Umbriel or anyone else could stand up to the power that had been entrusted to us.

These words seemed sufficient as we floated through the sunshine and as the confident melodies soothed my thoughts, but as soon as we landed in camp, we were struck by another tragedy that rocked my battered faith.

—◯—

Umbriel had not sat as quietly as we thought while the scientists tinkered with his bomb. At the same time we were fighting his army in the southwest, other parts of his army had struck at various other places on the southern front, making Pons's defense difficult. Then, on the morning before we arrived back at camp, one or several of Umbriel's terrorists managed, perhaps with help from traitorous Damonchokians, to slip past our camp's guards and barbed wire and trenches and other defenses and plant a bomb among our aerocarts. When it exploded, eleven of our soldiers were killed and forty aerocarts were either wiped out completely or damaged beyond repair.

The explosion was so loud and shook the ground so violently and spread destruction so quickly that some of the Damonchokian leaders thought it was *the* bomb they had so feared. Because our mission to the western part of Damonchok was still a secret to most people, the rumor also spread that Danuta and I had been killed in the explosion.

When we landed and walked through the rubble of our aerocarts, listening all the while to the soldiers giving their accounts of what had happened, my exhaustion from an almost sleepless night at Taron's house suddenly caught up with me, and I had to sit for a while on top of the hollowed-out underbelly of a demolished aerocart before I felt strong enough to go on. I was numb to grief. I felt only a wild, unfocused rage. I sat stiff, my head bowed, and listened even though my mind felt as if it were collapsing on itself. I fought hard to control even my most insignificant word or movement because I knew that in my state of mind anything I said or did likely would be the wrong thing.

Tarius Arc arrived at this garbage heap to tell me that my presence was urgently requested at a meeting of the Governors. Before I went with him I ordered that music shells be broken in the camp and that music be sung and played constantly day and night. I was determined that there would be no more silence. We would blanket the world with music.

When Tarius and I were by ourselves, walking through the halls of the Panjur, he said, "Actually, the Governors don't know that you're coming to this meeting. But I worked it out with Tully that we would be let in. I know Pons is there. We need to decide once and for all what we're going to do."

"I know what we're going to do. By tomorrow morning every aerocart in the camp is going to be in the air raining music shells all over the Known World, starting with the Rock of Calad and including every Amian fortress and building and camp we can find. I'm prepared to move on our own without the Damonchokians if that's what it comes to."

"I totally agree, and I'm glad to hear you say it. But it would be best to have them work with us. They know in pretty precise detail where Umbriel's forces are all over the Known World."

"Then why did they let his army cut a path of destruction most of the way up the western side of Damonchok?"

"The fact is, despite Pons's bragging, they're just not strong enough to stop Umbriel. Not if he strikes everywhere at once. Without us they cannot win."

"Tell me, Tarius, before we go in there. What about this bomb? Is Umbriel going to get it?"

"I think so, yes. Before now I didn't think it would ever be possible. But I think he is extremely close."

"Can we stop him before he wipes out everything, or will we be too late like we've been all along?"

"Jeremy, I believe we will win, but I don't know whether everything will be wiped out or not. From the time of the first War until now the entire purpose of Umbriel and his father has been to stamp out the voice of God forever. That's really what was always behind their moves in the Territory of Ur and everywhere else. It wasn't about grangicars and trade and all that. That's what

I could never get the people of the Rock to understand, and that's why they eventually fell. Umbriel wants to silence the voice of God, deny His existence, or at least make up a God of his own that is more palatable to him. He has gotten away with it for a long time, but now it is crashing in on him. The Amians are in a panic. Too many people have been turning to Emajus. Umbriel will not give up easily. He will fight and scream to stop us—and massacre anyone who opposes him—but still he will lose. The voice of God—His Spirit, His music—will be heard again in the Known World. There is a passage in one of the songs of prophecy that says, 'He shall grind the dog into the dust/He shall scatter His kingdom to the wind.' I've been thinking about those lines a lot lately. Maybe the Lord will start from scratch. Build a new world out of the rubble of this one. What does it mean, 'He shall scatter His kingdom to the wind'?"

"I don't know, but I want to do everything I can to avoid your interpretation. Let's get in there and talk to our buddy Pons."

—◯—

The Damonchokian guards under Pons's control tried to keep us out of the meeting, but when we finally persuaded someone to bring Tully out to us, he took us right in. Pons sat at the conference table with the Governors, not even trying to maintain the pretense of our first meeting when he had stood against the wall as if he were just an invited guest waiting to take orders. He did not look quite the heroic general that he had appeared to be at the earlier meeting either. He had shed the military jacket with all its decorations and wore a white shirt open at the collar. His hair looked as if it had been combed by merely running a hand through it once or twice, the goatee was scraggly and untrimmed, and stubble covered the rest of his face. Still, whenever he spoke, his whole body was so wiry and tense that you expected him at any moment to spring out of his chair like a cat and pounce right on top of you.

The meeting was not pleasant. When the Chief Governor, a ponderous old man, gave us a rambling summary of the report Pons had given them, it was clear that Pons had deceived his own people just as he had deceived us. Pons's story made what had happened in the west sound like a great victory for Damonchok, a victory brought about not by Caladrian music shells and aero-carts but by the great Damonchokian army that had swooped down from the north to crush the invading Amians.

I interrupted the Chief Governor to describe in graphic detail what I had seen—the burned out villages, the dead Damonchokian families, the Amian soldiers killing and burning with absolutely no resistance whatsoever. I described the paralyzing effect of our music shells on these invaders. I told how we chased the Amians northward until they fell exhausted and half dead at the feet of Pons's army, who finally cut them down.

Pons and I spent a great deal of time arguing over the particulars of this story, and then I said, "Governors, we trusted you, and we treated you as allies, but we have been deceived, and that deceit has cost us the lives of at least eleven of our soldiers, countless lives of your own people, and the destruction of forty of our aerocarts. What we came to tell you is that tomorrow morning every single aerocart we have will be in the air raining down music shells on Umbriel's soldiers. We will not stop until this war is won. We would like you to fight alongside us. We would like to know what you know about the best place to hit him because that would make victory come sooner. But no longer will we delay while General Pons dreams up schemes of his own."

Tully said, "Jeremy, we are all horrified by the killing that has taken place. But in all fairness, we want victory just as much as you do. If we have delayed, it has been for good reasons."

Tarius said, "The reasons were never adequate, and we should never have agreed to your delay. We have found out why General Pons wanted to wait. He has been trying to get our men to show him how our aerocarts worked so that he could push us aside and use the machines for his own purpose."

"A lie," said Pons with a brush of his hand, as if the charge were too ridiculous even to get angry about.

Tarius continued, "And some of Pons's people have been making plans for modifying the aerocarts so they could strap bombs to them, even though we forcefully have stated—and you have given your agreement—that the aerocarts would not be used that way."

Pons stood with his fingers spread on the table and leaned toward us, catlike, ready to spring, and said, "If winning this war is what you're interested in, gentlemen, then you'll stop fighting me and let me do it. With those aerocarts I could win this thing in a few days."

"I think you've shown your lack of good faith," said Tarius. "Those aerocarts are not yours. They belong to the people of Caladria, who were given the flying machines and the music shells as a blessing from God, to fulfill His plan for restoring His music in Persus Am. It is not the only way the Lord could have done it. He could have chosen your plan. Maybe you think He should have, but He did not."

Pons said, "For you this war is about music. For us it is about keeping Umbriel from wiping out the nation of Damonchok and controlling the entire Known World. I don't hold much with religion myself, though I have no objection to people believing what they want. But when that religion gets in the way of winning the war, then I think it should be set aside until the war is won. I don't know about any plan of God. Was it a plan of God that the Rock of Calad fall into Umbriel's hands? Is that what all you Emajians on the Rock were intending?"

"No," said Tarius, "the people on the Rock were idiots to deal with Umbriel. They lost faith. We don't intend to repeat their stupidity."

I said, "The point is, Governors, the issue of how the aerocarts and music shells will be used is not open for debate. We have demonstrated over the last few days that they will work as we said they would. We appreciate the camp you made for us here and the protection you helped provide us up until today. But tomorrow we start fighting, and if you wish to fight with us, we will be happy to have you join us in my barracks in the camp."

Tarius and I stood and left the room, with Tully and Pons chattering at us every step of the way.

—⊖—

Pons did not come to us, but a few hours after the meeting Tully did come, and he brought two of Pons's top aides, followed by four soldiers carrying maps and other material that they set up in my little barracks.

Tully said, "We have better rooms in the Panjur, if you would like to move everything there."

"No," I said, "we are quite comfortable here in our camp. Let's get started."

Tully called me aside privately and said, "Pons has great pride, and right now he is hurt and offended that we have chosen to cooperate with you. But these men know everything he knows and will help you until Pons has finished licking his wounds. We have seen him this way before. Don't worry about it. Despite these recent events, he is a great general. Damonchok is still standing, after all, even though the Rock has fallen."

"I do hope he will change his mind and work with us," I said.

"Victory will change his mind. If he sees you are going to win, he will be right there with you to take the credit once it's all over."

"The credit he can have. Once this is over, we'll be too busy with other things."

—◯—

The next morning more than two hundred aerocarts lifted from our camp and fanned out over Damonchok and the Rock of Calad. They were loaded with music shells and headed for Umbriel's army camps and the headquarters on the Rock where the bomb was being assembled. I watched in awe as wave after wave of the machines flew off. When they were nearby they looked like giant pillows in the air, and when they were far off they looked like fast moving clouds. There was nothing frightening about their appearance, but we prayed that the force they unleashed—the very voice of God—would so sting the hearts of Umbriel's legions that the Amians would not be able to take another step toward the slaughter they intended for us.

I stayed behind in camp to gather reports and plan the next phase. All day the news was good. In east and west Damonchok, and in the few places from the south where we received reports, the shells were wildly scattering Umbriel's soldiers in every direction. Those who did not run collapsed immediately, and those who ran fell eventually. Wherever possible, Pons's army moved in afterward to disarm the soldiers and take them prisoner.

By late afternoon we had still heard nothing from the Rock of Calad. I felt restless just sitting in the barracks, so I decided to fly south that evening to one of the temporary camps our soldiers had made after their day of flying.

Taron and I flew to the camp where we knew Rickeon, Tarius, Amandan, and Danuta were staying. We got there after dark, and as we landed I heard Rickeon's voice leading the music of the celebration in the center of camp. Rickeon was so attuned to the Spirit that he could sing so that the music would pick up and magnify his voice as well as break it into the sound of many voices. Taron also had this skill, and occasionally I too was able to do it.

The soldiers danced and sang not only because they were happy about the day's success, but also because they knew the sound was their best protection against the enemy. Dancing with them were some of the Damonchokian villagers, and as I made my way to where Tarius and Amandan stood, I even saw a few men wearing what looked like Amian uniforms!

"Why do we have Amians among us?" I asked Amandan as she reached out to hug me.

"It's the most amazing thing," she said. "Many of the Amians have been turning to Emajus and deserting Umbriel. The voice of God has so penetrated them that they have turned to Him in repentance. Many of the Damonchokians have turned to Him too. We are so happy."

Throughout the evening I met the new Emajians from Damonchok and Persus Am. They told me of the awakening of faith in Emajus over the previous few months across Damonchok and even in parts of Persus Am, especially in the Utturies. One Damonchokian woman said she knew Umbriel was lying when he said we had died in the desert. "I prayed for you every day," she said. "I knew the Lord would take you through that desert and that you would find Caladria and come back to us. But these flying machines! That I never dreamed of."

When I saw Danuta, who had been interviewing people all

evening and writing down their stories, she said, "The belief in Emajus started taking hold in these places before we came with our aerocarts and music shells. It's like the Spirit of the Lord was getting the people ready for us, revealing Himself to them more and more. No wonder Umbriel was scared. He saw people turning to the very faith he has spent his life trying to stamp out. People in the Utturies were risking death to follow Emajus, but it didn't stop them."

I stayed up most of the night celebrating with the people and listening to their stories.

At dawn I was interrupted by one of Pons's men who was working with us.

He said, "I'm sorry to bother you, sir, but I knew you would want to know. Boriock has been destroyed."

"What?"

"Boriock, sir, a town in the north, has been destroyed. It's their bomb, sir! They have it!"

"What do you mean 'destroyed'?"

"Hundreds killed. Rows and rows of buildings flattened. Even Umbriel's own terrorists were killed because they apparently didn't know how powerful the thing was."

"You're sure of this?"

"We have firsthand accounts, sir."

I sat up and pulled a robe around me. "Didn't we have music shells in the north?"

"A few, sir, but Umbriel's army hadn't penetrated that far. This bombing was the work of a small group of his terrorists, we think, not even a part of his army. They managed to squeeze through our defenses. It doesn't take many men to set up these bombs. If Umbriel sends such terrorist squads all over Damonchok and if they can target little places like Boriock that we haven't paid much attention to—"

"We've got to spread the music shells everywhere!"

"We have a message from the Panjur, sir. They would like to meet with you today if you can fly back."

I sat quietly, my thoughts flying in all directions.

He said, "What shall I tell them, sir?"

"Bring me Tarius Arc."

Tarius Arc did not come. I waited for him for the next two hours, gathering more reports and taking care of other business at hand. I sent for Tarius again, and still he did not come. Amandan did come, however, and asked, "Jeremy, what's going on? What have you sent Tarius to do?"

"I haven't sent him to do anything. I've been sending for him all morning to come and talk to me. Where is he?"

"He took an aerocart and two soldiers and left. He said there were some things he had to look into. He wouldn't tell me what he was doing. I'm very concerned. He has never kept anything secret from me before."

"Did he know about Boriock being destroyed by the bomb?"

"Yes. He was asking for all the details he could about it before he left. It worries me."

"He didn't say where he was going or when he would be back?"

"No."

"Did he know I wanted to see him?"

"Yes. I thought he had come to see you before he left. So you have no idea?"

"No. What did he think about the bomb that destroyed Boriock? Did he think it was *the* bomb?"

"He wouldn't say. He hardly said anything. He just kept asking those men questions and nodding and looking off in the distance. Then he ordered the aerocart and picked out two soldiers himself—two of the ones he liked—and left."

"Well, I sure could use his advice right now. But he must know what he's doing. I have to go to the Panjur now. When Tarius gets back, can you send him up to me?"

"I will."

The Governors were in a black mood when I met with them at the Panjur that afternoon. I pointed out to them that our music shells had stalled Umbriel's army nearly everywhere they fell. We had caused untold disruption on the Rock of Calad, and we had even lobbed some music shells into the palace at Persus Am, to give Umbriel himself a taste of the Lord's music.

But the Governors had only the bomb on their minds. After the devastation of Boriock that morning, the governors had received an ultimatum from Umbriel demanding that if the dropping of the music shells was not halted immediately, the entire nation of Damonchok would be leveled by the bomb one village at a time until the Governors surrendered. If the music shells stopped, peace negotiations could begin that would ensure the survival of Damonchok and its government.

I said, "He would be happy to negotiate with you the way he negotiated with the Rock of Calad, wouldn't he?"

The Chief Governor said, "We don't trust the Amians any more than you do, but we don't intend to sit and do nothing while they bomb our villages."

"We're not doing nothing. We're burying them in music shells. That's why they're so desperate. If we just keep it up, we'll weaken them so much that they'll never get through to bomb anything."

"Regardless of the music," said the Chief Governor, "which I admit is very impressive in its results, they still seem to be able to penetrate our defenses with just a few men, which is all it takes to wipe out a city."

"The answer, Governor, is to get them to surrender to us, not us surrender to them."

"No one is suggesting surrender, but I think it is the consensus here that if we could get the Amians out of our country for good, we would be satisfied with that."

"Of course, but I think you must realize that the only way to keep them out of your country is to defeat them. Umbriel will not settle for controlling only part of the world. He wants it all."

The Governor said, "If we negotiated a way to get Umbriel's army out right now, I believe we could keep him out if we had your flying machines to protect us. If he tried anything then, we could be ready with bombs of our own that we could rain down all over his empire. He wouldn't want to risk that. He has what he wants now, the main part of it. He got into this for the Territory of Ur. He has it. He also has the Rock of Calad. I believe we can use your flying machines as a force of deterrence rather than a force of destruction."

"With all respect, Governor, I believe that is very naive. I know Umbriel. He will not stop. And I know our people. They have come to restore the music of Emajus in the Temple of Persus Am. They won't settle for merely protecting Damonchok. This is a fight to the death now. I am sorry for the bloodshed, but there is no way to avoid it. The only way to win is just to play this out. I am asking you not to back down now. Play it out."

—⦶—

I could not get the cautious old Governors to unequivocally promise to see the war through to the end without compromise, but I did persuade them simply to try to stall the Amians for time while our music did its work. The aerocarts were so spread out by then and so many shells had already been dropped that putting an immediate halt to the operation would have been impossible anyway. As I remembered from my days as Prince of Persus Am, the Damonchokians were adept at dragging out even the tiniest detail of negotiations. They asked plodding, complicated questions, they repeatedly broke away from the negotiating table to confer among themselves, they raised endless nitpicky objections. The Amians would be frustrated but not surprised by the Damonchokians' seeming inability to come to a decision on Umbriel's ultimatum, or "cease-fire agreement," as he preferred to label it.

Tarius returned to the Panjur the next day with his aerocart loaded with boxes of materials that his two soldiers carefully guarded. Tarius asked for one of the barracks for his own use, and it was given to him. He asked that the barracks be declared off-limits to everyone but him and his assistants, and it was. He handpicked five soldiers to guard the building day and night. He told no one, not even Amandan, what he was up to. Almost immediately, however, the rumor sprang up that he was working on his own bomb, finally breaking his pledge never to build another one because Umbriel had at last unlocked the secret.

I did not believe the rumor. I did not believe Tarius would break his pledge for any reason. I also did not believe the bomb could be built just by gathering several boxes of supplies and throwing the stuff together in an empty barracks. If it were that easy, I thought, the Amians would have figured it out long before now.

Tarius did talk to me, though he would not explain what he was doing. He said he did not believe the Amians had yet figured out the bomb. "From what I've been able to find out, I think the bomb in Boriock was actually a series of bombs. But the Amians are close. They're very close. I have no doubt they'll break it now."

Over the next two days, as the music shells fell all over the Known World, and the diplomats sat at the conference table, and Tarius Arc worked nearly nonstop in his barracks, Umbriel's army managed to bomb two more small villages far from where we or the Amians had any troops stationed. On the first day the bomb killed thirty-eight people and injured many others. The one set off on the second day killed more than seventy. Tarius said the Amians did not yet have the secret, but with so many people being slaughtered, his assertion was small consolation.

After the second bombing the Chief Governor called me in and said, "We are losing patience with this strategy, Jeremy. We cannot afford to lose one village a day. The Governors want to call at least a temporary cease-fire until we can see if we can come to some arrangement with the Amians."

"Governor, it cannot be done. Our aerocarts are too scattered to call them back. By the time we could get them back, they could have finished their missions and this could all be over. We are paralyzing Umbriel's army. Persus Am itself is in an uproar with all the music. The Rock of Calad is chaos. We are winning."

"But they're getting through! They're bombing our villages!"

"They're getting through at the moment, but their days are numbered."

"How many more of our towns do you expect us to sacrifice?"

"Governor, we are trying to make it so that no town is ever sacrificed to Umbriel again. So that no one in the Known World ever has to live in fear of him. You can't 'come to an arrangement' with Umbriel. Didn't what happen to the Rock of Calad teach you that? He must be defeated. Our aerocarts will not be called back. It's out of the question. So you just keep those Amians talking."

———⊖———

The next morning I was awakened at dawn by a soldier who told me that Amandan demanded to see me at once. Before I could even get fully dressed and invite her in, she burst into my cluttered little barracks, which was scattered with maps and coffee cups and a couple piles of clothes. My guards trailed her closely, but they did not know whether to dare to restrain this great woman of Caladria.

I sent them away and invited her to sit down. She would not. Her face was flushed. I had never seen her so agitated.

"Jeremy, you've got to stop him. He's getting ready to leave again. He's packing everything into the aerocart right now. He won't talk to me or explain. We argued, something we have not done since the day he came to Caladria. You can't let him do this. It's insane."

"What is he going to do?" I asked, trying to catch up.

"I don't have the vaguest idea. He won't talk to any of us."

"What do you think it *could* be?"

"I think he's going to the Rock of Calad to try to stop that bomb. He thinks Umbriel doesn't have it yet but is close. I don't know what he's going to do to stop it, but I think that's where he's going. You've got to stop him. We can win this war without stopping that bomb. We're winning it already."

"I'll go to him," I said, standing.

"Jeremy!" she almost shouted. "He's not listening to anybody. You have to stop him. Take the aerocart away from him if you have to."

"Well, I don't think—"

"I cannot stand to lose him again, Jeremy. Not after all those years. I am pleading with you. Don't let me lose him again."

———⊖———

I asked Amandan to wait for me, and I went immediately to Tarius's barracks. He let me in without protest, but only because all but a few things in the building had already been packed away and loaded on the aerocarts.

"I need to talk to you alone," I said.

"The time for talking is almost done, my friend. I am ready to leave." He told the soldiers to take the last of the boxes out and said he would join them in a moment. "Now what do you have to say?" he asked.

"Tarius, you have that same look you always had when I talked to you in prison."

"What look is that?"

"Stubborn, confident, unalterable conviction."

His expression did not change.

"And when I saw that look I knew I probably would end up believing you were right even though I argued against you."

"I'm not as sure of myself as you think. But there comes a time when you have to decide what you think is right and then act."

"That's right. And I came here to find out what action you've decided to take."

"I am not going to tell you."

"I don't understand this, Tarius. Do you know what this is doing to Amandan?"

"My friendship with you is too deep for you to ask that question. You know how I love her."

"Then why don't you tell us? We will help you."

"Tell me the truth. Do you want me to tell you so you can help me or so you can stop me?"

"If you're going to do something drastic or unnecessary, then I'll try to help you find a better way."

"That's why I'm not going to tell you. You want to win this war, but you haven't decided how far you're willing to go to do it."

"I'm willing to do whatever it takes, but I'm not willing to sacrifice people unnecessarily."

"You still think we're going to get off easy."

"What do you mean? Nothing's been easy."

"You think the hard part's over now, don't you? You think we've given enough, the Lord should ask no more."

"Should I go looking for suffering?"

"I'm talking about you and me, Jeremy. The Lord is going to demand more from us than the others. Don't you understand that yet? Haven't you always known it deep down?"

"You act like He's *trying* to make us suffer."

"You and I, Jeremy, we can't quench His Spirit inside us. It goes on burning until it threatens to burn us up. You came to this world and shook everything up, didn't you, despite what you intended. At first you wanted to avoid the costs, be a peaceful prince, get everybody to sign a little agreement, forget their differences. But look what happened. You fulfilled your destiny. Now you can't stop it even if you want to. I can't stop it either. I'm not going to try. I'm going to do what I have to do."

He started toward the door, but I took his arm and stopped him. "The Lord is bringing us victory. We don't have to sacrifice ourselves to win."

"But victory doesn't come cheap, does it? It isn't guaranteed, is it? You couldn't have stayed with Umbriel in Persus Am and still have achieved the victory. You had to step out, take the chance of being caught and killed, take the chance of going to Caladria even though they said Caladria didn't exist. You had to suffer and nearly die to get there. You had to watch others die."

"Yes, but now we're winning. Just a few more days, a few weeks at the most. It's going our way now."

"Right. Except for the bomb. The only chance Umbriel has now is that bomb. And it looks like the Lord's not going to stop him. He's going to make us stop him—I invented the bomb. He's going to make me stop him."

"I almost think you *want* to sacrifice yourself."

Tarius shook his head. "What about you, Jeremy? What do you think is going to happen to you when this is all over? What do you think the prophecies say will happen to you once we win?"

"I will help rebuild the Temple."

"Then what? Who governs the people? Do you? Is that what the prophecies say? Did Dakin tell you that?"

"No. He never talked about that far along. He said the prophecies were too vague. Too symbolic. He said the meaning of the prophecies reveal themselves only as they happen, or close to it."

"The fact is the prophecies say nothing about you after they talk of the music being restored. The fact is the prophecies imply you don't even last that long. There is a line in one of the songs that says, 'Though he has drunk of the bitter cup You drank/ He will drink with You the cup of glory in paradise.'"

"Maybe the Lord will just take me back to where I came from," I said.

Tarius said, "I'm not trying to alarm you. I'm not saying I know for sure what the prophecies mean, and I don't pretend to know the Lord's plan. All I'm trying to say is there is a certain kind of person—and you and I are that kind—who is given a certain work to do, and it is a work that totally consumes us, as Emajus was totally consumed. When Emajus was in your land He didn't just preach His message and then retire to the countryside. You've got to realize, what we're trying to do is break the evil hold on the entire Known World so that the relationship the Caladrians have with Emajus will be possible for everyone. We shouldn't be surprised that all the evil forces in the world will try to defeat us. Now I have my task to do. I cannot let you stop me."

I sat down in Tarius's chair in the corner of the emptied-out wooden barracks. I said, "I am not going to stop you."

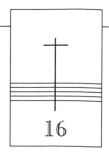

16

The day Tarius left was, ironically, one of our most successful days militarily. Hundreds of soldiers defected from Umbriel's army in Damonchok. Except for some terrorists, who always seemed to break through our wall of music, Umbriel's military effort in Damonchok appeared to be crushed.

We also had blanketed the Rock of Calad and the palace of Persus Am with music shells, but it was difficult for us to find out how much damage we had caused in those places. Rumors from Persus Am indicated the palace was in chaos. Our people had seen Umbriel's guards climbing around on the palace roofs trying to find and destroy the music shells, but they had to hunt through thousands of high and hard-to-reach nooks and corners, all the while suffering the music's furious onslaught. Many of them fell from the roofs to their deaths, and the palace continued to be saturated with music. We heard that Umbriel had ordered special earplugs made for him and his top aides, and that soundproof walls (which reportedly did not work very well) had been installed in the Dome.

The rumors from the Rock of Calad varied wildly and could not be counted on. We did believe that despite our shelling of the place, work on the bomb continued in underground shelters. We confirmed Tarius's suspicion that Boriock had been destroyed not

by one super-bomb but by a series of smaller bombs. The big
bomb, if it ever came, would be different in that it would not just
cause one big explosion but would spread a wall of flame and
destruction for miles in every direction. At one point in the day
we received a report from one of our best spies on the Rock that
Umbriel had abandoned the project in frustration and planned
instead one final massing of all his troops on the Rock, from where
they would spread across Damonchok in a giant human wall of
terror, able by sheer momentum to overcome the music. This
sounded not only unlikely but suicidal; and in fact, later in the day
our own source replaced this report with a new one. The idea to
abandon the bomb and instead use an all-out traditional attack
came not from Umbriel but from one of the chief scientists of the
bomb project, who claimed there were certain key secrets of the
bomb that could not be unlocked in time to win the war. Umbriel
had ordered him executed. We received no further information to
contradict this report, so we concluded that it was true. Such was
the degree of reliability of our information in those days.

One thing we knew for sure was that over the next three days,
Umbriel's terrorists managed to bomb three more Damonchokian
villages, one each day. After each bombing I had to meet with the
Governors and plead with them to stay the course and not to
negotiate with Umbriel. None of these bombings was as bad as
the destruction of Boriock, in which hundreds had died. All of the
villages were smaller and more isolated than Boriock, and in none
of the bombings were more than fifty people killed, a figure which,
although tragic, did not signal the destruction of the nation as
Umbriel had threatened. The Governors held firm.

Danuta traveled around Damonchok with Rickeon by day
and each night brought back amazing reports of people turning
to Emajus. Damonchok, which had always been skeptical of the
religion of the Rock of Calad, and whose believers had mostly
been underground, was almost overnight becoming an Emajian
nation.

Rickeon said, "If only we could build the Temple in Damonchok, we could start right now."

Danuta answered, "But right now the people are caught up in

the miracle and power of the music. When the war is over and things settle down, I wonder how many of them will remain believers."

I said, "Many of them will fall away. But still, many of them are getting their first chance to hear this music. We can't force them to believe. We can just let them hear the music and decide for themselves. We're doing what we came here to do."

"I only wish my father would come back," said Rickeon. "We're winning. He should be here to see it through with us."

—◯—

News about Tarius Arc did not come until three days after he left. The news came at night while I was at a celebration with new believers just a couple hours' flight from the Panjur. One of the Damonchokian military commanders, who had received word from one of our spies on the Rock, called me aside and said, "I am sorry, sir. We have been informed that Tarius Arc's aerocart has crashed on the Rock of Calad and he has been killed."

For a moment I said nothing, shoring myself up against the dread that was about to overwhelm me.

"Did our man see this firsthand?"

"I don't think so, sir, but—"

"Has anyone told Amandan?"

"No."

"Who else knows?"

"Only the messenger who brought the news to me."

"Is it likely he told anyone else?"

"I don't think so. He reported to me and then he flew directly back to his post in the Territory of Ur."

"I don't want anyone else to know about this. Not yet. I don't want Amandan to hear about it. These rumors are just not reliable enough. I don't believe Tarius is dead."

"I'm afraid it probably is true, sir. I am sorry. I know Tarius Arc was your friend. Our source is very reliable."

"That's what I hear about all of them, yet I listen to a dozen false rumors a day. Get it confirmed."

—◯—

I was tortured all that night and the next day as I waited for more news on Tarius. Why would that aerocart have crashed?

What was he carrying in it? What did he mean to accomplish by flying to the Rock?

Early the next evening after his first report, the general came back with more news.

"You were right to be skeptical, sir. We have another story about Tarius Arc, and now we are not sure which account is true."

He pulled out of his satchel a copy of Umbriel's informational, which he was still publishing sporadically from the Rock of Calad. The general said, "It says they have captured Tarius Arc alive. They have a shadow picture of him."

In the picture—stark and vague and painted over as all of these pictures always were, making them look more like drawings than photos—Tarius stood alone in front of a wall of gray blocks. His hands were bound with cords in front of him. He was not smiling, but he looked unharmed.

The general said, "They captured him alone, it says. Two days ago. The aerocart and the soldiers with him got away, but they did capture some subversive materials he had with him."

"What materials?"

"Doesn't say. But it could be a trick. They could have used an old picture."

"They could. But he was dressed this way. And the aerocart was loaded down with whatever he had been working on in his barracks."

"Well anyway, they say when they get from him the information they need, it will be the turning point of the war."

I said, "If they couldn't get it from him when they had him in prison, they'll never get it now."

"They say that Tarius Arc is a much changed man. They say he is disillusioned with the Damonchokians and—I'm sorry to say this, sir—with you. It says Tarius believes you are a fraud, who could not get Umbriel's throne one way so you're trying another."

"Obviously it's propaganda. No one will believe it."

"Obviously, sir."

But in the air hung the unspoken question, if Umbriel's story about Tarius is untrue, then what *would* explain why Tarius Arc would fly unauthorized to the Rock of Calad, land there, and get caught with "subversive materials"? The general stood looking at me until I dismissed him. I had nothing else to say.

———◯———

The appearance of Tarius's picture in the informational made it impossible for me to keep the rumors from Amandan until we found out the truth about him. I went to her right away to tell her everything we knew.

When I looked for her in our camp, I was surprised to hear that she had left it and had accepted the invitation of a Governor's wife to stay in one of the residences in the Panjur. Before Tarius left, Amandan, like the rest of us, had felt it more appropriate to stay with our soldiers in the barracks rather than isolate ourselves in more luxurious accommodations.

I found Amandan in a sun-drenched sitting room, reclining on a sofa and wearing a bright Caladrian dress. There was no trace of the agitation I had seen in her as Tarius had planned his departure. She was calmer than she had been since we left Caladria, but there was a hard edge to her unsmiling quietness.

I sat in a chair a few feet away from her and told her the rumors of Tarius's death and the later rumors and shadow picture in the informational.

"What do they plan to do with him?" she asked.

"I don't know. They seem to hope that because he is so unhappy with me, he'll help them finish the bomb."

"Which of course he won't."

"No."

"So I assume they'll kill him."

These words were spoken without emotion. The room seemed unnaturally bright, as if the sun were hurtling toward us and was about to consume the entire room with one fiery gasp.

"I don't think we should assume anything yet," I said. "We don't know the truth. Rumors from the Rock are often unreliable. Maybe this is all part of his strange plan, and when he gets back it will make sense to us."

"Tarius is never coming back, Jeremy, and you know it."

"Amandan—"

"It has taken me three days to come to grips with the truth, but now I have done it, and none of your empty words are going to turn me from it. Inside I am screaming against it, but I have decided to face it. Tarius is not coming back. He has decided to sacrifice himself. I don't why. Time will tell. But whatever's happening is exactly what he intended to happen."

"I don't blame you for thinking—"

"I just keep wondering why the Lord would let us lose him. I just keep wondering how much suffering it is going to take to satisfy Him. Surely it would be easy for Him to end this all right now and just let us build the Temple if that's what He wants us to do. I don't understand why we have to be in pain every last step of the way."

"We are in a war. Tarius believed it was his destiny, it was God's calling, to do what he has done. He believed that when the music is restored to the Temple, the relationship that the Caladrians have known with Emajus will be possible for everyone. He believed we should expect all the evil forces of the world to fight us to the death to keep such a good thing from happening. He said suffering was unavoidable."

She stayed quiet for a moment. "Does that answer satisfy you?" she asked.

"No."

"Thank you for coming, Jeremy. I'd like you to leave me alone now."

—◯—

Despite the loss of Tarius, over the next seven days our war effort with the music shells was dramatically successful. We now completely controlled Damonchok and the Territory of Ur. Umbriel's troops had either retreated to the Rock, been taken prisoner, died, or converted to Emajianism. General Pons, eager to get back into the forefront of the war, planned a final assault on the Rock of Calad. Our music shells had weakened Umbriel's army there, but still they somehow managed to hang on, both by crushing our music shells one by one and by hiding in the underground caves and bunkers that the Rock afforded. The Rock, we believed, would eventually have fallen by the power of the music alone, but Pons wanted to hasten its fall and stop any possibility that the bomb would be unleashed on us. Under normal circumstances a direct assault on the Rock would have been considered not only risky, but almost suicidal. However, Pons believed his enemy was so weak that the operation would be swift and smooth, with little loss of Damonchokian life.

The Governors were not so sure. Ever leery of shedding blood, they reluctantly agreed to allow Pons to move his army into position for the attack, but they did not give him final approval for it. They still believed Umbriel could be pressured into a "reasonable settlement."

Tarius's "defection" threw them into a panic, and after several days of false propaganda in Umbriel's informationals about how much Tarius hated me, I was summoned to the Governors' conference room to explain his actions. I told them the only thing I could be certain of was that Tarius had not decided to help Umbriel. I had no idea what his plan was, but I knew he was absolutely trustworthy. This did not satisfy them. They read to me the parts of Umbriel's informational that said Tarius believed I was a fraud and that he had decided to join the fight against me. Mere propaganda, I said. Ridiculous. They grilled me about exactly what Tarius had told me. What had we argued about? What was his state of mind? In the middle of their questioning Pons came in for a while and sat in the far corner of the room. Maybe it was just that the questions had made me paranoid, but it seemed to me as he sat there with his fist at his mouth that he was barely suppressing a smile. Finally I stood to leave and said, "I'm sure Umbriel would be delighted at how well his propaganda has divided us. I have nothing else to say."

Over the next two days two more Damonchokian villages were bombed. Seven Amian terrorists were captured and executed. Pons's army massed for the final assault.

—◯—

On the ninth day after Tarius was captured, we received two ominous messages from our sources on the Rock and at the palace of Persus Am. The message from the Rock was short and highly suspect: Tarius Arc had been executed the previous day. We, however, suspected that our own spy might have been caught and executed; our intermediaries told us that his message did not contain his usual flourishes, and they questioned whether it was really from him.

The other message was a little more believable. It said that Umbriel, though harassed and physically and mentally weakened by our endless barrage of music shells, had ordered a feast for his entire household and top politicians the previous night. The vapors, which had scarcely been used since the War began, were burst open for the "victory banquet." As his guests ate and drank and absorbed the colored vapors, the Father-King declared, "The secret of the great bomb finally has been unravelled. The Lord God has smiled on us. Victory is at hand."

The message further said that according to palace rumors, Umbriel would secretly leave the palace in the next day or two and go to the Rock of Calad, where he would personally oversee the "demolition of Damonchok."

$$-\!\!\bigcirc\!\!-$$

Umbriel never made his trip to the Rock of Calad.

For on the day he was to set out to admire his ultimate weapon of destruction, the Rock of Calad ceased to exist.

According to those witnesses close enough to see the holocaust but far enough away to live to tell about it, the Rock became a volcano, starting with an ominous rumble and eventually erupting its contents—bodies, buildings, trees, uncountable tons of dirt and rocks—into the air, blackening the sky. When it was over, the Rock of Calad was no longer a distinct geographical entity.

Not only was everyone on the Rock killed that day, but hundreds of others in the valleys that surrounded the Rock were also buried in its rubble. Among those killed were several hundred in Pons's army, who had massed for their assault. Several dozen of our Caladrian soldiers were killed when the eruption knocked their aerocarts from the sky.

Those far enough away to escape death said the first sign of the impending destruction was a rumbling in the ground, much like an earthquake, that brought them out of their tents and barracks and focused their attention on the Rock, from which the roaring and shaking seemed to originate. Then came the explosions, so massive that even in the distant camps water pitchers crashed to the floor and tents collapsed. As the terrified soldiers stared toward the cliffs of the Rock, they saw clouds of gray rise from somewhere near the center. It was not gray smoke, but gray rocks and dust and rubble of every kind. It was as if every particle of matter on the Rock had suddenly turned into a little bomb and had burst in unison, hurtling out in every direction.

Everyone hid from the destruction, burying themselves in trenches or under tables or anywhere they could find, and in doing so they were buried by the shredded remains of human carcasses or tree branches or pieces of furniture or a dish or a book or a child's doll.

When the Rock of Calad finally ceased its self-destruction it had turned into a soft mound of debris, charred and dead. It grew quiet, a tomb, with the only noise and motion coming from a few fires the rubble had not quenched. There were no screams and moans; everyone was dead. The sky was dark gray, choked with dust. If someone had been alive to stand at the center of the Rock and look as far as he could in every direction, he would have thought himself the last living organism on the planet.

We were never to know the part Tarius Arc played in the final events on the Rock of Calad. Perhaps in burying with himself the secret of his weapon, he achieved with that one magnificent explosion the atonement he craved for ever having invented the thing. Or perhaps his plan went awry and the bomb destroyed his beloved Rock despite his intentions to stop it. Whatever his intentions, the result was that Umbriel's best scientists, his best soldiers, his most important military base, and his best weapon were now buried forever. Our victory, it seemed, was at hand.

—◯—

Danuta, Taron, and I flew as close as we could to the devastated region around the Rock. It was dangerous to fly too close because all the debris in the air could clog the vents and engine of the aerocart and cause it to crash. But after we landed, we walked closer to the area of destruction. It was an eerie sight, dust-covered people scrounging through the ashes for who knows what, entire families squatting in the dust and wailing over the loss of someone whose remains they would never find, lost in endless acres of ashes.

General Pons's temporary headquarters was far enough from the Rock that it was not damaged, so we stayed there for the next few days while we decided what we would do next. Some of the key Damonchokian Governors also joined us, including the Chief Governor, who had not left the Panjur during the entire war until now. What had happened to the Rock, though horrifying, was also too fascinating for people to stay away from. They had to walk around in the devastation for themselves, feel the haunting coldness caused by the blocking out of the sun, feel the ashes burning their eyes and covering their skin. We huddled in little groups, saying the same trite phrases over and over about how awesome and horrible the destruction was. For me losing Tarius was like losing a father. I stood in the ashes with Danuta and Taron and cried for him. I cried for the others. All the loss we had known up to that point seemed to wrap around me like the cloud of debris that smothered the Rock—I grieved for Anne, for Dakin, for Jank, for all the others I did not even know.

On the third day after the explosion we held a memorial service for the dead, with music and prayers and tributes to the soldiers and civilians and to Tarius Arc. Amandan did not come. I had tried to speak to her just after I learned of the destruction of the Rock, but she would see no one but Rickeon. She stayed secluded in the Panjur, in the comfortable residence of her new friends. After two days she even sent Rickeon away, and he joined us. "She doesn't say a word," he said. "She just stares out the window and doesn't say a word."

Though from our perspective in the ashes it looked as if there could be no more war to fight, our enemy was not yet dead. Even as we mourned our dead, Umbriel shored up the defenses of his shrinking world and planned new strategies to thwart us. We received rumors from Persus Am that the music had finally eaten into his brain and made him lose touch with reality. He had become a madman, determined to fight to the death no matter how slim his chances for victory. I was skeptical of this report. Umbriel would *want* us to think him mad, it seemed to me. I believed we still faced a shrewd and supremely adaptable enemy. He still controlled Persus Am and the Utturies, despite our musical bombardment. He still had a formidable army protecting him. To me, our victory was assured, but we would have to march right into Umbriel's Dome and take it.

General Pons felt restless sitting among the ruins of the Rock. He was eager to move his army into Persus Am and finish his conquest once and for all. Persus Am was the last battlefield. Umbriel's forces in Wilmoroth, Damonchok, the Territory of Ur, and the Rock had either withdrawn or disintegrated. Umbriel now controlled only the land that had been his before the war, minus his precious piece of the Territory of Ur.

Though Pons did not trust me enough to discuss his concerns with me, I knew from my other sources that he was afraid that the Damonchokian Governors, with their bent toward negotiations and deal making, might try to put an end to the bloodshed before the full victory was won. Since Umbriel had been pushed back to his side of the mountain, they might say, maybe it's time to call off the war and start the rebuilding. Pons would have hated this scenario. He wanted to vanquish Umbriel indisputably. He wanted to march through the palace of Persus Am smashing Umbriel's furniture and drinking his wine. He wanted to sit in Umbriel's chair in the Dome and spin round and round, looking up to watch the jewels sparkle red in the ceiling. He wanted to explode Umbriel's vapors and feast on his steaks and gorge himself on the Father-King's fancy desserts.

He wanted victory, and he wanted his army to achieve it. So far the victories had been ours, not his. Our music shells had pushed Umbriel out of Damonchok. Tarius had destroyed the Rock. But Persus Am would belong to Pons. His soldiers marched the day after the memorial service.

We stayed with the soldiers on their march to Persus Am. The remnants of Umbriel's army were dug in around the Utturies and around Umbriel's palace, so we faced no resistance crossing the mountains into the desert region of Persus Am. Our aerocarts pounded the Utturies and the palace with music shells day and night. For all we knew Umbriel's army could be dead by the time we reached them. Even if they hung on and refused to surrender, we expected little difficulty shoving them aside and ending Umbriel's reign forever.

Our celebrations each night in the camps were intense. Though the horror on the Rock was never far from our thoughts, we were relieved to be physically away from the place and to be on the final march toward victory. The world seemed filled with the fabulous music of the Lord. Many of the Damonchokian soldiers had become believers, and they danced and sang with greater fervor than anyone. Not since the first War had the ground of Persus Am shaken with the Lord's voice. Even General Pons, who was not a believer, stood each night just outside the ring of torches that marked the celebration field and listened in amazement at the music that filled the night sky. Never did he complain about the celebrations or order his men away from them. The general controlled every detail of his men's lives during the day, but the Emajians controlled the night.

As we got closer to the Utturies, we began to pick up rumors of some sort of disturbance near the palace of Persus Am. At first we thought it was a riot by the people of Persus Am, and we hoped that maybe they would overthrow Umbriel themselves to avoid the needless final battle Umbriel was pushing them toward. But later one of the generals came to me and said, "We're still trying to gather information, but apparently Umbriel's troops were firing on each other within the palace walls."

"Firing on each other?"

"That's what we heard. And then apparently several hundred of them fled the palace and headed south."

"Are you sure they were fleeing, or is Umbriel just moving his troops toward the Utturies?"

"Supposedly those who fled were firing and being fired upon all the way."

"Unbelievable. Those soldiers at the palace are supposed to be the best and most loyal men Umbriel has. And he's losing even them."

"They're under constant torture from the music shells. And they must know that Umbriel can't win."

"It looks that way. Still, even with several hundred defectors, Umbriel still has plenty of soldiers to give us a good fight."

"That's right. Umbriel has surprised us before. I won't call it victory until the man is dead and we're standing in his Dome drinking his champagne. Or standing in the ruins of his Dome. Whatever it takes."

———⊖———

The one thing that had made the absence of Anne bearable to me was that no one ever mentioned her name. After my encounter with her in Caladria, Danuta, Tarius, and everyone else seemed to know without my telling them that I did not want to talk about her anymore. My belief that I would never see her again as long as I was in this world made discussing her simply too painful.

So the news that Danuta brought me on a hot afternoon in the desert of Persus Am was as jarring as anything I had ever heard. When Danuta came to me holding an informational from Persus Am, I sat under the awning of my tent talking to two of the Damonchokian Governors who had flown in to be with us for the day. Danuta asked the Governors if they could leave us alone for a while because she had something urgent to discuss with me. This was an unusually undiplomatic request from Danuta, who knew that the very image-sensitive Governors might take offense at being dismissed so abruptly.

As soon as they walked away, I said, "It must be bad news."

"I don't know," she said. "It may be nothing more than one of Umbriel's tricks, but I wanted you to hear it from me rather than someone else. We just got a copy of Umbriel's latest informational. It says that the woman you have talked about, Anne, is in his palace."

"What? That's ridiculous."

"It probably is. It says she came much the way you did, in a swirl of light—he doesn't mention music—and she came into the courtyard of the palace. He says there were lots of witnesses. He quotes them. He describes her a little."

"How does he describe her?"

"He doesn't give a description all in one place, but it says she has brown hair, shorter than most Amian women, and it's curled and loose about her shoulders, and her clothes were altogether foreign and colorful. He doesn't give much on her clothes. And let's see, she's about my height, her eyes are brown, and when she smiles her teeth are very white."

"All that is true. But it could describe lots of women. Does she say anything?"

"He doesn't quote her directly, but he says she has come to take you home. Umbriel's palace will be the end of the road for you. From there you will go home."

The air suddenly seemed so stiflingly hot that I could not breathe. I stood up as if to find more air to breathe. "So maybe this is how it ends," I said.

"Jeremy, Umbriel is very clever. He must have known how much you cared for this woman. This could be a final, desperate ploy."

"I know that. I know. We need to think about this. Do we have anybody who can confirm it?"

"I've already got people working on it."

"Does the informational say what he's going to do with her? Would he hurt her or—"

"It doesn't say. He calls her a Visitor, a guest. We don't know anything else."

"Let me know the minute you find out anything. I don't want to let myself believe this, but if it's true—God help us—then what?"

In just a couple of days we would be ready to strike the Utturies. I felt completely distracted by the unconfirmed news about Anne. We were unable to find out any more details right away, and events would not slow down enough to let me sort it all out in my mind. General Pons was eager to attack the Utturies as soon as possible, before Umbriel had a chance to recover from the devastation of the Rock of Calad. Some of the Governors, however, were in favor of trying to negotiate a surrender from Umbriel to avoid what could be a bloody battle in the Utturies. The region was thought to be filled with bombs that Umbriel could set off even if his army suffered humiliating defeat. Pons argued that it was a risk we would have to take. He believed Umbriel would never surrender as long as the Utturies provided a buffer between our army and the city of Persus Am. Only when we were at Umbriel's doorstep could we expect his surrender, and maybe not even then. Negotiating with Umbriel now was not only hopeless, but it also gave him precious time to strengthen his defenses.

As much as I hated bloodshed, I believed Pons was right. I did not believe Umbriel would surrender as long as there was the faintest hope that he could fight us off. He would not accept defeat to spare the people in the Utturies from suffering. They were born to suffer, to be his maids and gardeners and shoe shiners. And if they had to serve as a shield, well then, so be it.

As we debated our strategy, marching ever closer to the point where a fight would be inevitable, the group of Amian soldiers who had split off from Umbriel's army in the palace broke through our "wall" of music in the Utturies and headed straight toward us. After hearing of their skirmish at the palace with troops loyal to Umbriel, we had tracked them by aerocart as they marched toward the Utturies. There they picked up new recruits and had three more minor scuffles with fellow soldiers before they marched into the desert. By then there were nearly a thousand of them. Their leaders signalled to our soldiers in one of the aerocarts, who landed and took a message from them. The soldiers brought the message directly to me:

"Visitor Jeremy! The Amian soldiers who are marching toward us wish to announce that they are followers of Emajus who are willing to fight and die with their fellow believers in order to remove Umbriel from the throne of Persus Am. They wish to surrender to you and offer you their services. Their leader wishes to come to you ahead of the others and speak to you personally."

"Who is their leader?" I asked.

"We don't know, sir. She did not speak to us. She sent a messenger."

"She?"

"Yes, sir. The messenger pointed to the woman who wishes to speak to you."

"What did she look like?"

"Her face was covered with a veil because the sand was blowing. She was wearing a long Amian cloak to protect her from the wind. That's really all we could tell. Her clothes were very colorful."

"A woman."

"Yes."

We watched her ride toward us on her camuck across the desert, her soldiers barely visible in the distance. The wind puffed out her long, loose clothes in every direction, making her look as if she might float away like a hot air balloon. Danuta and Taron sat with me, and General Pons and some of his friends were nearby. Behind us our soldiers were on alert, in the unlikely event that the thousand Amians were there not to surrender but to fight. Music filled the air, but the Amians, as far as we could see, stood unflinching.

The woman's head was partially veiled. Before she got close enough for me to recognize her, I figured out one thing. She was not Anne. That is what I had hoped, of course, though I had said nothing to anyone. I had imagined Anne waiting for me in the palace of Persus Am, and then finding out that I was in the desert marching toward her. She would ask to be taken to me, but Umbriel would refuse. Some of his officers, though, would know that she wanted to leave, and they would rescue her as they too fled from Umbriel's crumbling kingdom. They would put her in front of their army, this new Visitor from God, and she would unite them with the prophet Jeremy and the Amians. This was the scenario I had constructed in my mind, but the woman was not Anne. The hair that flew out from her veil had a reddish tint. She was tall and thin, with a long neck that made her posture look unusually erect—

I jumped up and ran forward, startling everyone and prompting General Pons to send two of his guards after me. "It's Princess Shellan!" I shouted.

"Who?" asked Pons, close behind his soldiers.

"Umbriel's oldest daughter, Princess Shellan." I ran toward her, and she soon recognized me.

"Help me down," she said. "I just hate riding these things."

"Shellan! I can't believe it," I said, helping her off the camuck.

"I escaped," she said. "I got away from him. You did it, so I figured why shouldn't I? And about a thousand soldiers decided to go with me. It was their idea really. I'm just the mascot."

I introduced Shellan to Pons, Danuta, and Taron, who had caught up with us. "Shellan was always a rebel," I said. "It shouldn't surprise me that she would take a brave step like this. You could have been killed!"

"Well, it's a war, isn't it? I've been locked away most of the time anyway. Daddy somehow didn't think I believed in what he was doing."

While Pons took care of the soldiers, I took Shellan back to my tent to talk. As we sat on pillows on the ground and enjoyed a cool drink together, I asked, "Do you know anything about that report in your father's informational that says he has Anne there in the palace with him?"

"Anne? No. I did read that. I do know they've got somebody up there that they've been trying to keep a secret."

"But you haven't seen her?"

"No. I haven't even been allowed up there since shortly after you left."

"Did they keep you in the prison where they had held Tarius?"

"Oh no. Officially I wasn't a prisoner at all. It was like my grandmother's situation. I was given nice rooms and kept out of sight. I only heard rumors every now and then, and I haven't heard much about this secret person they have. But there is somebody. There's no reason it couldn't be Anne, but I didn't have time to worry much about that. We were just trying to get out alive."

"Do you think your father will have sense enough to surrender?"

"I don't think so. You wouldn't believe the insanity that has taken over that place. Some people say my father has lost his mind.

They say the music has eaten away at his brain. And the people around him—Vanus and that crowd—are just as bad. They still think they can win. They're willing to sacrifice everything and everybody."

"Will the rest of his soldiers stick with him?"

"Many of them will. Many of them passionately hate you and the Emajians and the music with all their might. But every day more of them turn to Emajianism and desert my father. And he's losing the support of most of the wealthy families in Persus Am, who can see the end and are afraid they're going to lose everything. They're ready to negotiate and give you your Temple just so you won't take away their houses and lands and fortunes. A lot of the soldiers who came with me are from those families. We haven't come empty-handed. We have weapons and food supplies and contacts with spies and sympathizers in the Utturies and Persus Am and loads of secrets about my father's military. You can beat him, but I don't think you'll get him to surrender. He'd rather go down fighting."

Shellan repeated her message to some of the Governors later in the day, but instead of persuading them that Umbriel would never surrender, her words made them hope that his situation had grown so desperate that he would have no choice but to negotiate. Pons, delighted with the weapons and soldiers and secrets that had been dumped in his lap, was exasperated with the caution of the Governors and was ready to proceed immediately with the liberation of the Utturies.

The Governors said no. They would give Umbriel one final chance.

———○———

Umbriel's chance was blasted into a million pieces that very night when a bomb rocked our camp not far from where I slept. Twenty-three of our soldiers were killed that night, and seven others died the next day. Dozens of others were injured. The force of the explosion caused my tent to collapse on me, and then a shower of debris fell on top of me, cutting me in several places but not seriously injuring me. I had a terrible time extricating myself from the tent and the debris, however, and my rescuers feared the worst when they first saw the garbage heap under which I was buried. Several of the Damonchokian Governors were in the camp. Though none of them was injured, this was their first sight of battle up close. They were dazed and frightened as they watched the soldiers pull dead bodies from the wreckage. To my surprise, General Pons personally escorted them around the camp to show them the bloody corpses and the screaming injured men whose legs or arms had been shorn off by the bomb.

The immediate suspicion for the act focused on Shellan's Amian soldiers, but before the night was over our soldiers caught a group of terrorists, stumbling through the desert because of the force of the music, carrying with them the evidence of their deed.

General Pons wasted no time in turning the tragedy to his advantage. He immediately sent out his troops to "find the perpetrators of the bomb," but they were really beginning their march toward Pons's carefully planned attack on the Utturies. When Umbriel's paranoid and desperate army in the Utturies learned that our men were on the march, they immediately tried to counterattack with more bombs. These fell harmlessly in the desert ahead of our troops, but they gave Pons the excuse he needed to press forward. There was no stopping him then. The Governors stood by ineffectually and waited for the battle. There was no talk of negotiation that night.

Our victory was swift and complete. Our soldiers met resistance at first, but the Amians were already so weakened and demoralized by the music that within a few hours they abandoned the dirty slums of the Utturies and fled toward the palace of Persus Am, their last stronghold. By early afternoon the Utturies were ours.

—◯—

Pons immediately set up his headquarters in the only section of the city that was not a slum—the abandoned military district from which the Amian generals were to have kept the Utturans under control and from which they were supposed to have directed the annihilation of the Emajian invaders. All that remained of the Amians were a few remnants of their pampered lifestyle in the midst of the poverty of the Utturies. The military buildings were made of stone, not the crumbly synthetic material from which most of the sagging structures in the Utturies were constructed. The offices and boardrooms were wood panelled, with high ceilings, luxurious carpets, paintings, and tapestries. There were pools and gymnasiums and lavishly decorated banquet halls. It was as if a piece of Umbriel's palace had been cut away and transported to the middle of this squalid poverty.

When I arrived in the Utturies by aerocart early on the morning of our victory, the military compound was so crowded that there was nowhere for my aerocart and the three others traveling with me to land. We had to land a few blocks away, in an empty lot in a smoky, chaotic slum. Danuta, Rickeon, and I were immediately besieged by Utturans, dirty and emaciated, who cheered and cried and grabbed at my clothes. The other aerocarts were filled with guards sent to protect me, but we were so vastly outnumbered by the throngs of Utturans that it was all we could do to keep moving slowly forward toward the military compound. The music from the shells played loud and fast, a whirlwind of strings and trumpets and drums. I shook the hands that reached across the guards to me, and at one point someone ripped off most of one of my sleeves. The people, though happy to be freed from Umbriel's grip, looked hollow-eyed and starved. Umbriel had hoarded food for his own troops and had given the Utturans barely enough to survive.

When I finally made it to the compound, I found Pons and the others drinking champagne and eating elaborately decorated cakes in one of the banquet rooms. They were rifling through some of the papers taken from the Amian generals' offices. Pons said, "I'm glad they didn't rip off *all* your clothes, Jeremy. Have some dessert. We're celebrating. We're reading their love letters. That's about all they left behind." This was the friendliest string of sentences Pons had ever spoken to me. For the moment he had dropped his suspicion of me. He was tasting victory. He had conquered the Utturies. His dirty boots left footprints on the plush carpet.

"It looks like Umbriel has been starving the people," I said. "Do we have some food we can give them?"

Pons said, "Plenty. We've captured their storehouses, every-thing. You can start passing it out this afternoon. And I'm sure he has a lot more stashed away inside the palace walls. In a few days, the Utturans can eat right in Umbriel's own dining room for all I care."

Just as a soldier handed me a piece of cake on a fancy china plate, our building was rocked by an explosion across the street. My plate crashed to the floor, and at first I had the illusion that the wall closest to the street was falling toward me. The wall held, but the blast knocked pictures off the wall and buckled the table that held the cake. One of the soldiers idiotically tried to catch the cake as it fell, and it smeared across his uniform and crumpled on the floor.

In the first moment of silence after the blast one of Pons's officers appeared in the room and yelled, "He's got more bombs hidden! They're in the walls! They're all over the place!"

"I thought you had cleared them all out!" shouted Pons.

"We did, sir, but those in the walls are so well hidden—"

"Get these people out!" Pons ordered, pointing at me and my entourage.

In an instant we were swept out the door, where the rubble of a building blocked our path. Across the street the bomb had peeled off the building's front wall, leaving its insides exposed to us. A fancy sofa teetered precariously on the edge of a third-story room while rich red drapes burned all around it. Paintings in gaudy gold frames melted in front of us. Bookshelves leaned slowly forward and then toppled, spilling their contents into the streets. The crowds were in such chaos that getting back to our aerocarts was like swimming through a choppy ocean. It took every soldier available to punch us through the crowd and keep them away from the aerocarts long enough to get us into the air. Many people in the crowd were angry at us because they thought, absurdly, that we had bombed the buildings ourselves. They screamed, "Why do you want to kill us? Why do you want to kill us?" As we floated above them, a wave of bodies jolting forward and backward like some bizarre, writhing organism, Danuta said,

"Look what Umbriel has done to these people! Even when we win, how will we ever get this place straightened out?"

"We're just here to build a Temple," said Rickeon. "The rest of it they'll have to figure out for themselves."

"That won't be good enough," she said. "The Lord's Spirit will never inhabit this kind of chaos. We're going to have to help them. This war is far from finished."

—⊖—

In General Pons's view, the war was only hours from being finished. The next battle would be the final one. There was nowhere for Umbriel's soldiers to retreat to. Unless Umbriel surrendered, his soldiers would have to fight to the death. It would be the bloodiest battle of the war. Therefore, the Governors were determined to use all their powers of diplomacy to elicit Umbriel's surrender. But first they had to hold Pons back. He was ready to attack while Umbriel was still reeling from the defeat in the Utturies. The Chief Governor told Pons that if he tried to launch an attack this time without permission, his command would be revoked and he would be arrested. This warning worked, at least for the moment.

We set up camp just north of the Utturies. All that stood between us and the walls of Persus Am were some factories, several shacks, and a few miles of empty space that the first Umbriel had established to keep the Utturan slums away from his doorstep. For me, though I had been able to confirm nothing about Anne's presence in the palace, every step we took toward Persus Am was another step toward her and toward going home. On the afternoon of our victory in the Utturies, Danuta brought me something that only fueled my faith and desire.

The soldiers were still setting up my tent when Danuta appeared with one of Umbriel's informationals in her hand.

"Where can we go?" she said.

I took her to Pons's tent nearby, where we sat at a table under his awning.

"He released this today," she said and handed me the paper.

Most of the page was covered with a shadow picture of a woman's face. It was distorted as all shadow pictures are, but the moment my eyes met those of the image I knew who she was. Her gaze was turned slightly away from the camera, as if she were embarrassed by all the attention. I looked at every detail—her smile, her hair, the shape of her face. I had no doubt.

"It's Anne," I said.

"Can you be sure?" Danuta asked. "You've barely looked at it."

"I knew the first instant. Incredible. So she's really here."

"But that's not a very good picture. Are you sure—"

"Danuta, when I looked at this picture, it was like looking at Anne herself. I know it's a bad picture, but it's her. It's like losing somebody in a crowd, and even in the hundreds of faces if you can just catch the familiar glance you've found them. You don't need to see their whole body close up to find them. Just that one familiar look. This is it. This is her."

"Is there any way they could have gotten her picture without her being here? Did you bring one with you?"

"No."

"Did you draw one?"

"No. There have been no pictures of her here. What does Umbriel say he's going to do with her?"

"It's not what Umbriel says that we're wondering about. It's what she says."

"What do you mean?"

"She has a message here, written in a language none of us knows. We assume it's your language."

Danuta opened the page and showed me the box in the upper left corner where English words appeared. The letters were hand written, but not in Anne's handwriting. They must have been copied by someone not used to writing English, and some of the letters were so distorted that it was hard to make out the words. I read the message and then translated it for Danuta:

"My dear Jeremy, The Lord has sent me here to stop the bloodshed and to take you home. Umbriel knows that all is lost. He knows that he has one last function to perform, which is to secure the dignity of his people and prevent their annihilation. He believes he can still play a role for the good and prevent everything he has built from being destroyed. You must stop the killing for the moment and come to speak for your friends. Umbriel knows that you and I have been sent by the Lord. He will listen to your friends only if they speak through you. He has agreed to a plan that will end the war and end our involvement in this place. No one else needs to die. I love you. Anne."

"So this is how it ends," said Danuta. "Maybe. Does it really say Umbriel knows all is lost?"

"Yes."

"Amazing. That is certainly something new. And in his own informational. I wonder if he really knows she put that in."

"I don't know. I wish she would say more. I wonder how she is, how they're treating her. I wonder what she means about us going home. I wonder what her plan is."

"We need to meet with Pons and the Governors."

"Yes. Let's call them together right away."

—◯—

We met an hour later around a table in Pons's tent. Tully, two other Governors, Danuta, Pons, and I were there, along with several of Pons's aides. I told them about Anne's message in the informational.

Pons dismissed it as a trick and argued that we should attack immediately before Umbriel had a chance to prepare.

He and one of the Governors argued about this for a while until Tully interrupted and said, "It's too late to surprise Umbriel, Pons. He's been prepared for weeks. We have plenty of time to attack, and the result will be devastating for all of us whether we do it now or later. So let's turn our attention to this informational. Umbriel seems to have combined Anne's promise with his own threat. In the same informational where he lets her say all is lost and it's time for peace, he also threatens us with the capacity for mass destruction that he says he still maintains. He wants this to end, but he's holding out for something."

"What do you think he wants?" I asked.

"I don't know," said Tully, "but it's worth listening to him."

Pons said, "We should not let him gain anything from this war. He has caused the death of thousands. We need total surrender from him."

"I agree," said Tully. "But I also want the killing to stop."

"So let me go in there, talk to Anne, talk to Umbriel, and bring their plan back to you," I said.

Danuta said, "It's too dangerous for you to go in there. If this is a trick—"

"If it's a trick, then you'll figure that out soon enough, and Pons can go in and attack."

"But in the meantime you could be killed," said Danuta.

Tully said, "Umbriel is looking for a way out. If his goal was just to kill more people, he could have waited until we attacked and then blown everything up. I think he wants to surrender. He has nothing to gain by fighting anymore."

Pons said, "But if anything goes wrong, we're going in immediately. No more stalling."

"I agree," I said. "Let's go."

—◯—

That night we worked out the details of my arrangements to meet Umbriel in his palace at dawn the next day.

I did not sleep that night at all. In the camp we celebrated. We all believed the war was over. I could keep my mind on nothing but seeing Anne the next day. I thought of her words about taking me home, and I wanted to say good-bye to my friends. The word *good-bye* was never spoken, but I did spend time alone that night with Taron, Danuta, Shellan, and Rickeon. None of them would speak directly about my leaving, preferring to believe it would not happen soon. But I could feel the place slipping away from me. I could hear it in the music.

Taron did not want to talk at all. She pulled me into the music. "Feel the Lord's pleasure," she said. "Feel what we have done. Feel His happiness that everyone will hear His voice."

I did feel it. I felt His love wrapping around me and charging through me. I was going home.

—◯—

My aerocart landed inside the walls of one of Umbriel's gardens just after dawn that morning. Nothing inside the palace grounds gave any indication that this was a war-torn, crumbling kingdom about to be surrendered to the enemy. The lawns were a bright green carpet of uniform height. Some of the sprinklers still spewed a thin mist. The bushes were trimmed, the walks swept, the flowers in bloom.

Accompanied by ten Damonchokian soldiers, I walked across the garden to the door of the palace, where Hamlin met me. He looked older, thinner. His eyes looked sunken and somehow hollow. The music from the shells swirled all around us. His ears were completely covered by a plastic device that looked like earmuffs. They apparently could not block out all the music, because his face was pained. He held out his hand and with a forced smile said, "Jeremy. Good to see you again. The Father-King is waiting for you in the Dome." As if this were yet another reception.

"Where is Anne?" I asked Hamlin as we walked.

"You will see her in the Dome."

The wide, heavy doors were opened, and I walked inside. Upon seeing the Dome for the first time, the soldiers escorting me were just as overwhelmed by its height and beauty as I had been. They stared openmouthed at the thousands of red jewels that shimmered in the light. The whole room radiated power.

Umbriel stood in the center of the room, by his desk, surrounded by several of his advisers. He was dressed in a magnificent red jacket covered with jewels. He wore a blue silk shirt and blue slacks. His shoes were shined, his nails were trimmed, and every hair was perfectly in place, but nothing could hide the fact that he had become an old man. His face was gaunt and ashen. His shoulders were slightly stooped, his arms and legs thin. The skin under his eyes was dark and puffy. He did not smile.

"Where is Anne?" I said.

"She will be here shortly," he said.

"I won't go any further with this until I speak to her and see that she's safe."

"Come and sit down, Jeremy. It's been a long time since we've talked."

"Anne," I insisted.

"I will send for her. Hamlin, will you ask her to come in, please? Now, Jeremy, come and enjoy this historic moment when you and I stand together for the last time under the great Dome of the Palace of Persus Am. Look around, Jeremy. If you had been smarter you could have inherited all this as my son. But instead you teamed up with the Damonchokians."

He shook his head. "Bad move, Jeremy," he said. "Just because they're not as savage as the tribes in Wilmoroth doesn't mean they're civilized. What's to become of this world after we leave it, Jeremy? Look at this room. Look at the Dome. Look at the palace. Do you think there was a Damonchokian who ever lived who could conceive such things? Can any of them think any bigger than a log cabin? These are the people you want to turn the world over to? I thought you had better taste, better sense."

"The war is over, Umbriel. You lost. I didn't come here to debate it with you."

"No. You came here to get your woman and to get the keys to the palace. Because you think God is on your side. You think God has defeated Umbriel, don't you? You think I will agree to your humiliations."

I did not answer.

Umbriel said, "Before Anne comes there's somebody else you might want to get reacquainted with." At the signal of his hand the door behind Umbriel opened and Tracian walked in. She clutched the arm of a large man with a beard and—

"Will!" I shouted, the jewels in the ceiling seeming to spin around me.

He was dressed in regal Amian clothes like those I had once worn. He would not look at me. He glanced at the floor and at Tracian.

Umbriel said, "Tell me, Jeremy, if God is on your side, then why did He deliver Will into my hands? Did God want me to win too? I'd like your analysis of this."

"Where is Anne?" I shouted. "Will!"

"We rescued him from your little gang in the desert," Umbriel said. "You had nearly starved him to death. We brought him here and set him up quite comfortably. He has taken a liking to my daughter Tracian. You might remember her. He's been quite a help to us. If the kingdom had survived, we would have given him a medal."

Will began to cry. He shouted, "I'm sorry, Jeremy! He tricked me. I would never have betrayed you."

"Betrayed me how? Will! Where is Anne?"

Umbriel said, "It will sink in before long."

Will turned to leave, but Tracian stood still and held on to his arm.

Umbriel said, "Don't feel bad, Jeremy. Even most of our people in the palace believed Anne was here. We even dressed a girl up like her and had her 'accidentally' show herself in public for a moment once or twice, just to keep the rumors going."

I turned to leave the room. I could have sworn the ceiling was spinning round and round. I stumbled into the soldiers. I pushed through them.

Umbriel's voice did not stop. "Will helped us with all the details. He was especially good with that picture in the informational, which apparently was quite—"

"I didn't know!" shouted Will.

I stopped hearing for a moment. I could not breathe well. I stared at the sparkling red in the top of the Dome and tried to breathe again. My chest felt as if it were being crushed.

Umbriel spoke paragraphs and then I heard him say, "Did you think I would just walk away and turn over the magnificence of my palace to Damonchokian swine who are not even fit to enter my stables? Did you think I would be content to spend the rest of my days in the squalor of whatever prison you would fashion for me?" He lifted his hands toward the Dome, as if praying. Two of his aides ran out of the room. "The great victory has been denied me, I admit it, but one victory remains."

The commotion began as soon as his voice stopped. From everywhere, it seemed, the room was pelted by a whirlwind of broken jewels and stone and glass. There was not one explosion but hundreds, all in the Dome as it erupted into a massive weapon. Each red jewel became a spinning, piercing bullet, while the walls themselves rumbled and began to crumble all around us. The soldiers tried to pull me away, but it was too late. No one was leaving the Dome alive. I saw one of the red jewels smash into Umbriel's skull, and then I myself was hit in the center of the chest and knocked to the floor.

The floor did not seem to stop me. That is, once I hit it I kept flying straight on through, with blinding pain, blinding darkness, or was it light? I kept flying straight on through, just as I had done the day I had fallen through the ice. Through the darkness toward the light. And when the pain stopped I knew that I was in a bed, and that beside the bed sat someone who held my hand. Umbriel had indeed reunited me with Anne, but not the way he expected to.

—◯—

My eyes flickered open and I saw Anne's face, though my mind was still too incoherent to stay focused for more than a few seconds. I squeezed her hand, and she drew closer. She knew I was back. She knew I had come home.

As I struggled to absorb the knowledge that I was finally with Anne again, my thoughts wandered back to Persus Am. Would all that we had worked for be lost in Umbriel's suicidal destruction of the Dome?

I didn't think so. With the Dome gone and Umbriel dead, Pons could sweep into the city and win his final glorious victory. The new Temple could be built on the site of the Dome, as the prophecies foretold. For all his scheming, Umbriel had managed only to do some preliminary demolition work in preparation for the Temple where the Lord's voice would be heard day and night in Persus Am.

I did not know how the starving people in the Utturies would be fed, or how the Rock would be healed, or who would take over the government of Persus Am. All I knew is that in the place where the Lord's music had been silenced for so many years, now His voice would speak to all who would listen.

When I was well enough to talk again, I started to tell Anne about my experiences in Persus Am, but then I stopped. To her and the others who stood around my bed, my words sounded like nothing more than incoherent babbling, a side effect of all the drugs they had pumped into me. I suddenly felt no inclination to reveal the amazing events I had been through. What had happened to me was beyond explanation. I believed, though, that it had been absolutely necessary for my spiritual survival. The Lord's Spirit embraced me in a new way. I would not go back to the old life, no matter how alluring it sometimes seemed.

Many details of my journey would fade from memory, but I would never lose the sound of the Lord's music, His own voice, His song of fire, that would burn in me forever.

About the Author

J oseph Bentz and his wife Peggy live in southern Califor-
nia, where he teaches literature and journalism at Azusa
Pacific University. In 1991 he earned a Ph.D. in American literature from Purdue University. He was born in Noblesville, Indiana,
and grew up in Indianapolis.